In This Hour

*A Story of World War II
and the Floods of 1953*

No longer safe behind the dyke

Wagon loads of sand for restoring the dyke

The dyke is going to be closed again

Help came from land, sea, and sky

In This Hour

*A Story of World War II
and the Floods of 1953*

by

Rudolf Van Reest

Translated by Theodore Plantinga

**INHERITANCE PUBLICATIONS
NEERLANDIA, ALBERTA, CANADA
PELLA, IOWA, U.S.A.**

Library and Archives Canada Cataloguing in Publication
Reest, Rudolf van, 1897-1979.
   In this hour : a story of World War II / Rudolf van Reest ; translated by Theodore Plantinga.

Translation of: In dit uur.

ISBN 1-894666-68-2

   1. World War, 1939-1945—Underground movements—Fiction.
2. Netherlands—Flood, 1953—Fiction. I. Plantinga, Theodore, 1947-
II. Title.
PT5866.R54I513 2006   839.31'362   C2006-900437-4

Library of Congress Cataloging-in-Publication Data
Reest, Rudolf van, 1897-1979.
   [In dit uur. English] In this hour : a story of World War II and the floods of 1953 / by Rudolf van Reest ; translated by Theodore Plantinga.
   p. cm.
   ISBN 1-894666-68-2 (pbk.)
   1. World War, 1939-1945—Underground movements—Netherlands—
Fiction. 2. Netherlands—Flood, 1953—Fiction. I. Plantinga, Theodore,
1947- II. Title.
PT5868.S84I513 2006
833'.914—dc22
                                                          2005037007

Originally published as *In dit uur* by Uitgeverij Bosch & Keuning N.V,
Baarn, The Netherlands

Translated by Theodore Plantinga

Cover Painting *Landing of the Allied Forces on Walcheren* by Peter J.
Sterkenburg

Published simultaneously in U.S.A. by Inheritance Publications
Box 366, Pella, Iowa 50219

Available in Australia from Inheritance Publications
Box 1122, Kelmscott, W.A. 6111 Tel. & Fax (089) 390 4940

Printed in Canada

Contents
Part I
Struggle

Part II
Despair

Part III
Triumph

*Queen Mother Wilhelmina
came to encourage the people in Zeeland in 1953*

Part I

Struggle

Queen Juliana visited Zeeland in 1953

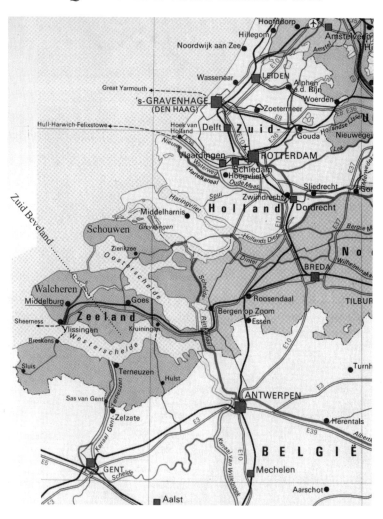

Chapter 1

The little Walcheren church was completely full, just as it was every Sunday. The women, each wearing a white cap with golden spirals along its side, sat in the middle part of the church. The men, each holding a large Bible open before him, sat apart from their wives along the two sides of the church in high, straight benches. The older ones were wearing Walcheren garb — a cloth jacket with gold buttons.

The minister was dealing with a passage about persecution drawn from the prophet Jeremiah. He had come to chapter 27:12-13, where it is written: "I spake also to Zedekiah king of Judah according to all these words, saying, Bring your necks under the yoke of the king of Babylon, and serve him and his people, and live. Why will ye die, thou and thy people, by the sword, by the famine, and by the pestilence, as the LORD hath spoken against the nation that will not serve the king of Babylon?"

The year was 1941. Rev. Verhulst was convinced that since the Netherlands was now under German occupation, its people were in the same position as the people of Israel during the days of Jeremiah. Because of the people's sin and apostasy, the land was being subjected to German control. Therefore the people were not permitted to resist the Germans. They would have to bow willingly and carry out the orders of the occupying forces.

Week after week, the Walcheren congregation got to hear the same kind of admonition: You have sinned, and God has now visited you in judgment. Bow down in the dust and kiss the rod of your affliction.

The people sat silently. They were calm and composed as they listened to the judgment. There was the same stern and quiet respect as always. There was no movement to be detected in the stiff caps of the women — it was as though they were carved out of marble. As for the men, they were staring straight ahead at the pulpit. Not one allowed a muscle on his face to move and thereby uncover what was going on in his heart.

Were all those men and women in agreement with the minister? Or were they resisting his message? Did they really understand what he was saying, or did it go right past them without touching them? From their posture and what was written on their faces, no conclusion could be drawn.

But when it came to the young people, who sat mainly in the back of the church, it was a different story. Meaningful glances were exchanged. Sometimes a small movement of the head could be detected, as if a message was being sent to the man in the pulpit. It was as though someone was saying: "Just listen to that!" The young people were not about to accept such preaching.

When the service was finished, the duty elder, as always, shook hands with the minister when he came down from the pulpit. The handshake signified that the consistory took responsibility for the sermon. Then the members of the consistory disappeared one after another into the room set aside for their use. The people headed home on foot or on bicycles or in some sort of buggy or automobile.

But before the minister left the consistory room, elder Melse coughed a few times, cleared his throat, and said: "Reverend, it's about time to quit preaching on those passages from Jeremiah. There are other things in the Bible too."

Suddenly there was tension in the room. Just then elder Francke was just in the process of bringing a burning match to the tobacco in his pipe; he forgot to suck on the pipe, and so the match burned out without lighting the tobacco. He quickly threw the little match into the ashtray, for the tips of his fingers were being burned.

Deacon Flipse has already taken hold of the doorknob and was in the process of leaving the room, but he turned around and stood at the table. The other members of the consistory followed his example. Almost all of them agreed with elder Melse: it was a great relief to them that he had finally taken the bull by the horns.

Rev. Verhulst looked at his elder with open eyes, full of amazement. "Have I not preached the Word this morning, brothers?" he asked.

"You preached a word *out of* the Bible, Reverend. But what I just said is that there's more in the Bible than what you have been finding in Jeremiah."

"Yes, that's true, but I believe in *concrete* preaching. The message in Jeremiah applies to our time."

"I rather doubt that, Reverend."

"You must leave it up to me to decide such things, brother Melse. *I* have been called to preach the Word here — not you."

"Reverend, do you mean to say that the elders are not allowed to offer criticism of the preaching?"

Rev. Verhulst turned red. "Criticism is good, but it needs to be based on the Word, Melse."

"Then preach sometime about the midwives of Egypt, Reverend," responded Melse. "That passage is also in the Bible. Those midwives refused to do what the king, the Pharaoh, demanded of them. Remember that Egypt also had a government given by God. The midwives allowed the children born to Hebrew mothers to live, and they even proceeded to *lie* about what they were doing. Yet we read in the Bible that God *honored* the midwives because of the resistance they offered and built up their houses. Preach a sermon about that passage sometime, Reverend. May we expect such a sermon next Sunday?"

Rev. Verhulst jabbed his index finger into the farmer's broad chest and said: "Just listen, brother Melse! I don't like to be criticized the moment I come down from the pulpit. If you have something to say to me, come over to the parsonage or bring up the subject when the whole consistory is present. Good day, brothers."

Once the minister had disappeared, the brothers all looked at each other. "I'm glad you finally brought up the subject," said Francke, and the others nodded in approval.

*   *   *

David Melse and Bart Francke walked side by side as they left the church. They lived near one another. Francke had quite a large spread, while Melse had only a small farm.

"What you said just now moved me very deeply, Melse," said Francke.

"To think that it finally had to come to this!" said David Melse. "It couldn't go on the way it was. The minister is driving us apart as a congregation. It's becoming harder and harder to get the young people into church. We'll have to discuss it at a consistory meeting sometime."

"I stand right with you."

The two men left the solitude of the street on which the church stood and were now at the edge of the village. On Walcheren it was customary for people to remain inside their homes as much as possible on Sunday. Although the young people were beginning to think differently about such matters and were taking walks in the meadows and along the pathways outside the village, the older people did not approve of such conduct. The life of the people on Walcheren was still stamped by a strongly conservative attitude. The farming population continued to cling to deeply rooted customs which the people were not about to surrender. Intuitively they sensed that there were dangers threatening them if they tried to move the old markers setting limits to what is permitted.

Now that they were outside the village, the two men had an unobstructed view of the Walcheren dunes. The northern dunes led toward the very strong sea dike of Westkapelle. The squat, square lighthouse of Westkapelle was set off clearly against the blue sky.

For a moment they stood before Francke's place. Melse lit his pipe once more and looked out over the farms in the distance, to where the sandy-colored dunes separated the land from the water.

"And now they're busy digging under the dunes."

Francke understood what Melse was talking about. He added what he knew: "The Germans have begun to build bunkers. One of the leading officers in Middelburg has decreed that the island of Walcheren is to be made into an even stronger fortress than Gibraltar. Everything that can be seized will be used to construct those defenses — material, but also people."

"This week they called up my son to work on those defenses."

"And is he going?" asked Francke.

12

"Would your son go?" responded Melse, looking inquisitively at his neighbor.

"I don't think he would."

"Not even if the minister said he must go?" asked Melse.

"No, not even then. That's not for the minister to decide — it's my decision."

"That's what I believe too," said Melse. Then, with a nod, the two men went their separate ways.

*   *   *

Melse stood for a while and stared over the flat land of Walcheren. He was looking toward the dunes. A grim expression covered his face.

Melse was the type of farmer that people would look upon as typical of Zeeland. His thick cloth jacket encased his heavy-set body like armor. The pants around his strong legs resembled pipes coming from a stove. When he set his feet on the ground, there he would stand — and it would not be easy to budge him. His countenance was lined. Deep furrows were clearly visible on his forehead. His graying eyebrows hung over his recessed dark-brown eyes.

He was having trouble coming to terms with the conditions he now lived in. In May of 1940 he had watched as Middelburg burned. And on the very same day the Queen had fled . . .

Whenever David Melse looked beyond the edges of the dunes, his eyes would seek the land to the west where the Queen was living as an exile. That land — England — was now the seat of our government, for it was there that the government appointed for us by God conducted its operations. As for the Germans, they were interlopers and evildoers who had to be chased out of the country as quickly as possible.

And now his thoughts returned to his deep, principle difference with the minister. He knew it was a difference that could never be bridged: eventually there would come a conflict. He could not let things go on as they were. He realized that he did not have enough knowledge to be able to argue successfully against the minister, but intuitively he felt that the minister was wrong.

* * *

David Melse walked onto his own farm and entered his house. The family was already seated and drinking coffee. Dirk, his oldest son, who had just turned twenty, had been called up to work on the bunkers to be constructed in the dunes.

Melse had five children. In addition to Dirk there was another son, Henry, and three daughters: Tina, Janet, and Laura.

David Melse had made a fine marriage, but in other respects life had not been easy for him. First there were the four years of mobilization, lasting from 1914 to 1918. During that time of crisis, he could not get a proper start in life. In 1928, when prices were at their highest, he bought the little farm on which he still lived. He'd had a hard time getting the previous owner to release his hold on it, and so he eventually offered a price that was actually too high. One consequence was that the little farm was excessively taxed. During the period of economic depression lasting from 1932 to 1936, prices fell so far that he came up short every year. Only during the last few years had things gone a bit better for him. He managed to get an orchard going, and he was now getting some fruit from it. Moreover, prices were higher than they used to be. In 1939 Melse was able to say to his wife Beth: "Now we're finally getting ahead, wife! As long as there's no fresh setback, we can say that the worst of it is behind us."

The Melse family also included a seventy-two-year-old grandfather. The old man was still strong and took an intense interest in everything that went on around him. After his wife died, an event that took place three years before, he had come to live with David and Beth. Beth had suggested it herself. After all, what was an old man to do on his own? Grandfather Dirk was a man of good character and sensible judgment. He still undertook many of the tasks that were always lying around on a farm waiting to be done.

Just then mother Beth was pouring the coffee. Young Dirk opened a conversation topic by saying: "Wasn't that a dandy this morning?"

14

At once everyone understood what he meant. Almost every Sunday the sermon was criticized in the Melse family circle, even though David Melse tried to protect the minister as long as he could.

"What do you mean?" asked mother Beth.

"As though you don't know . . ."

Tina then spoke up: "Oh, let's talk about something else — you always make such a fuss about the sermon."

"You only want to hear about *nice* things," murmured Dirk. "If I were to do as *he* says, I'd have to go and help turn those dunes into bunkers."

"You mean you're *not* going to go?" asked eight-year-old Laura.

Mother Beth frowned and gave her elder son a warning glance. Then grandfather Dirk spoke up. He took his clay pipe out of his mouth, looked directly at his grandson, and proceeded to warn him gently not to be too critical of the minister. After all, the minister is the Lord's anointed who is called to proclaim the Lord's judgment to the people. We must remember that whoever touches the Lord's anointed touches the apple of His eye. When we are critical, we are opposing the working of God's Spirit. And when such a thing happens, God may well decide to release even more severe judgments over the land.

The result of the old man's words was silence in the room. But Dirk could not accept what his grandfather had said. "So are we supposed to bow before the Germans and do whatever they ask?" he demanded. "What if the Queen tells us over the radio that we must *resist* the Germans? To whom are we supposed to be obedient? I'd like to have an answer to that question."

Mother Beth frowned again and sent her son a silent signal that he was not to argue with his grandfather. She did not like skirmishes at her table.

Grandfather had his answer ready: "How all that works I'm not precisely sure. What I do know is that the minister has been put here by God to preach the Word. We must all listen to him."

Dirk stubbornly kept up his side of the argument: "So, what you're saying is really what the Roman Catholics teach. The laymen have to do *exactly* what the priest says. Perhaps I'm simple-minded, but I thought we had a different understanding of these things."

Dirk then proceeded to light a cigarette. He looked to his father for support. But mother Beth wanted to see the discussion end. "Just look at the clock, son. Don't forget that the animals still need to be fed. All of you get out of here and look after those animals. It won't be long before I set the table, and then we'll have to sit here waiting for you."

Dirk stood up, and father Melse went with him. Once they were outside, they continued their conversation.

*   *   *

All that Sunday the tension continued to hang in the air. No one came right out and said it, but they all understood that Dirk would be going into hiding the next day. And what would happen after that? Where would he go? Would he be picked up by the Germans? Would the Germans take measures when they found out that he had fled? The future was uncertain. Making things even more uncertain was the conflict with the minister that loomed on the horizon.

That evening, when the father and son were together again feeding the animals, David Melse said: "You don't have to tell me where you're going, my boy."

"No, Father, it would be better if you didn't know."

But there was still something that David Melse wanted to say to his son. There was no need to leave Zeeland if he did not wish to go far away. It might be possible for him to be helped on his way by his own family. On Schouwen and Duiveland it had been more peaceful up to now than on Walcheren. There were no bunkers to be built over there.

Dirk assured his father that if something were to happen, he would somehow get word to him. And that was as far as he went in giving assurances. Father Melse was satisfied, but the older man felt compelled to add: "I hope you don't get any strange ideas in your head, Dirk. Think about what you are doing. Remember that

16

you have a mother who will be on her knees every evening praying for you — do you understand?"

"And a father!" Dirk added, giving his father a loving clap on the back. He went on to assure him: "It's only for a little while."

*　　　*　　　*

It was a difficult night for father and mother Melse. They did not get much sleep. Although they did not talk much about what Dirk was about to do, each was aware what the other was thinking. In difficult times — and they had gone through a great many difficulties during their marriage — they could understand each other without using a lot of words. And now they were both lying there awake. Father Melse held his wife's hand, and it was as though thoughts were exchanged silently through their clasped hands.

Early on Monday morning, when it was still hazy out in the fields because of the mist, Dirk made ready to depart. His mother gave him some bread to take along, and Tina packed some underclothes for him. At the last moment his mother shoved a small Bible into his rucksack as well. "Read the Bible faithfully, my boy, and never forget what it says — do you hear me?"

"I'll do just as you say," responded Dirk, touching his mother's shoulder gently. He was trying to act excited, as though he was going on a pleasant little journey. But it was camouflage — they all knew better. Dirk always had a hard time being away from home.

When it looked as though they were about to step out the door with him, he stopped them. "I don't want any of you to be seen with me," he told them. "When they come checking up on me, you must act as though you know nothing. Then you won't be able to tell them anything. That's the best way. So you stay right here in the house, Mother."

Mother Beth symbolically shut her eyes and stepped back. Father and Tina did the same thing. Staying out of sight behind the curtain, they watched as the young man went on his way. Finally the mist concealed him from their sight. Then mother Beth let out a sigh: "He's really just a boy."

"But he's in God's hand," answered David Melse.

*　　*　　*

Two days later they had the Germans at their door to inquire about Dirk and take a good look around. Nothing was told them. When they left, they threatened to return.

On Wednesday evening Rev. Verhulst came to see them. "Is it true, brother Melse, that your son has gone into hiding?"

"I'm staying out of his business, Reverend."

"But you are his father, and so you should know what the boy is up to. Did he get your approval?"

"I'm telling you again that I'm staying out of the boy's business, Reverend."

"If there's something going on in your son's life, you are responsible for it."

Melse nodded.

The minister then asked: "Did he really find it such an awful thing to help build those bunkers?"

"Yes, indeed, he was strongly opposed to the idea," said Melse.

"But why, brother Melse? He doesn't have to take the responsibility for the bunkers. He would just be following orders."

"I don't believe that, Reverend. The Germans have no right to put up such fortifications. If Dirk were to help them, he would become a traitor to his own country, and that's not something I'd like to see my son doing, Reverend."

"That's a rather rough expression, brother Melse — 'traitor.' How could you call someone a traitor if he's simply obeying the government? I would rather not hear such language from the mouth of an elder."

"I maintain that such work as building bunkers is treason against our land," repeated David Melse. "The bunkers have a definite purpose: when armies come to liberate us from the power of the Germans, the bunkers are supposed to hold them back. Each bunker could help sink one of the naval vessels approaching our coast. And on those vessels are our friends — perhaps even our own soldiers. Reverend, you should think carefully what those bunkers represent."

18

Rev. Verhulst shook his head. "You people have completely the wrong idea about those bunkers. Do you really believe that Germany will one day sink to its knees before England? If you do, you're completely mistaken, brother Melse. Germany will take control of all of Europe and will never let itself be overthrown. Germany is much too powerful to be defeated. Moreover, if you had listened carefully to last Sunday's sermon, you would know full well how I think about these matters. The apostate covenant people spent seventy years in the grip of Babylon, and I'm sure that our time under foreign domination will not be any less. You and I will not live to experience our liberation, brother Melse. The Germans will remain in control here — you'd better just believe what I'm telling you. You have to look at these matters in more *spiritual* terms. As a free people, we have thrown away our freedom through our sins. Because God is now coming in judgment, we are to become the servants of a foreign power. This is not something pleasant for the flesh. But whoever kisses the rod and bows before the judgments of the Lord will have peace. In the peace of Babylon you can also have peace — that's what God said to His people Israel through His servant."

"I'm not as good at talking and arguing as you are, Reverend, but I want you to know that I don't agree with you." David Melse was determined to make it clear that he thought there was something wrong with the minister's line of reasoning. There would be an opportunity in the consistory meeting to talk further about these things.

* * *

As the minister headed home, he thought about his conversation with the farmer. On the one hand, the people of Zeeland did not particularly enjoy arguing, but on the other hand they didn't budge from their position either. You just couldn't do anything with them!

The minister was feeling disconcerted. His colleagues also opposed him and had warned him against the course he was following. They told him that if he continued on the path he had chosen, he would eventually run stuck and find he had no way out.

19

But as he considered his colleagues' words, he noted a parallel between his own work as a minister and the things that had happened to Jeremiah, who faced opposition from false prophets. Jeremiah, too, could easily have lost his life. Well then, he would emulate Jeremiah's faithfulness and take his stand alone! He was not a herd animal — no, he would swim against the stream. And if his congregation kept opposing his preaching, well then, he would express his convictions in still stronger language. He knew that by doing so he could avoid besmirching himself with the blood of the flock entrusted to his care as a shepherd.

As for the Germans, he simply did not believe that they would ever go away. Nothing in the world could block their forward march. Germany was the great Babylon of the twentieth century — it would rise up in its great power and crush everything that stood in its way. It would not be destroyed until the hand cut out that great stone of which the Bible speaks.

Such was the firm conviction of Rev. Verhulst. Therefore he was convinced that the Bible passage that applied to this situation was: Seek the peace and welfare of Babylon — there you will find your own peace. But all who opposed Babylon would be struck with misery and pestilence, hunger and death.

*   *   *

The next time the consistory met, the elders did not get any further with the issue. The minister dug in his heels. Again and again he shook his head and said: "Here I stand, brothers — I cannot do otherwise. God help me!"

He was never altogether free of the tendency to be theatrical. But this time the consistory members, with only a couple of exceptions, were not taken in by what he said. Now that they had finally spoken up and expressed themselves, they held their ground. They pointed out that the minister was destroying the unity of the congregation. He was bringing God's Word in a one-sided manner and causing the young ones to turn away from their calling.

The clock struck midnight as the men finally headed for their homes. The room in which they had met was still thick with the smoke of home-grown tobacco. And in the heads of the brothers things were not very clear either. Debating with the minister was very difficult work. They would rather clean out a stall — at least, then you could see you were getting somewhere.

"So what do we do next?" Melse asked Francke on the way home.

"There's nothing I can think of — I wouldn't know where to begin," said Francke. "He's a good talker, sure enough, but he's completely wrong."

"Wrong? He couldn't possibly be more wrong, man!" said Melse. "If there was nothing else in the Bible than the Book of Jeremiah, then there might be something to his position. But think about it: there are many other passages in the Bible that we have to consider as well. The sad thing in this situation is that *we* don't have enough learning; we're just ordinary people. And even if you know the most important things to know, you can't always find a way to *express* them — you just don't have the words. Still, I know the minister is wrong. We don't know exactly where the hole in his argument lies, but we're going to find it — that's for sure."

"Right you are."

They wished each other good-night in front of Francke's place. Melse took another look around before he went further. Again his glance sought out the dunes. That was where the hated enemy was dug in — not even four kilometers away. There the Germans were getting ready, waiting for the friends of our people. They were digging themselves in like rats in a dike. All of Walcheren was enveloped in a night as black as pitch. There was no light anywhere to be seen. All was dark. The light at the top of the Westkapelle lighthouse no longer rotated and shed its familiar beams. The searchlight had been put out of action: it no longer shed light over Walcheren.

"All works of darkness," grumbled Melse, as he walked on toward his farm.

Chapter 2

On a beautiful Sunday evening in May of 1942, Jacob Jobse and his wife came to visit the Melses. Jacob worked for a carpenter and was a very familiar figure in the congregation. He was known to speak his mind; he did not hide his feelings from anyone. And he knew what he was talking about. He was an active member of the church and cared deeply about the lives of others. When someone said something to him, he always had an answer.

Joan, his wife, fit in very well with Jacob, just as a lid fits on a pot. She was a somewhat quiet, withdrawn person, friendly and gentle, very bright, and she knew what she was doing. She had a growing brood of children to whom she was giving an excellent upbringing. Some even thought she was raising Jacob along with the children.

Joan was a friend of Tina Melse, who was now working for a family in Middelburg. Joan was a few years older than Tina, but they had gone together to girls' society and catechism classes. If Jacob had not come along to ask for her hand, Joan would probably be working for a family in Middelburg too, where she would continue her friendship with Tina. Even so, the bonds of friendship were being maintained. Jacob and Joan were welcome visitors on the small farm of David Melse, where all the family members enjoyed their company.

But on this particular Sunday evening, Jacob was not in the best of moods. Food had by now become scarce and expensive. It was hard to get hold of wheat. The bread that was made available through the authorities was of poor quality, and it was rationed. It was a good thing that Joan was an outstanding baker. The bread that emerged from her oven was highly regarded in the village, just as her dark-brown molasses candies were.

Jacob Jobse was a strong man with jet-black hair — a pure Walcheren type. He had piercing dark eyes in which everything going on in his mind was reflected. During the week before, he had had a small dispute with Dupre, who was one of the richest farmers in the neighborhood and a member of the church. Dupre had wheat, and Jacob knew that he was selling it to strangers for an extra high price — selling it for more money than the people in the village could afford. It was not that Dupre did not want the people in his own village to get his wheat, but he did not dare ask his fellow villagers to pay the high price — that would cost him his popularity. But neither was he willing to sell them his wheat for the normal price.

He said he was willing to make an exception for Jacob Jobse, provided Jacob kept the price secret. Jacob paid him eighty cents per kilogram. Now, that was below the black market price, but according to Jacob's thinking it was still far too much money. Twenty cents per kilogram would have been a more reasonable price, he thought.

Jacob was telling all this to Melse. He explained: "And then I said to him: 'You just hang on to your wheat and use it to get rich.' One of these days Dupre should read what it says in the Levitical laws about how the laborer is worthy of his bread." Jacob paused for a moment, and then added: "Just suppose he winds up sitting beside me the next time we celebrate the Lord's Supper. Then he would really have something to think about. Oh boy!"

When Jacob used the phrase "Oh boy!" you could be sure he was worked up over something and did not know quite what to say next. "Oh boy!" was a signal to others as to what he was feeling.

David Melse shook his head. On Joan's small, well-formed mouth a faint smile was to be seen. Joan wanted to make the situation right. "You shouldn't get so upset over this," she said, gently admonishing her husband. "We'll still manage to get enough to eat — wouldn't you say, Mrs. Melse?"

"I'm sure we won't go hungry," answered mother Beth, but then she added that it was nevertheless a shame when so rich a farmer as Dupre took advantage of wartime shortages.

David Melse was silent. He also thought it was a shame.

But Jacob was not done talking: "You know, Melse, sometimes I think that greediness is a folk-sin among us here on Walcheren."

He was wondering whether his own people were not too materialistic in inclination, and so he put the issue before Melse. "We're always scrambling to get more, and we're never satisfied with our life. Every cent we earn we hang on to. As to just how we came by our money — well, no one asks us about that."

Jacob had not excluded himself from the criticism he was uttering. He knew that if he had been in Dupre's place, he might well have done the same thing. Wasn't that the way it went with many of the people on Walcheren?

The conversation continued. Mother Beth told Joan that ever since Tina had started working in Middelburg, she found her mother's house old-fashioned. Tina would like to see her mother

get rid of the things on her mantelpiece — they didn't fit the times we live in. As for the tea service that she keeps on the table in the living room, that sort of thing just isn't done anymore. There should be a small tea table instead. In the summertime, when the furnace is not in use, Mrs. Melse puts a small cloth on top of it, but this, too, was wrong in Tina's eyes.

"You just keep things the way they are, Mrs. Melse," said Joan with a laugh, displaying her row of small, white teeth.

"You're a fine one to talk," said Jacob, inserting himself into their conversation. "Do you know what Joan wants to do? She wants to stop wearing our distinctive Zeeland costume and walk around every day in ordinary clothes — isn't that true? Oh boy!"

Joan blushed as she realized that all eyes were fixed upon her. She tried to save herself by saying: "But I'm not doing it to act grand or to put on airs. I want you to know that."

"Well then, what would your reason be?" her husband asked.

"I've told you many times," answered Joan. "Those special Zeeland costumes are far too expensive. You almost need gold to pay for that stuff, and where would we get the money? There are all kinds of special items you'd need to wear if you wanted to be decked out properly as a woman of Zeeland, and then think of all the work that's required. It takes a great deal of time to get all of that special clothing on, and then you have to keep it neat all the time — otherwise people are scandalized."

Joan then turned to Mrs. Melse and asked: "Would you find it such a terrible thing if I wore ordinary clothing?"

Mother Beth was hardly in a position to criticize Joan on this score. Tina had dropped the distinctive Zeeland costume as well, and she was looking fine. She now had more clothing to choose from, and when she took a journey she did not become the object of attention. If those English and American visitors were so eager to get a picture of her in Zeeland garb, then maybe they should wear it themselves — then they could find out first-hand what it's like to dress in such an old-fashioned way. She turned to Jacob and asked: "What do you have to say on the subject?"

Joan laughed and nodded contentedly as she looked at Jacob. "I got you, my boy," she thought to herself. Her clear blue eyes glistened with pleasure.

"Well, I suppose we'll see," said Jacob. "But if Joan thinks it's all right for her to set aside all that special Zeeland garb, she can be sure I'll follow her example. What we men are supposed to wear — especially that strange underwear — well, you can be sure that

I would set it aside too. Then I would come to church on Sunday dressed much more simply. You can be sure that I wouldn't be walking around in a Zeeland farmer's costume if Joan were wearing ordinary clothes and looking like a young girl. Oh boy!"

Joan had no other response to offer than a laugh. She winked at mother Beth as she tried to smooth things over. It was as if she was saying: "Jacob is not as bad as he likes to act." But they already knew that.

At about nine o'clock, Jacob and Joan went home. They knew that work would begin very early on the Melse farm, and so they allowed their hosts to get to bed on time.

*   *   *

Very early the next morning David Melse got on his bicycle and set out for a piece of land he farmed. The land he was headed for was half an hour from the village.

Melse farmed a number of small pieces of land that were scattered here and there. But there was nothing unusual about his situation: he was in the same position as most of the farmers. Walcheren had been divided up into little pieces of land lying here and there and everywhere; in the course of their work, the farmers often had to move from one field to another.

This situation, which had come about gradually over a long stretch of time, was far from economical or practical. Farmers who had all their land right around their home were an exception to the rule. On the other hand, the island had been made beautiful by this parceling out of the land. The little roads and pathways connecting the pieces of land ran this way and that, making the whole island look like a beautiful garden. The sides of the winding pathways were flanked by tall bushes. Anyone who rode through Walcheren on a bicycle would repeatedly encounter entirely new and surprising vistas to enjoy.

And it seemed that no pathway ran in a straight line. According to an old story, when the pathways and roads through Walcheren were being laid out, the idea was to make them as straight as possible. Therefore a long string was stretched all the way from one village tower to another. But because people pulled too hard on the string, it snapped and wound up on the ground in all kinds of curving patterns. The roads and pathways were then laid out along those curving lines. Now they no longer ran from village to village but rather from little farm to little farm. They were intimate, lovely to behold, as though begging to be painted — but they were certainly not practical.

Melse biked along a small, winding pathway to a little field where he planned to work that morning. Now that Dirk was gone, he was very busy, and he did not see how he could possibly hire someone to replace him.

He was thinking about the previous evening's conversation with Jacob. The farmers on Walcheren are materialistic — at least, that's what Jacob said. Melse had to agree: what Dupre did was not right.

After a final bend in the winding road, David Melse stood before his small field. He put his bicycle under a hedge to keep it out of the sun and walked over to a small shed from which he pulled a tool for weeding.

While he worked, his mind was occupied with the same topic he had discussed the evening before. He wondered whether it really was fair to say that we are materialistic. The minister certainly thought so and had said it often. According to him, our materialism was part of the reason for the judgments God was now sending over the world.

Melse found it a strange way of reasoning: the minister seemed to believe that the whole world had to be involved in a world war just because Walcheren was guilty of a certain sin. Of course, the minister did bring some other factors into the picture as well. Still, the idea that the love of money had a deep hold on the island of Walcheren was not something David Melse was about to deny. Moreover, he knew he was guilty on this score himself. As he came to this realization, it was as though Jacob Jobse suddenly stood before him with those dark eyes looking into his soul. He almost felt a finger poking him in the chest. It was as though he could hear

Jacob saying: "But you are also guilty of that sin, David Melse. Oh boy!"

"Oh boy!" Then a seeming flash of lightning suddenly enabled David Melse to see what his life really consisted of. His father had been a steady worker all throughout his life, but he had always aspired to something greater and higher. For years he had labored to get a little bit of money together in order to buy a small place of his own. He would then quickly get rid of his mortgage and expand his herd of cattle. But stop — didn't David himself, right at that moment, have some three hundred guilders in the cabinet which he was planning to use to buy a young cow? Man shall not live by bread alone — that was what the Bible said.

It was not as though he never received an admonition. The elder Melse's pride in his son's achievements did not keep him from giving his son a warning when he thought he needed one.

"Just think of Uncle Joris," the older man said to his son one day. Joris, his younger brother, had been bound and determined to get a place of his own. And when he had an opportunity to take over a farm alongside the outer dike of Schouwen and Duiveland, his father, who was David Melse's grandfather, was past the point of being able to work. As for Dirk Melse himself, he was supporting a household of little children by that point. When Joris Melse was asked if he could spare a few guilders a week to help support his aged father, he responded: "That's what we have deacons for." And so he never sent any money to assist his father in his old age.

Some years later, the family on Walcheren heard that Uncle Joris had gotten married. He worked hard his entire life, but he never achieved much prosperity or success — neither with his farm nor with his family. His wife died while she was still young, and he lost his daughter as well.

In recent years Uncle Joris was hardly able to work anymore because of rheumatism, and his only son, who was also named David Melse, wound up looking after him and the farm. "I'm sure he often thinks back now on what he did to his own father," mused the elder Melse, "or rather, what he *refused* to do for him. The Lord has punished him."

David Melse rose from his knees. His legs were stiff, and so he stretched. Yes, he thought to himself, he had certainly taken good care of his aged father. Even so, he wondered whether he might not possess some of Uncle Joris's characteristics. Could it be said of him, too, that he was overly concerned with earthly things and possessions?

The small eyes under his heavy eyebrows stared intently at the coast, where the enemies of his people were busy making their position ever stronger by digging bunker after bunker in the dunes and fortifying the beach with heavy barbed wire. It was almost impossible to go down to the water now. The Germans were in charge — no question about it.

Walcheren was a deep basin, and on its edge the enemy was dug in. Just one order from Hitler, and they could crack open the basin's edge. Then the entire island would be flooded.

Melse was all too aware of the danger. He had thought about it so often. And when his gaze turned from the sandy dunes in the distance to his own field and he began to think of his house standing some distance away, he looked at his property with different eyes than before the year 1940. In some important way, his possessions had now become relative. All his plodding, all his labors during countless days and nights and inconvenient hours, all his thrift, his calculation, his care — it no longer had a firm foundation. It was all hanging by a thread. It made him think of what the Bible teaches: you must hold your possessions as though they are not yours. He realized that what the Bible said here applied to everything — his wife, his family, his house, his fields, his cattle. He was to possess them as though they were not really his . . .

David Melse now began to understand something of the deepest meaning of this theme in the Bible. Should he not also possess his oldest son as though he were not really his?

By this point he knew where Dirk was. On his most recent birthday he got a letter from his cousin David — which otherwise never happened. Included among the best wishes and congratulations was a quotation from Psalm 133. Behold how *good,* how lovely it is, when the sons of the same house *dwell together.*

The words "good" and "dwell together" were underlined. Something was being communicated through those underlinings. David figured out that it meant that his son Dirk was now on Schouwen and was doing well.

But could he still say that he *possessed* his son? He pondered what might happen to Dirk at almost any time — or, worse still, what might *already* have happened to him. After all, the boy was rash and impulsive, and David, being a son of Uncle Joris, was also impulsive. For all David Melse knew, they might both be working for the underground by this time. He had long worried about this prospect, and it had cost him many a sleepless hour.

Possessing as though you do not possess — *now* he began to understand something of it. The enemy had it in his power to take away everything just by issuing a single order. And then David would have to be happy if he could manage to hang on to his wife and children. The problem was that Walcheren is a deep basin whose edge is so small and vulnerable, whereas the sea is huge, powerful, mighty . . .

David began to ask himself whether he had given enough to the church and to the fund for the care of the poor. His whole life lay open before him like a book, and it almost seemed that Jacob Jobse, with his penetrating eyes, was looking through that book. But wait — was it really Jacob? Was it perhaps Another who was approaching him here?

Again Melse straightened up. He threw his weeding tool against some clods of mud and once more looked at the dunes at the island's edge. The dunes were glowing in the spring sunlight.

He was feeling warmer. But the warmth did not come entirely from the outside. Melse was getting warm from within. He knew that he would have to talk with Dupre about the business of Jacob Jobse and the price he paid for the wheat.

He also knew that he needed to have a good talk with himself. He was facing the fact that his whole life was geared to working hard — planning and calculating and building up his own possessions. That was the sort of thing that took priority for him, and the church came second. First myself, then God — that was

30

how it had been in his life. He had held on to his possessions as though they really were his own: he had been completely unwilling to surrender them. He had tried to assemble ever more possessions and had struggled to get ever fuller control of them — that was the meaning of his life. Yet the Bible said that we were to seek first God's kingdom and its righteousness — then all the other things would be added unto us. David Melse was painfully aware that he had not made an honest effort to live by that text. He knew that he was living in the grip of materialism.

Such was the judgment he had to make about himself on this Monday, now that he was working alone in his field. He began to sense his great guilt before God, until finally, behind his little shed, hidden from view by a thick hedge, he fell on his knees and folded his callused hands and cried out to God: "Be gracious to me, a sinner . . ."

*   *   *

That very evening David Melse called on Dupre. He asked to see him alone, and so they went to his big barn for their talk. There he told Dupre what Jacob Jobse had said. Dupre nodded. "You're right, Melse," he admitted. "That was not a good thing I did. Later on I regretted doing it, but I could hardly have done otherwise, because if I had made an exception for Jacob Jobse, the others would say that I was playing favorites."

"You should not make anyone pay those higher prices, Dupre. There's no way to justify it."

"Well, they all do it, and you have to take account of the risk you're running."

"You have to be willing to take the risk, Dupre."

"This is all fine talk, Melse, but I'd like to know: don't you ever sell anything without declaring it?"

Melse told him that wasn't the point and explained that he did help people as much as he could. And although he knew he was speaking the truth, in his heart he decided that he needed to do better.

Dupre observed: "To me it's a question whether the people really appreciate it."

"That's not for us to worry about. All we're responsible for is making sure we do what God asks."

Dupre shrugged his shoulders. "I'll see what I can do. Jacob is a nice fellow."

"Even if you didn't find him a nice fellow, you should never be asking those high prices."

They were standing and talking in the doorway of the big barn. Dupre had a first-class farm, and when David Melse took a look around, he was almost ashamed of his own little place. But he thought to himself that he should not be jealous of this farmer, who was well known to be a money-grubber.

"What we need to do, Dupre," said Melse, "is see that we're not so attached to our money."

"Hmm. That old song — Dupre is attached to his money. Listen, Melse, I've heard that sort of talk before. But I know what I'm able to do for others, and if I help someone out, I try not to embarrass him in the process."

Melse knew there was not much point in talking any further with the farmer. "Straighten things out with Jacob, Dupre, and you'll sleep better," he said.

"There's nothing wrong with my sleep — I'm sleeping as well as anyone could wish."

"All the better."

The next day Dupre informed Jacob Jobse that he could now buy wheat for twenty cents per kilogram.

"Well, thanks so much, Dupre," said Jacob. And then he added: "Now we can sit next to one another at the Lord's Supper — right?"

The farmer nodded stiffly. He did not grasp the full significance of these words from Jacob Jobse's nimble tongue.

*   *   *

The little village, normally so peaceful, was uneasy. The tension had been increasing steadily.

From one thing came another. Rev. Verhulst seemed to have only one arrow in his quiver nowadays. He was always telling the congregation that we must humble ourselves before the German occupying forces. Everything else fell away. It seemed that young people's societies were no longer needed. It was a time for sitting in sackcloth and ashes and crying over the sinful life we have been leading. It was a time to bow before the rod of chastisement being wielded by Hitler.

David Melse was having a hard time with all of this. On the one hand he did not permit his children to talk in a rebellious way when they discussed the minister's sermons, but on the other hand he had to admit in his heart that they were right.

*   *   *

One evening Jacob Jobse came over, wanting to talk. He fixed his large, piercing eyes on David Melse and addressed him very directly. His question was: can this go on forever in the congregation? Didn't the consistory have a task here? Was it right for them to just let things run on and on? Melse had no other answer to offer than a despairing shrug of his shoulders. He said to Jacob: "It's very difficult, my young friend."

"What's so difficult?" asked Jacob. "If the consistory does not want to tackle the issue, then I'll do it myself. There has to be an end to this business! The congregation is being destroyed. The minister seems to have no compassion whatsoever for the sheep entrusted to his care. What happened to the comfort which the holy Gospel offers the poor sinner?"

Jacob was asking difficult questions. Could David Melse, in good conscience, shake hands with the minister each Sunday after the service? By doing so, he was sharing in the responsibility for what had been proclaimed.

Jacob continued: "You should just listen sometime to what the people in the congregation are saying. If the consistory members continue to remain silent, there will finally come a point when the congregation makes itself heard. And then it will be an ugly scene — you can count on it."

"I'm sure it will be an ugly scene if you fan the flames, Jacob. My friend, what you need to do is to take control of yourself and be patient. Don't imagine that the consistory knows nothing of what goes on in the congregation. That's simply not the case — I want you to know that."

Melse was quite concerned about Jacob Jobse. He knew that when his friend sank his teeth into something, he was as stubborn as a bulldog. The minister might get a long way with his usual tactic of pouring a flood of words over people, but if he tried it on Jacob it would not work. Melse realized from this latest conversation with Jacob that his friend would not keep silent much longer. Jacob Jobse was wrought up, and the explosion could not be far away.

*   *   *

One night David Melse was lying awake for a couple of hours thinking about these things. He wanted to preserve the peace of the congregation. Finally he decided he would propose to the minister that the two of them make an official home visit to Jacob Jobse. David would then be in a position to smooth over the waters, if need be, and in any case he would be witness to their conversation. Later on it might prove useful to know just what was said.

It turned out that Rev. Verhulst was not in favor of making the proposed home visit. He had already made quite a number of home visits during the winter season, and they had not gone all that well. Moreover, he was well aware that he would not get a warm reception from Jacob Jobse. But when Melse kept pressing him gently, he gave in.

One day they stood together outside the small day-laborer's cottage at the edge of the village. When they were let in, they saw that Jacob Jobse was dressed in the Zeeland Sunday-best costume that he wore to church. His wife Joan had a clean, freshly starched cap on her head and was also in her special Sunday clothes. The children were already in bed.

David Melse could see at once that Jacob had his defenses up. Jacob was taking the measure of the minister from head to toe with his large, dark eyes. The furrows in his forehead were deep. Joan was a little nervous.

The small talk at the beginning of the visit was anything but smooth. Jacob Jobse wanted to get right to the main point. When the minister began to talk about all sorts of things, Jacob decided to take the initiative. He observed that he was surprised to see the minister making this home visit himself, as opposed to sending a pair of elders. He had heard that the minister often sent out the elders on their own.

"You shouldn't pay too much attention to what people say, brother Jobse," said Rev. Verhulst. "Again and again, you find out that what they are saying is wrong. And why should I not take part in a home visit myself?"

"Reverend, there's no need to act as though everything is normal here. Let's not try to hide the truth. You know as well as I do that the congregation does not agree with your preaching."

"Yes, that's public knowledge. But brother Jobse, what is your own position? Do you not agree with the preaching?"

Jacob Jobse raised his eyebrows as high as he could, with the result that the furrows in his brow looked even deeper than usual. "No, Reverend, I certainly do *not* agree with your preaching." Jacob then explained how much he would appreciate it if the minister would once again bring the Word of God from the pulpit. It would do the congregation a lot of good.

"You mean to say that I *don't* bring God's Word from the pulpit, Jobse? That's a very serious accusation."

"Indeed it is, Reverend, and I hope you respond to it in the spirit in which it's meant. Will we be hearing something different this coming Sunday?"

"On Sunday you will hear the same thing that you hear every Sunday, Jobse. What I preach is the Word of God, and you just have to bow before it."

"If I was convinced that it really *is* God's Word, I would surely, through God's grace, bow before it. But because you're bringing *your own word,* I cannot make my peace with it."

"You certainly don't pull your punches, Jobse."

"I can do so if need be, but today I feel I should not restrain myself."

"So tell me — do I preach anything other than what Jeremiah had to say to the covenant people of Israel?"

"But, Reverend, you're not Jeremiah."

"Well, that's true, I suppose, but I have the same message as Jeremiah."

"When and where has God charged you just as He charged Jeremiah to bring exactly that message?" asked Jobse. Then he pressed the minister further: "Can you tell me just where you were when the Lord called you and what the Lord said to you on that occasion?" Jacob's eyes flickered and did not leave the minister's face for a moment.

"Well, no, in the exact manner of Jeremiah — well, I can't say that I was commissioned in that way, but . . ."

"You just listen to me, Reverend! Now we're at the heart of the issue." Jacob drew a breath and then continued: "You think you have to bring the very same message as Jeremiah, even though you did not get a commission to bring that message, as Jeremiah did. Now, you're a very learned man, and in my life I have never had anything else in my hands than a saw, a chisel, and a hammer. But now you must listen to something I have to say, Reverend, and it's this: There are no Jeremiahs anymore with special messages received from heaven, and there are no prophets anymore who hear a special voice telling them what they are to preach. In the time of Jeremiah there was not yet a Bible. Jeremiah had to help produce what we now call the Bible, but you have no calling to do such a thing, because the Bible is now complete, thankfully, and it does not need any words from you added to it."

"Brother Jobse, may I also lay something on the table now?" asked Rev. Verhulst.

"In a little while, Reverend. I'm not done talking yet — far from it." If the minister was indeed willing to listen, Jacob knew he could keep him occupied until the next morning, for he had a great deal on his heart. "Just let me add a little bit to what I've already said."

Again the minister tried to interrupt the stream of words, but with no success. The condemnation kept washing over him. He got to hear about the things he had done to the young people, and about what he was withholding from the people, who are the sheep of Christ's flock. Jacob went on to tell him that he was letting down the resistance fighters in the land, and added that he was being disloyal to the royal family. Jacob even talked about the misuse the minister was making of God's Word, which he was using for his own purposes.

The stream of words continued to pour through the little room. Pearls of sweat formed on Jacob's forehead. He got very warm and wiped off his face with a colorful handkerchief. But there was no letup in the torrent of criticism he unleashed. He kept on going and going.

It was a stinging indictment, but it came forth from a heart that was full to overflowing, a heart that had been weeping for years, crying over a shepherd who no longer understood his task, a shepherd who was busy scattering the sheep instead of gathering them.

The minister bit his lip. A couple of times he made a fresh effort to cut off the stream of words, but in vain. Finally he stood up. "We're going home, brother Melse. I've had enough of this." He wiped the sweat off his pale face.

"Shouldn't we first ask a blessing?" said Melse hesitantly.

"No! I can't pray here. This man is opposing the work of the Holy Spirit. He's a wolf in sheep's clothing, and he's scattering the flock."

"Now, now, Reverend, what's that you're saying?"

The minister did not give his elder an answer. Without saying goodbye, he left the room. But Jacob was not about to let matters rest. "What you just said was spoken before God's countenance," he stated firmly.

The minister's statement would indeed have consequences. Brother Melse would have to make a report to the consistory about this visit.

Jacob wished the brothers good night. When he stepped back into the little room, he saw that Joan was crying. Her apron was over her face. The coffee she had poured had not been touched by the minister. She had prepared a special cookie to go with the coffee, and he had ignored it as well.

Jacob muttered something under his breath, but he found no relief. He was still very tense.

*   *   *

"Yes, that's exactly right — that young man knows what he's talking about." It was Francke talking, after David Melse reported to him what had happened at the home visit to Jacob Jobse. "Now someone has finally taken the bull by the horns."

They both understood what the issue was for the minister. He seemed to think he was a second Jeremiah. He did not understand that there are no Jeremiahs anymore — no more prophets with a special message from heaven. Still, they would have to talk about the matter further at the consistory meeting.

It turned out to be a rather hot meeting, but the minister shook his head and stuck to the message he had been proclaiming from the pulpit all these months. "I am the shepherd here, and I have the words of the Spirit. You must all change. You brothers will have to subject yourselves to that Word . . ."

The minister also uttered many complaints about the conduct of brother Jacob Jobse. But he could not be persuaded to make another visit to the Jobse home. "God will visit him in His own good time," he said.

Chapter 3

Time had moved on, and it was a stormy evening in the fall of 1942. The Melse family was sitting around the wood stove. David Melse's stocking feet were resting on a bench by the stove. Thor, the dog, lifted his head and began to growl.

"What can be bothering that beast now?" asked mother Beth anxiously.

"It's probably nothing — maybe some kind of mouse in the attic," her husband replied.

But Henry said: "I hear something just outside the window." He stood up. Just as he was opening the door to leave the room in which they were seated, they heard the outside door opening. Mother Beth turned pale and followed her son into the hallway.

"Dirk, my son!" she cried out. "What are you doing here?"

It was indeed Dirk standing in the doorway to the little room. He laid his finger over his mouth. His first question was whether all the curtains were properly drawn so that no one could see anything from outside.

David Melse jumped to his feet and shook his son's hand warmly. He was having trouble remaining calm. But a Zeeland farmer knows what self-control is.

Dirk took off his long coat and ran his fingers through his hair. Then he kissed his mother and Janet and Laura. As for Henry, he got a clap on the back.

"How good it feels to be home at last!" he sighed, as he looked around the room. His eyes fell lovingly on all the familiar things, while the eyes of all his family members remained fixed upon him.

Mother Beth had recovered from her fright and was already bustling about. She got some first-class coffee out of a little tin; she had been saving it from the old days for a special occasion. "We were not expecting you, my boy," she said.

"No, I had to come without giving you notice," said Dirk. "That's the way things are nowadays. How happy I am to be home once again!" Once more his eyes swept the room. "I see that everything here has remained just the way it was."

"That's right — nothing has changed," said his father. "How are things with you?"

"With me? Everything's fine!" Then he added: "It's just that I'm rather busy."

"So, tell us first what you're up to and why you're back here today. Are you planning to stay here with us? I'm sure the Germans aren't looking for you anymore. That bunker project was given over to other hands some time ago: the ones who were seeking your soul have disappeared." As David Melse talked, echoes of Biblical phrases came through. "To tell you the truth, I expected you home long before this."

By this point Dirk was sipping his coffee with great enjoyment. His mother observed: "You must be hungry, my boy"

"I'm as hungry as a horse."

He looked happy as he stretched out his long legs and let them come to rest alongside his father's legs. They both had their feet on the bench by the stove. It was just like the old days.

"You've gotten skinny, Dirk," observed Janet.

"No, I wouldn't say he's skinny," said mother Beth, as she looked in concern at her son who had been away from home for so long.

As Dirk ate and drank, he told them his tale. He was now connected with the underground and had been assigned to go to Middelburg. While he was there he talked with Tina. He was pleased to report that Tina had a good place to stay. And now, taking advantage of the darkness, he decided to visit home for a little while. The next morning he would leave, and no one was to admit to seeing him. As far as they knew, he had not been home.

"Why must everything be so secret, my son?" asked Melse.

"There's no way around it, Father. There's just too much that hangs on our maintaining total secrecy."

Father Melse threw some more coal into the stove and lit a fresh pipe. It was not the best tobacco by any means — homegrown. Still, he found that he could smoke it.

40

At that point Dirk took a package of English cigarettes from his pocket and threw them on the table. "Those are for whoever wants them," he said.

Immediately Henry took one. "How did you come by these?" he asked.

"That's for me to know and for you to find out." More he did not say. But father Melse, who otherwise did not care for cigarettes, also took one and set his pipe aside.

Then Dirk proceeded to tell about his experiences. He had followed his father's advice by going to Schouwen. The reception he got there from Uncle Joris, his grandfather's older brother, was not all that warm. When they got around to the subject of the bunkers being built in the dunes, which Dirk gave as the reason for his coming to them, Uncle Joris took the same stance as Rev. Verhulst. He wanted to know on what grounds Dirk could refuse when his services were demanded. He argued that if Dirk refused to do the work, the Germans would simply get someone else in his place, and in the meantime Dirk would be forced to live away from home.

But David, Uncle Joris's son, soon took Dirk aside for a private talk. He wanted Dirk to know that he thought along entirely different lines than his father. He assured Dirk that if he was determined *not* to cooperate with the Germans in building their bunkers, other work could be arranged for him to do. And he promised to find a place for Dirk.

The place assigned to Dirk was not on the Melse farm but on another farm in the general vicinity. Dirk went to . . . no it would be better not to mention any names here. Dirk simply told the family that it was a rich farmer with a place of his own.

Dirk had made it clear to the farmer that he was quite willing to pitch in with the work on the farm. But as time went by, he got more and more assignments of another sort to carry out. Indeed, he had been on Walcheren once before, but on that occasion he had not dared to come home.

"You can never be careful enough!" This point was stressed by David, Uncle Joris's son.

That David — what a fellow he was! It seemed he was willing to try almost anything. "I'm just an old bachelor — I take more risks than another man can." That was how he would talk when he was warning others to be careful. But the truth was that he had barely reached the age of thirty.

Dirk was of the opinion that Uncle Joris did not know what was going on in the way of underground activity. Not only did he talk along the same lines as Rev. Verhulst when it came to cooperating with the Germans, he also seemed to share the minister's other opinions. It was too bad for him that he never had an opportunity to hear those sermons about Jeremiah. Then Dirk paused to ask whether the minister was finally done preaching about Jeremiah. Continuing his story, Dirk explained that in order to give Uncle Joris some pleasure, he had laid out everything that he remembered about those sermons, which amounted to quite a bit. This happened one evening when he was at Uncle Joris's place for a visit.

"You should come here more often and tell us about those sermons," said David, just before Dirk departed. They were standing in the barn by themselves talking things over. David thought it was a fine idea to have Uncle Joris go on and on about Jeremiah and how we have to humble ourselves before the Germans as God's rod of chastisement. He figured it could not do any harm if people got the impression that Uncle Joris and his family were very obedient people, willing to humble themselves before the Germans.

As Dirk was talking about David Melse, his father's cousin, he got excited. They all listened to him intently.

Mother Beth had a great deal to process that evening. She did not say much, but she watched her boy very carefully, as only a mother can do, and she noticed that he was no longer the young fellow he used to be. He had become much more independent, just as though he had experienced a great deal. His features had become more distinct, more masculine. And he did not seem at ease; rather, he gave the impression of being a hunted man. She wondered to herself what her boy had gone through.

"Do you all know enough to keep quiet about what you've heard here tonight?" asked father Melse, looking at his children one by one. They nodded. As far as they were concerned, there was no need to ask such a question.

It was almost two o'clock in the morning when the family finally went to bed. Before they turned in, they all sank to their knees in front of their chairs as father Melse asked a blessing over their night's rest and thanked God that Dirk had been spared.

But Dirk decided to sit down just a little longer and proceeded to smoke one more cigarette. Just then Thor laid his big head on Dirk's knee and looked at him inquisitively with two large canine eyes. Dirk responded by laying his hand on Thor's head. That was the endearment the dog was waiting for, and now he was satisfied.

When Dirk decided to go to bed at last, his mother got an extra kiss, which brought a pale smile to her face. But when she was in bed where it was dark, Melse heard his wife crying quietly. He reached out for her hand, as he did more often when he was lying next to her in bed and they needed to comfort one another.

*   *   *

The next day Dirk stayed completely out of sight in the Sunday room. No one was allowed to enter that room on weekdays. While he was there, mother Beth had a chance to be alone with her son.

He gave short and often evasive answers to her questions. Nevertheless, she came to understand that he was involved in underground work in which he was risking his life.

"If I were you, I would stay home now," mother Beth repeatedly urged him. But he shook his head energetically. "I can't do that, Mother," he said. He felt he could not let the other fellows continue with the difficult and dangerous work while he folded his arms and waited for the Americans to come and liberate them. In his eyes that would be as bad as committing treason.

While he was in the Sunday room that day, he also had a private talk with his father. Later David Melse would often think back to what he had discussed in that heart-to-heart conversation with his son. And he would often ask himself whether Dirk had made that risky visit to his parents' home precisely for the sake of what he said to his father in the Sunday room: "Father, did I hear you complain once about doubting whether you are really God's child because His hand has chastised you your entire life? No, I won't mention any names, but from the farmer with whom I have been staying for some time I heard a whole different slant on this question. According to this farmer, it says in the Bible that God chastises His children. He then asks: Now, I have enjoyed prosperity all my life, so how can *I* be His child?

There was no opportunity to finish the conversation properly, for mother Beth called out that dinner was on the table. Yet it made no difference. David Melse would not have been able to find words to give expression to the joy that filled his heart. Just think — he had a son to whom the spiritual struggle meant so much! That day he decided that, one day, when he got a chance, he would seek out that man on Schouwen and have a talk with him.

Toward nightfall, when it was completely dark, Dirk disappeared just as mysteriously as he had come. Outwardly, there was nothing unusual to be noticed about Melse and his wife as they took leave of their older son. They said goodbye to him just as though he was merely making a journey of a few days. But that night mother Beth did not sleep a wink. She lay there silently on her back next to her husband, who pretended to sleep . . .

*   *   *

It was at about this time that Jacob Jobse fell from some scaffolding alongside a house under construction and broke his leg. When Joan brought the news to the minister, he said: "Tell your husband, Mrs. Jobse, that I cannot come to his sickbed. He has fallen into God's hand because of the hardening of his heart. I'm not about to get in the way of the work which the Lord is now doing with him."

When Joan came home with this message and reported it to Jacob in the minister's exact words, the injured man was lying facing the window with his leg in a cast. As the minister's words sunk in, he forgot all about his pain and declared: "I did not fall into God's hand! And if I had, it would be much better than falling into the hands of that minister!" He remembered what David Melse had said to him: Please do not let me fall into the hands of man, for then I will be in a very bad way indeed. Jacob decided that once he had made a partial recovery from his broken leg, he would go and have a talk with that minister . . .

*   *   *

A couple of weeks later David Melse got an unexpected visit from his oldest daughter. In the evening twilight he found Tina standing by one of the sheds, waiting for her father. "What are you doing here all of a sudden?" asked Melse, puzzled.

She laid a finger over her lips and gave him a signal to enter the shed. She was breathing hard as she whispered to him: "Father, an English pilot crashed not far away, and tonight he has to have a place to sleep. May he sleep up in the hayloft? In a few days he will be picked up by someone from the underground. But for the moment they don't know what to do with him. The Sloedam is being carefully guarded. The Germans are looking for the pilots who flew the burning plane they shot down."

Tina was still panting. She had come all the way from Middelburg in a great hurry without stopping. The tension added to her exhaustion.

"Now you're really asking something of me!" responded Melse. "Do you realize, my girl, what could happen if such a thing became known? It could cost all of us our lives!"

Of course Tina knew that perfectly well. She told her father so, and then added that Dirk was aware of it as well. Yet Dirk had assured her that Father would be willing to help.

"Dirk is right — let the man come. But see that you don't tell anyone, and make sure to wait until it's completely dark."

Tina departed on her bicycle. No one knew where she was headed.

It was about midnight when she returned with a young man in uniform. Her father then took the young man into the barn. With a lantern in one hand he clambered up a ladder. The pilot followed him. Not a word was spoken. The ladder was taken away and the barn was closed.

Tina slept in her parents' house that night. She told them that she had to get some clothes for the pilot. His uniform would have to be buried; no trace of his possessions could be left anywhere around, for the Germans might come looking for him. She explained that some false papers were being prepared for him. Then, somehow or other, he would be picked up and sent on his way toward the south.

And so Melse found himself with a diver on his property.[1] He made a point of bringing food and drink to the man in the hayloft himself. But on the third day, early in the morning, when he brought the pilot his breakfast before going out onto the land to do his daily work, he found the Englishman standing before the barn door, clothed in the Zeeland costume Melse had provided for him.

Melse asked the pilot what he planned to do. The pilot replied in English that he intended to take a look outside.

Melse knew no English, and so he understood not a word. He repeated his question. And the pilot repeated his answer.

Melse mumbled something about having no idea what the man wanted. Then he tried to communicate by shrugging his shoulders.

The pilot pointed outside. Then he pointed to the hayloft where he had been staying. He complained that it was dark up there.

But Melse, who still did not understand what the man wanted, grabbed him firmly by the shoulder and spun him around. He pointed to the ladder and began to show him what to do, indicating that he was to climb the ladder. The pilot got the idea and soon was back up in the hayloft, where it was completely dark. Once again he complained that it was dark.

Melse still understood nothing of it and went below. Once he was back in the house, he told mother Beth what had happened, explaining that the man was talking about "dark." Melse suspected that this was a reference to their son Dirk.

---

[1] The term "diver" is commonly used to refer to people of all sorts who had reason to hide from the Germans during the occupation of the Netherlands. The Dutch refer to a diver as an "onderduiker." —Trans.

Melse did not know what to do, and so he took away the ladder leading up to the hayloft. Then he paid a call on the local schoolteacher and asked him what it meant when an Englishman said "dark."

"Dark? Dark?" The schoolteacher thought for a moment, uncertain of Melse's pronunciation, and then told him what it meant. He asked: "Why did you want to know that, Melse? Have you been listening to English radio broadcasts?"

The teacher had supplied Melse with a diversion, for he did not want anyone thinking he was hiding an Englishman on his farm. "I might just do that someday, teacher," he said, and then he disappeared.

Now Melse understood what the pilot was talking about. When he got back home and climbed up the ladder, he created a makeshift window that let some light into the pilot's living space. When the sunshine finally penetrated the hayloft, the pilot blinked a number of times. His eyes were not used to all that light. Melse then made the opening still larger. The pilot put his face right in front of the opening and looked across the island of Walcheren all the way to Middelburg, with its severely damaged carillon tower right next to a prominent church.

The pilot was very grateful and enthusiastic. He made sure to say how nice the view was. But again Melse failed to understand him. The pilot tried once more: "Yes, very nice, thank you, sir!"

Melse pointed to the ladder and shook his head. He raised his finger by way of warning. The pilot understood at once and shook his head, indicating that no, he would never do such a thing. Thereby he put Melse at ease. Then he pointed again to the view now available to him. "Very nice, indeed!"

Melse departed, muttering once again that he had no idea what the man was talking about.

*   *   *

After a few days Tina came again and reported that there was no underground worker able to come out to the farm just then because the Germans were keeping a very close watch on everything in the neighborhood. Dirk, especially, should stay away.

She had been sent to instruct the pilot to let his beard grow. She also had glasses for him to wear as part of the disguise he would need. His head would have to be shaved, and he would be wearing the garb of a Roman Catholic priest. In such a disguise he would be moved to his next destination.

By this time Jacob Jobse was starting to get around again, and so Tina thought that he might be able to smuggle the pilot to Bergen op Zoom. Others would take charge of him once he was there.

"It's a dangerous assignment," sighed Melse. Together Tina and her father climbed the ladder into the hayloft.

The pilot saluted as soon as he saw Tina. In his Zeeland garb, he looked like a bit of a clown, for the outfit was too big for him, especially in the arms and legs.

When he caught the drift of Tina's message, he showed her with a gesture that he was already beginning to grow a beard. But Tina shook her head: she wanted more than stubble.

Thinking that she had not understood him, he repeated his gesture. But she shook her head again and held her hand far beneath her chin; then, with her other hand, she acted as though she was stroking a set of long whiskers.

The pilot found it a funny sight. He slapped his knee and laughed out loud. Melse put a finger over his lips to stress to him that he was supposed to keep still. Then the pilot took hold of some hay and held it under his chin, as a sign that he now understood what Tina wanted. Despite himself, he burst out laughing again. And Tina had great difficulty to keep from following his example. She found him most amusing.

Melse and his daughter went below. It was time to contact Jacob Jobse and inform him about his assignment.

Melse thought it would be best to begin by asking him to come over to the farm. Within a matter of minutes Tina was back with Jacob in tow. He stared with big, dark eyes at Melse as if to ask: "Have I done something wrong?"

"How's your leg, Jacob?" asked Melse.

"It's getting a lot stronger. I think that by next week I'll be able to do some real work again. But before then I want to have another good talk with the minister, Melse. I can't take much more of what he's been dishing up."

Melse cut him off as if to reprove him gently. He advised his friend to be more long-suffering. "Be thankful that it was not any worse."

Jacob replied: "But I don't imagine you summoned me so that you could call me to account for my attitude toward the minister, did you?"

"No, I have something I'd like you to do. But, my friend, you have to realize that it's a matter of secrecy. You see, I have a diver up in my hayloft."

"Well, that puts you in the very same position as me," said Jacob. "I've had one for about a year already. Only, mine is not up in the hayloft, because I'm not rich enough to have one. Mine is in the attic of my house, and he peels potatoes for Joan, but she finds that he takes too much off the potatoes. Still, she lets it go, because the poor guy has to have something to do; otherwise he'll eventually go crazy. And now, what do you want me to do with your diver? Is he going to wind up in my attic as well?"

"No, not that. My diver has to be brought over to Bergen op Zoom, and the underground is asking you to do it."

Melse then explained that the diver was an English pilot. And so it was a dangerous assignment which could cost Jacob his head. "Therefore you must first think carefully and decide what you are — and are not — willing to undertake. If you say no to this request, let nothing be said about this matter. But then, Jacob, your lips will have to be sealed — do you understand? No one in the whole village may know anything about this."

Jacob was offended: "David Melse, can you think of a single instance in which I have let out some secret by talking freely? Oh boy! All you have to do is tell me what needs to be done, and you'll find me ready and willing."

"All we're asking you to do is to accompany the man to Bergen op Zoom on the train. He'll be dressed as a Roman Catholic priest. He already has quite a beard, and tomorrow evening you must shave the top of his head. You do know how to do that kind of thing, don't you? Don't you cut your own children's hair?"

"Do you want me to cut the hair off the top of his head or shave it?" asked Jacob Jobse.

"I don't know anything about such things, Jacob, but I think it would be best if the top of his head was completely bare. And his beard needs to be trimmed and brought to a bit of a point."

"Do you want me to do his fingernails too?"

"This is not a matter for joking, Jacob. Life and death are at stake here."

"Listen, I'm just as serious as that goat over there," said Jacob, "But I need to know just what you want me to do. How's the pilot's Dutch?"

"He doesn't speak a word of Dutch."

Jacob's eyes opened wide when he heard this. "What am I supposed to do with this fellow on the train if he doesn't understand a word of what I'm saying? They'd be on to him in no time!"

"I really don't know. I suppose it would be best if both of you would decide to remain silent for the whole journey. We should see to it that he takes along some kind of Roman Catholic book. Maybe he could recite his prayers during the journey."

Jacob sighed. Finally he said: "Of all the things that a fellow could be called on to do!" Then he left, promising to come back the next morning to give the pilot his new hair-do.

The sun was not yet up the next day when Jacob came by. With Melse right behind him, he climbed the ladder to the hayloft. The makeshift window was completely closed, and so they used a barn lantern to provide some light.

The pilot immediately asked who Jacob was. Clearly the sight of a stranger standing before him caused him some consternation.

"What did he say?" asked Jacob.

"If you tell me, we'll both know," answered Melse calmly.

"There you have it already! As soon as he says something, I'm in a pickle. How in the world is this supposed to work? How do you imagine we're ever going to get this fellow safely to Bergen op Zoom?"

Jacob then took a good look at the diver. His cool, black eyes seemed to bore into the young man, who was feeling uncomfortable under such intense scrutiny. The pilot turned to David Melse again and asked who Jacob was.

This time David Melse figured out what the question must mean. He made a gesture to indicate that Jacob had come to cut his hair. He then took off his Zeeland cap and pointed to the top of his own head, which was already quite bare.

The pilot now understood him and began to laugh. He fell to his knees and bent forward to make his head available.

"He looks like a joker, if you ask me," said Jacob, who unpacked his implements and set to work. The young pilot had quite a head of hair. Jacob removed a circular portion from the top of his head and began to shave it. Next he tackled the beard, which had grown quite a bit while the man was in hiding. He made it symmetrical so that it came to a point below his chin, which did not take him long. The pilot then ran his hand over the top of his head. He stroked his beard and asked for a looking-glass.

"What's he saying now?" asked Jacob. "What does he want with a class? What kind of a class would he be talking about? Or could it be that his name is Klaas?"

"I have no idea," said Melse.

The two men then nodded to the pilot by way of saying goodbye. Down the ladder they went. Once they were below, they took the ladder away.

*   *   *

Tina came by on her bicycle, bringing with her the costume of a Roman Catholic priest. That evening the pilot was to accompany her to Middelburg, where he would spend the night. The next morning Jacob would join him there and take him along on the train.

The first part of the journey went well. The English pilot had been transformed by his disguise. Moreover, he seemed to be an excellent actor. He even walked like a priest, and he looked at his surroundings in a compassionate but reserved way that suggested he was a very devout man.

When they got on the train, he sat directly opposite Jacob in the corner of a rundown compartment whose windows had been shot out. At the last moment, a young lady entered the compartment and sat opposite him. She promptly began to read a book. The pilot then took out his rosary and began mumbling something that was supposed to resemble a series of prayers. And so the train pulled out of Middelburg without incident.

When it stopped in Arnemuiden, Rev. Verhulst, of all people, got on. He glanced into the compartment in which they were seated and seemed about to enter it. But when he recognized Jacob, he nodded stiffly and withdrew. He would seek a place in another compartment.

It was not exactly friendly behavior on the minister's part, but Jacob was relieved. Then he racked his brain to try to figure out why in the world Rev. Verhulst would be getting on the train in Arnemuiden. Finally he decided it was the minister's own business.

After a while the priest seemed to be finished with his prayers. He took a look around the compartment. He coughed and drew the attention of the young lady, who looked up from her book. And now it appeared that nature was stronger than doctrine. The pilot gave the young lady a fetching wink. She responded by blushing and quickly burying herself in her book again.

Jacob's heart was pounding. He tried to signal to the pilot that there was to be no more of such nonsense, but the young man seemed to have forgotten that he was in Jacob's custody. It had been a very long time since he had enjoyed an opportunity for contact with a beautiful girl. And so he coughed again. When the young lady looked up, he gave her his most charming smile, once more accompanied by a wink.

Jacob then placed his big shoe on his travel companion's toes and applied some pressure. But the pilot acted as though he didn't get the point; instead he continued to enjoy the beauty of the young lady sitting opposite him.

"If this continues, we'll be lost before we get to Goes," said Jacob to himself. He looked around anxiously, as though he were a mouse caught in a trap.

They managed to get through Goes without mishap, but then the trouble began anew. Before the train got to Kapelle, Jacob decided to take action. He had noticed that the young lady was wearing an orange ring on her index finger. That was enough for him.[2] He stood up and signaled to her to follow him into the passageway outside the compartment. "You're a true patriot, aren't you?" he asked, with his big, dark eyes focusing intensely on her face.

"And what are you?" she responded.

"It happens that I'm accompanying an English pilot to Bergen op Zoom. That's who the man dressed as a Roman Catholic priest really is. You know how to keep a secret, don't you?"

"So that's what's going on!" she said. Earlier she had found him a very unusual priest, for he sat there winking at her. But now that she understood the situation, she was quite willing to cooperate. She promised that she would not betray him. Still, she thought that the pilot should be more careful. Before long the train would arrive in Kreekkrak, and there it would be inspected by the Germans. If the pilot did not watch out, the Germans would catch on. After all, what sort of priest winks at young ladies?

She laughed. Now that the danger seemed to have passed, Jacob laughed too. Together they enjoyed the moment.

Just then, Rev. Verhulst came toward them along the passageway. He paused and said to Jacob: "What are you doing flirting with a young woman? And you the father of three children!" He walked on immediately, leaving Jacob behind with a beet-red face.

"And who would that be?" asked the young lady.

"That's my shepherd," answered Jacob. "He's on his way to look for some lost sheep."

The young woman went back into the compartment to retrieve her luggage. She gave the pilot a final wink and disappeared to another compartment so that she would not lead the poor young man into further temptation.

---

[2] The royal family of the Netherlands is called the House of Orange. A person wearing the color orange during the occupation could therefore be regarded as demonstrating loyalty to the Queen. —Trans.

Still red with embarrassment, Jacob went back into the compartment and sat down opposite the pilot. He was no longer enjoying the journey. He was offended to the depths of his being. Before the train reached Bergen op Zoom, some Germans came aboard to check on papers. Everyone had to produce identification documents of some sort. One of the Germans came into the compartment in which Jacob and the pilot were seated. He made a polite bow toward the priest. When the priest made as if to produce some papers, the German signaled that it would not be necessary. Jacob's papers were found to be in order. The German then nodded again to the priest and carefully closed the door of the compartment. This time the priest gave Jacob a wink.

When they got to Bergen op Zoom, a man with a Brabant newspaper in his hand was standing on the platform, as arranged. Jacob turned the pilot over to him. He was relieved to have come safely through his dangerous assignment.

*　　*　　*

The next evening, when Rev. Verhulst was sitting in front of the window with his wife, he saw Jacob Jobse approaching. The minister led him directly to his study and said: "So, Jacob, after what I observed on the train yesterday, I did not expect to see you at my door for quite a number of months. I was very disappointed in you — I have to tell you that. Or have you come here to confess that you did wrong?"

He invited Jacob to sit down, but Jacob chose to remain standing. His imposing physical presence filled the little room. His eyes were wide open, and he was looking directly at Rev. Verhulst.

"Reverend, there are people who think they have seen something when actually they have seen nothing. Even though they have their eyes wide open, they might just as well shut them, for then they see just as much."

"What are you trying to tell me — that yesterday I did *not* see you in the train making jokes in the passageway with that young woman, who, by the way, does not have such a good name?"

Now, Jacob Jobse did not know the young woman, but it was true that he had stood talking with her in the passageway of the train, where they exchanged jokes. Nevertheless . . .

As the minister talked, he drew on some official church language regarding discipline. He then asked Jacob Jobse whether he really expected him to keep his eyes closed.

Jacob made it clear that he had come to the minister to ask him to take back his sharp words of reproof. If he refused, the matter would have to be brought to the consistory meeting.

By the time he heard all of this, Rev. Verhulst had risen from his chair. And although he was quite a bit smaller than Jacob Jobse, he felt he was much better able to tell this unruly brother a thing or two when he was on his feet than when he was looking up at him from a low chair.

"I really have to say that you're a rough and inconsiderate fellow, Jacob Jobse. When I ponder what I saw with my own eyes and what you have just told me now, I see that there's only one possible interpretation of that scene in the train yesterday. Now, I don't mean to draw the conclusion that there's already an improper relationship between you and the girl, but I do have to say that the way you were talking with her is out of bounds for a married man. And to think that you have only just gotten off your sickbed!"

"You don't know anything about this matter, Reverend, but once I tell you just what was going on in the train, you'll see that I was not doing anything wrong."

Jacob then proceeded to tell enough of the story to bring the minister around. Rev. Verhulst saw that he had indeed made a mistake, and he admitted his error in a generous way. He extended his hand to Jacob and said: "I beg your pardon. I acted on the basis of appearance, and I was too quick to draw a conclusion. I take back my words."

But Jacob declined to shake his hand. "There's another matter that stands between you and me, Reverend. You have characterized me as a wolf in sheep's clothing. Is that still what you say today?"

Rev. Verhulst's face became very somber. "You know very well what I think about underground resistance work, brother Jobse.

What you need to do is bow before my preaching and quit criticizing me."

"I asked you whether you still look upon me as a wolf in sheep's clothing, Reverend." Jacob was not about to let the matter go.

"What a bulldog nature!" said the minister to himself spitefully. "Once Jacob sinks his teeth into something, he never lets go." Still, the minister knew how to stand his ground. "You know how I think about these matters, brother Jobse."

"So you're sticking to your position?"

Jacob turned to leave, and when he had reached the door he said: "Then it will be up to the consistory to determine which of us is right. You realize that you cannot celebrate the Lord's supper with wolves wearing sheep's clothing. If you are a true shepherd, you must drive the wolves out of the fold, for they will devour the sheep. And so it becomes a question of church discipline — if, indeed, you truly mean what you said."

Jacob Jobse departed and left the minister alone in his study. "That fellow really gets on my nerves," thought Rev. Verhulst to himself. He could feel his heart pounding anxiously. Of late he was having a lot of trouble with headaches.

*   *   *

More months passed. Then, one day, the Melses received a short, clandestine message to the effect that Dirk was all right.

But when more than a year had gone by since Dirk's last visit, they saw the dreaded German automobiles pulling up in front of their farm one day. In marched three Germans, two of them in uniform. The Germans announced that they were there to search the house. Everything was pulled apart and turned upside down, and father and mother Melse were interrogated sternly. Finally the three Germans left without having accomplished anything. There was nothing to be found on the farm, and the parents knew nothing.

Three days later the mailman brought a little letter in stenciled form. Above it, in German, stood the words "Police Detachment Amersfoort." Their son had written — or signed — some sort of German declaration which David Melse could not decipher. And so he took the declaration to the principal of the local school, who translated it for him as follows:

"The following conditions apply to me: each month I am allowed to write one letter and receive one letter. I am not permitted to receive packages. Money may be sent up to the amount of two guilders per month. Making inquiries of the commandant of the camp is futile, for they will not be answered. Prisoner D. Melse, Block 4D, #312."

Now father Melse knew that his son was a prisoner and was locked up in the dreaded camp in Amersfoort.

Later they got more short messages from Dirk, always including the stereotypical phrase "I'm doing fine." David Melse wondered whether there were any victims in the camp at Amersfoort who were not "doing fine."

Letters of this sort with the phrase "I'm doing fine" were also being received by Joris Melse on Schouwen. Uncle Joris's son David had also fallen into the hands of the enemy.

When the news about Uncle Joris's son reached the family on Walcheren, Henry said, a bit scornfully, that Uncle Joris would now have to humble himself even more. His father admonished him for his attitude.

Now that both families were in the same position, there was some exchange of letters between them. This was a change, for it had been years since the two families had written to one another regularly. Even so, the new circumstances did not bring the two families closer together — not yet . . .

*   *   *

That summer David Melse began to turn gray, and his back, which had always been ramrod-straight, became somewhat bent. He could stand before the window for long stretches of time looking out over the flat land of Walcheren, and sometimes he simply did not hear mother Beth's voice when she tried to tell him something.

Chapter 4

Once the Allies landed on the beaches of France on June 6, 1944, hope revived in the hearts of the people of Zeeland. Those who had a forbidden radio in the house made sure to listen to every broadcast that came from Radio Orange in England. But in other respects, the summer went by as usual.

David Melse heard nothing more from his son Dirk. There wasn't even a little note or an indication from someone or other that he was alive and well.

Jacob Jobse was the one who brought them the illegal newspaper in which they could read the names of the underground fighters for the fatherland who had been executed by the Germans. One day the name of David Melse appeared on the list, but Dirk's name was not there. Yet, David Melse from Schouwen and Duiveland and Dirk Melse from Walcheren had worked in the same underground group and had been taken prisoner at the same time . . .

Father Melse realized that he would now have to act on his father's behalf by making a visit to Uncle Joris. But it would be a difficult assignment. It was not so much the journey itself that would be hard, for in the summer of 1944 travel between the islands had not yet become particularly arduous for the people of Zeeland.

As long as David Melse was biking over Walcheren and North Beveland or standing with his bicycle on a ferry, his mind was occupied with the purpose of his journey. Would he find words of comfort for the bereaved father? He was well aware that he might be asked to make the same sacrifice that his uncle had now made, and he wondered whether he was truly prepared for it. In his heart he thought the answer was no. But in that case, how could he be of comfort to his uncle?

But David Melse had an additional purpose in making this journey to Schouwen and Duiveland. His secondary purpose was one he hardly dared admit to himself. Somewhere in the neighborhood of Uncle Joris's farm lived the man who had been asking himself anxiously whether he could really be a child of God in view of the fact that God's hand never chastised him. David Melse wanted to meet that man and talk with him, for he hoped that this unusual man would be able to give him the comfort he needed more than ever, now that God's hand had afflicted him by allowing his son to be taken prisoner by the Germans.

When Melse was back on land at Zierikzee and was biking away from the town, he saw something that diverted his thoughts. In *Faithful* (*Trouw*) and *Free Netherlands* (*Vrij Nederland*), the underground newspapers, he had already read that Schouwen and Duiveland had been partly flooded by the Germans, but now he beheld the situation with his own eyes. The water had been allowed to come through the sluices, but only to a certain level. The Germans made sure that nowhere was it deeper than one foot. Yet it was *salt* water, and so it ruined everything that lived. Even though there were trees that still had green leaves above the water level, they would slowly die, and the ground would surely be poisoned.

*   *   *

David Melse had brought along some words of comfort from Walcheren, and he intended to address them to Joris Melse, his uncle. But when he got to his uncle's place, he found that what the old man was crying over like a child was the ruin of his land. He had been told that he would have to abandon the land. The Germans had just issued a decree to the effect that the farmers were to get off their farms. And so Uncle Joris would have to await the end of the war far away from the island on which he now lived.

His whole life he had slaved so that he could own a farm of his own. The members of his extended family knew him to be completely preoccupied with his work. Earning money was what really counted: he ignored everything else. Now that he was bent over with rheumatism and could hardly work anymore, he would see all his work come to naught in a single season.

David Melse was not even sure whether his uncle was still thinking about his son David who had been put to death by the Germans. Could it be that disappointment about the land had caused him to forget his grief over his son? Could this forgetting be God's gracious way of easing his pain as a father? Or did it mean that the land meant even more to him than his own son? Was it possible that God's hand of judgment had now struck him by taking away the very thing that was most precious to him? David Melse knew what it was to feel God's hand of chastisement, for his son was in German hands. But he still had his land . . .

"Your son died as a hero," said David Melse, trying to comfort his uncle.

"My son? I'm glad I don't have a son anymore, now that I'm losing my land."

And then the words David Melse meant to speak about his own son died on his lips. He did his best to help his uncle with all the work that had to be done in great haste before the farm was abandoned. It appeared that under the circumstances, there would be no opportunity for a visit to the neighbor on whose farm Dirk had hidden. The farmer in question was named Bart de Vaat; Uncle Joris explained that Dirk had stayed on his farm longer than in any other hiding place. David Melse wondered whether he would get a chance to talk with Bart de Vaat on a later occasion. It might happen sometime, if it was God's will.

*   *   *

The people were living between hope and fear. "Mad Tuesday" came and went: it was the day when rumors raced all around the country that the Germans were on the point of being chased out by the Allies. But the people's hopes were dashed. No one knew how those rumors had gotten started.

On the very next Sunday, dozens of Lancaster bombers, flying at frightening speeds, swept low over the Western Scheldt, and on the way back to their bases in Britain they flew over Biggekerke. By mistake they released some of their bombs when they were right over the village. As a result, many houses were destroyed. Fifty-one people were killed.

From his home, Jacob Jobse could clearly see the plumes of smoke rising in the air. He also heard the thunderous sounds that made the windows rattle in their frames. "Joan, I've got to go down there," he said. "There will be work to do."

60

His wife nodded. Within a couple of minutes later he was hurrying on his bicycle to the neighboring village. He helped to dig up victims of the bombing in the midst of all the smoke and fire and ruins. Mothers and their children were lying dead with bricks and smashed fragments of stone all around them. Using his own shovel, Jacob dug out a mother who had her lifeless infant at her breast. The next day was devoted to making caskets.

Jacob Jobse was very quiet that Sunday evening as he looked at his wife and children. There was one question that kept coming up in his heart: why *those people* and not *me?* He had no answer to this question. But before he went to bed on that memorable Sunday, he sank to his knees with Joan to thank God that his little family had been saved and to pray for the loved ones of those who had perished in the neighboring village.

*   *   *

Finally September was over, and October was upon them. Jacob Jobse was sitting on the roof of the unique little church in Biggekerke, where repairs were needed after the bombing. From his perch he could see over all of Walcheren: the paths that led to the dunes were directly in his line of sight. And what he beheld was a remarkable sight: people everywhere were moving in the direction of the dunes — people with carts and wagons loaded with household goods. There were mothers leading their children by the hand. Once he came down from the roof of the church, he was told that Radio Orange in England had warned the people of Zeeland to move to higher places because quite a bit of Zeeland was about to be flooded.

"What do you think we should do, Jacob?" asked Joan.

"I'll discuss it with David Melse." It turned out that Melse had also heard the report, but he thought the flooding would not be all that extensive. A great many reports were sent out with the intention of making the Germans nervous.

Melse's own farm was not on such low land, and he figured that the Allies would not let in very much water. And so, if Jacob Jobse was not able to stay in his own house, he was welcome to come to the Melse farm with his wife and children.

61

"But we're not alone," said Jacob Jobse.

"Not alone? What do you mean?"

"I have three divers up in my attic. They're Poles who were forced to serve in the German army and have deserted."

"What? What's this you're telling me, Jacob?"

"They've been sitting in my attic since February. They're fine fellows, even though I can't understand a word they say. Would it be all right to bring them along if it becomes necessary?"

"Well, if you really have to, I suppose so. But please be very careful, Jacob." Melse felt he had to add a word of warning.

It was October 3, at exactly 12:30. Jacob Jobse and his wife and children were enjoying their noon meal when they heard a strange rumble not far away. Jacob ran out the door and across his yard. Then he caught sight of the dreaded Lancasters. They circled above Domburg for a moment and headed back in the direction of Westkapelle. It appeared that their flight path would take them directly overhead in just a matter of minutes.

Jacob watched as the heavy bombs fell on the strong sea dike. There was a muffled rumble. Then smoke and flames could be seen rising into the air.

The first hole had been punched in the wall protecting Walcheren from the sea. Salt water would now stream over the land.

"Shouldn't we be fleeing to the dunes, Jacob?" asked Joan.

"The dunes are full of Krauts. And what would we do with our Polish divers over there? Have you got an answer to that one?"

Joan did not know what to say. They decided to wait calmly for a while. The Melse farm was not far away; they could always go there for shelter. Maybe the water would not rise very high.

But a few days later there were more holes in the dike — in the Nollen Dike and by Rammekes and by Veere. The beautiful island of Walcheren, wounded on all sides, could no longer hold out. It seemed to be sinking away into the sea, like a ship taking on water.

*　　　*　　　*

It was halfway through October by then, and Jacob Jobse was standing on his land in front of his house one evening looking at the water as it crept ever closer to his home. He saw that the water was higher than usual. He was somewhat uneasy, but he did not want to communicate his apprehension to his wife and children. When he came inside, Joan asked him what he thought of the situation.

"I think we're all right for now. We can go to bed." He assured her that the water would not flood their land just yet. But he hardly slept that night. At 5:30 in the morning, he was summoned from his bed by David Melse, who informed him that the water was now up to the front steps.

Jacob Jobse got dressed and put on some boots. Joan and the children also got out of bed. Jacob went up to the attic to make it known to the Polish deserters that they should get ready to depart.

Within an hour the water was coming into the house. The children's toys were afloat. The stove was still burning, but there was water in the ashes compartment.

"We'd better bring all the bedding upstairs, Joan. It's not safe here anymore." Jacob also moved the stove upstairs, along with as much of the furniture as he could get up there. They didn't have a lot of furniture, and so the job was soon done. He made a new hole in the chimney and ran the stove-pipe through it. The stove could burn just as well upstairs as downstairs.

"Now I'm going out for a while," he announced.

"Where are you going, Jacob?" asked Joan. "Everything is closed — surely you can see that."

"I have to try and save my animals. They're God's creatures too, and they don't know how to save themselves. I can't just let them drown."

Wading through the water in the yard, Jacob gathered some branches and twigs and piled them on top of his lower barn. Then he moved the cages holding his rabbits and chickens up there. He forced the goat up the walkway to the higher level of the barn. The goat put up a lot of resistance, and so Jacob was sweating profusely. He dried off his face with his colorful handkerchief. The Polish divers were laughing and making some sort of gestures that seemed to have a bearing on the milking of goats. But Jacob was not in the mood for jokes. Somehow he had not expected that the water would get as high as it now stood. And there was no telling how much higher it might yet rise.

But for the present, the water went no higher. When high tide was over, the water level fell as quickly as it had risen. It did remain about half a meter deep in the living room, but when Jacob put his boots on, he could still get outside and save his carpenter's tools and get some feed for the animals out of the little barn and drag it up to the roof. He still had potatoes and vegetables and some fuel left over. And so he knew they would be all right for a few days. He hoped these conditions would not last long.

*   *   *

Time kept marching on, and soon it was winter. The Germans were entrenched in their bunkers in the dunes. They directed their guns over the villages of Walcheren toward the positions occupied by the Canadian troops beyond Middelburg. And the Canadians kept shooting right over Jacob's little house in the direction of the dunes. The noise of the guns and the bursting of the shells continued night and day.

The situation became critical. There was less and less to eat now that there was nothing to be obtained in the village, where all

the needy people were huddled. And the water was poisoned because of the dead farm animals floating around in it.

One Sunday evening Jacob and his household were sitting up on the second floor with just a little bit of light from a petroleum lamp. They just could not get used to the sound of the guns above their heads, accompanied by the sound of the water sloshing around in the room on the first floor, and the sound of the cabinet endlessly bumping against the bedframe. Finally it was too much for Jacob. He began to think of the sermons of Rev. Verhulst, the ones in which the minister had appealed to the people to repent. By this time, Rev. Verhulst, who had been having trouble with his nerves, had left Walcheren for Brabant, where conditions were much better.

Jacob began to wonder whether the minister might not have been right after all. Is the Lord an angry God who comes in judgment? Jacob had no defense against the fear that had sprung up in his heart. He looked out the square second-floor window and saw an opening in the clouds. Through that opening he caught sight of a star in God's spacious heavens. Just at that moment, a stanza of Psalm 66 came to mind. He had learned it back in his school days, but he had hardly heard it sung in church or at home since then:

Into the net Thou, God, hast brought us;
Thou heavy burdens didst impose.
Thou didst let man upon us trample;
We have been humbled by our foes.
We went through fire, we went through water,
Yet Thou didst show Thy power and grace.
Thou hast delivered us, Thy people,
And brought us to a spacious place.

"Joan, do you remember that stanza from Psalm 66?"

"Which stanza do you mean, Jacob?" asked Joan. She knew so many psalms.

"The one that begins with 'Into the net . . .' "

"Of course — why wouldn't I know that one, Jacob?"

"Would you sing it with me, Joan?"

Jacob did not have a very good singing voice. He was usually somewhat hoarse, but he loved to sing all the same. As for Joan, she had a firm and clear alto voice.

The Polish divers found the singing strange, for they did not understand a word of it. Even so, they listened respectfully. And when the stanza was done, they clapped spontaneously and asked that it be repeated. Jacob and Joan wound up singing all the well-known stanzas of Psalm 66.

At that moment a strange warmth stole into Jacob Jobse's heart. It was as though the cobwebs had been cleared out of his brain. It was as though he was living in a completely different world — that's how close he felt to God just then. He now felt ashamed of all his worries. When the Polish divers withdrew behind their curtain and he knelt down with Joan before their bed spread out on the floor, his prayer was so simple and childlike, so full of trust, that Joan was also greatly encouraged. A couple of tears trickled down her cheeks.

It had been a long time since Jacob had slept so well and soundly as he did that remarkable night, when the water sloshed about beneath him in his own house and the fire above his head was not from the sky.

*　　　*　　　*

As for David Melse, he was not having much trouble with water on his farm. His farm was a bit closer to the village and thus was on higher ground. He had brought his animals to a field in the village, where they joined the animals of many other farmers. His farm implements and the feed for his animals were piled up around the church. The village had become a small island in the middle of a hungry sea.

The church was being used to house refugees. There was enough to eat since many of the animals were being slaughtered, but the supplies of wheat and barley were rapidly dwindling. The cows were still giving milk, and so the village community was safe for the present.

But the land . . . that was another story. Melse thought repeatedly about Sodom and Gomorrah, the two cities which God has turned into a salt sea. He also thought about what had happened to Schouwen and Duiveland. He had seen it with his own eyes.

And then he thought about Uncle Joris, who had been punished with the loss of both his son and his land. Now David Melse knew it was his turn. Walcheren would suffer the very same fate — no, an even worse fate. For on Schouwen and Duiveland the Germans had at least made sure that the water level did not rise too high, but on Walcheren the dikes had been broken through, and so it was no longer possible to control the water level. The ebb and flow of the tides was just the same now on their island as it was at sea. And that would mean devastation for his farm — a catastrophe whose effects would linger for years.

He knew that he would never recover from the loss. He still had a mortgage on his property. He needed every harvest just to be able to exist and to meet his mortgage obligations. He did not have any savings, as Francke and some of the other men on bigger farms did. The next summer he wouldn't be able to get a cent from anything he grew on his land. And would it be any better the summer after that? How long would it be before the earth again allowed something to grow? And when the time of growth returned, what sorts of crops would he be able to plant and harvest? No, he would never recover from the catastrophe. Whatever he had managed to build up in the course of his life through hard work and thrift and careful planning was lost — that much he knew. How would he ever manage to find a new way to make a living as he got older?

Such were David Melse's worries, and his aged father worried along with him. "It's a visitation from the Lord, my son," declared the old man. "Just read what the prophets have to say. If oppression from the enemy doesn't help, then there is sickness among the animals and famine and drought. God has more than one stick with which to beat us. I just hope we come to understand these things in time. There's no escaping the hand of the Lord, says an old proverb. We'll simply have to submit ourselves to this chastisement. Dirk isn't here anymore, and the farm is standing under water. And we have no idea what else may yet happen. Do you really think our minister was off the mark when he preached those sermons on Jeremiah?" It was clear that Grandfather didn't think so.

His words were not exactly encouraging for David Melse. He, too, had lost his certainty.

*   *   *

One Wednesday afternoon Jacob Jobse came along on a raft he had built for this time of flooding. He tied up his raft by the barn and walked through the water in his boots as he made his way over to David Melse's house. "I've come to see if I can help you, in case you have need of anything. And I also want to bring you greetings from Joan. Have you heard anything from Dirk?"

Mother Beth shook her head. "No, we've heard nothing."

"Well, the thing to do is keep your spirits up," said Jacob. "It may turn out for the best after all."

"It may also turn out for the worst," observed Melse.

"If we leave it in God's hands, it always turns out for the best," answered Jacob.

"You're taking these matters too lightly," said grandfather Melse. "I have already told this to my son, and now I need to say it to you: it may well turn out that the minister was right when he preached those sermons appealing for repentance. The Lord has more than one stick with which to beat us."

Jacob looked at him for a moment with eyes wide open. "The Lord also has more than one ointment with which to heal our wounds," he responded.

68

Jacob thought to himself that the Melse family did not have all that much reason to complain. After all, they were still living in their house, and their farm animals were safe in the enclosure by the church. They had enough to eat at home, and they could still pray every day that their own son would be spared.

They should think once about Uncle Joris. His whole farm was standing under water, and the Krauts had already murdered his son. And now Uncle Joris had been driven from his land and was sitting somewhere in Dordrecht in an upper room peering out the window while the farm he had worked for lies abandoned and might well be destroyed or looted. The thing to do, thought Jacob, was to look to those who were having an even harder time of it than you, for then you would realize that there was reason to be thankful. And so Jacob believed they were guilty of a great sin if they sat there murmuring about their lot.

As for Rev. Verhulst, he could be left out of the picture. He had talked about the seventy-year exile in Babylon, but he turned out to be far off the mark. In just a little while the people of Walcheren would be liberated, and then they would again fly the Dutch flag. Even with all the misery they were suffering at the moment, there was more reason for them to be thankful than to complain. Those were the thoughts Jacob was trying to express.

"How are you folks coming along?" he was asked.

"We're getting by," Jacob answered. But he knew that he had quite a problem with one of his legs. He went around the neighborhood on his raft because there were people almost everywhere who were trapped on their second floor. He would check on their chimneys and, if need be, connect their stove pipe to the chimney on the second floor. He also did other odd jobs for his neighbors. He cobbled together rabbit cages up on the roofs so that the rabbits would be safe from the water — that sort of thing. But in order to do all that work, he often had to wade through the water. And sometimes he would open a leg wound when he brushed against that awful barbed wire. And so he was now walking around with an open wound.

"You people should have a look at my leg sometime." Jacob rolled up his pantleg and let them examine his left leg. It looked awful. They could all see a couple of open, festering wounds. The filthy sea water seemed to have caused an infection. As long as he kept the leg wet, he could endure the pain, he told them, but once it became dry, the skin lost its elasticity, and it was all he could do to keep from crying out.

Mother Beth had said nothing. At once she went to her medicine cabinet and got out some iodine. She put a few drops of the brown ointment on the wounds. Jacob did not wince but allowed her to do what was needed. As she put a makeshift bandage over his wounds, she told him that he would now have to keep the leg dry.

"That's easy for you to say," replied Jacob, "but how am I supposed to help the people then? How can I go to the village with my raft to bring supplies to the people and pick up the things we need? I can't very well do like those Polish divers, who sit day and night in my second-floor rooms looking out the window. And I can't very well expect Joan to do all the work alone." And so it was clear to him that he would not be able to follow her well-meant advice. Nevertheless, he made a point of thanking Mrs. Melse for the medical assistance she had rendered, and he assured her that he would be most happy to do something for her in turn.

*　　　*　　　*

It was November 1944 . . . Goes and Middelburg and Vlissingen had already been wrested from the grasp of Hitler's Germany. The Canadians were approaching from the east, following the Kreekkrakdam corridor. Some English troops had landed near Westkapelle, in the midst of an inferno of water and fire. Many brave soldiers had lost their lives in the waves.

The village surrounded by water did not get much news. There was no electricity, and so the people could not listen to the radio. Only a few meager reports got through to the people. They did know that there was still fighting going on. The Germans were putting up a stubborn defense in the dunes and were making good use of the bunkers they had built.

And now the November storms were testing the island to the utmost. The fierce northwesterly wind, which was so much feared by the people living on the island because it could drive mountains

of water out of the North Sea against the coast, was blowing hard and sending water streaming toward the houses. Sometimes the water level was almost up to the eaves troughs.

The little house of Jacob Jobse was struck repeatedly by free-floating wood from fences that had been uprooted and from houses that had already fallen apart. The house creaked and groaned as the doors and windows were tested. The water was ice-cold, and at night the people huddled up on the second floor had to endure freezing temperatures.

Jacob did his best to appear brave before Joan and the children, but as a carpenter he knew all too well the endurance capacity of houses of that sort. It would not be very long before his house, too, would begin to collapse.

Using his raft, he still tried to keep up contact with the village and the houses in the vicinity, but his leg was making it almost impossible for him. As soon as he got out of the water and the skin dried up, the pain became unbearable and left him trembling. At nights he could not sleep.

*   *   *

One stormy morning, at daybreak, he was looking out the window when he observed that a small worker's house about a hundred meters away on the other side of the road had developed a big hole in one of its corners. Its inhabitants, who were also huddled up on their second floor, were probably not even aware of the danger as yet. Jacob took a good look and saw that the house was beginning to give way before the water. The blood streamed to his head. "Joan, get my boots," he cried. "The Aernoutse family is in big trouble. Those people have to get out of there at once — otherwise they'll drown before they even realize what's going on."

The three Polish divers also came to take a look. By this point they were beginning to understand just a bit of the dialect spoken in that part of Zeeland. They looked at each other and then fixed their gaze on what Jacob had observed. One of them made gestures to Jacob indicating that he was to stay home this time. The Pole pointed to his own leg and shook his head very firmly. He made it clear that the three of them would take care of the situation. It would be the very first time that they showed themselves in public since going into hiding, but they were willing to risk it. It had been a number of days since any Germans had been seen in the vicinity of the village.

At first Jacob refused, but then he gave in. The condition of his leg left him no choice.

The Poles climbed out the window and jumped down to the roof of the little barn that had been built directly onto the house. They released the raft from its moorings. They proved quite good at making their way around obstacles, and soon they were propelling the raft over to the threatened house. The people they rescued climbed out the window, and the result was that Jacob had six more people joining him in the confined space of his second floor.

"This had better not last much longer," he sighed. "We hardly have a place left to stand — never mind lie down."

Somehow arrangements were made. As the day went on, they kept the little Aernoutse family house in view. Before evening arrived, it seemed to slump to one side — the side where there was a big hole. Mrs. Aernoutse put her hands up over her face and cried out: "My poor little house! My poor furniture! Now we have nothing left!"

"You still have your husband and your children," said Jacob. "Thank God for them, and everything else will work out in the long run."

One morning the dreaded Lancaster bombers came flying very low over the flooded fields. The children cried out in terror, for they remembered the horrible bombardment that had struck Biggekerke. But Jacob and the Polish divers stood right in front of the window to get a good look. What they saw made them rejoice: the pilots dipped both wings. Clearly it was a signal: Walcheren was now free!

The Poles looked at each other in amazement. For them liberation meant the end of imprisonment. As quickly as possible they wanted to make contact with the Allies. They, too, feared the water. Their small, damp prison had kept them safe from the Germans long enough, they thought.

That day, at about noon, a man in a little boat came from the village and informed Jacob and the people with him that all who wanted to be evacuated were to make their wishes known at once. They would soon be taken away in an amphibious military vehicle.

Jacob did not need to think about it very long. He informed the man in the boat that they *all* wanted to be evacuated — the whole family, and also three Polish soldiers who had been in hiding with them for many months.

Melse got the same invitation at his farm. By that point, his family had also been forced to abandon the first floor of the house and take up residence on the second floor. The flood had gotten higher and higher: it stood at some thirty centimeters in their living room.

"I'm staying here," said Grandfather.

"Why would you want to do that?"

"I'm staying here with the animals and with our home," the old man repeated. Many of the old people of Walcheren said the very same thing once the liberation came.

"But the animals are all safe in the village!"

"That may be, but I'm staying here anyway. I'm staying with the animals."

Matters were discussed for a little while. They would all have preferred to stay, but mother Beth had one objection to staying. When she expressed it, she was also articulating what lived in her husband's heart: "If we stay here, we might not hear anything about Dirk."

She then looked at her husband in an inquiring way. He said: "That's right — we have to see what we can find out about our son."

It was decided that Grandfather and Henry would stay on the farm. All the others would evacuate.

*　　　*　　　*

Two days later, when the amphibious vehicle arrived to pick up Jacob Jobse, David Melse and mother Beth and their children were already seated in it. The Canadians were very sympathetic to their distress. They had all kinds of supplies with them — clothes and food and chocolate for the children. They distributed their supplies generously.

Melse had taken five baskets of locally grown apples from his attic. Now the Canadians were enjoying them. They sank their teeth deep into the apples, and through their gestures they made it clear that they found them very tasty.

By this point a channel of sorts had been laid out through the farmland, because earlier some of the rafts and boats had capsized or been punctured. Under the murky water were unseen obstacles that posed a deadly threat. One raft carrying cattle went down, and three people from the village lost their lives.

Jacob could not walk anymore. By this point he was lying on some straw, and despite the cold, there was sweat on his face. The pain was unbearable. Joan saw it and tried to wipe the tears from her eyes.

Melse was standing at the front of this curious conveyance, and when it passed once again along his beautiful orchard, he looked at the baskets of apples on board. Those were the last apples he would ever pluck from those trees. He had picked them only six weeks before. But now the trees were standing in water up to their crowns. Like a drowning man in need, they seemed to be extending their bare, knobby arms on high.

The trees were doomed to destruction. Melse took a last look at them and then let his eyes follow the little waves which the amphibious vehicle made in the murky water as it passed through. The branches bobbed a bit in the waves. It seemed that there was no land — everything had become sea.

Mother Beth watched her husband looking at the trees and knew what was going on in his heart. Just as Joan had sought the nearness of Jacob, so she went to stand by Melse and laid a hand on his shoulder. In silence they watched as their possessions disappeared from sight. "It's quite something," sighed Melse. More he did not say.

*   *   *

It was a strange experience for the evacuees to arrive in Middelburg. They saw people walking down dry streets with shoes on their feet! Just as strange were the houses with their neat curtains in front of the windows, houses that were occupied by people living normal lives. The evacuees had lived with the flood for so long that they were no longer accustomed to ordinary life.

Jacob was housed in a trade school along with his family. Melse was placed in the home of the lady that Tina worked for.

The very same evening a doctor arrived to examine Jacob's leg. He frowned when he got a good look at its lamentable condition. He then bandaged it himself and said: "Tomorrow I'll return and bring another doctor with me. In the meantime, keep it wet with some water that I'll have someone bring you."

Now that the leg was no longer in contact with sea water, the pain subsided somewhat. When the doctor was examining the leg, Jacob could see for himself that the wound was so deep that it went all the way to the bone. But he did not mention this to Joan.

The trade school was filled with evacuees; each had his own tale of woe. It turned out to be a restless night. Children cried, and there were always people coming and going.

The next morning, when the two doctors came, Jacob was feverish. Just then he saw Rev. Verhulst entering the room. The minister talked with some other people while the two doctors looked at Jacob's leg.

After the doctors conferred with one another, the specialist said: "Your leg will have to be amputated below the knee, Jobse. It would be best if your wife and children went to some other address." He then suggested a home in a village not far away. "And as for you, you should go directly to the hospital — there's no time to lose."

Joan became even more pale than she usually was. Her eyes were full of fear as they moved between the two doctors and Jacob.

No one said a word. Jacob now had to make a decision. He knew a great deal depended on what he decided. As happened so often, his thoughts returned to that wondrous evening up on the second floor, with the flood waters down below, when he and Joan had sung that stanza from Psalm 66 with the final lines:

Yet Thou didst show Thy power and grace.
Thou hast delivered us, Thy people,
And brought us to a spacious place.

At once his decision was made. "That leg is not coming off, Doctor," he announced. "I'm going to get better, and I'm going to keep both my legs so that I can continue to work and support my wife and children. Oh boy!"

Joan knew from long experience that Jacob's "Oh boy!" was a powerful signal. She felt encouraged. When he put his "Oh boy!" behind his words, Jacob never failed.

The doctors looked at one another in perplexity. The specialist shrugged his shoulders and said: "If you refuse to do as I say, Jobse, we will later have to take your leg off *above* the knee, and then your prospects of working to support your wife and children will be even dimmer than if you had allowed us to take it off below the knee. I'm warning you."

"Thanks for your warning, Doctor, but I'm *not* going to allow it. I'm going to keep this leg. Someday I'll come and thank you for the well-meant advice you have given me here today, and when that day comes I'll be walking on both legs!"

"How can you argue with someone like that?" said the specialist to the other doctor. It was clear that he was irritated. Then he addressed himself once more to Jacob Jobse: "If you won't take my advice, at least promise me this: as soon as you are placed with your family at an evacuation address, seek a doctor's care."

"You can count on it," said Jacob, writhing in pain and eager to get this encounter over with.

The doctors withdrew. Then Rev. Verhulst came and stood next to Jacob Jobse's bed. He had become quite thin. Jacob surmised that he must have gone through quite a lot in Brabant before he returned and found the members of his congregation in such difficult circumstances.

"It looks as though you're not doing so well, brother Jobse," he said. He seemed to have overheard something of Jacob's conversation with the doctors.

Jacob still had enough energy to open his dark eyes wide and fix them on his shepherd. Then he said: "And what am I now, Reverend — a brother or a wolf in sheep's clothing?"

"Brother Jobse, I did not mean it in a bad way. Sometimes, when you're angry, you say things that you really shouldn't say. Doesn't that happen to you once in a while?"

"There are things that cut a man to the quick, Reverend. So what about it: am I a wolf in sheep's clothing — yes or no?"

"All right, I'll say it: you're *not* a wolf in sheep's clothing, brother Jobse. Can we shake hands on it?"

"Yes indeed, Reverend." Jacob then extended his hand and proceeded to shake the minister's hand in his usual energetic way. For just a second, he saw Rev. Verhulst wince.

Then the minister said: "But you will have to admit, brother Jobse, that the Lord is afflicting you very severely right now. That you have come to lie on this painful sickbed means that the Lord has a message for you. You need to be attentive and give ear to what He is saying, brother Jobse. You see now that the Lord no longer wishes to use the Germans, but He has various other means with which to visit His rebellious children with the rod and other bitter herbs. Do you really think it was wise to reject the doctor's advice the way you did just now? When two doctors agree that the leg needs to come off, is it right for you to refuse? Isn't that also a form of hardening, brother?"

Jacob was in a great deal of pain. Joan was standing at the head of the bed; with her small hand she was gently caressing the top of Jacob's head. Jacob's eyes were staring straight into the minister's eyes. Then he lifted up his head a little bit and said: "You will *not* succeed in taking away my comfort, Reverend. I know I'm a sinful creature and not worthy of God's grace. But I also know that I belong to Jesus Christ, in both body and soul. That's what my catechism tells me, and I say amen to it. As for my leg, it's *not* coming off. And even if it did have to come off, even if both legs had to come off and I had to be pulled down the street in a little wagon, even then I would continue to recite the catechism. The Lord has delivered us from the Krauts, and He has delivered us from the flood. He will also help us further. But right now I am in a great deal of pain, and so I ask you to leave me alone to rest."

Rev. Verhulst shook his head and looked helplessly at Joan, who gently indicated to him that it was time to depart. She thought to herself that Jacob spoke rather roughly at times; after all, a minister always remains a minister. But she continued to run her hand over his feverish head.

Rev. Verhulst shook hands with Joan and disappeared.

*   *   *

When they arrived at their designated evacuation address, the doctor in the village also looked quite disturbed when he took off Jacob Jobse's bandages and got a good look at his leg. It seemed that all the colors of the rainbow were present in his wound, and the open spots ran deep into his flesh. The doctor wrote a prescription and told Joan that she was to go twice per week to Wolfaartsdijk to pick up two bottles of a special water that was to be used to keep Jacob's leg wet.

The woman in whose house they were staying had a lot of possessions and kept everything very neat and clean. It was only in response to a great deal of pressure that she had taken a family into her home.

Jacob was laid up in a small room on the top floor. Through a window he could look far out over the polders.

Twice per week, Joan had to make the long journey of an hour and a half on foot to Wolfaartsdijk and back, carrying a shopping bag containing two bottles for the water. The woman in whose house they were staying had a fine bicycle, but it was too beautiful for poor Joan. When Joan asked to borrow it, the woman said: "I think you'd better not do that. You can't get new tires nowadays, and my bicycle is still so new. You'd better just walk."

And so Joan walked. Jacob watched her as she departed, dressed in her Walcheren costume. From her pale arm hung the shopping bag with the two bottles. Her white, starched cap remained visible from Jacob's window for the first part of her journey. Jacob always watched her as long as he could as she disappeared in the distance. First she walked along a dike, a forlorn dike, and then disappeared from view, but then she was visible again for a while. Gradually her cap became ever smaller, until there was nothing more to be seen.

After that Jacob would lie on his bed waiting. His watch was suspended from the wall right by his bed: by keeping track of the time, he knew roughly when Joan's white cap would become visible again. She never disappointed him, for she never took a minute longer for the trip than was strictly necessary. When she came into view and realized that Jacob would be able to see her from his window, she would already begin waving, even though she was still quite a distance from the house. Her greeting put a smile on Jacob's face.

He smiled the happy smile of someone who was recovering. His leg was indeed getting better. The wounds were getting smaller, and the flesh was slowly returning to its normal color. The pain was subsiding. His prayer had been answered.

Joan's white cap became very precious to him, each time he saw it disappearing in the distance and approaching again. He loved to watch Joan swaying as she marched along indefatigably, with her white cap buoyantly moving from side to side.

*   *   *

Elsewhere in Middelburg, mother Beth was staying with her daughter. The woman in whose home Tina had been working was very good to evacuees and was willing to let them have anything they might need.

David Melse was away. Now that everything below the Moerdijk was in the hands of the Allies, he traveled from city to city, seeking contact with military authorities and with officers of the Canadian and English and American armies. He placed inquiries in all kinds of papers. He asked for the help of the Red Cross. He extended his inquiries all the way to the front, which was close to the German border at this point. He talked with refugees who had survived the German concentration camps. He did not weary of his labors.

But there was no trace of Dirk. No one had heard of a Dirk Melse, and so no one could help. As for the occupied territory to the north of the Moerdijk, there were no contacts there at this point.

Finally David Melse returned to Middelburg and mother Beth. They sighed as they carried their heavy burden together. David Melse's hair had become grayer, and he was somewhat stooped as he walked. His struggle with God had been difficult. Sometimes it was such a severe struggle that doubts began to eat away at his assurance of faith.

Part II

Despair

Chapter 5

It was February of 1945. North of the great rivers of the Netherlands, the "hunger winter" dragged on. The border between the liberated territories and the land still occupied by the Germans cut right through the Eastern Scheldt. Schouwen and Duiveland were still in the hands of the enemy, who flooded the island and evacuated most of the people.

The Western Scheldt had been liberated, but at a frightful price: 40,000 Allied soldiers had lost their lives. The convoys bringing more men and material for the war against Germany kept arriving from the south.

Walcheren lay sunken in the sea, whose high and low tides crossed over it every day. The beautiful garden of Zeeland had been leveled — it was not much more than a pool of muddy slime in which the murderous salt from the sea ate away at everything that still had life.

*   *   *

Jacob Jobse quickly recovered from his dangerous illness. His wife Joan was the very best nurse he could wish for. His general health and strong constitution also contributed to the recovery of the tissue that had been devastated by the deep, ugly wounds in his leg.

Now he hardly had the patience anymore to wait for his doctor's approval to get out of bed. He yearned to return to his little house on Walcheren, where he would try to save what he could of his household goods. He had heard stories from other evacuees: some of them had saved quite a bit, whereas others had been able to recover almost nothing of their possessions.

Joan wanted to restrain him from carrying out this plan. When he managed for the first time to stand on the wounded leg and walk a few feet, there was no holding him back: he saw that he could actually do it!

From the military authorities he got permission to return to Walcheren. His doctor, still under protest, reluctantly gave in as well. And so, halfway through the month of February he set out. The doctor stressed that Jacob was to keep the leg dry and make sure it did not come into contact with the poisonous water that now covered Walcheren.

Jacob went to Middelburg and there made a connection with a boat service that had started providing transportation around the island of Walcheren. Some English military men who were running the boat service brought him to his village. As they steered the boat, they seemed to know just how to get past the dangerous spots.

Jacob reached his little house and found that it was still standing erect. To him this was a great miracle, because everywhere in the neighborhood he saw houses that were newer and stronger than his that had sunk away or fallen apart completely. Some of them still stuck up a bit above the waves, whereas others had completely vanished — there seemed to be no trace left of them. But his humble worker's house was still standing just as he had left it.

In his high boots he was able to get over to the barn. He climbed up on the roof and managed to reach the window of the second-floor room where he and his family and the Polish divers had spent so many anxious days and nights.

He waited patiently for low tide and then went below. Because the water on the first floor was not very deep, he knew he could get out the door and walk across the yard over to the barn. He found some boxes and crates and used them to pack things in the house that he still considered worth saving. He also found his carpenter's tools. He retrieved linen and china from the cabinet and put it all in crates which he then moved to a high point in the little barn. He figured that when the boat came by again, he could easily transfer the boxes and crates into it.

And so Jacob kept busy until high tide came in. Then he had to go back up to the second floor of the house. He had told the men operating the boat service that he wanted to spend the night in his house so that he could pack up all of his goods.

Jacob wanted to do as much work as he could during the hours of darkness, using his kerosene lamp. But it proved far from easy. He was no longer used to working with his hands, and his body did not have enough strength to keep going for so long. Soon he was utterly exhausted.

When deep darkness fell, the wind picked up and soon grew into a powerful storm. The waves smashed against the thin walls of the little house, and Jacob could feel the house trembling as though it were a nervous colt. From the small window in the upper room he could see banks of clouds moving rapidly by, driven by a northwesterly wind. It was a turbulent atmosphere.

Darkness had covered all of Walcheren. There was no small point of light to be seen, no sign of life anywhere. But he did hear the sound of furniture smashing against the walls. It was the same ominous sound that had frightened the children so much and had kept Joan from sleeping.

When Jacob opened the trapdoor and used his lamp to look at the scene below, he discovered to his consternation that the sea water was only about thirty centimeters below the first-floor ceiling. Clearly the dreaded high tide of spring was upon them, the high tide during which almost anything can happen.

Now he no longer worried about the boxes and crates he had packed so carefully, which by this point would also be covered with water. Instead Jacob thought of himself and his wife and his children. The house was starting to shake and tremble on its undermined foundations. He figured it might well give way that night, just as so many other houses had done. Jacob knew that if that happened, he was lost. Because of the high water level and the storm, deliverance was out of the question if the house should collapse.

As the minutes crept by, Jacob was consciously experiencing each second. Every blast of wind, every strong wave smashing against the walls could mean the end for him. The minutes and hours were frightfully long.

Jacob's life seemed to pass before his eyes. If God were to call him during this stormy night, what then? Would he be ready to appear before God's face? Jacob thought about his wife and children who would be left behind. Who would take care of them? It was as though the howling of the wind and the ceaseless dashing of the waves were the wrath of God coming at him.

In his despair Jacob stood in front of the small window from which there was nothing to see but a frightening tableau of banks of clouds rushing by, with sometimes a small, light patch of gray between them. And below them was the raging sea in which high waves with a white foam on their crests kept charging toward him out of the deep darkness of the night.

Without pondering what to do next, Jacob fell to his knees and appealed to God out of his deep need. It was a short, sober, and very direct cry of the heart to God, in which he confessed his sins and acknowledged that he deserved condemnation — but he also asked for grace. He asked to be allowed to continue living for the sake of his wife and children. And when he came to the point of saying "Amen" at the end of his prayer, the little room on the top floor became to Jacob — for the second time — a true paradise of peace. All fear had fallen away. He now knew with great certainty that he had found God back — the God who had preserved him when he was threatened by water and fire. He found that he could again sing psalms in the night, for God had also given him the assurance that his leg would be healed.

In the midst of the raging storm, while the waves smashed against the little house, Jacob Jobse lay down and slept peacefully until the first morning light began to shine through the little window in the upstairs room. The weather was now a little calmer, and his house was still standing. Again he was amazed: it was truly a miracle.

The waves were still smashing against the walls and the storm stirred up turbulence in the water. Jacob understood that in these circumstances there would not be a boat making a regular patrol to pick up his boxes and crates. Staying here was also out of the question. There was no food, and he was not sure how much longer the house could hold out. And so Jacob attached a white sheet to a long pole used for drying clothes and stuck it out the window. From his window he could not see the village; the window only allowed him to look in the direction of the dunes, where he could see the water flooding Walcheren. But the white flag waved above the roof. He hoped the people in the village would be able to see it.

An hour passed, and nothing happened. The water remained high, and the storm continued. Then, suddenly, a small boat appeared alongside his window. The man rowing the boat shouted to get Jacob's attention and asked if he needed some help. Jacob requested transportation to the village, but the man in the boat replied that he had no time to go to the village. Because someone in the village was deathly ill, he had been sent to Middelburg to get a doctor. Jacob was welcome to go with him to Middelburg if he wished.

Jacob had no choice. He crawled out the second-story window, slid along the roof-tiles over to the eaves trough, and then jumped down onto the roof of his little barn. From there he was able to lower himself into the boat.

The two men then moved over the restless waves as they headed for Middelburg. When they got to the other side of the little house, Jacob could see the village straight ahead. The fierce weather had caused great devastation all around and had done damage to the houses that were still standing. A corner had been knocked out of the Melse farmhouse, and part of the roof was now hanging down into one of the rooms.

"That farmhouse has had it," observed the man rowing the boat." Jacob nodded. His voice stuck in his throat, and he could not speak a word. When he took a last look at his own house, he wondered whether it had been a miracle of God for him to have survived the night.

They arrived safely in Middelburg, and there he hitched a ride with an English military vehicle that brought him almost all the way back to his evacuation lodgings. Joan greeted him at the door and saw that he had his hands extended to indicate that he was bringing nothing back. When she inquired about their property, he explained that it was all standing in water. Would they ever see any of it back?

But Joan did not think about her worldly goods. She threw her arms around his neck and kissed him on the lips. "I'm so glad to see you standing before me again," she laughed.

*   *   *

A week later the water had subsided somewhat and the sun was warming the earth again. Joan stood before the window of the little room in which they were being housed. Jacob looked at her pale face. The pensive expression in her eyes, seeming to stare at something far away, did not escape him. "What are you thinking about, Joan?"

"Nothing in particular, Jacob."

Jacob didn't believe her. "You don't expect me to believe that!" he replied. "A person's thoughts never stand completely still. How is it possible for you to be thinking about nothing whatsoever? A person is always thinking, even if he's sleeping. I believe I know what you're thinking about: you're thinking about your household goods back on Walcheren. I'll tell you what — I'll go back and see whether it's possible to save anything of that stuff."

Joan blushed as she looked at her husband. How had he managed to guess so precisely what was occupying her attention?

She told him that he should stay where he was. After all, there was nothing more to be saved. It would all be gone by now. Still, if only she had the wedding pictures and the pictures of the children . . .

Jacob was listening carefully. It seemed to him that she was saying two things at the same time. On the one hand she was telling him to stay put. On the other hand she wanted him to go and determine whether it might be possible to save the photographs.

Of course by this point in their marriage Jacob was very familiar with his wife's way of thinking. And so he decided he would go. The weather was fine, and the house was probably still standing. He would see what there was to be salvaged. He hoped he would come back with more to show for himself than the previous time. As for Joan, she should set her heart at rest, for he was planning to leave for Walcheren the very next day.

When Jacob arrived at his village, he could see that his house was still standing. Yet his carpenter's eye discerned that it had shifted slightly. And when he got onto his property, he could still walk around wearing his deep boots. He even got into a part of his garden.

The little barn was still largely dry, and for the first time he could see the entry to his living room. On the floor was a thick layer of black, slimy mud, on which he almost lost his footing.

In the little barn there was chaos. His boxes and crates had been dislodged from their high place by the spring tide and the storm. When they fell, a number of them opened, allowing their contents to spill out. There were some books and an album with photographs lying on the muddy floor, drenched with sea water. Linen goods were spread everywhere, and the carpentry tools had somehow gotten out to the yard, where they were rusted by the sea water.

Jacob began to assemble everything that might yet have some value and pack it up. It did not amount to a great deal. Once again he moved everything up to the loft in the little barn. Then he waited for the boat that would come by his house every now and then as it brought threshed wheat into the village. The boatman let him come along to the village, where he could try to find someone who would take his goods over to Middelburg.

The village square was unrecognizable. It was full of farm implements that had rusted and were starting to fall apart. He found people living in the church; some of them had spent the entire winter there.

Among the people he encountered was grandfather Melse, who had steadfastly refused to leave the farmstead. Finally, when the Melse farmhouse was badly damaged, he had permitted someone to bring him to the village.

The baker was still baking bread every day for the people who were left in the village. At high tide he would stand in his boots, for the water then covered the entire floor in his bakery. The village was a curious island in the middle of the sea.

Jacob succeeded in getting the use of a barge. The owner of the barge agreed to let it be towed to Jacob's house so that he could pick up his goods. He told him to have everything ready by four o'clock, for at that time an English motorboat would be along. The boat could then pull the barge to Middelburg.

Jacob was happy with this offer. Zealously he undertook to carry outside everything that was still of value to him. The borrowed barge was tied up against the little barn. He even looked at the cabinet which was Joan's pride and joy; it had been given to her by her mother as a wedding gift. It was now in pieces. He brought the pieces into the small barn so that they could also be given a place on the barge.

The water now began to rise, and so he took off his trousers in order to keep them dry. His boots were no longer keeping all the water out. In his short underpants he kept working zealously, repeatedly wiping the sweat from his forehead.

Suddenly the English motorboat approached at an amazing speed. The man who owned the barge was standing in the motorboat. He shouted to Jacob to throw everything onto the barge at once if he wanted to take it along. Word had been received from Middelburg that a storm was coming, and the Englishmen did not wish to take any risks. They wanted to get out of there at once.

The English soldiers helped load the barge, but they were rough about it. And so the boxes and crates were thrown down without any care. The men did not pay any attention when Jacob begged them to be careful. They were in a big hurry!

The operator of the motorboat kept looking at the sky and shouting to Jacob to jump into the barge because it was time to leave. Whatever had not yet been loaded would just have to stay where it was for now. Jacob indicated that he needed to fetch his trousers from the upstairs room and pull them on. But he was not allowed the time it would take to do this. The Englishmen were not prepared to risk their lives anymore for the sake of some Zeelander's trousers. And so, wearing his short underpants, Jacob had to jump from the roof of the little barn onto the barge. Almost before he knew it, the motorboat was tugging the barge away.

The sky to the northwest was indeed looking very threatening. The air was getting cooler. Because Jacob was not wearing trousers, he felt the chill keenly and began to tremble. He seated himself among his goods which had been thrown down here and there and tried to use them for shelter. He saw that the parts of the big cabinet were all on board; this fact gave him some satisfaction. He knew Joan would be very pleased to see them.

In due course they arrived in Middelburg. There were a lot of people at the dock where they tied up the barge. When Jacob appeared in his short underpants and his boots, with the laces of his underpants hanging down along his legs, it was quite a sight. The top part of his body was well provided with clothing: he wore the usual Zeeland upper garments.

The people looked at Jacob as though he had stepped out of another world. Their scrutiny made him very uncomfortable. And so he decided to address the people who were staring at him, and he used his usual Walcheren dialect:[3] "Yes, people, it stands to reason that you have never before, in your entire lives, seen a fellow in his underpants. So now you're going to take a very good look so that you can tell the people at home just what a man in his underpants looks like. But once you're done gawking, I'd appreciate it if you folks would go home and see whether anyone has a pair of pants in the closet that he can spare for a little while. That way I could at least walk through the streets again like an ordinary man. Or would you rather see me walking through Middelburg as I am right now, so that everyone can get a good look? Wouldn't such a sight bring dishonor to the city? And now I'm leaving it up to you folks."

By making this speech, Jacob recovered a degree of dignity despite his embarrassing lack of trousers. And it was not long before an old gentleman came back in triumph, carrying a first-rate pair of pants that even had a sharp crease. Jacob put on the pants while standing on the dock.

---

[3] The Zeeland people in this story speak in dialect much of the time, but I have made no effort to imitate their deviation from standard Dutch by having their English words spelled in unusual ways. And so, although Jacob is presented at this juncture as addressing the people of Middelburg in standard English, readers are encouraged to use their imagination and consider the social significance of the fact that Jacob was actually speaking in a regional dialect while addressing people in the provincial capital under rather embarrassing circumstances. —Trans.

Then he had to find a way to get over to the village where he and Joan were staying as evacuees. Once again, it was a military vehicle that gave him a ride.

"Now I'm a farmer from above and a gentleman from below," said Jacob, when he told Joan his story. Carefully he took off his borrowed trousers and folded them exactly as he had seen people wearing such pants do before.

The next day they went to Middelburg together because Joan was eager to see what had been saved of her possessions. It was not a great deal. But she was very pleased to see the cabinet, which Jacob would soon be able to repair to the point that it would be almost as good as new.

When she ran her hand over the water damage done to her wedding photos, she said softly: "Jacob, how blessed we were not to know all the time what was hanging over our heads."

"Let's be thankful for what we still have," said Jacob, "We still have our friends and our children." And then, voicing deep conviction, he added: "Oh boy!"

*   *   *

Now it was May of 1945 . . . The peace treaty ending the war had finally been signed. The Nazi monster had bowed before superior force, and the world could breathe easily again.

Walcheren was still under sea water. Overhead were clear skies that nowhere looked quite so clear as above this island. The water rose and fell each day with the tides.

The fruit trees were in full bloom. Their branches displayed a rich array of blossoms, but it was a false promise — really, no more than a lie. When a person is suffering from consumption, his cheeks may be red and his eyes may seem to shine, but these are false signs of life, for the truth is that death is approaching ineluctably. Every Walcheren farmer knew that the blossoming meant that the dying trees were pushing the last of their sap outward to the twigs. The roots and the stem were already poisoned by all the salt, and soon the crown of the tree, blossoming so beautifully for the moment, would die too. No fruit would ever ripen on those trees again.

David Melse knew these things too . . . Even though the gaps in the dikes would be repaired within a matter of weeks, it was too late to get any fruit from those trees. Walcheren, the proud garden of Zeeland, was doomed to lose all of its fruit trees. And that wasn't the end of it. Walcheren itself would never again be what it had been for so many centuries.

When Melse looked out over the island from the outskirts of Middelburg, he saw small villages partly submerged in the water. Everywhere he saw churches surrounded by a small group of houses. On the edges of the villages he saw flour-mills, usually white in color.

The trees marked off the winding paths that led from the one farm to the other and ultimately made their way to the villages. The paths looked like threads of a web that came together at various connection points. There were so many twists and turns that a stretch of about seven kilometers would include no fewer than forty turns, some of them greater than ninety degrees. As for the little pieces of land, they were marked off from one another by ditches or hedges. It looked like a richly laid-out mosaic.

But all this was now slated to disappear. The island would indeed become dry again. The newspapers and the radio passed on this firm promise from the government. But what would happen after the land was dried up?

Melse already knew what the authorities were planning. At low tide one could see endless slime and mud-flats on the outside of the high sea dikes. The slimy mud had also filled the ditches and had left a layer of salt on the earth, destroying all boundaries and demarcations, devastating the fruit trees, and making the ground unfruitful for years to come . . .

And there were reports that all the land on Walcheren would be parceled out afresh to the farmers. No farmer could be sure that he would get his lawful property back. Cutting through the land would be new waterways and ditches and canals — all of them as straight as an arrow. Moreover, there would be broad new roads leading directly through the island. Everything would be modern; everything would be geared to the new transportation needs. But when all of this was accomplished, the new island would no longer be Walcheren.

Every farmer would now get land right around his own farmstead. The property holdings would be exchanged on a sensible basis that would save a great deal of time and money in the long run.

Yet all this reallocation of fields and rebuilding of the transportation network would entail the loss of hundreds of acres of the finest agricultural land. And which farmers would have to suffer the bulk of the damage when all of this took place?

The Walcheren farmers saw what was coming and what would happen. Their beautiful island would be turned into a new, modern polder. It would be flat and bare, and its former charm would be gone. It would be just like the polders in other parts of the country — nothing more. No one would ever go out of his way again to see Walcheren.

When David Melse stood thinking these things over, a question kept coming up in his mind: will there still be a place for *me* on Walcheren? Will I get all my land back? If there must be land exchanges, will the land assigned to me be of a lower quality than the land I used to own? Everything had now become uncertain. No farmer knew what to expect.

In the meantime, heavy equipment had been brought over to the holes in the dikes, and the work was underway. The authorities were determined that the holes would be repaired before winter.

It proved to be a slow, painful struggle with the rising and falling of the tide. Millions of cubic meters of water poured into the island each time there was high tide, and low tide meant that a massive amount of water had to flow out again through those holes in the dikes. And so the holes continued to function as powerful channels.

Nevertheless, the belief that the island would be restored was unshakable. That was why the small band of people who had lived through the hardest times huddling around the church remained exactly where they were. There was no way to move them. They were waiting for the land to dry out. They wanted to see the water subside with their own eyes, until the last high tide came and the last low tide pulled much of the water away for the last time. They would chase after that water as it disappeared, just as they would pursue a fleeing enemy. Step by step, they would then see their land rise again and dry out. The well-known little paths would appear again, along with the hedges and trees and bushes which were being reduced to dry wood. What they were waiting for was to see all of this restoration begin. They wanted to behold it with their own eyes and touch it with their own hands.

Among the stubborn ones was grandfather Melse. When he was finally forced out of the dilapidated farm, his son David pressed him to come along to Middelburg. But he shook his head and pursed his lips tightly. "No, my son," he said, "I will stay right where I am. You must never transplant an old tree, for that would mean its death."

David Melse knew it was true. During the worst times on Walcheren, many of the old people had been transported to other parts of the country; some of them were as far away as Haarlem. And now the people back on Walcheren were beginning to read the death notices. When people are above the age of sixty or perhaps sixty-five, such a change is too much for them.

Many of the old people had never been away from home for as much as a night. There were many who had never been outside of Walcheren. And now such people were being put into a small room on the second floor of a house in a big city. Inevitably, this meant their death. No, those hardy Walcheren people in the village would rather be heaped together in a little clump in a few dilapidated houses in the middle of an ocean of water. They would rather do without everything, lacking even suitable drinking water, light, and fuel, than be transplanted to some place that was unknown to them.

How could anyone who was not part of the local scene possibly understand such attitudes? One day a high-ranking American officer visited the village. He looked around in amazement at this small, packed little island with a big church right in the middle. He looked at the dilapidated houses at the edge of the village and at the shabby remains of what had once been prosperous farms. He saw small remnants of those farms sticking out above the still water. He understood nothing of it and shook his head. Then he asked: "Why don't you abandon this miserable territory to the sea?"

He put his question to a member of the Zeeland provincial government who was accompanying him. "Why spend millions in an effort to dry out this little piece of land again? Why not let these people emigrate to the United States or Canada, where there are hundreds of thousands of hectares of the very best land lying untilled, just waiting for the hand of some skilled farmer? Why do these people remain here in a little heap?"

The government official could not make it clear to him. How could one ever explain to such a man the deep feeling in that old Zeeland song?

My heart would nowhere prosper,
And nowhere find its rest,
Except between your rivers,
Near the wide ocean . . .
That's where my heart breaks out in song;
That's where the voice of my blood is heard . . .

Just as the government official was racking his brain, trying to come up with a suitable answer, grandfather Melse came along. The official detained him for a moment and said to him: "Tell me, old farmer, what's your name?"

"I am Melse, Dirk Jan Melse, sir. What do you want with me?"

"This American officer has just asked me why all of you are sitting here in a little heap instead of giving up on Walcheren and going to the United States. What would you say in response, Melse?"

The old man looked at the government official, and then at the American officer. Again his eyes sought out the official. He remained silent while his eyes, just as clear as they were when he was thirty years old, once more surveyed the spacious waters flooding Walcheren. Then, after a little more reflection, he said cautiously: "Look, I'll tell you in just a few words. We have remained here because there's nowhere in the world that's as nice as Walcheren. If you could make him understand that, he would know enough, I would say."

Grandfather Melse put his cap back on his head and walked on. The American officer smiled when he heard the translation of the answer. But it was the smile of someone who didn't understand because he *couldn't* understand.

Grandfather Melse was somewhat annoyed that his son had made no effort to move back to the farm. Was it really so bad that a corner of the house was damaged, with part of the ceiling hanging down? It would not be difficult to provide some support for that ceiling, he thought. And even if that should prove impossible, they could move into the small part of the house that still seemed to be sound. A farmer ought to be with his stuff, just as a captain belongs on his ship.

Each time low tide came along, grandfather Melse and his grandson Henry went to the farm, where they set to work clearing the slimy mud out of the rooms and the barns. Even though each high tide would undo all their work, grandfather Melse was quite prepared to repeat the task each day. The Walcheren farmer never gives up in his struggle against water.

But David Melse remained at his evacuation address in Middelburg. He did come out to his farm from time to time to assess the damage. Then he would stick around for a while during low tide and talk with the people who had remained in the village, people who, just like grandfather Melse, were not inclined to surrender their isolation. They really didn't find it so bad where they were. They had enough water to drink because they were using various barrels and tubs to catch rainwater. They maintained that their rainwater was tastier than tap-water. As for the distribution of food in the cities, they had nothing to do with it. They still had enough wheat, and the baker stood there in his high boots three times per week baking bread in his ovens. Moreover, there were many farmers who needed to kill some of their farm animals. There were plenty of cattle around the church which could also be slaughtered if need be. So why should they leave the village? Weren't the cows giving excellent milk? Hadn't they remained healthy all through the winter?

And when they stood talking together, they would look at their possessions, their farms and workers' houses standing outside the village covered with water, some of them still sound, some of them partially collapsed or without a roof. There were also some who saw nothing whatsoever when they looked at the place where their house used to stand. The water rose with high tide and then subsided with low tide, but there was nothing for them to see — there weren't even foundations anymore. They would turn their back to the place where their house had stood. They would thrust their hands into their pockets and suck in their cheeks and begin talking about the weather. Or perhaps they would start talking about what the Allies were likely to do with the German war criminals.

*   *   *

"Come back," grandfather Melse pleaded with his son when he visited the village once again, making use of the ferry service. But David Melse shook his head. He would like to come back, but as long as he heard nothing about Dirk he would not do so. He was thinking about making more inquiries on his own.

David Melse was torn in two directions at once. If he just had some certainty with regard to Dirk, he would not hesitate for a moment to return to his village and his possessions.

In Middelburg he once again walked the route that he had already followed so often to the building where the Red Cross had set up its office. The people there knew him well, and he did not need to say anything to them. They simply shook their heads, sometimes as soon as he walked in the door. It was always the same report: we haven't heard anything.

"Do you suppose I should go and take a look for myself and see what I would be able find out?" he asked.

"But where would you propose to go, Melse? If there was a report, we would be the first to get it. Your son's name is on our list of people for whom we are looking."

"But I hear that a great many people are arriving at our borders, and that first they are held there for a time so that they can get stronger and be checked over. Do you know anything about that?"

The Red Cross man shook his head. "There's really no point to it," he said. "We're working hard to track down all of those who were imprisoned in Germany. It would be best for you to wait at home. Moreover, we don't have any certainty that your son is in Germany, do we? You never heard anything to that effect, did you?"

Melse shook his head. He had no certainty on that score. But he did not want to contemplate the possibility that his son was among the many hundreds of victims who perished in Amersfoort without ever leaving the Netherlands. And so he had gotten the idea into his head that his son had been transported to Germany, and that one day he would return from Germany.

Finally he said: "If you people are of the opinion that there's nothing I can do myself, I'll just have to wait."

At home there was not much talk about Dirk. Mother Beth was not the kind of woman who tells people about her sorrows. Yet there was no radio report or piece of war news that escaped her attention. Everything that was made known about the victims who had perished in the camps and the mass graves and the instruments of torture discovered by the Allied soldiers who liberated those who were still alive in the camps — all of this she pondered in her heart. She was afraid to talk about these things with her husband, but her mind never let go of them. In the long waking hours during the dark of the night, she folded her hands in prayer for her child. More she could not do.

*   *   *

And then, suddenly, they got news. David Melse did not hear it by checking in at the office of the Red Cross; rather, a Red Cross official came and sought him out. And the news was that Dirk Melse was alive! He was very sick, but he was improving, and he would be transported to Middelburg as soon as possible. Just a few days before he had come across the border with a convoy of soldiers who were ill. He was now in a hospital in Brabant.

It was very difficult to travel there. Train connections were still very bad. But David Melse and mother Beth would not let such obstacles hold them back. At the very first opportunity they wanted to rush to their son's sickbed. They couldn't wait to see him. There was only one thing that filled their hearts — Dirk was alive and they would soon see him again!

During the journey, David Melse tried to prepare mother Beth for the reunion. She was not to think that Dirk would look as well as he did when he last took leave of them. David Melse hesitated as he explained these things. But mother Beth had long ago prepared her mind and heart for the reunion. She expected that her boy would be visibly weakened, famished, and in ill health because of what he had suffered. Nevertheless, he was alive, and his health would come back in time.

They did not have a hard time getting to his sickbed. Very little was demanded in the way of formalities. The people involved in the care of the victims thought only of the horrors which the victims had suffered; they did everything they possibly could to help them and their families.

Dirk had indeed changed. It was as though he had been sick for years and was still very sick. He was deathly pale, and his cheeks were sunken. His eyes were vacant.

Father and mother Melse knew that it was a time to be strong. Their emotions would have to be held in check. But because they were Walcheren farm people, the art of self-control was not foreign to them.

"My son," said Melse, "here we see you again at last! Hasn't God heard our prayers?"

Dirk nodded, and then he felt his mother kissing his lean face. "We're so, so happy!" said mother Beth as she ran her hand through his black hair.

Eventually she got around to the question that was in their hearts: "Did you suffer a great deal, my son?"

Dirk waved the question away with his hand. He smiled, raised his head from the pillow, and assured her: "Not any more than the others did, Mother. We won't talk about that now. I'm still alive, and I'll soon be coming home. So how are things with the farm? Are the buildings still standing?"

Father Melse then began to talk about Walcheren. Mother Beth listened, but at that moment her eyes became sensory instruments that did the work of her motherly heart. She observed everything very carefully. She realized that what Dirk said might well be camouflage, but what she saw with her own eyes told her the truth. She observed little wrinkles around his eyes, and also a nervous twitch at the corner of his mouth. The twitch was new: she had not seen it before. These things spoke to her of the suffering her son had undergone. She took hold of his hand and held it fast — just as if that hand could somehow tell her things of which Dirk himself would not speak.

"Are you still in pain, my son?" she finally asked.

"Not very much. It's going well. There's no need to feel sorry for me. I'll be all right. Let's be thankful to God that He has heard our prayers."

"That's just how I feel," said David Melse.

* * *

They waited in the hall until they had a chance to talk with the doctor. The doctor did not make much of David's illness — it was partly due to malnutrition, and the emotions also played a role. Within a couple of weeks he should be able to go home. "Your son has an iron-strong constitution," said the doctor. "That constitution got him through the horrible times."

"Do you think he suffered a great deal?" asked Melse.

"He probably did. Those scum made exceptions for no one. But it would be better not to think and talk about these things very much. It's all in the past. You've gotten your son back as though from the dead. There are thousands of people today who cannot say that."

* * *

Some weeks later Dirk arrived in Middelburg. At first things appeared to go fairly well. Of course he was weak and had to rest a great deal. He did not take any pleasure in eating, and the doctor was quite reserved.

One afternoon, when the doctor was alone with Dirk, he asked him: "Did they ever mistreat you?"

"Well, no, not really — at least, if you don't count the fact that they starved us and you don't consider that business of getting us out of bed at all hours of the night."

"Did they ever hit you or kick you?"

Dirk looked at the door, which was closed at the time. "Will you promise me not to tell Mother anything about this?" The doctor nodded reassuringly.

"There was this one time at the very end — we could already hear the heavy guns of the approaching American army — when we had to stand at attention for a full three hours. I was utterly exhausted and could no longer keep it up: one leg began to give way. One of them came along and gave me a good one under my chin. When that happens you can't help it: your head snaps back, which means that your stomach sticks out somewhat. Well then, he did the usual thing: at once he gave me a tremendous kick in the groin with the point of his boot. But when you feel that kind of agonizing pain, you just crumple up."

The doctor could see that Dirk was having a hard time bringing these words over his lips. And now he pressed his lips together. He did not want to talk with anyone about what he had suffered, for it then seemed as though he had to go into that dark tunnel again. It was bad enough that during the night, in frightening dreams, he would again fall into the hands of his cruel tormentors.

The doctor nodded. He understood. He continued to probe Dirk's abdomen where he had been probing before. Then he told the young man that he would be going to the hospital rather than back to the farm.

*   *   *

"It's not going well with our boy," said mother Beth repeatedly, almost every time they left the hospital.

"It may yet turn out well," said Melse, trying to encourage his wife. "He's strong — that's what the doctor said." But mother Beth shook her head.

By the time September came around, they both realized that they would have to surrender their son. Dirk was not going to recover, and he knew it. He didn't seem to have any interest in life anymore. He just let things happen to him; such passivity was foreign to his character.

When Melse sat at his son's bedside, it was as though he was looking into the eyes of someone in a different world. And whenever Dirk talked with mother Beth or with Henry or his sisters, they got the impression that he no longer regarded himself as one of them.

No one could get him to talk about what he had suffered in the concentration camp. He saw no reason to talk about it — it was in the past. He was beyond the point where people could harm him or do him evil. He was going to heaven — he knew it.

In the quiet hours he thought a great deal about the other David Melse, the son of Uncle Joris, who had suffered the same sort of thing, but in greater measure. Somehow, God seemed to regard such agony as necessary for certain of his children. And so it was good that those things, however painful, had happened. In due course, the difficult questions would all be answered.

As for Dirk, he had only one desire — to make it as easy as possible on his parents and his brother and sisters when it was time to say goodbye. He talked with them all separately in short sentences that said a great deal, sentences they would never forget.

When the end was near, he took his mother's hand as she was visiting him one day. "Now, you mustn't always sit there puzzling over the things that have happened," he said. "If I were at the beginning of all of this again and I knew then what I now know, I would make the same choice. We *had* to do what we did — it was part of God's plan for us."

He then explained to his mother how he had been obedient to God and to the Queen, and as for all the consequences of his actions, he was not responsible for them. It was *God* who judged these things to be necessary. As for us, we had to accept them as good.

Dirk urged his mother not to regret his departure. "After all, I will be ahead of you for only a short time, and then you and Father and the others will also come — isn't that so? What you must do is look ahead and not think too much about the past, Mother. And if Father sometimes has a hard time of it, Mother, then you must point heavenwards. Remind him: that's where Dirk is. And then you should tell him that all the things that have happened are good — they *had* to happen. Bring the same message to Uncle Joris. Will you do these things, Mother?"

Mother Beth nodded. Her large eyes were open wide, but they were still dry as they looked lovingly upon her son. Her hand was in his. Her love for her first-born son was so deep that it was beyond words. She remembered how difficult his birth had been. And was this the purpose for which she had raised him? God's ways were indeed shrouded in mystery, and yet she knew that it was all for the best. It was for heaven that she had carried this child under her heart. He was ahead of her — far ahead of her. He was ready for heaven, but she was not — not yet. "God, grant that I may have peace with the path Thou hast decreed for us," she prayed. Then, as she had done so many times before, she laid her hand on his head and ran her fingers through his dark hair. Gently mother Beth kissed her son's dry lips. Then she departed.

*　　　*　　　*

When the hour of death was near, the whole family stood around Dirk's bed. Grandfather Melse was there too. It was an amazing deathbed. All who were present were in control of their feelings. It was just as though Dirk was about to make a long journey, and the people around his bed were there to say goodbye. Not many words were spoken. And there really are no words for such an occasion. Dirk had already addressed all of them one by one and said what needed saying.

As his dying eyes rested on his father, he was aware that his father would have an even harder time of it than his mother. He knew that in David Melse's heart doubt was deeply rooted. David

Melse did not have quite the same firm foundation that mother Beth possessed.

Father Melse looked at his son and nodded. His lips were tightly pressed together. His heart seemed to be shrinking from the intense pain he was feeling, and he did not know what else to say. Finally he spoke up: "Are you certain, my boy, that you're going to heaven?"

"I know it as surely as I know that Christ's blood has washed me from all my sins, Father." Just a few moments later he passed on. Dirk was home.

Father Melse felt his knees knocking as he walked down the stairs of the hospital. Grandfather walked next to him on the street and said: "Never in my life have I seen such a deathbed. What a royal departure it was for the boy! It's enough to make you jealous. I just hope we can also enjoy that kind of certainty, my boy."

Chapter 6

The sea fought a grim and furious battle against all attempts to wrest the newly won territory from its grasp. When the dike near Vlissingen was finally closed again after a long and weary struggle, the storm of a single night ripped out the materials that had been used to repair it: with enormous force, it hurled them hundreds of meters inland. And so the sea, with renewed strength, once more streamed over the land.

But the determination of the Dutch, who were greatly aided by modern technology, finally prevailed over the strength and stubborn resistance of the sea. The holes in the dikes were closed. Then, for the first time, high tide did not sweep across the island.

The task of draining the water left on the island could then be undertaken. Pieces of land that had been under the waves for months gradually dried out. The Walcheren farmer could finally see what he had so long hoped for: the water slowly subsided, and it was not coming back. Any piece of land that dried up remained dry — first the high pieces of land, the yards around the farms, then bits of the road which happened to be higher, and then the other sections of the road. The pastures and the land on which crops were grown also dried up in due course. The water level kept going down.

But what became visible as the waters subsided was not the Walcheren of old. Because of all the slimy mud, it was chaotic in appearance. No flowers bloomed and no blades of grass shot up. Nowhere was there a tree with leaves, and no bush was able to grow. As far as the eye could see, there was nothing but that dark gray material that had made the entire landscape the same — nothing but a wilderness of mud.

After a few weeks, the slimy mud dried up and became a gray-white crust, a layer of salt. The drying of the land eventually opened fissures which made the land look like the dry, diseased skin of a poor sufferer afflicted by stinking wounds from which the odor of death emanated. The decaying corpses of farm animals which had been caught in the rusty barbed wire were lying around. Pieces of walls and roofs and doors and windows were everywhere, along with items of household equipment that was half rotted away.

As long as the sea covered the island, it managed to camouflage its destructive work, which was what the Germans had also attempted to do. It was only now, when it was forced to give way, that the extent of its destructive power was clear for all to see.

*   *   *

The people came back to their villages and tried to make their houses habitable once again — at least, if their houses were still standing. Their amazement at the destruction stimulated them in the zeal with which they attacked the work. The women scrubbed and swept until they got the mud out of the houses and the floors and walls were visible again. They scraped the mussel shells off the outside walls and looked around for their kitchen equipment. Everything worthless was thrown away, and the rest was repaired and restored making it fit for use again.

And so the people repossessed the land that had been under the waves for months. Again they trusted in the dikes that formed a thin wall between themselves and the ocean of water. They began to look around for that special place where once a cradle had stood or where a loved one had been buried.

*　　*　　*

Like the others in his village, David Melse pondered how he could best restore his house. He tried to figure out what it was going to cost him. But before he had a chance to confer with Jacob Jobse about this matter, the mayor said to him: "Melse, I do not have a pleasant message for you. I have to advise you not to spend any money fixing up your house. The land on Walcheren is all going to be reallocated, and a waterway is going to come right through the place where your house is now standing. Of course you'll be compensated for the loss of your house, but you will have to build somewhere else."

"Are you trying to tell me that I am not the boss over my own house anymore?" David Melse was very upset at this intervention.

"No, Melse, you're indeed the boss, but you should realize that personal interests always have to give way to the common good." As the mayor talked, he switched over to the local dialect; that way the two men could understand each other more easily.

"Well, I'm not going to take this lying down," said Melse. "I'm going to fight it. Why does it have to be *me* and not someone else? Why does that waterway have to go right through the place where *my* house stands?"

"What you should do," replied the mayor, "is come to a meeting of the commission in charge of the reallocation process. Then everything will be explained to you." That his message was quite a disappointment to Melse came as no surprise to the mayor.

David Melse did as he was told, but his appearance before the reallocation commission did not make things any clearer to him. He did understand from the papers and drawings shown to him that some higher authority had made this decision, and he was told again that his own interests would have to give way to the "common good," as they called it. He was also told that he did not need to fear monetary loss, for he would be fairly compensated. He would get the opportunity to choose some other land, and if he cared to, he was welcome to take up residence in the Noordoost Polder, which had been reclaimed from the Zuyder Zee. Quite a number of

Walcheren farmers had chosen to go there. There was excellent land available in the Noordoost Polder, and a good future lay open for anyone who knew how to roll up his sleeves and get to work.

The men on the reallocation commission were not exactly at a loss for words. They explained their position quickly and easily. They knew just what they were talking about, and Melse was unable to find fault with their argument. No one seriously believed that the Walcheren they had known would again rise from this flood. It would be foolish to try to restore it just the way it was. The old island was gone. What now remained was in effect a polder which had just dried out and needed to be divided into land parcels. If Melse — or, for that matter, any one of the hundreds of farmers on Walcheren — felt hard done by through this process of restoration, that was indeed too bad, but it was surely a small loss when one considers the fact that untold numbers of soldiers and citizens had lost their lives during the war years. That was simply how matters stood. And Melse had to admit that things were bound to change.

But the human being is not just a machine for thinking sober thoughts. A human being has a soul and a character — he has a spirit as well. Much that goes on within him escapes the grasp of sober logic.

Let's say that you are a Walcheren farmer. Your parents and grandparents lived on your land before you. Here the history of previous generations was played out, and it was here that you played as a child. When you were a young man, you sought out a young woman here as your life's partner. Here you married and formed a family. You had good times here and laughed in happy days, and you also shed many tears here when your soul was overwhelmed. You became so accustomed to the silhouette of the dunes you beheld at the edge of the island, and also to the things you saw when you looked around in the direction of the Walcheren villages, that you cannot help but be reminded how much you have come to love the little steeples of the churches that stand out against the sky.

David Melse was not the kind of man who would transplant himself willingly to some faraway, unfamiliar territory. He knew that his wife was even less inclined in that direction than he was.

He decided to discuss his difficulties with Francke, his neighbor, who was permitted to keep his large farm and would have all his land right around his house. He asked him: "What would you do in my place?"

"It's hard to advise you in this situation, neighbor," replied Francke, who was a thoughtful man. "Where would you wind up if you chose to remain on Walcheren?"

David Melse had been told that he would be permitted to build a house making use of the stone fragments left over from his former house. He would then wind up living about a half-hour outside the village, but he would only be occupying a little house built under emergency circumstances. Who could say how much time would pass before a new farm would be made available to him?

Francke asked: "But in any case, you don't wish to live in Middelburg any longer than you have to, right?"

"What else can I do? They forbid me to fix up my house. And I don't know any other place in the village where I could live."

Francke thought for a moment. Then he said: "I'm going to go and talk with my wife. And we can get a nice cup of coffee at the same time."

Mrs. Francke soon had the coffee ready and poured a cup for the men. Francke said: "I thought, as long as my wife agrees, that you folks could come and stay with us in the meantime. Tina and Janet are now working in Middelburg, and I heard that Henry is going into the military and will be sent to Indonesia. Is that correct?"

David Melse nodded. They got the news about a week before, and it was part of the reason why he was so anxious.

"Well then, that leaves just the two of you, plus Laura. Our house is big enough to accommodate you three temporarily. What do you say, wife?"

Mrs. Francke was of the same opinion as her husband. She said: "I've been thinking along these lines for some time. You folks should come and stay here. Then, at least, you'd be back in the village and close to your own place, and you could see what's happening."

"It's a wonderful offer," said Melse. "And that's also what my wife would say. She's getting awfully tired of sitting there in Middelburg. She's not the kind of person to stay long in the city."

"There's another factor in the picture," said Francke. "Somehow we have to see to it that we get the church services going again, and for that purpose we really can't do without Melse. Various of the consistory members are still away, and the minister is still living in Middelburg. And so we'll have to make do with reading services, and Melse is better at reading a sermon than any other elder. I won't pull any punches here, neighbor."

"You can read just as well as I can," said Melse modestly.

Francke waved away the praise. "You must be kidding! Whenever I have to lead a reading service, I get a pain in my stomach. What do you say, wife?"

"You get that pain because you let your nerves get the better of you," replied Mrs. Francke. "You should take something for your nerves — that's what I've always told you."

"Nerves are nerves, but if Melse were with us again, my nerves would be at rest, and that's part of the reason for this offer I'm making. So what about it — are you coming or not?"

"I think it's too beautiful an offer to be refused. In any case, I know that my wife will be very happy with this offer."

"Then you people had better come just as quickly as you can," said Mrs. Francke. "Even tomorrow would be fine."

*　　*　　*

The one who was having the hardest time with the new situation was grandfather Melse. Each day he walked back and forth between his son's dilapidated farm and the village, where the cattle were still housed in the barracks next to the church.

What was going on in the old man's mind? One day he stood next to his son on the mud that still covered most of the farm. "That all of this should have happened to us . . ." he sighed.

Melse looked at his father and saw something he had never seen before: there were tears trickling down his weathered, deeply lined face. For him, too, it was almost too much.

"Who can resist what God has ordained?" David Melse had once read this saying in black letters on the white fence of a Walcheren farm that had twice been struck by lightning and was being rebuilt yet again. He found it remarkable that this truth came into his mind just then.

The old man repeated the saying after him as though lost in thought. They were standing before the dilapidated farmhouse. The planks of wood covered with black pitch that used to form the walls of the barn had largely come off and were lying on the ground. What was left of the barn resembled a skeleton without flesh. The hayloft had sunk somewhat, even though much of the hay was still in place. Melse remembered throwing the hay up there with Henry through the upper-level opening. Later the hayloft had served as living quarters for the English pilot who disguised himself as a priest in order to be brought to Bergen op Zoom by Jacob Jobse.

In the stables for the cattle there was almost half a foot of the slimy mud. The hayrack for the horses, formerly attached to the outside wall, had sunk to the ground and was now lying in the mud.

Half of the house had sunk away. Because of the water streaming in and out with the tides, the ground had been undermined and had turned into no more than a soft bed of mud, in which the foundations of the house could no longer find much support. The upper portions of the walls still looked neat, and the chimney, by which Grandfather had always enjoyed sitting, was intact. But because of the corner that had fallen away, there were rays of daylight penetrating the interior of the house, thereby robbing it of its familiar intimacy.

David Melse felt an intense pain for which he could not find words. He felt as if his intimate life had been opened up to the cruel inspection of the world. Again those words came to his lips: "Who can resist what God has ordained?"

"We deserved it, my son," said grandfather Melse. "The minister was right — these are the judgments of the Lord. We have not bowed enough and humbled ourselves the way we should have. We should never have stood up to the Germans."

These words again sowed doubt in Melse's mind and heart. He felt inwardly torn. Then what about his son Dirk? He could hardly be expected to believe that the boy had departed this life with a lie on his lips. And so David Melse said to his father: "I can't believe that."

"The Germans were sent by God, my son," grandfather Melse replied. "Just pay attention to what I'm telling you. There you see all the stuff you've worked for all your life. You still have a big mortgage, and where's the money going to come from to pay it off? Dirk is gone, and Henry has to go to Indonesia for military service. As for you, you're not getting any younger. Are you in a position to hire strangers to help you with the work?"

As David Melse listened to his father, he realized that his words expressed clearly and concisely just what he had been wrestling with in his own soul for some time. "We'll just have to wait and see, Father," he said. He did know what else to say.

They walked together over to Francke's farmhouse. At the Francke place, the work of restoration was underway. By this point Melse's cattle were housed also in the spacious stalls. Henry was busy restoring and repairing what was left of the farm equipment.

The English had made a special tool available to the farmers, and they were using it to get rid of rust quickly. The special tool also served to preserve metal against further corrosion. But for many of the tools, the services of a smith would be needed if they were to be restored to working order, for sea water is as hard on metal tools as lye.

*   *   *

Jacob Jobse was not thinking about going back to Walcheren. One day he found an employer in Beveland who was willing to pay a good wage for so capable a workman as Jacob.

He also turned his attention to Joan's cabinet and set to work to restore it thoroughly. Carefully he scraped everything off the cabinet, concentrating especially on the inlaid portions. Of course the sea water had also removed a good deal of the finish.

"Joan, my girl, you're going to get a *new* cabinet!" he said, after he had spent an evening fussing over the cabinet. It was a point of honor for him to restore the cabinet so completely that it would look as good as new.

Jacob had also worked on the children's toys, which somehow survived the sea water and regained their former glory. But it was a different story when it came to the carpets — especially the red carpet with black stripes. Once all the mud was scraped off them, they just fell apart. "We'll burn all that garbage — then we won't have to look at it anymore," he said, comforting Joan. "We'll get some new stuff in time."

One evening, while Jacob was working on the cabinet, Joan asked: "When do you plan to return that pair of pants the man lent you, Jacob?"

"What pair of pants are you talking about?"

"Don't you remember that time in Middelburg, when you appeared on the dock in your underwear for all to get a good look?"

Now Jacob remembered. Quickly he turned his head to the right and looked straight at his wife: "Now, now, enough of that!"

He added that the man had told him to keep the pants. Apparently he had about ten pairs of pants hanging in his closet.

"But what good are such pants to you? They are not part of our native Walcheren dress. What do you say — shall I make them into pants for the children?"

"For the children?"

"Yes, is that so strange?"

"But I regard those pants as my own," said Jacob resolutely.

Joan had the coffee pot in her hand and was about to pour two cups, but then she got lost in thought. She asked Jacob: "Do you propose to wear the Walcheren costume from the waist up and ordinary civilian clothes from the waist down? If you ask me, you could better walk through the village in your underpants."

Jacob shook his head. "You just don't get it, do you?"

"Why? What do you mean?"

"Why can't you understand that I'm planning to switch to regular civilian clothing? I'll stop wearing the Walcheren costume altogether. I got tired of that fancy stuff a long time ago. And now that it's clear that we're not about to return to Walcheren . . ."

As Jacob said these words, Joan was still holding the coffee pot in her hand.

"Watch out!" warned Jacob. "If you're not careful, you'll wind up pouring the coffee on the tablecloth."

The timely warning brought Joan back to her senses. She poured the coffee. After handing Jacob his cup, she said: "Well, in that case I may also want to switch to ordinary dress."

Now it was Jacob's turn to be dismayed. He put down his screwdriver and looked intently at his wife. "I suppose you might as well," he said, after a moment of silence.

"Yes, and why not?" asked Joan, with her clear, blue eyes fixed intently on Jacob.

"I didn't say anything, did I?"

"It was *the way* you said it," responded Joan, imitating his tone of voice.

"So, am I not allowed to say no once in a while?"

"Oh sure — it's all right to ask a question," replied Joan.

"I was just thinking to myself what you would look like if you weren't wearing the Walcheren costume anymore. At the very least I would think to myself that I had gotten a new wife."

"You'd get used to it soon enough."

"One gets used to anything, according to the proverb," replied Jacob.

"It would be even stranger for me than for you."

"Why would that be?" asked Jacob.

"Because I would then be done with those heavy skirts and petticoats."

"You could use the material to make clothing for the children," suggested Jacob.

"And so you approve?"

"What is there for me to approve? If you say it's going to happen, then it's already been decided — right? What point would there be in my raising an objection? I'd be wasting my time."

"Well then, if you approve, we'll just go ahead and do it — right? We'll both dress in ordinary civilian clothes." At once Joan walked over to a closet and pulled out a flowery dress.

If ever Jacob was caught without words, this was the occasion. He stood straight up with a copper screw still in place between his pearly white teeth. "Now, what's this I see?" he finally asked.

Joan laughed, but she was blushing deeply.

"What's this I see?" he repeated. His eyes were wide open in amazement.

"How do you like it?" asked Joan.

"It's beautiful," said Jacob, without even taking a good look at it, even though Joan was holding the flimsy dress right in front of him.

"You really mean that?" she asked

"If I say something, I always mean it," he replied. But now he began to wonder whether Joan had somehow tricked him. First she had asked him with a perfectly straight face whether he would approve of her going around in ordinary civilian clothes, but all the while she already had this nifty dress hanging in her closet. Jacob reflected that there wasn't a man in the world who would ever understand women. "How did you come by that dress? That's what I'd like to know."

"That's for me to know and for you to find out. Shall I try it on?" She looked at him with the excitement of a young girl. Her head was slanted slightly to one side, and there was mischievous mirth to be seen in her clear blue eyes.

It was almost too much for Jacob. "If it really gives you pleasure, then go your way. I'm not about to say anything against it."

Joan went to the little bedroom on the upper floor and soon returned. But now she was a different Joan, decked out in a flowery little dress.

"Now, what was it I was just saying?" asked Jacob. "Do I have a new wife or not?"

But Joan said not a word. She could see from his eyes that he approved of the dress and was proud of his wife in civilian clothes. "Shall I keep it on for this evening?"

"You're just like a child, aren't you? When they have something new, they want to wear it right away, whether it fits the occasion or not."

Jacob was teasing her. But he still did not have an answer to the question where Joan had gotten the dress. Had she saved money from her household belongings? If that was the case, he figured he could give her a little bit less in the future. Who knew what other purchases she might have made by saving on household expenses?

"No, Jacob, I came by it honestly — just as you did with that civilian pair of pants. But if I'm no longer to dress in Walcheren costume, I'll need many more new clothes. One dress is not enough. And so I thought I should perhaps sell my gold. It's certainly worth a lot of money, and then we could both buy suitable civilian clothes and even have some money left over to buy clothing for the children. There are three of them, and they're all going to need new shoes, as you know."

Together they sat down to figure it out. Once they were finished with the money side of it, Joan took the box with the ration coupons to see how things stood with their clothing allowance.

As for Jacob, he forgot about the cabinet. It pained him to think that Joan would have to part with her gold, but he understood that for the moment there was no other way for them to scrape together enough money to buy new clothing. And Joan had assured him that in the long run it would be much cheaper to dress in civilian clothing than to continue to wear all those expensive Zeeland costumes.

"Well, just bear this in mind: I don't want you to sell that special necklace of yours, and I want you to hang onto your brooch as well. The rest of the stuff I don't care about."

"The stuff you don't care about is hardly the nicest stuff," replied Joan. "Of course, those are not the most expensive items, and we might not get much for them."

"That makes no difference to me — you should hang onto the necklace and the brooch. One day you'll make our children happy by passing them on." And so the decision was made.

*　　*　　*

117

A couple of weeks later, Jacob and Joan, wearing ordinary civilian clothes, set out on their first journey back to their village on Walcheren, where they would look up their friends. When they stepped out of the rickety train in Middelburg, a train whose windows had not even been restored, and walked over the windy bridge into the city, Joan said: "I have a strange feeling that I'm not wearing much of anything."

"It's no wonder when you consider just how many clothes you used to wear. It will take a while to get used to this new way of dressing. Just see to it that you don't catch a cold today."

The wind was indeed sharp. Jacob fumbled with his collar, a collar that still seemed as strange to him as the thin skirt did to Joan.

When they got to their village, they stepped out of the bus and walked over to the Francke farm. Francke was just coming out the door, accompanied by Melse; the two men were on their way to look at the cows. But when they caught sight of Jacob and Joan, they both remained standing right where they were. They did not recognize Jacob and Joan.

Jacob was amused and took off his hat in a gesture of exaggerated politeness. "May I introduce myself to the two gentlemen?" he asked.

Then Francke finally clapped his hands together. Without saying a word he went back into the house and brought out the two wives, followed by grandfather Melse. The two wives also clapped their hands, seemingly in unison, as though they had planned it in advance. "Well, well, this is really something!" said Mrs. Francke. "Jacob and Joan wearing civilian clothes!"

"It's something you never expected to see — right?" said Jacob. But he was a bit embarrassed. Joan was also embarrassed. Now that they were back on old, familiar territory, they began to feel like strangers in their own environment. It was as though they no longer belonged here.

"How did you two ever come up with that idea?" Melse finally asked, with a smile.

"Well, how am I supposed to answer that question?" responded Jacob. He had already inserted his carpenter's finger into his collar and was trying to wiggle his way to more breathing space.

"Come inside, people," said Mrs. Francke. "I've got a pot of coffee ready. You arrived just in time."

Once they were seated, Jacob took the time to tell about all the things that had happened to them. He also explained how they had wound up in civilian clothes. He began with the day when he arrived at the dock in Middelburg and had to step out of the boat in his underwear. But as he proceeded with his story, he adopted the tone and manner of someone who is trying to make excuses for something. The further he got into the story, the more he was overcome by the uncomfortable feeling that he had somehow committed treason against his Walcheren ancestry. Now that he was back in familiar surroundings, his conscience was not as much at ease as it had been on Beveland.

But his listeners nodded and agreed with what Jacob and Joan had done. "You probably aren't completely used to it yet," said Mrs. Melse, "but that will come in time. I think you folks are right. If I were faced with such a choice, I would do it too." Then she turned to her husband and asked what he thought. David Melse quietly shook his head, but he did not say a word.

Grandfather Melse spoke up: "If only you folks had waited until they brought me to the cemetery," he said. "If you ask me, it's sinful."

"Sinful?" said Mrs. Francke. "You mean to tell me that all people who wear ordinary civilian clothes are thereby sinning?"

"No, that's not quite what I'm saying," responded the old man. "But if we, who have so long dressed in Walcheren costumes, one day take them off and then start walking around in ordinary civilian clothes, we are putting on airs, and when you put on airs, when you pretend to be something that you're not, you're sinning."

"Now, I can't agree with you on that," said Mrs. Melse. "If we had been *born* in our Walcheren costumes, that would be something else, but consider the situation now. The truth of the matter is that we *choose* to wear these costumes. When you really come down to it, what is more a matter of putting on airs — the very ordinary civilian clothes that Jacob and Joan are wearing, or the expensive costumes with all the decorative gold and other finery that the rest of us are currently walking around in? What do you think, Jacob?"

But before Jacob could utter a word by way of agreement, the old man spoke up again: "If you ask me, it's exactly the sort of thing that our minister always warned us against. It's conforming to the world."

Jacob had forgotten about his civilian clothes, and the tight collar did not seem to be bothering him anymore. His eyes opened wide as he fixed them on the old man. Joan knew all too well what was about to happen, and so she used her civilian shoes to put a little pressure on Jacob's toe, which was out of sight, under the table.

With a pained expression on his face, Jacob pulled back his foot. But he paid no attention to Joan's signal. Instead he said: "I'll tell you something, Melse. The humility that should be in our hearts is not in the civilian set of clothes that I or someone else might wear. Neither is it in the special costumes that you people here on Walcheren wear. That's my view, Melse."

Jacob leaned forward as far as he could in the direction of grandfather Melse. He pointed to his own chest, where his heart was. He then said: "Look, this is where the heart is, and if things are right with the heart before God's countenance, then we can wear whatever kind of clothes we choose — whether you folks with your Walcheren costumes, or this tight collar that I have around my neck today. What really counts is whether your heart is right before God. Oh boy!"

Grandfather Melse shook his head and responded: "But our minister told us . . ."

The mention of the minister led Jacob to interrupt the old man: "Please don't talk to me about that minister! He may be a fine fellow, but if you ask me he could better have become a shoemaker. Then he would have been in a position to give people a better foundation than what he's doing now as a minister. That's what I think. He told us that we would have to suffer for at least seventy years in exile, just as the Israelites did. But it turned out that the German occupation lasted exactly five years. I'll tell you what I believe: the minister was completely wrong about this matter, and now he's suffering from some kind of nervous exhaustion which may well be connected with his mixed-up ideas. Give me a fellow like your Dirk or that cousin of his on Schouwen. Those are real men, if you ask me! And if the minister ever has such a wonderful and rich sickbed and deathbed as your Dirk did, well, I'll get on my knees and thank God for the change. Oh boy!"

Now the collar was feeling tight again. Jacob had turned red as he talked, and no wonder: the veins in his neck had swollen from his excitement. Again he inserted his index finger between the collar and his neck. He gave the collar a good tug, with the result that a button popped loose. Suddenly he had lots of breathing space.

It was a strange sight. He looked helplessly at Joan, who quickly tried to restore the collar.

Grandfather Melse shook his head as he watched the struggle with the collar. He stood up from his chair and said: "I'm going to milk the cows. It's about time."

He paused by the door and then shook his head once more as he watched Joan struggling to adjust Jacob's collar. Those young fellows don't even know how to dress by themselves. "Vanity of vanities — it's all vanity. That's what the Book of Proverbs says."

Jacob had turned beet red. He removed Joan's hand from his collar, made a partial turn toward the old man, and said: "You're wrong about that, Melse. That text is in Ecclesiastes — not Proverbs."

Joan turned Jacob's head toward herself and glared at him. "Why must you always have the last word?" she said, admonishing him.

Jacob did not get a chance to answer, for just at that moment Joan pulled the stubborn collar so tightly around his neck that he couldn't even swallow.

And so grandfather Melse had the opportunity to have the last word. He said: "Proverbs or Ecclesiastes — it makes no difference.

Either way, it's in the Bible, and that's enough for me. I just hope that the Bible also has something to say to you."

With that said, he left the house. He went over to the shed to get some equipment for milking. He carried his pails to the barn where the cows were waiting.

He did not bother to tie the back legs of the cows. When he did the milking, the cows remained calm. He knew just what he was doing, and the cows were used to him. The righteous man knows his animals — that was in the Bible too. Melse thought about that verse from time to time. And although he did not dare reckon himself among the "righteous," he did consider himself a "seeker" after righteousness.

But because grandfather Melse was a "seeker," he had a hard time understanding those who could say so easily that they had "found it." Among the ones who were too easy on themselves in this regard was Jacob Jobse.

While his pale and practiced fingers pulled at the cows' teats, his thoughts returned to his wife, who had left this life in darkness. She had also been one of the "seekers," but throughout her entire life she struggled without ever taking hold of what she was seeking. She died just as she had lived. Yet his wife took these matters much more seriously than Jacob did — to say nothing of those other young people nowadays who were so glib when it came to talking about these matters.

No, grandfather Melse could not understand the younger generation. It seemed that they simply wanted to take hold of salvation without ever experiencing anything. They could not give you any sort of account of what had happened within them. Indeed, they had the idea that you were not supposed to talk about your spiritual experience.

Such were the thoughts that went through grandfather Melse's mind as the creamy white milk spurted into his pail. When he was done with the work, he poured the milk into larger cans. Then he walked into the yard and straightened his back. His eye moved in the direction of the village, where the family graves were located. Time and again he had asked God in prayer to allow their graveyard to remain dry. And his prayers had been heard: the water got right up to the edge of the black fence around the graveyard, but it went no further. And so his wife's grave had remained dry. He thanked God on his knees for this fact. Now it was his continual prayer that when the time came, God would give him a place next to his wife where he could lay down his head.

Yet there was the fear that he would have to leave his village. Would they wind up going to the Noordoost Polder? He was not familiar with the strange world over there. It was far away, and everything would be new and strange to him. He knew that it would mean his death if he had to leave Zeeland. He would never be able to thrive in that foreign region.

He had seen the death announcements of the old Walcheren farmers and their wives who had been completely healthy but wound up dying not long after they were evacuated to some strange territory. And so there was fear in his heart when he thought about leaving Zeeland. What could he, as an old, lonely man, do here all by himself in the village?

He struggled with this question from time to time and often talked to himself. Henry sometimes heard him and could see his lips moving, but what grandfather Melse was dealing with remained a complete mystery to him and to the others.

*   *   *

A number of weeks went by. When it came time for Melse's little farm to be flattened, the catastrophe that had overtaken the land became irrevocable. The walls of the house were demolished, and the fragments of stone and brick were pulled apart and piled up for further use. They would wind up as part of some temporary housing that would soon be put up. As for the beams and planks that were still solid, they were also piled up to be used again. But when you looked at the piles carefully, you could not help but be surprised at how little was left of such a house when the materials were taken apart.

The heavy equipment that had been brought in was now put to use. Ditches and canals that were straight as an arrow were cut through the land. Such a waterway also passed through the piece of land on which the Melse family had lived and farmed.

The old, winding road leading out of the village was gone. A new road, completely straight, had taken its place. And so, through these measures, the deeply furrowed, wrinkled countenance of the island, in which an age-old soul with all its suffering and struggles came to expression, was irrevocably mutilated and transformed as straight lines were cut into the earth. To grandfather Melse, it was as though the new lines in the earth, which to him made no sense, cut right through his soul.

But Henry could not understand his grandfather's sorrow. As far as he was concerned, the reallocation of the land put an end to an awful lot of foolishness. Things were now being made more economical. When you stopped and thought about it, it was simply foolish to have one farmer working as many as four or five separate pieces of land scattered around as many different villages. A great deal of time and effort was wasted moving from one place to another. This modern age demanded efficiency. That word — "efficiency" — was often to be seen in the newspaper, and the people who were responsible for the reallocation of land on Walcheren also liked to use it.

But grandfather Melse just shook his head. "You folks, as young people, just can't understand these things," he said. "It's like what you read in the Bible. When the people of Israel came back from exile, Jerusalem and the temple were rebuilt. The young people were happy when this was done, but the older ones wept, for they recalled the way the city used to be and remembered how glorious the previous temple was. The new city and temple were not nearly as beautiful as the temple and city before them — they were convinced of it."

To these arguments Henry could offer no other response than to shrug his shoulders. Grandfather thought in Biblical terms. No matter what you pointed to in this world of ours, Grandfather always managed to haul the Bible into it. But David Melse said to his son: "Let's just hope that when you're as old as he is, you'll also think in Biblical terms the way your grandfather does."

124

Again Henry could do nothing but shrug his shoulders by way of response. And so, just as there was a very deep difference between the old Walcheren and the island that was now being reshaped, so there was an unbridgeable gulf between old and the new the generations.

*　　　*　　　*

"What are you thinking of doing?" grandfather Melse asked his son.

"I don't know yet," answered Melse. People told him that it would be best to go to the Noordoost Polder. It could be the chance of a lifetime, they suggested. He would get wonderful land there and a beautiful new farm. But he found it quite something to undertake. It would surely be a whole different kind of farming than what he was used to on Walcheren, and so it would be a major reorientation for him. And then he would be in a strange world. He had no idea what kind of people he would get for neighbors. And so he did not know yet what he would do.

"You shouldn't leave, Son. Stay here in Zeeland. This province is our home."

"That's easy for you to say, but what is there for me to do here?"

It was indeed a good question. Was there any possibility for David Melse to make a new start on Walcheren? A good deal of farmland had been lost in the process of reallocation, a process that involved laying out new roads and waterways. And then you had to be satisfied with whatever they gave you. He had already heard it said that some farmers who had given up excellent land had received rather poor land in exchange. And if you wanted to appeal the decision, you had to wait and see what came of your appeal. You could be sure that the high and mighty knew how to pull strings and get their way.

"But you shouldn't stay on the Francke farm indefinitely," said grandfather Melse. "It's wonderful that these people were willing to help us, but this can't go on forever. Something is going to have to happen."

That was also what David Melse thought. But just what should happen he did not know. Often he would lie awake at nights thinking about it. When Henry left for Indonesia, maybe he would then consider moving to the Noordoost Polder. But what could he begin there with just the two of them — and his father already an old man? Where would he get the money to hire people to help him on his farm? He had lots of debts, but no assets.

The time was approaching when Henry would have to take leave of them to begin his military service. After a period of basic training, he would depart for the far east.

The young man seemed to like the idea; he saw something beautiful in it. Indonesia needed to be set free, and the chaos there had to be ended. If the Dutch army did not intervene, Indonesia would fall prey to revolution.

And so Henry idealized his mission to Indonesia. He seemed quite light-hearted when he took leave of his family for basic training. But his parents looked at each other when their boy departed, and each could read the same message in the eyes of the other: now we no longer have a son at home. God has demanded a great deal of us.

Chapter 7

One evening grandfather Melse said to his son, while the two of them were milking the cows: "I think I'm going to make a visit to Uncle Joris."

"What do you propose to do there?"

Grandfather shrugged his shoulders. "I'm just going to go there and take a look and see how he's doing. We haven't heard anything from Joris since his return to Schouwen. I'll only be away for a few days — no longer."

When grandfather Melse arrived on Schouwen and Duiveland, he decided to make the rest of his journey on foot. It would take about an hour and a half, but the prospect of a long walk did not bother him. He followed the winding route along the solid sea dike, a route that had him walking right on top of the dike much of the time.

A fresh sea wind from the southwest was blowing over the water onto the land. The sun was shining brightly, and the seagulls swooped and dived over the dike on their beautiful, silver-white wings as they headed down to the water near the shore and fell upon the foamy sea in quest of their prey.

The outside of the dike was reinforced to about the halfway point with heavy basalt boulders. At regular distances there were sea-breakers whose shining tops could be seen protruding just a bit above the surface of the water. The heavy waves played endlessly with the breakers.

At the top of the dike was a concrete wall about one meter in height. The people of Zeeland called this fortification the De Muralt Wall. After the catastrophic flood of 1906, it had been built on the initiative of a man named De Muralt, who was the engineer in charge of the dikes for the province of Zeeland. Such a wall could now be seen on top of almost every dike in Zeeland. It was an enterprise that had cost millions at the time, but it seemed to be doing the job. Since that time, there had never been another occasion when the sea water got above the level of De Muralt's concrete wall.

Old Melse walked along the inside of this wall. It was just as though he was walking inside the battlements of a high castle wall. On the outside was the enemy watching for a chance to attack, but within the wall you felt secure — completely safe.

The enemy . . .

Then Dirk Melse paused and stood still. He stuffed some of his homegrown tobacco into his pipe, held the bowl of the pipe in the hollow of his two hands, and sucked gently to get the tobacco burning properly. He leaned over the concrete wall and stared out over the wide expanse of water.

How familiar this view was to him! Sky and water, a stretch of sea dike, and solitude. Right where he stood, in front of the dike, was a great sand-bar, and the light shade of the water indicated just how far out to sea the sand-bar extended. Beyond the sand-bar was a deep navigation channel marked as such by buoys.

On the horizon he could see a stripe that indicated the dike protecting another island. Behind it, sticking up into the hazy sky, he saw the church steeples and windmills of the villages on the island. He knew that in the distance, behind this hazy line, lay the islands of South Beveland and Walcheren. They were still within view. That's how it was in Zeeland: you could travel for hours and then come to the realization that you could still see your own village.

Further to the west lay the North Sea. In the southwest, the storm winds could sometimes build up and sweep over the islands of Zeeland. But if the wind came a little more from the north or if the northwesterly winds were unleashed, it was as though the seas were being rolled up at high tide, and once they got moving, one feared that they would sweep right over the coast of Zeeland. It was at such times that the sea dikes showed their immense value.

Old Melse could talk at great length about these matters. Woe betide the polder when the dike gave way during such a northwesterly storm! If the battlements of the De Muralt Wall developed as much as a crack, the enemy, lurking in the neighborhood, would immediately discover the breach in the fortifications and force its way inland with irresistible power.

But just now the sea looked friendly and gentle. It was lying at the foot of Zeeland's land mass like a submissive, defeated enemy who was aware that he had no opportunity whatsoever to overcome the strong dikes.

The sun deposited a layer of silvery gold over the peaceful waves. The waves allowed patches of light and dark to play across the mirror that was the sea. The play of light on the sleeping water was both moving and fascinating. It reminded one of the innocence of a sleeping child.

Then old Melse turned his attention to the land behind him. Right below the dike was a steep descent. The slope was covered with a heavy carpet of grass on which all kinds of wild plants grew. Hard as was the side of the dike facing the sea, its inner side was gentle and soft. From the outer side came the danger that demanded firmness and strictness and earnestness on the part of the people, but on the inner side a joyful play of unconcern was to be seen — grass and flowers, gentle and loving.

The polder below the dike was deep and broad. The little villages looked as though they had been given their location through the willfulness of a small boy setting up his toys.

From where grandfather Melse stood, it was obvious that the life of those villages and farms lay well below the surface of the sea water. The whole place was encircled by a thin, small ridge — a dike topped by the De Muralt Wall, which was only about thirty centimeters thick.

It was wonderful, rich soil that lay inside this ridge. The ground was always willing and gave abundantly — as much as a hundredfold in terms of return on the seed it received. And with this ground wrested from the sea, the people had done well for themselves. They had built their churches, raised their children, and established their schools; they had worked and slaved, suffered and struggled, laughed and wept. Here were their cradles and their graves. Here their cattle were pastured and their birds sang.

And all that colorful movement on the part of seemingly insignificant people, who had been created for eternity and yet were so much bound to the earth, was protected only by a thin wall composed of a number of meters of earth. Outside the wall was an ocean of water rising above the heads of the people, an ocean that covered more than half of the earth's surface. If that gigantic ocean were to be given just the smallest opening, an opening of only a few centimeters, it would move right through it and quickly gouge out a channel many meters wide. And then the entire struggle against the sea which the people had waged for centuries to make the earth habitable would be over: the sea would swallow up the earth. Yet the sea itself would not be changed by such an event. It would not be made either lower or higher. As for all that man had worked so long to establish, no trace of it would be left. Later generations could then speak of the land that had "drowned."

* * *

Old Melse continued his journey down the small concrete path along the wall. The path continued the entire length of the dike.

The friendly, transparent light that was reflected on the water also caressed his old, lined face. Finally he turned his attention in the opposite direction, and when he came to a bend in the dike, he saw below, close to the slope, a few houses and a café. He walked down a small path to get to the bottom and entered the café.

It was a new building; the old one had been smashed by the Germans. When the Allies were getting close to Schouwen and Duiveland, the Germans had claimed the land on which the café had stood for their artillery. After the war, the owner had quickly rebuilt his café.

The owner turned out to be a talkative man. When he handed old Melse his cup of coffee, he sat down opposite him and took a good look at him. "If I'm not mistaken, I've seen you before, but I don't remember the occasion."

"That may well be," said Melse. "It was some years ago when I was last here with my brother, Joris Melse, who lives in the neighborhood below the dike."

The café-owner now remembered the occasion. "Wasn't it at the beginning of the occupation? And wasn't David, the son of Joris Melse, with you as well? There were some Germans in the place at the time, and I was a little nervous. In those first days of the occupation, David Melse spoke quite freely when it came to the Germans — he didn't try to hide what he was thinking. He came right out with it. He later learned to be more cautious — and with good reason. We now understand very well why he was so cautious. With Joris Melse it was a different story. As long as that man has lived around here, he's been very cautious about speaking out — even more so after the death of his wife. Things simply did not go well for that man here. He lost his wife while she was still fairly young, and then his only son was murdered by the Krauts . . . So, now his brother has come from Walcheren to visit him. That's a fine thing to do. Does Joris Melse know you're coming?"

"He doesn't know anything about it," replied Melse. "But that's the nice part. An unexpected arrival can be such a wonderful surprise."

But what Dirk Melse was really after was to get the café-owner to tell him how Uncle Joris was doing. Back on Walcheren they had not heard from him for a long time, even though he had returned to his farm. He had never been one for writing letters.

Now the café-owner was in a position to do some talking, which was an activity he particularly enjoyed. He told old Melse that his brother Joris had some sort of heart condition and walked with a stoop because of rheumatism. He was somewhat run-down in appearance and did not take much interest in his farm, now that his only son was gone. With him on his place now was only a housekeeper. The farm looked as though it was being neglected.

Grandfather Melse listen attentively. Sad as the facts were, these were the kinds of things that he had come to find out. And so he saw that he had chosen wisely when he decided to enter the café and drink a cup of coffee.

"You people were fortunate to have been liberated already in 1944," observed the café-owner. "We had to wait until May of 1945 to get rid of the Krauts. There was a German post here, which consisted mainly of Russian prisoners of war — they were not bad fellows. At the very end they even began to chum around somewhat with the men of the underground. They wanted to liberate the island and chase out the Krauts. But somehow the Germans picked up word of what was going on, and then they began to call up all the men between seventeen and forty years of age. A group of underground fighters tried to flee to South Beveland, but they were captured. The Germans demanded that every parish on Schouwen turn over five of its men at the Moermond Castle near Renesse. The family members of the victims gathered there as well, and what they saw was a beam supported by two big trees, and from the beam ten young fellows were hanging. One father saw his only son hanging there, and the death convulsions were still going on. It was too much for the poor man and he fainted. The bodies had to remain hanging there for two days. Still, there's this to be considered: because David Melse had been arrested much earlier, this horrible experience was not something that Joris Melse had to endure. Yes, I'm telling you, those rats surely did some horrible things here. And then they put all this beautiful land under water — not all that high, mind you, but just enough water to make sure that we couldn't do anything here. Some years will have to go by before our land is fully restored in terms of getting the crop levels that we used to achieve. But it will all come out well in the end — I'm sure of it."

By this time old Melse had finished his coffee, and he started a fresh pipe. He continued to listen to the stream of words from the café-owner. Every now and then he would nod approvingly. Finally he said: "Well, it's about time for me to move along."

"It's not far anymore," responded the café-owner. He added: "I wish you a pleasant journey."

Old Melse felt rested. His journey had worn him out more than he expected. Now he felt fresh again. He did not want to arrive at his brother's farmhouse looking exhausted.

As he undertook the last part of the journey, his thoughts returned to his youth, when Joris was still at home with them. Joris had always been something of a loner; he was a boy who lived only for himself. He was egoistic in nature and did not concern himself much with his surroundings. And yet he had been eager to try looking after himself.

And so the lives of the two brothers gradually followed separate paths. Before long Joris went to Schouwen and Duiveland and got married there. They did not hear much from him after that. There were only a few times when the two brothers saw one another, and they were special family occasions, such as funerals and weddings. After that the two went their separate ways and were almost strangers to each other.

When they drifted apart, it caused their parents a great deal of pain. It was indeed strange how children who had slept in the same bed and had eaten dinner at the same table and had enjoyed the same upbringing could become so estranged from one another. But when you got older, you began to change in this regard. While you are in the prime of your life, there is so much in your family and your job that draws your attention that all the rest is easily forgotten. But when your life begins to draw to a close and the years of youth become much more vivid in your memory, the bonds of blood also speak more than they had before. And so, when he heard his grandson Dirk talk about Joris, Dirk Melse came to the conclusion that the death of Joris's wife had really changed his brother. The Lord had visited him again in the death of his son and the devastation of his farm land. Did Joris bow under those judgments and accept them?

With these thoughts running through his mind, grandfather Melse arrived at the farmstead. He walked down the stone pathway and onto his brother's property.

Joris was sitting in front of the window. Just at that moment the sunlight was falling on his weathered face. Grandfather Melse raised his walking stick by way of greeting. When he reached the door, Joris tried to get up out of his wicker sitting chair. With his head leaning far forward, he stared from under his bushy eyebrows at his unexpected visitor. He was leaning on his cane, and his hands were trembling.

When he recognized his brother, a look of relief and a bit of a smile came over his face. "Well, well, what do we have here? Is it really you? I'm glad to see you!"

He then turned to his housekeeper and informed her: "This is my brother Dirk from Walcheren."

"Well, well," he continued, "this is really something! Just last week I was talking about you to someone, and now I find you standing here before me! I do hope that it isn't bad news that led you to make this unexpected visit." There was no hiding Joris Melse's pleasure at receiving this visit.

"We all have our cross to bear," said grandfather Melse. "And that's probably necessary too. But the question is whether the Lord will be pleased to use that cross to work sanctification in our hearts and lives."

"It's just as you said," responded his brother, seemingly eager to agree with him. "If only we could get some certainty about these matters on this side of the grave!"

His brother looked at him attentively. Then he sighed.

Lana, the housekeeper, poured tea and gave them each a cookie from a black cookie tin. But she said nothing. She looked on and listened.

"How long are you thinking of staying here?" asked Uncle Joris.

"Well, I suppose, a day or two — not longer. They really can't do without me back on the farm. I want you to know that I still help with the milking."

There was a bit of pride in grandfather Melse's words — the pride of an old man who knew that he had not yet been put on the sidelines by the younger generation.

"I've gotten rid of my cows," said Uncle Joris. "I just have one cow left, for my own use, so to speak. I can't keep up with the work anymore. I'm almost crippled from my rheumatism."

"I hope you can still get around outside," said grandfather Melse.

"Yes, leaning on my cane, taking it step by step. But you mustn't ask me just how I manage it."

"As for me, I'm still as fresh as a young buck," said grandfather Melse. "I had to walk for an hour and a half to get here. If you have no objections I'll milk your cow for you after a while. And if there's some more work to be done around the place, just let me know."

"I do have a hired hand on the place, but you know how these things go. They act as if they're their own boss, and they take advantage of the circumstances."

After two cups of tea, the two old men walked out into the yard. Uncle Joris was curious what it was that had prompted his brother to make this unexpected visit. He could not bring himself to believe that he had come without any particular reason. But grandfather Melse did not let his purpose be known.

Uncle Joris slowly made his way through the barn and around the yard. They stood looking at the cow and then at the horses. They estimated the weight of the pigs and watched the chickens in their coop. And when grandfather Melse went to bed that evening in a room on the second floor, Uncle Joris still did not know what had prompted the visit.

The next day grandfather Melse got up early. He had slept very well and felt as fit as a young man. He went out onto the land and looked at what was growing there. He talked with the hired hand, milked the cow, and fed the pigs. Joris was amazed at his vitality.

They talked about the farm, and grandfather Melse gave Joris some advice and hints. When the opportunity came up, they began to discuss spiritual matters as well. But neither of them got any farther than the heartfelt wish that it might happen for them, or that the change might come — the change that would give them a bit of certainty with regard to the most important things. They both agreed that to arrive at the end of your life without any hope of eternal salvation is a dreadful thing.

On the morning of the third day, grandfather Melse began to make preparations for departure. He stood with his brother looking at the cow, which was grazing in a pasture not far from the house. Joris sensed that now he would finally hear what his brother had in his heart. Both men got some tobacco for their pipes from Uncle Joris's tin.

"Shall I tell you now what I think you should do, Joris?"

"I have no idea what you have in mind, Dirk. How can I guess what you're thinking?"

"Well, what I've been thinking is this: you should let my son take over the work on your farm. You could then keep on living here peacefully, and both of you would have a roof over your heads."

Uncle Joris had not expected such a suggestion. "Where did you get that idea?" he asked in amazement.

"Well, the one hand washes the other, and they both become clean. Because of the reallocation of land that's going on, my son has to leave the area where he's now living, and he really doesn't want to move to the Noordoost Polder. But if he were to come here, he would still be in Zeeland. He only has one son left, as you know, and that son has gone off to serve with the military in Indonesia. And so he could very nicely handle the farm here with the help of your hired hand. As for you, you'd have an easy and undisturbed life. My son's wife would look after the housekeeping, and so you would not have any strangers in your place."

Grandfather Melse went on to explain that the two brothers could then enjoy one another's company. For he, Dirk, planned to come along, of course.

Joris had already seen that, if necessary, Dirk could give a good account of himself when it came to farm work. He did not need to take second place to anyone.

Dirk did not press Joris for a decision just then. It was too important a matter. He suggested that Joris sleep on it for a couple of nights and then let him know his decision by way of a letter.

As to just how he proposed to arrange matters in case the answer was yes, that could be worked out later. He could make the farm over to David, but if he wanted to remain the owner he could let David rent the place, on the condition that he, Joris, would be allowed to remain living there.

"I've given this matter a great deal of thought, and I believe that the solution I'm proposing is best for all parties." Then grandfather Melse blew a big cloud of smoke into the air.

"It's a very important matter that you've dumped into my lap just now," said Joris. "I'm certainly going to have to think it over for a while. There are some important implications which I cannot immediately see through. But as I look at it today for the first time, I have to admit that it does have possibilities. And so I'm glad to follow your advice. I'll think it over and send you a letter once I've made my decision."

When the conversation was over, grandfather Melse departed. This time he walked past the café by the dike. He made the journey to the bus stop without pausing to rest along the way, and he got home safely. But he did not say anything about the purpose of his visit. Soon enough there would be an occasion to talk about it.

*　　　*　　　*

When Uncle Joris's letter arrived in the mail and grandfather Melse proceeded to open it, he was tense. A great deal depended on what his brother had to say.

It turned out that Joris Melse had given the proposal a good deal of thought and had come to the conclusion that it wouldn't be a bad idea after all if his nephew David took over the farm. He invited him to do so by way of a rental arrangement, but with an option to buy the place. Uncle Joris said he would wait for an answer, and if the family said yes, he would find it best that the move take place quite soon.

When it was evening, grandfather Melse told his son and daughter-in-law about the letter and explained to them what his real purpose had been in going to visit Uncle Joris. David Melse gave mother Beth a wink and said: "See, wasn't it just as I said? Grandfather didn't go over there without a good reason. He had something up his sleeve. And now we know what it was."

By making these remarks, David Melse avoided giving a direct answer to his father's question what he thought of the plan. But grandfather Melse was not to be diverted from his purpose quite so easily. He said: "Naturally, I can understand why you can't make up your mind at once. Uncle Joris also had to sleep on it for a couple of nights. But I must say that he has come to the right conclusion after thinking the matter through. For him this is the best solution. And the beauty of the situation is that for you folks just as for me, it's the best solution. This way we'll all get out of the tough situation we now face — true or not?"

"I can't give you an answer just now," said David Melse. "But it's certainly worth thinking about."

"In this way we could all remain in Zeeland."

"That's true, but over there it's not the same as it is here on Walcheren, Father. It's an entirely different people over there than we're used to here. They're more liberal — they don't take God's commandments as seriously as we do."

"We don't need to let ourselves be influenced by them," said grandfather Melse. "We would live our own life, and what the others do is their business — true or not?"

After a few days David Melse made up his mind. Mother Beth did not have a hard time agreeing with him. It was also the best solution for Henry. When he had his years of military service behind him and returned safe and sound from Indonesia, he would know that there was a farm for him to take over one day. Nowadays it was almost impossible for a young man to get hold of a farm that would one day be his own. In this way, the future would be laid out for him.

And so a letter was written to Uncle Joris. Francke was also told about the important decision that had been made.

*   *   *

The weeks went by quickly. Grandfather Melse wandered through the village quite a bit, visiting places that brought back recollections of his earlier years. He thought about his school years, and about his years as a young man when he walked with his girlfriend along the paths outside the village on a Saturday evening, which was the only evening in the entire week that they could be together, even though they lived in the same village.

A number of times he went to the graves in the churchyard where his wife lay. Now that the time for departure was coming close, it became ever harder for him to contemplate taking leave of her. On the one hand, it was a victory that he and his family did not need to leave Zeeland after all and that he would wind up living not all that far from his beloved Walcheren. But on the other hand, now that the time was almost upon them, he was no longer so sure of the decision and not so happy with the outcome of his plan as he had been earlier. A question kept coming up in his mind: am I somehow running away? Was this decision made prematurely? Have I been thinking too much in earthly and fleshly terms? Could it be that God was preparing some other way out for us and that we didn't wait for Him?

And it didn't get any easier for him when Rev. Verhulst, who by then had recovered from his nervous breakdown, came along to strengthen his doubts. "Are you folks really sure that this is what you must do?" he asked. "Lot also chose the better of two places to live, and look what happened to him. He wound up fleeing, while his wife remained behind as a pillar of salt."

David Melse did not know what to say in response. For some reason, the minister's words made an even deeper impression on him than he realized they would when he first heard them. In some hidden corner of his heart, they found resonance.

Mother Beth was more sober about the situation. She turned to the minister and said: "I'm not in a position to make a judgment about Lot, Reverend, but I do want to tell you this: my husband need not fear that he will have to leave *me* behind as a pillar of salt. I won't look back at Walcheren for a single moment. Instead I'll think about the words that came into my heart this week: 'Go tell the children of Israel to leave.' I believe we'll be able to serve the Lord just as well on Schouwen and Duiveland as we have done on Walcheren. What do you say, Husband?"

David Melse nodded, but at the same time he looked toward the minister apprehensively. He wondered what sort of impression these words were making on the minister.

*   *   *

A reception was arranged at Francke's house for the local people to say goodbye to the Melse family. When various friends and acquaintances arrived, they noted that Jacob Jobse and Joan happened to be sitting near the minister.

Jacob said not a word. It was not like him to do a lot of talking if it was not strictly necessary. Normally he would listen.

On this occasion it was again evident that there are very strong ties between the people living in a Walcheren village. All afternoon the house was full of people. David Melse was a man who was much appreciated by the people in the village, and everyone lamented the fact that he was moving away. They would also miss grandfather Melse: many had trouble imagining him living in some other village. The Melses and their village belonged together.

The conversation got into all kinds of subjects, especially the developments right after the end of the war. The people talked about the way the government was handling the compensation for all the loss of land and property on Walcheren. They also talked about the evacuation and the reallocation of land. In time they got around to the people who wound up victims in the process and touched on those who had already left for the Noordoost Polder or were about to do so. And then they went on to talk about the struggle in Indonesia and all the chaos over there. There were plenty of topics to get into.

Grandfather Melse did not have much to say. He drew the tobacco out of the bowl of his pipe and blew clouds of smoke toward the ceiling. He was having a harder time of it than he was willing to admit to himself, and his son was in the same frame of mind. The future on which they were about to embark was uncertain, even though the circumstances looked good.

Tina and Janet, who were both living in Middelburg, were not too pleased at the thought that their father and mother would be living much farther away than before. Both of them were engaged to be married, and Tina was hoping that her wedding day would come soon.

Laura, the youngest, who was now fourteen years old, did not know what to think about the new developments. When she looked at the faces of her father and grandfather, she got the impression that the move was more of a mistake than something for people to rejoice over.

As for Henry, who had returned from basic training, he was strutting around in his military uniform. He did not care much where his father and mother would wind up living. After all, he was about to depart for Indonesia, and when he came back in a couple of years, it would be quite clear to him what he was to do.

Tea was offered with the cake. The women were busy talking about the houses that had been flooded and were still damp inside. Then their conversation went around the neighborhood as they reviewed how all the people had fared in 1944, that catastrophic year. They paused to mention those who had lost their homes completely.

The discussion among the women gave Rev. Verhulst an opportunity to put his stamp on the conversation. "You people are talking about the catastrophic year of 1944. You're right to call it catastrophic, Mrs. Karelse. It's just too bad that we're so reluctant to recognize the catastrophe as something sent to us from above. Instead we keep looking at our neighbors to the east, as though *they* were the cause of the catastrophe, whereas the real cause lies in our own hearts. In the final analysis, it was not the Germans' fault that they ruled over us for some five years . . ."

Jacob Jobse interrupted the minister: "I can't agree with you on that point, Reverend, for then it would have had to be just like the Babylonian captivity, in which case it would have lasted at least seventy years."

"What I always miss in your reasoning, brother Jobse, is humility."

Jacob responded at once: "That's because you don't understand that humility can be accompanied with the determination to fight back against the Germans and to chase them out of our land."

No, that was something the minister could not understand. He shook his head and replied: "The trouble is that you don't see the Lord's hand of chastisement in these things."

"Oh yes, I do see it, Reverend, but in my Bible it says that there can be a hand of chastisement from the Lord at the same time as a fatherly and merciful hand toward those who fear Him. According to my way of thinking, you are approaching these matters with a one-track mind — *that's* where you're wrong. And for that matter, if we were to insist on reasoning just the way you do, we could also ask what kind of sin *you* are guilty of. Why was it that you suffered from nervous exhaustion for so long and could not do your work as a minister in the church? According to your own reasoning, the Lord's hand of chastisement would have to be behind that situation. The idea would be that He wanted you to repent of your sins — true or not?"

The minister stared at the edge of the tablecloth and felt the eyes of all the people fixed upon him. What was he to say?

"Jacob, I think that should remain a matter between God and my conscience."

"I can happily agree to that, Reverend, but then, when it comes to what our people have suffered, you should let the question of the German occupation also remain a matter between God and our conscience. You should not be hitting the congregation over the head every Sunday. Oh boy!"

This time the "Oh boy!" was a very positive way for Jacob to end what he had to say. Rev. Verhulst was happy for an opportunity to let the matter go and consider the conversation closed. He stood up and shook hands with the Melses and wished them God's blessing in their new place of residence.

He left the room and walked across the yard with his head bowed. Joan watched him and shook her head. All she said was: "Jacob, Jacob, why are you so quick to speak out? Don't you think you should have watched what you said?"

"I'll watch what I say when the minister changes his tune," responded Jacob.

Now the conversation turned to other subjects. But Francke was very appreciative of what Jacob had said. The young man could always find the weak point in dubious reasoning. Once Jacob had stated his position, there was usually nothing left for others to say than: "Just so — that's exactly right!"

Grandfather Melse was also listening intently. He did not know which way to turn when it came to these questions.

* * *

When it was finally time to depart, the last walk David Melse took was to Dirk's grave. As he stood before the grave, he thought again about what Jacob had said to the minister. He remembered that his son Dirk used to talk the same line.

"My boy, to think that I now have to leave you behind!" he sighed. He knew that Dirk had been a support to him in more than just his earthly existence.

* * *

As they left the village, there were various friends on hand to wave goodbye to them. Melse could not help thinking of Naomi, who said when she returned to the land of Canaan: "Do not call me Naomi any longer but call me Mara, for the Lord has dealt very bitterly with me."

He took a last lingering look at the barren stretch of land where his farm had stood. The digging machines were already busy cutting a deep waterway right through his former farm. Soon there would be nothing left to indicate that a farm had once stood there. The Walcheren he had known and loved was gone. There were no trees left, and no bushes to mark the paths. No flowers blossomed in small gardens in front of the houses.

The bus took them to Middelburg, where Tina was waiting at the station to greet them. "Next spring we hope to get married!" she said. "Willem has been able to find a place for us to live. We'll be staying with an old couple. I'll do the heavy housework for the lady, who is ailing. The one hand washes the other. I'll write — you can count on it! Goodbye! Keep your chin up!"

It appeared that Tina had no problems. She was looking forward to getting married, and beyond that prospect there was not much in the world that concerned her.

143

Mother Beth looked out the window of the train for a long time, keeping her eyes fixed on her daughter, who stood there waving. The train barreled away in the direction of Goes. Walcheren was behind them . . .

*   *   *

The cows and the farm implements that Melse had managed to save from the ravages of the flood waters had already been sent ahead. Now that Uncle Joris was getting some solid help on the place, it would be possible to keep cows again. There would be a couple of strong Zeeland horses pulling a plow through the soil. The cows could enjoy the pasture, and so new life would come to the neglected farm.

For all of these reasons and more, the new residents were very welcome at the home of Uncle Joris. In the meantime, the housekeeper had moved in with her sister and was collecting a small pension. These arrangements had also made the separation somewhat easier.

Uncle Joris was hobbling next to one of his fences, leaning on his cane, when he saw his brother Dirk and his son and son's family approaching along the dike. He pulled the black, heavily used pipe from his mouth and waved it in the air, thereby giving them a welcome from afar.

Uncle Joris's farm was right at the foot of the dike at a point where the dike made a gentle bend outwards. There was a winding path along the bottom of the dike and a set of stone steps leading to its crown, along which ran the De Muralt Wall. The big dike looked like a powerful arm that encircled the farm to protect it against the treacherous power of the mighty enemy on the other side of the dike.

The table in the farmhouse was covered with a bright red-and-white checkered tablecloth. Through the small window the approaching Melses could see a teapot with steam coming from it.

Mother Beth felt at home immediately. With the practiced eye of a housewife, she could tell that the kitchen had been well maintained. At once she took off her short, heavy coat, put on the apron that was hanging ready for her, smoothed it out, and said: "It looks as though the tea is already prepared, and I would certainly enjoy a cup. Shall I pour for all of us?"

"You're the boss in the house now," said Uncle Joris. "You just do as you see fit. As for tea, yes, I would also like some. There's a tin with cookies in the cupboard on the middle shelf — the black tin. That's where my wife always had cookies ready when visitors came."

"But we're not visitors here," said mother Beth.

"And that's just the way I want it," responded Uncle Joris. "Still, because you have just now arrived, I thought to myself: they must have something sweet to welcome them. What do you think?"

David Melse chuckled as he refilled his pipe from the brass tobacco tin his uncle held before him.

"And where is Grandfather now?" asked Uncle Joris.

They looked through the window into the yard, but there was no sign of Grandfather. He had gone into the barn where the cows were kept. He was caressing the animals' heads between their horns. "At least you have your own stall again," he said.

The large, vacant eyes looked back at him. The damp noses of the cows rubbed up against his jacket. It was clear from the sounds the cows had made when he entered the barn that they were glad to see him.

He walked out of the barn and into the carriage shed, where the farm implements were kept. Everything appeared to be in order. The cart that had been used to transport the implements was still standing out in the yard, although there was room for it in the shed. There was plenty of room on this farm, he saw. He wandered past the firewood shed over to the chicken coop and then to the hog barn. He also took time to scratch the bristly heads of the pigs.

And so grandfather Melse had taken the trouble to greet the livestock. Then he looked over the yard at the fine land that had indeed stood under water but had not suffered nearly as much as the land on Walcheren. Here it was largely a matter of the land becoming swampy. There was not the daily alternation of high and low tide doing its destructive work. His experienced eye told him that the land would soon be very productive again.

Over his head he could see white clouds sailing along. They had come from the Eastern Scheldt and were moving in a northwesterly direction. The sun peeked out from time to time between the clouds. Grandfather Melse knew that this was a real Zeeland sky. The clouds overhead connected him with Walcheren. After all, it was a single sky and a single land, even if the Scheldt came between them.

A warm feeling of endless gratitude welled up within him. He went back to the barn where the cows were kept and fell to his knees onto a pile of hay. He folded his bony old hands and mumbled a prayer of thanksgiving. He thanked God that he had been allowed to come here, and then he asked God to allow his brother's farm to be the place where he would die.

Meanwhile, in the house, mother Beth said: "Now one of you should go and see where Grandfather is. Tell him that his tea is getting cold."

David Melse looked in the carriage shed and then in the hog barn. He walked across the farmyard and eventually wound up in the barn with the cows, and there he found his father on his knees in the hay. He could see that the old man's lips were moving. Without a word, Melse turned around and left the barn. "Father will be along soon enough," he said in response to mother Beth, who gave him a questioning look as he entered the house.

Chapter 8

Since the day Uncle Joris had received his brother and his brother's son and family into his house, his life had become different and much better. Mother Beth brought some domesticity and family atmosphere back into the place. She was a born farmer's wife. Now that young Laura was done with school, the two of them looked after the housekeeping, although there was also a girl who came from the village to help out during the morning hours. But for the rest they did all the housework between the two of them.

Once a week mother Beth baked, and her results were always first-rate — soft bread without hard crusts, never too hard, never doughy or underdone, never too much salt or too little. She was also in charge of killing the animals for meat. She knew how to make sausage and headcheese, and she used brine and salt to cure the pork.

If necessary, she also helped with the farm work. She fed the animals some leftovers, helped with the milking, and looked after the yard where the vegetables, including peas, carrots, lettuce, cabbage, and radishes, were growing. She also raised flowers and always saw to it that a little bouquet of flowers was standing on the table next to the window. She prepared the famous Zeeland molasses candy with some chocolate powder running through it, giving these wonderful sweets their unique striped appearance.

For Uncle Joris, all of this was an unexpected turn for the better, which sometimes led him to forget about the great pain in his life. He could hardly find adequate words to express his gratitude, but his smile said enough.

*   *   *

One Sunday morning, when the family was drinking coffee and Uncle Joris was blowing into his cup, he asked mother Beth: "Do you know what the difference is between now and the time when I lived here on my own?"

"Why don't you tell me? Then we'll all know."

"The difference is only a tee."

"What did you say there?"

"It's only a tee," repeated Uncle Joris.

Mother Beth shrugged her shoulders and looked at her husband, who was smiling as he listened to the conversation. She asked him: "Do you know what he means?"

But David Melse didn't get it, and neither did Grandfather. "Am I not saying it clearly enough?" asked Uncle Joris. "The difference is only a tee!"

"But what is a tee?" asked mother Beth. "Who has ever heard of a tee?"

"Isn't there a tee in the alphabet?"

"I can see that Uncle Joris loves riddles," said Laura. "Why don't you just tell us what you mean, Uncle Joris, for not one of us will get it."

"All right then, I'll tell you. When my wife was still alive, my dwelling was a home *(thuus)*. When she died, it became a mere house *(huus)*, and now it's a home *(thuus)* again — a house with a tee. Now, isn't that a difference of just a tee?"[4]

Now mother Beth nodded. She understood. "You're right," she said, as she thought carefully about what might lie buried in these few words that had come forth from Uncle Joris. "There's quite a difference between a house and a home."

"But let's hope that for all of us it will remain a home," she added. With her mind on the sermon they had heard that morning in church, she went on to say: "It could be a home until the day that a house with many rooms is prepared for us in heaven."

"Yes, as long as there will actually be a place for us there," said Grandfather.

"Nowhere in the Bible does it say that there would be no place for you there," said mother Beth resolutely.

"We should not think too lightly about these things," said grandfather Melse, and Uncle Joris agreed with him. "There would

---

[4] In the Zeeland dialect in which the characters speak much of the time, the difference between home and a house is the single letter T. In Dutch the respective words are *huis* (house) and *thuis* (home). —Trans.

have to be some personal knowledge before we could say such a thing, girl."

"I'm aware of that, but it says that there is a house with many rooms. Well, that also applies to you, Uncle Joris. It's all a question of whether you are willing to believe that the Lord has prepared a place for *you* too. With all that sighing and doubting we don't get any further. We *must* have faith."

"And faith is a gift of God," said Grandfather.

"Just because it's a gift of God, you can share in it too. That's what the Lord promised you in your baptism."

"My baptism, my baptism," sighed Grandfather.

"That was a long time ago," Uncle Joris remarked, with a smile on his face.

But mother Beth was not smiling. For her it was a very serious subject. "In your baptism the Lord says that He wants to accept you as His child. That's what you have to believe now. And if you don't believe, you are disappointing the Holy Spirit."

"I can't follow you in your reasoning, girl. Your thinking is too superficial. There has to be something else in the picture besides that little bit of water on your forehead."

"If you wait for that something else, you'll wait in vain, for the Lord already provided sufficiently for your salvation when He let His Son die on the cross. With all of that sealed to you in your baptism, I don't know what more would need to be done."

"You're forgetting about appropriated grace, girl, which must be given to us by God. It's something that does not come into our lives automatically."

"You're talking nonsense!" said mother Beth resolutely. "You must tell me where in the world you find those ideas in the Bible. What I read in the Bible is that we have to believe like children — we are supposed to be full of faith. That's what gives the Lord pleasure. But to reason the way you're doing — it's really nothing but unbelief!"

"How I wish I could think about these matters the way you do, girl!" sighed Uncle Joris. And therewith the conversation came to an end.

David Melse had listened in silence. He was quite familiar with the respective standpoints of his wife and the two old men. But how did he think about these matters himself? Under the influence of his wife, he had come to a somewhat sounder point of view. And so he did not share the standpoint of his father and his uncle. But he was not able to be as resolute as his wife was.

Sometimes he asked himself whether he still had the old trust that he used to have. Had he perhaps lost it? Wasn't God against him now? Wasn't everything being taken from him? His farm on Walcheren, his oldest son, and now Henry was in Indonesia.

Often he thought back to the sermons of Rev. Verhulst, which had left an even deeper impression on his thinking than he had been aware of at the time. When he looked at these matters soberly, he came to the conclusion that he was not much further ahead than Grandfather and Uncle Joris.

As for the congregation in the village where he now lived, it was not the kind of church that could help you in such a struggle. The group was too small to have a minister of its own. Sometimes a minister from some other place would preach, but in many of the services an elder would have to read a sermon. Moreover, the village was rather superficial and not much interested in church life. There was indeed a big church in the middle of the village, but it did not have much of a place in the hearts of the people. At Easter and Christmas and New Year's Eve, there were still many who attended a worship service, but for the rest they used the Sunday to get some extra sleep and to loaf. The younger people liked to take a walk on the dike or even go to Zierikzee on their bicycles.

At the beginning of the war, there seemed to be an improvement in spiritual life, and during the first weeks the churches in the village were full. But the improvement did not last long, and now, after the liberation, conditions were worse than ever before. Most of the people had been evacuated for a while, and when they returned, they brought with them the customs and lifestyle of other places. They tried to transplant some of the patterns of larger cities into their life in the village. But those city patterns did not include faithful church attendance, and so there was an increasing moral decline, especially among the rising generation of young people.

150

David Melse was well aware that when it came to matters of this sort, the situation was much better on Walcheren. The people there were more conservative and restrained. They also took the church much more seriously. When it was Sunday on Walcheren, it was evident throughout the entire village. But here you could hardly tell that it was Sunday. There were even farmers who went out to work on their land on Sunday!

When David Melse thought all of these things over, doubts arose in his heart as to whether he had done the right thing in leaving Walcheren. Had he not strayed from the path, as some people had suggested he was doing? The only thing that could reconcile him with the situation in which he now lived was the great thankfulness in the heart of Uncle Joris.

*　　*　　*

One afternoon, when he was up in the hayloft throwing down some hay, he saw Uncle Joris standing on the barn floor. He was bent over, leaning on his cane. He shouted a warning to his uncle to watch out for the hay coming down. Then he threw down some more hay with his fork, and it wound up right in front of his uncle's wooden shoes. Uncle Joris took hold of a hayfork and tried to bring some hay to the cows, even though he was bent over. Again and again he tested his strength, only to discover that he was no longer up to doing productive work.

When David Melse came down from the hayloft, he saw that Uncle Joris was sitting on a crate. He was panting. "You shouldn't let yourself get so busy, Uncle Joris," he said.

"You're right, my boy, but if my eyes see some work lying there waiting to be done, my hands have an awful hard time staying away from it."

"But now there are hands enough on the place to do the work that needs to be done."

David Melse was sitting next to his uncle on the crate. He put some tobacco into his pipe and offered his tobacco tin to Uncle Joris. The old man shook his head. He then stuck out his right hand and let his nephew look at the curved fingers. "Just take a look," he said. "What hands!"

David Melse nodded. He had often noticed those hands. It appeared that his uncle could no longer stretch his fingers out until they were straight.

"How I wish this condition had come about through the work I have done," said Uncle Joris.

"What else did you think it could be caused by?"

"I'll tell you, my boy. It's the punishment I have received for my sins. All my life long I've been a grasping creature, and now my hands are good for nothing but grasping. But let them also be a warning to you, my boy."

More Uncle Joris did not say. And David Melse did not ask any questions. Again he was amazed at how Uncle Joris could come up with those stimulating, pithy sayings that would get a person thinking. When the pipe was finished, David Melse continued with his work of feeding the animals, while Uncle Joris wandered around the barn a little longer.

Grandfather Dirk then entered the barn. Uncle Joris sat on the crate again, and Grandfather went over to sit next to him. "I've just shown these two hands to your son," said Uncle Joris. "And I told him that they are the punishment coming to me for my sins. You know much more about this than he does. I've always been a grasping creature, and now my hands are good for nothing but grasping. Just take a look." Again he extended his hands and showed that he could not straighten his fingers.

Grandfather was silent. The past was vivid in his mind now. It was true that his brother Joris had been an egoist from childhood. He had lived for himself alone, but now that he was an old man, he was different.

"Have you ever thought about how strangely things sometimes go in the world, Joris?" he asked. "When you and I were boys, we drifted apart. Years went by when we did not see each other at all. But now that we're old, we've come together again."

"Indeed, it's amazing. I often stop to think about it, and when I do, our younger years come to mind for me. And then I see our mother and father before me. Where in the world has the time gone? Can you understand why the years go by so quickly?"

"Yes, they go by quickly," said grandfather Melse.

Uncle Joris was in an unusual mood: he wanted to talk. "I know that I was a miserable character when I was a boy," he said. "I lived for myself. I caused our mother and father a great deal of grief and disappointment. I was greedy and acquisitive; I took things for myself and did not pause to consider that there were other people in the world too. But now I have been punished for all of this. Because my fingers were only busy hauling things toward me, just look at them now! They've turned into hooks. Every moment of the day my hands remind me of my greediness. They show me what I deserve."

Grandfather Melse listened but did not respond. Uncle Joris continued: "And what have I achieved by being so acquisitive and greedy? My wife was taken away from me, and also my only son. I was here all by myself. And as for that little piece of land, what does it really mean? You know as well as I do that it's not the best land around. The land near Brouwershaven and Zierikzee is much better. You have to work very hard here to coax just a little bit of harvest from the ground. Well, I've worked hard. I worked until I became lame and crooked. You can see that for yourself. Day and night I sweated, and my wife with me. I stood before the Lord with clenched fists. And in the bad years before the war I said: 'I'm going to triumph even if I die trying.' I've known times when I couldn't even get two cents for an egg, times when I couldn't get rid of my hogs because no one wanted to eat pork. There were times when I could get almost nothing for my peas and beans. And so I had no money left over to make it through the winter. Even so, I survived. I got through it somehow. Day and night I drove myself, through rain and wind and cold and heat. And now I sit here with this twisted body on a crate in the barn and I find myself admitting to you that when you add it all up, I'm no farther ahead than when I began. Many years ago I acquired this farm, and now things are going fairly well again because the prices are better than they were before the war. But what good does it do me? My wife is in the grave, and my son is gone too. If you and David had not had mercy on me, I'd be sitting here all alone with a strange woman as my housekeeper, and with a body crippled by rheumatism, waiting to die. And that's the end, Dirk. But the question remains: is it really the end? For if we must one day stand before Almighty God to give an account of our deeds, what then? I won't be in a position to show Him much more than these two greedy, crippled hands attached to my body like a pair of hooks."

Grandfather Melse was still listening silently to his brother's confession. In his mind, too, the past was again clear. He could see his brother Joris standing before their father with clenched fists and hear him screaming: "I'm just going to go *my own way*. I'll make my way through the world relying on my own strength. I'll see how far I can get using my own muscles."

Their father had shaken his head, saying no more than: "Joris, Joris! What a conceited fellow you are!"

And Joris did indeed go his own way. He refused to help keep his father's farm going when some very difficult days came along. He looked out for himself instead. If the old man had gotten some help from Joris, he might have made it. But when he was all alone and in great need, it was his other son, Dirk Melse, who was already married and was struggling to support his family on the meager wages of a hired hand, who had to take responsibility for the old people, along with the deacons of the church. Joris did not bother with his parents. In later years they saw almost nothing of him. He wound up on Schouwen and Duiveland and went his own way.

"We're both sinners, and so we have to appear before a righteous God," said grandfather Melse gently.

"But you've led a better life than I have, Dirk."

"There's no one who leads a good life, Joris."

"Well, you led a better life than I did, Dirk. I was a greedy, acquisitive egoist."

Grandfather remained silent. When he heard his brother's favorable judgment about his life, he shrank back, because he knew it was not true. He thought back to his youth and remembered the sins of those days, which still weighed heavily on his conscience now that he was an old man. Just as Joris had ignored his father's warning, he had turned a deaf ear to the warnings given him by his

154

mother. He could still see her so clearly in his mind's eye. It was as though she was yet standing before him, waving her finger in the air and saying to him: "Son, be careful! You have a girlfriend now. Don't let the devil take the beautiful crown from your head. Keep your body pure and make sure you have a clear conscience on your wedding day."

But he had not kept himself pure. And his sins cost his mother a lot of tears — he knew that.

It surprised grandfather Melse that even when he was an old man, these events were clear in his mind. It was just as though it had all happened yesterday. He continued to feel deep pain over what he had done. If Joris's sins lay in the area of serving Mammon, his own sins had to do with fleshly lusts. No, he knew he was no better than Joris.

"We've both sinned, Brother," he said again. "And now I hope that we'll both be able to count on God to be gracious to us."

"Yes, that's what we must hope for."

*   *   *

David Melse was finished feeding the animals. He turned a milk can upside down and sat on it across from the two old men in the barn. "What are you two talking about?"

The two old men were a bit embarrassed as they looked at each other. Yes, what was it that they were discussing? Although they had been very open with one another, they clammed up now that someone from a younger generation came along and started asking questions.

"I want to tell you something," said Uncle Joris.

"What would that be?"

"If you two had not come here to live, I would probably have sold my little farm to Koster!"

"To Koster?" asked David Melse in amazement. He knew that Koster was a rich farmer who lived a little farther along on the polder. He was one of the wealthiest farmers in the area. For years he had been asking Joris Melse to sell him his farm so that his son could take it over. But Uncle Joris never gave the proposition any consideration. And now Koster's son had moved to Canada, for he was convinced that the Russians would one day march into the Netherlands, and he did not want to live under foreign rule for a second time.

Because Koster's second son also wanted a farm, Uncle Joris was once again presented with an offer. Just before Dirk's unexpected visit, Uncle Joris had decided to have a talk with Koster, for he realized that with the way things were going, he could not continue indefinitely on the farm. But now he understood that things had turned out in a way that was much better for him and for his family, even though Koster didn't like it.

Koster was a stubborn fool who was not accustomed to seeing his plans frustrated. And so he would probably come back at some point to make still another effort to buy the farm. However, it now appeared that the farm would stay in the family.

It didn't matter what Koster did — he could stand on his head if he wanted to. He would just have to leave them alone, even if he thought he could get whatever he wanted with all his money. And he did indeed possess a great deal of money — more than the three men had ever seen together in their lives. These were the things that David Melse now heard from Uncle Joris.

"I wish him much happiness with it," said David Melse.

"Happiness is just what he's never had," replied Uncle Joris. "All his life long, he's never been satisfied. He always wants more. And his wife is just the same. No hired hand ever lasts long at their place. He just squeezes everything he can out of them."

Then Uncle Joris suddenly fell still. There was a pained expression on his face as he rubbed his sore leg. He continued: "But I shouldn't be talking about someone else, for I'm no better myself. If I hadn't been kept small, I would have gone in the very same direction as Koster. I would have continued to scratch and claw, just as he does." He sighed.

David Melse stood up and went back to work. Slowly Uncle Joris rose from the crate on which he was seated. With grandfather Melse at his side, he walked back to the house.

156

David Melse could not help but notice how the two old men seemed more and more bound to one another and sought out each other's company.

With a basket of chopped beets he now walked over to the barn and gave the cows something to eat. Faithfully they chewed on their favorite food, as Melse rubbed their foreheads between their horns. The slow process of chewing the beets, their favorite food, produced the familiar sound that Melse loved to hear.

And then he began to ponder what Uncle Joris had said about Koster, the wealthy farmer. He had met the man once in the city, when he was with his son, the one who went to Canada, the one who was afraid that the Russians would take over.

Was there any reason for the younger Koster's concern? As happens so often, Melse's thoughts went back to Rev. Verhulst, who had said so much about the judgments of God over the apostate Dutch people. Could it be that Rev. Verhulst was right after all?

Melse was in a somber mood, and his heart was in the grip of doubt. He saw no way out of the labyrinth of difficulties in which his heart was entangled.

*   *   *

A few weeks later David Melse was returning by bus from the city, where he had visited an exhibition. As he took his bicycle from the rack, he found the wealthy farmer Koster standing before him. Koster was a big and sturdy man who seemed to be in full possession of his strength. From his round face radiated the desire to control others, and he appeared to be looking down on Melse.

"You're David Melse, if I'm not mistaken."

Melse nodded and stood ready to pedal away on his bicycle.

"If you don't mind, I'd like to walk along with you a little ways. You have to pass my farm anyway. Then we can get acquainted."

Melse nodded. Together they walked out of the village along the road that led to the polder.

"Perhaps you've already heard of me?" asked Koster.

Melse nodded and said: "Yes, I certainly have."

157

"You still dress in that Walcheren costume?" asked Koster.

"Yes, I plan to go on doing so."

"So, does that mean you don't plan to stay here? I can well understand it. Farmers from Walcheren don't seem to adjust very well to life here."

"I'm not planning to go back, but that's not a reason why I can't keep wearing the Walcheren costume, is it?"

"My position is that you have to honor the land in which you are living. That's what I said to my son when he left for Canada recently. I said: Make sure that you learn English quickly and that you adapt yourself to the country where you're going to live. That's just the way it is, I would think — true or not?"

"Well, Schouwen and Duiveland isn't exactly Canada, I would think. And if I take a look across the water when I'm standing on the dike, I can see a good part of our province. We're all Zeelanders — that's what I think."

"There are Zeelanders, and then there are Zeelanders," said Koster proudly. He waited a couple of seconds and then lit a fresh cigar. "You have a son in Indonesia if I am correctly informed."

"Yes, I do."

"Is he coming back, or will he be staying in the army?"

"The former, I think. He'll come back. He's not a soldier by nature, and I can certainly make good use of him here."

"As long as he doesn't get shot first," said Koster with a thoughtless grin, as though he had told a clever joke.

"We'll hope and pray that he's kept safe while he's over there."

"Praying doesn't help much," responded Koster. "There are more parents who prayed for their son, but their son got murdered by the Krauts anyway. Just think of what happened over there in Renesse. And you also had a son who was murdered by them — right?"

Melse nodded. It was not easy to talk about his son Dirk with this man who came across as crude and insensitive when discussing painful matters. And it bothered him deeply to realize that all his praying for Dirk to be spared had not helped. His many petitions turned out to be unheard prayers, he thought to himself. In this respect the free-thinking farmer was right. But praying had to be done in faith, and David Melse asked himself whether he really had faith. It was as though a sharp, stinging barb had penetrated his heart during the discussion with the wealthy farmer.

Koster was enjoying the distress he was inflicting on this insignificant farmer from Walcheren. It irritated him that Melse wanted his son back with him on the farm. If only the son would stay in the army, Koster would still have a chance of acquiring the land and farmhouse that belonged to old Joris Melse. He had already surrendered one son who sought his fortune in a faraway land, and that was bad enough.

"I think it's kind of risky for you to come over here and start farming," he said. "The land you're working on is by no means the best, and your Uncle Joris has already suffered enough from poverty while farming there. You just ask him about it."

They were now standing before the long lane leading to Koster's farmhouse. Before the war, there had been high trees around the house, which was quite some distance from the road. The big elm trees had towered over the house. One could look through a green tunnel of trees on both sides of the lane leading to the spacious patio in front of the steps. When the Germans put the land under water, the beautiful trees and all the finery around them suffered greatly. Koster had planted young trees in their place, but the young trees were fresh growth that did not make much of an impression. And so the large house looked somewhat bare and forsaken. The land around the house, which had once been a beautiful orchard, now looked like a barren spot.

The former glory of "Rest Haven," Koster's farm, had passed. The Germans had done a thorough job of ruining everything. Each time Koster took the road from the village back to his farm, he had plenty of reason to hate everything connected with the Germans. Often he arrived on his own land with clenched fists in his pockets.

"I suppose, to some degree, I'm standing in your way," said Melse with a smile on his face.

Koster proudly shrugged his shoulders. "There's no man able to get in my way," he said.

"But I've heard it said that you wanted my uncle's land for your son."

"Oh, yes, that would have been handy. I could have used it all right, but now that you've got it, I would say: just keep puttering along there until you're bent over with rheumatism, like your Uncle Joris."

"You sure are a nice fellow — that's all I have to say," answered Melse.

"People may make of me what they will," said Koster, shrugging his broad shoulders to signal indifference. He waved to Melse as a goodbye and headed down the lane toward "Rest Haven."

*   *   *

As far as Koster was concerned, it was the fault of other people that he had become the kind of man he now was. He would never forget what it meant for him to have to bow his stubborn head before the Krauts. Never before in his life had he needed to bow before anyone. And that he had been forced to do so before the hated enemy was like a consuming fire in his soul, a fire that just would not go out.

In 1944, when he and his family had been forced to abandon their farm, he had resisted to the uttermost. Finally the German soldiers drove his livestock out of the barn and stood before him with their guns drawn. They *forced* him to leave — he had no choice. And then his possessions, his Babylon, remained in the hands of that hated people. With a curse in his heart, he finally gave way to their superior power.

While he lived far away in territory that was foreign soil to him, he was tortured by the thought that his possessions, his livestock, and his beautiful farm were being handled in a rough and arbitrary way. If only he had not been so foolish as to go to North Holland, if only he had gone instead to Brabant, which was in the south, he would already have been on free soil in October of 1944! As it was, he wound up waiting until May of 1945 before the Germans finally took to their heels. And when he returned to his island, he found that his farmland had been heavily damaged by sea water.

It had taken years before things began to grow normally again, and crop yields were still not back to the levels that the farmers had been able to count on before the flood. While he was gone, his farm had turned into a sea of mud, and his home was no cleaner than a stable. His beautiful elm trees and his fine orchard had to be cut down and used as fuel.

After the war things continued to go completely wrong. The policies pursued by the government had the effect of chasing the younger farmers out of the country. His own son emigrated to Canada, believing that it would not be long before the Russians moved in and dealt with the local people just as the Germans had done.

Anger and hatred dominated Koster's soul so completely that his wife finally said: "Johan was never the same after the war." She could not accept the fact that he never showed up in church anymore. Before the war he had not gone very often either, but on special occasions he was always in attendance. As a prominent member of the community, he made sure that his broad figure was to be seen in a special pew near the front. He never missed a Christmas or New Year's Eve service.

His wife thought it was a bit much that just on the days when the church was most full, he insisted on sitting in a prominent pew at the front. Of course the family in which he was raised was quite church-minded. Years before, he used to talk with pride about how his father was a special friend of the minister and often went to the parsonage to play billiards with him. But ever since so-called democracy had come to their area, the special position and privileges of the wealthy farmers had gone into decline. Government policy decisions were no longer made in the clubs, and the candidates for a seat in the national legislature or the municipal councils were no longer nominated in private meetings.

As far as Koster was concerned, the church doors could now remain closed. With his luxurious carriage he could still cut quite a figure in the city, where something of the old glory of the time of the clubs still lingered. In the city one could find the carnival and comedians and stage entertainers. There was still something of the spirit of the closed club in which the leading citizens could be sure they would not be disturbed by people who were their social inferiors.

And that he, Koster, after enduring so much grief at the hands of the Krauts, should now have trouble with that miserable little man who was bent over with rheumatism as he wandered over his land — all of this was a new torment for his proud spirit. Whenever he drove in his automobile along the outer dike, the bitterness welled up in his soul. He could just see what would happen: his second son would also emigrate to Canada once the first one began to send back good reports. And then he would be left on his farm without anyone to carry on his name, the farm that went back in his family for many generations.

*   *   *

Melse was riding his bicycle along a small road in the direction of the outer dike, the dike that formed a very visible border with the land. When he got to the dike, he followed the path that led to the top and then cycled further on top of the dike toward Uncle Joris's little farm.

The tide was out as Melse looked over the concrete De Muralt Wall. Below he saw mud-flats over which the sea gulls flew as they sought food.

The view over the spacious waters always fascinated him. Under the sunlight from the west, the water shone as though it were silver. The view made man feel small in the face of the majesty of God's creation. How could anyone ever hold out against God's wishes? Melse simply could not understand how and why a man like Koster could live as he did. The dike — it was really a small dike when you thought about it carefully — divided the island from this arm of the sea. Its assigned task was to protect the polder against the mighty forces of nature. If there was anything that preached strict dependence on God, it was surely this small ridge that had to stand up for life in the face of death. Just a small signal from God's finger, and everything would be lost.

As these thoughts coursed through his mind, he thought again about Koster's words: "Praying doesn't help much . . ."

He did not dare take Koster's words on his lips, but when he thought carefully about them, he had to admit that in his heart he had already said amen to Koster's callous observation. Had he not found out in his own life that praying did no good? How he and mother Beth had struggled together in prayer to save the life of their son Dirk! First Dirk was arrested, and they knew he was being held in the camp at Amersfoort. Then came the frightening time when they heard nothing more from him. After the war he returned, and they thanked God that they had him back. It looked as though their prayers had been heard, but then came a new pain when they could see with their own eyes that their son was withering away before them. They prayed and prayed, but what had God done? Why was it that He first let the boy come home, only to take him away later in death?

Melse asked himself the same question he had asked so many times before without ever getting an answer, the question that led to endless doubting and wondering. Could it be that *his own* guilt and sin were behind all of this? Could it be that God no longer wanted anything to do with him and was abandoning him to his own doubts? God's hand was resting heavily upon him.

No, a conversation with that farmer Koster was hardly the thing Melse needed at this point. Mother Beth could tell immediately from his eyes and his sad face that he was doubting again. She did not know what else to do than shake her head and run her hand through his graying hair.

That evening he told the family about his conversation with Koster. Uncle Joris nodded. He understood, for he knew the proud farmer quite well. "That man did a lot of resistance work during the war," he said. "But my David still did not appreciate him. I have heard tell that Koster once killed a local traitor. But there was also a time when he stood before the Germans with clenched fists, and he wasn't afraid of them at all. Indeed, it's a miracle that he escaped being sent to a concentration camp. After the liberation, he had a chance to meet the Queen, and she thanked him for all he had done for the fatherland."

Those words made a deep impression on Melse's soul, also when he and mother Beth went on their knees together in their room before they went to sleep that evening. So Koster had been involved in resistance work, just as their son Dirk had been! But how could a Christian and such a freethinking, indifferent farmer have been involved in the very same work? Could a Christian have communion and fellowship with a worldly person? Again Melse began to think about what Rev. Verhulst used to say about these things. If a worldly person does this or that, does it mean that a Christian may do the very same thing? Can that ever be right?

Once again doubt took possession of his soul and his thoughts. What if Dirk had made a horrible mistake? What if he had done something wrong and then God took him away? In his thoughts Melse placed the wealthy, worldly, indifferent farmer Koster next to his son. The two had done the very same work during the war. Could God have taken pleasure in that? A farmer like Koster could not possibly have seen the punishing hand of God in the German occupation. He would have been blind to the judgments of the Lord. But surely a Christian ought to be able to recognize such things! What if Dirk had based his short life on mistaken ideas? What if he had made a fundamental error?

It became very difficult for Melse. He did not want to consider the possibility that Dirk had been wrong and had sacrificed his life in a sinful cause. And so he thought back to the last words he had heard from his son. Dirk had said that if he had it to do all over again, he would do the very same thing. Could that have been hardening on his part? Had Dirk blinded himself to the sinful path he was following even when he stood at the gates of death? Or was it faith on his part? Melse did not know where to go with his questions.

He tossed and turned in bed and simply could not get to sleep. "What are you worrying about so much tonight?" asked mother Beth.

"I'm not lying here worrying," he said as he turned over once more.

"Oh, yes you are. You can't fool me."

"Just leave me alone. I'll be all right. Sometimes a man just wants to lie in his bed and think."

"A fellow like you, healthy as you are, working the way you do all day — I would think that you'd sleep like an ox when you got into bed."

"I'll get to sleep in time. But just now, I think I'll go and have a look outside. Then I'll be ready to sleep when I get back."

She said nothing but let him go. Melse pulled on some clothes and stepped out the door.

The moon was shining and the sky was clear. It was a peaceful night. He walked across the farmyard and over to the stone steps that led to the outer dike. He stood on the dike and looked over the Scheldt toward the horizon. In the hours that had passed since his return, the tide had come in. The water was now lapping halfway up the basalt stones that made up the slope of the outer dike. He sensed a deep restfulness over the broad arm of the Scheldt. A gentle night wind caressed his hair. He felt the cool air was doing him good.

He wandered a ways along the top of the dike, and in the distance he made out the silhouette of someone else who was out walking, someone who was coming toward him. It was a man with a cane in his hand. At first it seemed strange, at this late hour, to encounter someone out on a walk when he himself was all alone. When the figure came a little closer, he realized that it was Bart de Vaat, one of the richest farmers in the village.

He knew that De Vaat had served as an elder for a number years and that he was respected by both young and old in the congregation. Shortly after moving to Schouwen and Duiveland, David Melse and his wife had made De Vaat's acquaintance. During their visit to his large farm, they had heard stories about the time their son had spent on Schouwen and Duiveland during the occupation. As for Dirk himself, he had not been inclined to talk much during the last months of his life.

David Melse thought back to the conversation he had hoped to have with De Vaat during the occupation, after hearing about him from his son Dirk, but there had as yet been no opportunity for such a talk. And now this late-night meeting . . .

"So you're out walking too!" observed Bart de Vaat, once he had recognized David Melse in the moonlight.

"As you can see. I was tossing and turning in bed, and so I said to my wife: 'I'm just going out for a little while to have a look on the outer dike.' That's what I do if I can't get to sleep. But now, this is quite something — running into you here."

"Well, it was the very same way with me. And so I also got out of bed."

"Shall we walk a little ways together?"

The two men walked on through the stillness of the night. At first both were silent, but then Bart de Vaat began. From Dirk Melse he had heard a few things about David, and so he felt he knew him well enough to talk about some things that were deep in his heart. Bart de Vaat admitted that he, too, was subject to doubts.

"What is it that you're doubting, if I may ask?"

"Well, I'll tell you. From the outside everything appears to be in order with me, but that's not how it is from the inside." Out came the story, and it was quite a story indeed. Melse listened sympathetically and said little, since he had already heard a good deal of it from his son Dirk.

Bart de Vaat was a man who never seemed to run into rough weather in this world. It was as though the wind was always at his back. His farm was flourishing, and his cows and barn were always in first-class order. What his land produced was of the highest quality, and he could always count on getting the best prices. He had a wonderful wife, and his children had all grown up normally and were doing well. But it is written in the Bible that the Lord chastises the one whom He loves, and Bart de Vaat had known nothing of chastisement in his entire life. "And then you finally come to ask yourself: 'Does the Lord really love *me? Am I really His* child?' People in the congregation may think that Bart de Vaat is a fine fellow, someone for the congregation to be proud of, but I know better. That's what sometimes drives me from my bed at night and has me walking on the outer dike. So what do you think about my situation, Melse? I understand that you have been an elder on Walcheren. Perhaps you have experience with this sort of thing."

Melse walked along with the wealthy farmer in silence. The impression he had formed when listening to Dirk's account of De Vaat's situation was now more than confirmed. Bart de Vaat had come to basically the same conclusion that he, David Melse, had reached, namely, that he was not a child of the Lord but an outsider. Melse felt he was an outsider because he had experienced *only* the Lord's hand of chastisement in his life, whereas Bart de Vaat had come to that conclusion because he had *never* felt the Lord's hand of chastisement.

"So you have nothing to say," observed Bart de Vaat. "I suppose you're disappointed in me. I can well understand that. If you look at someone only from the outside, you can easily get the wrong impression. I was hoping you could understand me somewhat, Melse."

In Melse's ears, it sounded like a cry of need. But how could he possibly speak a word of comfort or deliverance to this man?

He proceeded to tell De Vaat that he had heard many of these things years before from his son Dirk. Still, he did not know what to say in response. What Bart de Vaat had told him seemed to turn everything upside down. Melse explained that he also had many doubts, but that he had been cast into doubt because he seemed to encounter the Lord's hand of chastisement everywhere in his life. And so he could not help but think that he was dealing with an angry God. "And then I doubt, just as you do, whether I'm really a child of God. And so, what would I be able to say to you, my friend? It looks to me that we are in the same boat, even though we got there by following two entirely separate routes."

Bart de Vaat remained standing where he was. In silent amazement he stared at the face of Melse, which he could now see clearly in the moonlight. He laid his hand on Melse's shoulder and said: "Melse, I have to think about these things. I wonder whether you're wrong, or whether I'm wrong, or whether perhaps we're both wrong. But I do know that doubt is a frightening thing, Melse. It has driven me from my bed tonight. It grips me in my heart, because I cannot live without knowing that I'm a child of God. I have to know how things stand with me. Is it the very same way with you, Melse?"

Melse nodded. The two walked further together. "Strange that I should meet you here at this hour, Melse," said Bart de Vaat.

"Yes, it really is strange," responded Melse.

"We'll both have to think about it."

By now they stood in front of the stone steps that led down to Uncle Joris's farm. "It's a beautiful night," said De Vaat.

"It sure is."

"We'll just have to think these things over and talk about them again," said Bart de Vaat. And then he waved with his thick cane in the moonlight by way of saying good night.

Melse walked down the stone steps toward the farm. Thor, the dog, began to growl when he heard someone walking in the yard, but when he recognized his master's footsteps, he laid his head down again peacefully on his front paws.

Melse got back into bed. While he was gone, his wife had lain awake, thinking, wondering what was wrong with her husband. Once he had stretched out next to her, she said: "I've been thinking that I should do what Martin Luther's wife did — I read about it once in a book."

"What are you talking about now?"

Mother Beth then proceeded to explain that Luther's wife had once decided to dress completely in black. It seemed that her husband was in the grip of doubt. He walked around every day with despair written on his face, and he did not know where certainty was to be found. At last she said to him: "I think I'll put on my mourning clothes." And when Luther asked her why she would do such a thing, she responded: "Well, because God is dead." Mother Beth then told her husband that she was also beginning to think that God was dead.

Melse had hoped to fall into a deep sleep after his late-night walk, but his wife's words stimulated his thoughts again and kept him awake for quite some time. They did not serve to dispel the doubts in his soul.

Part III

Triumph

Chapter 9

When the boat steamed into the North Sea Canal, something seemed to break free deep within Henry Melse. It was a hot summer, and the meadows in the polders along the canal were dry. But Henry's eye could see only the blossoming beauty he had missed in Indonesia. The farms with their trees, the cows lying there chewing their cud, the windmills, the church towers wherever there was a group of houses nestled together on the flat land — all of it spoke to him again of Holland, of beautiful Holland, for which Henry had felt such homesickness. In comparison with Holland, what did the smoking mountains and impenetrable jungles and rice paddies really mean?

The soldiers pressed against the rail and tried to pick out family members and friends among the people on bicycles who were accompanying the boat along the canal. Henry knew his family was waiting for him in Zeeland. A bus would take him and the other Zeeland soldiers to their home province.

The Henry Melse who returned from Indonesia was a different fellow than the one who had left. The adventure that had appealed to him so much before his departure had proven an illusion. He had come to know the world — also the world of young Dutch fellows who went to Indonesia to live it up and had no way to hold back when they faced the dangers over there.

Henry had become older. He had been in hospitals where he saw his friends succumbing to their wounds. He had found three of his best friends lying wounded in a ravine where they had walked into an ambush. He had served in a firing-squad in which he had to point his gun directly at the heart of a soldier who had married a rich Indonesian woman and then shot her in order to inherit her wealth. The soldier was condemned to death after a court-martial. For many nights, the face of the wayward soldier as he saw it for the first and last time when serving on the firing-squad kept Henry from sleeping. When you are still so young and you are given an order to point your gun right at the heart of a young fellow who has given in to temptation in this land of so many temptations, and then you have to hold your gun ready for the moment the command is given to fire, and then you see him crumble and collapse — at that point all your desire for adventure in this foreign, hellish country vanishes.

Henry yearned for Zeeland's soil; he yearned for the cows and horses and tools and implements; he yearned for his mother's eyes and the feel of his father's hand; he yearned for the rest that flooded his heart when he beheld the wide-open distances of the flatlands of Zeeland, when you could see all the way out to the massive dikes that kept the sea at bay.

As the young men continued their journey in the bus, they sang songs they used to sing in Indonesia when they had time off. But once they were through the hills of Brabant and the bus began to enter the polders of Zeeland, there was no holding them back. The young men might well have danced if there had been room in the bus. And then one of them began to sing Zeeland's own anthem:

No dearer place for us on earth,
No region is of greater worth.
Protected well by dike and dune.
The fields and woods shout forth a tune.
Where from of old the union stays,
And blessings crown the landman's ways.
The Zeelander's strong voice doth say,
"I struggle on and swim away."

Thou, Zeeland, art our own dear land,
We will allow no stranger's hand
To rule us; and we stand on guard
For freedom dear; as in our heart
We know we have but this one choice.
"Orange and Zeeland," says our voice.
With heart and mouth we thus will be,
Body and soul, while Zeeland's free.

Henry joined the singing joyfully — his heart was right in it.

The bus stopped at various villages where one or more of the young men would jump out. The whole village would be present for this festive occasion. Many of the people would be standing on the dikes. In the village streets shouts of rejoicing would rise whenever a familiar figure jumped out of the bus. In front of the soldiers' homes stood welcome gates made of flags and greenery, and there would be a large sign in special lettering: "Welcome home!"

Henry did not think his father would be quite so effusive about welcoming him home. It was simply not his way. But in this regard he was mistaken. Although Father did not take the lead, Mother and Laura were also in the picture. When Laura began to tell her family what was done in the neighboring villages when a young fellow came home from Indonesia, mother Beth decided that she was definitely *not* going to be left behind. And so, at the Melse home there was also a welcome gate that included the three-color flag of the Netherlands and the Zeeland emblem — the lion that struggles and swims away.

If you stood up on the dike, you could get a good view of the village and see the bus coming from quite a distance. That's where Grandfather and Uncle Joris were standing, each with a smoldering pipe in his mouth. But father Melse had his hands in his pockets and said nothing. There was only one thought in his mind: how would he find Henry when he got him home again? His letters were good: in them he found no indication that something had been lost in Henry's soul. Moreover, the letters included quite a few references to sermons he had heard, and also talked about spiritual life in the far east. If the boy had wandered from the path, it was not likely that such words would be flowing from his pen. David Melse knew Henry too well to be fooled in that regard. But he still felt he needed to look him in the eye before he could know for sure that all was well with him.

Finally, the bus came into view. It rolled to the bend in the road just outside the village and pulled up to the sea dike. There were not many young men in the bus anymore. Most of the soldiers were already home.

David Melse stood on his spot, seemingly immovable. The black head of his pipe was hanging down, and the pipe was out. His hands remained in his pockets.

Laura danced and cried out: "There he is! There he is!" Mother Beth could not see very well at this point because of all the mist before her eyes. This moment was an answer to prayer, she realized.

The bus put on the brakes, and a smiling soldier jumped out, landing on the grass below. The first person he saw was his mother. He ran over to her and threw his arms around her and kissed her on both cheeks. Then he shook hands with his father — but if he had followed his inclinations, he would have embraced him as well. Henry gripped his father's hand tightly. Father Melse then said to him calmly: "So, my boy, you're home again." It was almost as though he was returning from a little trip to Bergen.

But while his hand held on to Henry's hand, David Melse's eyes looked deep into Henry's soul. Henry would never forget those eyes. At that moment, he sensed deep-seated feelings in his father's eyes. Not until David Melse got to the very bottom of his son's soul and became convinced that Henry had remained upright during his time in Indonesia did he let go and say simply: "Let's go inside now. Mother has the coffee ready."

Laura put her hands on Henry's shoulders and implored him: "Now say something about the welcome gate!"

Henry laughed and kissed his sister. "How delighted I am to be home again!" he said. Within an hour he was wearing civilian clothes and walking with his father across the farmyard. He looked at the hogs in their pens and scratched their backs. He looked over the pasture where he saw the cows grazing and said: "You don't see such cows anywhere else in the world. The scrawny beasts they have in Java are nothing in comparison. How are the prices nowadays?"

"Just fine," replied his father. "We can't complain. We're being well paid, and the land has certainly not been a disappointment.

But I'm so glad to have you with me here again because I can sure use you!"

"Well, I can start tomorrow," said Henry.

"Was it really awful over there?" asked David Melse cautiously.

"Well, I got by," said Henry. For the present, that was where he left it. His father understood that weeks would pass before Henry would begin to tell bits and pieces of his experiences during the years in Indonesia. Those bits and pieces he would carefully remember, and then he would try to put them together as though assembling a jig-saw puzzle, until at last he had a complete picture of his son's years of service in Indonesia.

*   *   *

The next day, when Henry wanted to go to the village, Laura begged to be taken along for company. Henry was glad to have her at his side.

Before he departed for Indonesia, Henry had of course been in the village quite a number of times. Still, he was not as familiar with it as he had been with his former village on Walcheren. Even so, he remembered the village's main street quite well. But when he got there, he saw that things had changed tremendously since his departure three years before.

Laura was eager to tell him all about the improvements that had been made during his absence. It looked to Henry as if the merchants in the village were experiencing some golden years, for almost every store had been rebuilt and made to look new. With his own eyes he now saw his father's words confirmed: the prices for agricultural products seemed to be quite good. Would the merchants in such a village be doing so well if the farmers were not also prospering?

But Henry did not have much understanding about such matters. He knew that his country had lost Indonesia. He had expected the country to be poorer as a result, but now that he was home it appeared that everyone was prospering — and then on Schouwen, of all places. Schouwen had suffered immeasurably during the war years! Yet the soil had recovered very quickly from the consequences of standing under salt water. Not only had everything been rebuilt, there was also considerable new construction. A large furniture store had some hyper-modern furniture on display. Laura found all the renewal beautiful, and she drew her brother's attention to the latest things. The conversation was quite one-sided. Henry had a great deal to think about.

They stopped to visit a smith who was putting a horseshoe on a workhorse. The smith was eager to talk: "So, you're a son of Melse? And now you're home again?"

"Yes, I'm back."

"And are you planning to stay on the farm, or will you be going away again?" The smith seemed quite interested.

"I'm staying home. There's no better place in all the world."

"So, Koster will not be very happy to hear this."

Henry did not know who Koster was, and so he looked at the smith in puzzlement. The smith proceeded to tell him about the rich farmer who still hoped that Henry would decide he had had enough of farming, now that he had seen more of the world. Then Koster would be able to watch for an opportunity to buy Uncle Joris's farm.

"Well then," replied Henry, "I suppose he won't be very glad to see me here. I'm planning to stay on the farm. They're not going to lure me away a second time. That whole world out there is a rotten place. There's nothing better than to be on the farm with the cows and horses."

"I do believe you're right," responded the smith, with a smile on his face, while he hammered a few more nails to attach the horseshoe. In the meantime, the horse tried to pull back. Henry did what he could to calm the horse by putting his hand on its neck.

"A beautiful animal," he said. "Whose is it?"

"It belongs to Koster. But he doesn't have very many horses anymore. He, too, is moving forward with the times. He's now having all the work on his place done with machinery because labor costs have gone so high. You folks will also have to make the switch, if you ask me."

Now that he had gotten these things said, the smith was of a mind to keep going. "Anyone who doesn't keep up with the times will eventually fall far behind, and he may not make it."

He went on to explain that he now had a dealership that supplied tractors along with machinery for mowing and threshing. It was a good business — better than shoeing horses. Last year, just in the local area, he had sold no fewer than fifteen new tractors. The average cost of such a tractor was about 15,000 guilders. Some of them went as high as 20,000 guilders. But it appeared that money was hardly a problem anymore. The people were earning plenty.

He revealed that he had discussed the question of a tractor with Henry's father, too, but David Melse wanted to stay away from tractors for the present. "He's quite a careful follow, if you ask me," said the smith.

He advised Henry to take up the issue of using a tractor with his father. Perhaps Henry could get further with him than the smith had managed to do. "But let me give you this piece of advice: if you want to keep up with the new developments, you really have to believe in them. The labor costs and the social taxes are much too high right now. And you hardly dare ask what workhorses like this one cost nowadays. When they're doing nothing the whole winter but standing in the stable, they go right on eating. But farm machines don't cost you anything when you're not using them — true or not?"

Henry nodded. Then Laura, who was not interested in what the two men had to say about business and farming, managed to pull Henry away and lead him over to a beautiful store displaying the sorts of things a young girl finds appealing. She almost talked Henry's ear off. It did not seem to bother her that she heard almost nothing from him in response.

Henry was experiencing so much that he did not have time to process it all. He was amazed at the many changes in farming methods that had taken place in just a few years. It looked as though all the people were well off in terms of money. The stores were full of goods. As for the system of regulated distribution that had been in full swing when he left for Indonesia, it seemed to have been relegated to history. The pressure our people had been feeling because of the war's aftereffects seemed to have lifted.

And the people were now totally different. The Netherlands had forgotten the misery of the war years. It appeared that the young people were immersing themselves in the enjoyments life had to offer. Most people were busy making money and assuring themselves of economic security of a sort they had never possessed before the war.

All in all, it looked as though the Netherlands could get along quite nicely without Indonesia. As for all the sacrifices our boys had been called upon to make in that strange land, no one was interested in hearing about them. It seemed that those sacrifices had been made in vain.

It was a number of weeks before Henry could digest this amazing fact and adjust to it inwardly. He did not talk with anyone about it, for he sensed that people would not understand him.

*   *   *

When it was Sunday, Tina and Janet, who were both married by this time and living in Middelburg, came home to see their brother and welcome him back. With so many people about the house, it was a busy day on the farm, but Uncle Joris was enjoying it greatly. He slapped his older brother on the back, which was a liberty that grandfather Melse was not accustomed to and did not seem to appreciate.

"It sure is busy on the farm today — what do you say?"

"As long as it's not too busy for you."

"No, not at all. I find it refreshing. If I were still living here all by myself with that housekeeper, it wouldn't be much of a life. After my wife was taken away, there was never any coziness here in the house — no family feeling. But now we sit here together as family again. I can never be thankful enough to the Lord for this."

On Sunday morning they all went to church. Uncle Joris hitched the horse to the covered carriage. The old horse knew just what to do on a Sunday: it pulled the carriage along the dike right into the village. The young people chose to go to church on their bicycles and left the carriage far behind.

There were three different churches in the village. They were only small churches, but then it was a small village. The biggest of the three was in the very heart of the village and drew the most people. But the minister in that church preached light sermons.

In the small church outside the village, there were three reading services each Sunday. In most cases the sermon was drawn from one of the eighteenth-century writers, and it was contained in a book with parchment binding. The fact that there was no minister to do the preaching did not seem to affect the attendance. Almost all the services, which lasted about two hours, were well attended. The two older Melses sometimes attended this church, but they did not feel altogether at home there, even though the truth they heard proclaimed did have some appeal for them.

The church to which the Melses belonged was still without a minister. Although the congregation was small, it was growing, and the people were willing to sacrifice for the church. And so there were hesitant discussions underway: would they dare to call a young minister who did not yet have a sizable family to maintain?

But today there was a minister — at least, what some people called a minister. Actually, he was a candidate, a young fellow who had begun preaching here and there just a few months before.

Earlier in the week, Bart de Vaat had discussed the candidate with Melse. He did not seem to expect much from him. "You've been an elder, Melse," he said, "And so I'm asking you to listen very carefully. Next week you can tell me whether you think he might be the man for this congregation."

The little church was full. The custodian had to set out some extra benches. The people sat close together in uncomfortable pews with straight backs.

When Bart de Vaat came into the consistory room, the candidate was already there, as was his host, elder Davidse, who, as a municipal employee, got to wear a collar all week long. Davidse was good at getting along with visiting ministers, and so the consistory preferred that they lodge at his home.

The candidate was standing by the window, trying to strike a minister's pose. It was clear that he was both embarrassed and shy. He was a very pale, tall, thin young fellow in a jacket with tails. He was wearing a high collar with pointed studs and a silver-gray tie. His flax-colored blond hair was immaculately combed and parted. Although his jacket was no longer than it needed to be, it did look a little loose as it encircled his thin body. Perhaps the tailor hoped that the young minister, once settled in a parsonage, would fill out the jacket.

There was an oppressive silence in the consistory room. Zeelanders are not a talkative people, and so the elders did not know quite what to say to the embarrassed young man. As for Davidse, he was not saying anything either: before, during and after breakfast he had already discussed a great many topics with the candidate in an effort to keep the conversation alive. Elder Davidse was out of ideas.

All the men in the consistory room were longing to hear the sound of the church bells at the large church. The two little churches always took their signal to begin from the sound made by the bell in the large church. Because the clocks around the village were not well synchronized, the signal from the big church that it was time to begin the service was accepted without question.

When the slow, heavy chimes from the big church tolled out over the village, the brothers folded their hands and Bart de Vaat, who was the duty elder that Sunday, led them in prayer. The custom was that once this prayer had been offered, the office-bearers would form a row in preparation for entering the church. But at the last moment the candidate touched his host's arm and whispered: "Could you show me where the washroom is?"

Bart de Vaat looked around and saw that the minister, instead of following him into the church, was going out another door. He seemed amused as he looked at the other office-bearers.

"Nerves, nothing but nerves," whispered Davidse. "At my place he had to make many visits to the washroom this morning."

The brothers waited patiently. Soon the pale candidate took his place behind the broad back of Bart de Vaat. Just before he entered the pulpit, he got the usual handshake.

The people, restless in their pews, strained to get a good look. Then there was complete silence. In a timid, almost whispering voice, the candidate asked a blessing on the service.

Bart de Vaat looked at Monica, an elderly woman who was hard of hearing and already had her hand cupped around her ear. She was hunched forward, almost as though she despaired of hearing. If that situation did not improve quickly, he thought to himself, the candidate's visit wouldn't come to anything. If Monica went around the village telling people that the minister could not be understood, there would be no point in his returning to the village and there would be no chance of calling him to serve as pastor.

In the meantime, there was singing, praying, and Bible reading. The text came from Luke 21, verse 28: "And when these things begin to come to pass, then look up, and lift up your heads; for your redemption draweth nigh."

Things were not going smoothly for the candidate that morning. The little church was so full that people were sitting very close to the pulpit. Every little gesture, every nervous tick on the candidate's pale face was noted and criticized. He would have been better off in a large city church with hundreds of people seated some distance from him than here in this little country church with one hundred twenty people right around him like a wall.

Then the candidate had a small accident to deal with. The pale young man had scarcely begun with the introduction to his sermon, which came before the collection, when one of the two pointed studs holding down his collar came loose. The collar curled up, and the stud wound up embedded in the flesh of his cheek. It was a very strange sight indeed.

He immediately noted that the young people were having great difficulty to keep from laughing out loud. That such a thing should now happen to him! It had been his fiancée's idea for him to wear that fancy collar and special studs with his preaching jacket.

His pale face turned beet red. With his left hand he held down the point of his rebellious collar. Then he hurried on to the next element in the service — singing, followed by the collection — so that he would have an opportunity to repair the damage.

The people of Zeeland are well known for their self-control: even the young girls were able to keep from giggling. Each person in the church did his best to make the embarrassed candidate feel more at ease and give him a fair chance. During the singing, the candidate slouched down as far as he could behind the large pulpit Bible, which gave him cover as he tried to hold down his collar with his stud in such a way that it would stay put once the congregation was done singing and the collection had been taken.

Then it was time for the sermon. Again there was shuffling to be heard in the church; people were peering carefully at the candidate. But before long everything was still — very still.

Gradually the candidate's voice increased in volume. Bart de Vaat took a surreptitious glance at Monica and observed that she no longer had her hand cupped around her ear. Things were starting to look up.

The rest of the service went very well. In fact, it looked as though the preacher, standing in that small pulpit, had undergone a transformation. He forgot all about the pesky collar and the confines of the pulpit and the close proximity of the people.

As for the people, they now found a young man standing before them who had come to bring a definite message: he seemed well aware that he was there for a purpose. Lift up your heads, for your deliverance is near! Would that not be a worthy message?

There are some strange people around: no matter what happens to them, they bow their heads ever more deeply. When the Germans came and took over our land, they seemed to forget all about Psalm 124. All they could think about was the judgment of an angry God who had struck them down. When they are sick and in pain, they rack their brains and ask themselves: how can I possibly escape the horrible wrath of God that seems to have come over my life? When they stand by the grave of one of their children, all they can talk about is the flaming justice of God that has struck them. When a flood streams over their land and their hopes for their farm are dashed, all they know how to do is crawl along in the dust because of the grim fury revealed from heaven. On the other hand, when things go well for them and they enjoy prosperity and God makes things smooth and light and joyful on their pathway through life, a frightening question comes up in their hearts: can I really be God's child if He never chastises me? And so, through such thinking, *the facts* are made normative. All reasoning proceeds from the facts. Instead, explained the candidate, we should be listening to the Word of the Lord in our text for today . . .

Do you hear it, grandfather Melse? Are you listening, Uncle Joris? What about you, David Melse? Are you getting the message, Bart de Vaat?

It certainly looked as though they were listening. Their heads were slightly to one side, and their mouths were half open. They seemed to be drinking in the words. This was a sermon from which everyone could benefit. It seemed that the candidate was right on target. But no, they realized that it was not a matter of the candidate hitting the bull's eye — it was *God Himself* who, through this pale, thin young man, was accomplishing His purpose in the church.

God was touching the hearts of these poor people with all their doubts and questionings. He was shaking them and waking them up and saying to them: now listen once to My Word, the Word you read every day in your homes but do not seem to understand. Listen to this young man who lays his hand on that thick book and stands in the pulpit proclaiming the truth. After all, he is not speaking on his own account, for who is he, really? I, the Lord, your Deliverer, your Redeemer, am speaking to you today. It was for *you* that I went down the path of suffering all the way to the cross. Have you forgotten the Via Dolorosa?

God had seen the doubts and anxieties of the people. He knew just what sorts of horrible things it would take to shake them up. He knew how the devil would try to make use of those horrible things as he tried to pull the people away from God's fatherly heart. But there is no reason to fear when these things start to happen. Look up! Lift up your heads, for your deliverance is near!

Does this mean that there is no longer any punishment here on earth, no judgment, no flaming wrath because of sin and apostasy? Of course there is — but it's different. It's not what you are thinking of, congregation. The wrath of God always rests on everyone who does not turn to Him, regardless of whether he is enjoying prosperity or adversity at a given moment. If the farmer does not fear God, his rich harvest is cursed. Then everything which he undertakes and in which he succeeds is cursed by God. The curse of God works through his health as well as through his sickness, through his fruitful years as well as his barren years, for everything in his life is cursed.

And that's how it is — but just the other way around — for God's people, for those who fear Him. When it comes to those who believe in God and fear Him, there is no longer such a thing as wrath or judgment; there's only prosperity, the blessing that flows from the cross. And whatever may happen in this world by way of horrible things, whether it be wars, years of occupation, earthquakes, famines, epidemics, floods, persecution, or other terrors — lift up your heads, for your deliverance is near.

All the things you have suffered and will yet suffer are coming to pass because your deliverance can only be achieved through the birth pangs of this world. God is, in Christ, your Father. Do not grieve His fatherly heart. Do not spoil your own joy by showing that you are lacking in faith. Be afraid of only one thing — committing the sin that causes a separation between you and the Father . . .

The words came quite freely from the candidate's mouth. Of course, he had preached this sermon in other churches too. And once he got going with this sermon, he could recite whole sections of it without paying any attention to his typed sermon notes. Still, this sermon was not just a little speech he had memorized.

Bart de Vaat sensed all of this very keenly. He knew that the young man stood behind his message with all of his heart. He wanted to hammer it into the people: Do not disappoint the Father by having so little faith. Live by His Word.

That morning, the energies of the Holy Spirit were poured out in the small congregation. God was at work among His people: it was obvious that He was present.

"The Holy Land," thought Bart de Vaat.

"Father, is it really so?" prayed David Melse.

"If only I could consider it all as applying to me," sighed grandfather Melse.

Uncle Joris prayed: "If only I might have the assurance that Thy chastising hand in my life, a life full of faults and inadequacies, is being raised in love."

And so, that morning, they all drank from the spring that gave them the water of life.

When you are listening to such a sermon, it is nothing to sit for an hour and a half in church. The time flies by. The people seemed surprised when the candidate abruptly said: "Amen."

David Melse looked over to Bart de Vaat in the elder's bench. When De Vaat stood up for the prayer of thanksgiving after the sermon, he quickly took his handkerchief from his pocket and used it to wipe his lined face. Melse's eyes were also misty. But even though the rugged farmers had all these feelings coursing through them, their hoarse voices were able to break out in jubilation when the organ announced it was time to sing: "Let all the streams in joyous union now clap their hands and praise accord."

In the consistory room the men stood facing one another silently — the elders and the young candidate. Now he was again the shy, awkward, embarrassed young man who fingered his collar to make sure it was still in place. He turned red when he thought back to the ridiculous figure he had cut up in the pulpit.

He had not the slightest idea what sort of impression his sermon had made. And the people of Zeeland are not much inclined to speak an encouraging word to a young man or to give him a firm handshake or even to say to him simply: "Thank you so much for that wonderful message this morning. Your feet were like the feet of those who bring good tidings."

No, the elders seemed somewhat embarrassed. They remained silent as the one looked at the other. They seemed to be waiting to hear what the young man himself would say.

But the candidate also remained silent. Moreover, he completely misinterpreted the silence on the part of the elders. And so he left the consistory room with his host, elder Davidse, and headed home after saying timidly: "Until this afternoon, brothers."

Once he was outside, he looked at the young girls, afraid that they would laugh at him even now as they remembered how ridiculous he had looked in the pulpit with a collar stud embedded in his cheek. But all he saw were earnest, composed faces.

Meanwhile, his host, who was racking his brain to think of a way to get a suitable conversation underway as they walked home, began to tell about his family in Zierikzee. He went on to talk about an old grandfather, well into his eighties, who — miracle of miracles! — had managed to survive the evacuation of 1944 quite well.

The candidate listened with half an ear. He kept thinking about his sermon. Was it the right emphasis for this congregation in its situation? Did the sermon give the people something to take home and think about? The elders had been so frighteningly quiet after the service! It seemed that the people in these parts were not free to express themselves, and the young candidate was still so uncertain of himself. Had he made a mess of the sermon that morning? Had he been speaking to the four walls? Why didn't Davidse say something about the sermon? Why didn't he come right out and say whether he found it a good sermon or a bad one? He seemed willing to talk about everything under the sun, but not about the sermon. It was just as though he had not heard the sermon. The candidate felt like a visitor who was subjected to all kinds of interesting stories about the family.

As the young man, in his perplexity, pondered all these questions in his mind, he did not realize that the people of Zeeland talk about everything except that which touches their soul at the deepest level.

*   *   *

"What did you think of it?" asked Bart de Vaat, when he stood talking with Melse for a little while after the service.

"What I thought of it? Well, if you had the same reaction as me, then you'd say that you had a good Sunday. I haven't had a chance to think it all through as yet, but I can tell you that I certainly came away with enough to keep me occupied for the whole week."

Bart de Vaat nodded. "That young fellow has a lot of promise for the future. For me he had a separate message, one that I can do something with."

Melse understood what he was talking about. "It was the same way with me, and probably with all of us."

*   *   *

The sermon preached during the afternoon service also met with the people's approval. That evening there was quite an assembly of people visiting at the Davidse home. Zeelanders always want to get to know a candidate as a person before they consider calling him.

There was much conversation and drinking of coffee. But the candidate wasn't saying very much. As the farmers were busy talking about this, that and the other thing, the candidate noted that spiritual matters did *not* come up for discussion.

Then he heard Bart de Vaat addressing him directly: "So, Reverend, did you feel comfortable standing up there in the pulpit?"

The candidate smiled. He had certainly not felt very much at ease in the pulpit that day. But he couldn't very well come out and say so. "I hope the congregation derived some benefit from my sermons," he responded, dodging the question.

"That's what we all hope," said Bart de Vaat.

Another neutral answer telling him nothing. Then came a lull in the conversation: there was no word to be heard in the room.

*   *   *

When the candidate left the village on Monday morning, he thought to himself that he would never be invited back. That evening he visited his fiancée. "And how did things go over there in Zeeland?" she asked. "Were they nice people? What sermon did you preach? Did the people like your sermon? Do you think you might get a call there?"

He dismissed her last question with a wave of his hand and said: "What a host of questions! But I'll give you one answer to them all: never again will those people invite me to preach for them, and it's *your* fault."

"*My* fault?"

"Yes, you're the one who talked me into that silly collar that came loose and started flapping around just as I was getting into my sermon. Just imagine — there I was preaching without a collar. They were all sitting there grinning, and the edifying atmosphere was completely shattered. But that's the last time: from now on I'll choose my own collars!"

His fiancée couldn't believe it. She shrugged her shoulders, and then she started to laugh. "Of course you're exaggerating again. Because you were nervous, you didn't attach the little stud properly. It was your fault, not mine."

"Well, whether it was your fault or mine, I'll never get a call from that church — just you wait and see. And it's all because of that strange collar you told me to wear."

He wanted her to have the last laugh, but in his heart he knew he had not made a favorable impression on the people. He could tell that there had been no genuine contact. His sermon had not hit home. There was no reaction whatsoever. There wasn't even anyone who asked whether "the minister" would like to come back and lead another service sometime.

* * *

During that week a congregational meeting was arranged, and the consistory came forward with an important proposal. If the congregation was willing and able to give concrete evidence of its intention to sacrifice further, it would be possible to call a candidate.

And if the congregation had no objection, the idea was to call candidate Zomer by acclamation.

"Is that the candidate who was here last Sunday — the one whose collar came flapping loose?" asked a young farmer's son.

There was some muffled laughter. Bart de Vaat nodded.

Someone spoke up and said: "So let him come. His wife will see to it that he has a more reliable stud on his collar."

Many people nodded. No one seemed to be in disagreement.

"No one has an objection?" asked Bart de Vaat. No objection was stated. Apparently all the people had found it a wonderful Sunday.

"But there's still the issue of the money. We will need an additional eight hundred guilders if we are to be able to issue a call."

"I can come up with one hundred fifty," volunteered Uncle Joris.

"I'll give a hundred," said David Melse.

"I can manage two hundred," said Bart de Vaat.

"I'll put in twenty-five," said Davidse. The congregation knew that this brother, with his large family and very limited income, was cutting his budget to the bone.

The money to call the candidate came rolling in. There was even a special contribution to cover his moving costs — provided that candidate Zomer accepted the call. "That's what we must all hope for," said Uncle Joris. But the people did more than hope: they also prayed for a favorable response.

*   *   *

When it was evening and candidate Zomer was visiting his fiancée again, he placed the telegram before her. "They were all in favor!" she said, as she stared at the telegram in amazement.

"I don't understand it at all," said the candidate.

"Are you going to accept the call?" she asked.

"How can I say at this point? I have more calls, and I suppose I first have to find out where the need is the greatest — right?"

"Yes, that is indeed so," she said, feeling a bit ashamed of herself. "But . . ."

"Well, what?"

"Zeeland is so far away from here. I don't know anyone there, and if those farmers are as stiff as you say they are . . ."

"I guess I don't understand the farmers there. But if God is leading me to Zeeland, I'm going to go, and you'll go with me. Together we'll do what our hand finds to do."

*   *   *

Candidate Zomer visited the village one more time and learned more about the consistory and the congregation. Then he made up his mind. "We're going to Zeeland, Dear," he said.

His fiancée answered: "Yes, we'll go there, and as far as I'm concerned, you don't have to wear any more fancy collars."

Chapter 10

When Rev. Zomer arrived in the village, he brought not only his wife but also his wife's twenty-year-old sister, who was planning to stay with them in the parsonage for a while to help set up housekeeping. Her name was Corinne. She had light blond hair and clear, blue eyes.

Corinne regarded her stay in Zeeland as a pleasant change, a diversion from her usual life. But she was not thinking in terms of a vacation consisting of loafing. She worked hard to get the parsonage ready for habitation.

One afternoon, when Henry came to the parsonage and propped up his bike against the fence and made ready to ring the bell so that he could speak to the minister, he looked through the open window and saw two blue eyes. This one encounter with those eyes made such an impression on him that he would never forget that day. Instead of ringing the bell, he continued to look into those eyes.

The girl he was looking at came over to the window and asked: "Are you the baker?"

"No, I'm not the baker," Henry responded. He then said quickly that if she was in need of bread, he would be happy to go and get her the most tender Zeeland bread to be found anywhere in the village. He looked right into the girl's eyes, and a smile came over his face.

She blushed. "Oh, that wasn't what I meant. I thought that you were the baker. My sister told me that when the baker came by, I was to ask for a small loaf of bread. And now I thought . . ."

"Yes . . . yes," said Henry, as he secretly tried to think of a way to keep the conversation going. "How do you like our Zeeland bread?" he asked.

"It's delicious and nourishing, but the slices are too thick."

"You could try making one slice into two."

"Yes, I suppose I could. You know some more things, I suppose?"

"Yes, I know many things, but I wish you wouldn't look at me so sternly."

The girl laughed, and the sight of the pretty white teeth between her red lips excited Henry. He asked: "Are you getting used to living among us here?"

"As long as my stay doesn't last too long and the people don't keep me talking as long as you do. So what can I do for you?"

Henry screwed up his courage and said: "The nicest thing you could do for me would be to talk with me a little longer."

"Look, you didn't come here today to talk with *me*. Moreover, I have no time for talking. I'm here to help my sister. And you're keeping me from my work. I thought you were about to ring the bell."

Henry did not dare stretch out the conversation any longer. He said: "I'm Henry Melse, and I would like to talk with the minister, if I may."

She left the room, walked over to the front door, and let him in. A little later, when Henry was done talking with the minister, he hoped he would see Corinne once more. But she seemed content to let him find his own way out.

He noted that she was in church twice the next Sunday, and during the week he passed by the parsonage on his bicycle more often than he needed to. But he only caught a glimpse of her on one occasion, when she was out in the yard. She did not notice him.

The next week, when he saw her again, he talked to her over the fence and asked whether she would like to go bicycling with him along the outer dike. Corinne had no more forgotten the young farmer's son than he had forgotten her. Those faithful, dark eyes, reflecting his youth, appealed to her. "I'll come with you," she replied.

She made no delay, and soon she was right next to him with her bicycle. They cycled out of the village and took the road that led to the high outer dike. On the outside of the dike was a small walking path that could also be used for cycling. It ran right alongside the basalt De Muralt Wall.

They bicycled for half an hour, and then Henry stopped. Corinne pulled up next to him and stepped down from her bicycle. "What now?" she asked.

"I'd like to sit here for a little while in the grass," he said. "Look at the beautiful view over the water!"

She sank to the ground next to him, and in doing so she laid her hand on his shoulder for support — for just a moment. She quickly withdrew her hand and looked out over the water. Yes, it was indeed beautiful here.

Henry proceeded to talk about his years in Indonesia and told Corinne how much he had missed the flat Zeeland landscape while he was out there. Bushes and mountains are beautiful, he told her, but in the long run they leave you feeling confined. You want to climb up the highest mountain in order to get a good view of things.

"You Zeeland folks really love water, don't you?"

"Naturally! Just imagine what Zeeland would be like without water. But the water is not only our friend; often it's also our enemy."

"I know that, but I can tell that you people aren't afraid of it. As for me, I shudder at the thought of living here. How could one ever rely on such a small dike? What if the water is really determined to get in here? It's just a little border of earth that has to keep out the mighty sea. But I believe you people don't even think about things like that. In the province of Gelderland, where I'm from, the sea can't reach us. But here . . ."

At that point Corinne turned to look over the Scheldt. Then her eyes turned back to the land that was protected from the sea by the dike.

"Big breaks in the dike don't happen anymore nowadays," Henry assured her. "All of Zeeland is protected by the De Muralt Wall. The outsides of the dikes have been strengthened with basalt, and the water never gets high enough to be able to wash over the concrete wall. There may be a small leak in the dike at this point or that, in case we have not been careful enough inspecting the dikes, but that's only a local situation, and nowadays it doesn't happen anymore. The men in charge of the dikes and polders are very watchful. There are always watchmen on duty. There's really nothing to worry about."

Henry was chewing on a piece of dry grass. He looked into Corinne's blue eyes. "Do you suppose you would enjoy living in Zeeland?"

She said nothing but shrugged her shoulders.

"Or are you so afraid of the water that you would rather remain high and dry in Gelderland?"

"Well, do you suppose you'd like to live in Gelderland?" she asked, as she looked at Henry intently.

"Never! Those eternal, huge, green trees you have there would make me feel somber. Give me the Zeeland skies and horizon. And the Zeeland clay soil."

"And the Zeeland cows and pigs as well, I suppose?" she asked, teasing him.

"There's nothing finer in the world than to be a farmer," said Henry. She could sense that this remark came straight from his heart.

The two of them were silent for a moment as they looked out over the water. Then Henry said: "Do you suppose you could ever be a farmer's wife?"

Corinne could not suppress a clear laugh. "I can just imagine it! Me with a Zeeland cap, with thick, bare, red arms, wearing a bunch of skirts, and sitting there under a cow at five o'clock in the morning. Tell me, what do you think I am anyway?"

She looked at him mischievously and tickled his neck with a little piece of straw.

Again Henry fell silent and looked earnestly over the water. Corinne on a farm? How would that go? He asked her: "Do you like animals?"

"Questions, questions, and more questions! How am I supposed to answer a question like that? I love our dog, named Harry — his name is almost the same as yours — and I love our cats. But I suppose you were wondering whether I like cows and horses."

Henry kept looking at her intently. "Would you like to come and see our farm?" he asked.

"Still another question! Tell me, did you take me out to this dike in order to subject me to an examination?"

"You're not answering my question."

"Of course I'd like to see the farm. Just tell me when it would be convenient for you."

"Saturday afternoon," he said spontaneously.

"You sure don't let any grass grow under your feet!"

"Well, I'm a farmer."

"Just look across the water to the other shore," she said. "Do you see a dike there?"

Henry shook his head. Corinne then observed: "It's just as though the church towers and the windmills are rising straight from the water. You get the same impression with the roofs of the houses. You don't really see a separation between water and land."

"It's an optical illusion," said Henry.

"Such a sight makes me feel uneasy. I don't see a dike anywhere."

"But the dike is there, sure enough. It only *looks* as though there is no dike."

"Yes, I'm sure there's a dike there, but I can't see it. And the people who live on that side must think the very same way when they look at our island. They don't see a dike over here either — only water, with a church tower and a windmill floating on the surface."

"Nonsense! Do you like sailing?"

"Another question, Mr. Examiner!"

"Well, what about it? Do you like sailing?"

"I'm crazy about sailing."

"Then we'll go sailing together. It's important to work up the courage to look your enemy in the eye — then your fear melts away. When we were in Java and we could look the rebels in the eye and fight them hand-to-hand, not one of us was afraid anymore."

"Listen, I'm not a chicken!"

"Next week we'll spend an afternoon on the Scheldt — okay?"

"I'll first come on Saturday afternoon and visit your farm. After that we'll see further."

"And so, young lady from Gelderland, you really are afraid of water?"

"Don't think you can lure me from my tent, farmer from Zeeland!"

*   *   *

By the time Corinne left the village three weeks later, the two of them had come to an understanding. In the fall they would announce their engagement, and so Corinne would become a Zeeland farmer's wife after all.

For Henry this meant that life took on a new excitement. Now he had perspective for the future: he knew what he was working for as he toiled on Uncle Joris's farm. Every week, on Tuesday morning, he received a letter that had been written the Sunday before.

He now had to get used to addressing the minister, who was about to become his brother-in-law, as William. And Rev. Zomer's wife was to be addressed as Ida.

As for William, he was doing very well in this Zeeland village. The tailor who had spoken up for him saw that his optimism was not being put to shame. Whereas the minister's clothes had once looked a bit baggy, he now filled out and seemed to fit them very nicely. William enjoyed Zeeland bacon and the potatoes grown in the rich Zeeland soil and the pure wheat bread. The farmers saw to it that he suffered no shortages.

But it still remained a mystery to him why the congregation had called him after that distressing morning when things went wrong and his collar came flying free. That collar never appeared on the pulpit again, for he got permission from his wife to wear a flat collar that she herself secured around his neck each time he went to church. And so he was safe in that department. But he often thought back to the sermon he had preached that Sunday morning. What in the world had the people seen in that sermon? And he knew that when the congregation called him, it was not a matter of choosing between two candidates. Moreover, the vote in his favor was unanimous.

On his birthday, the consistory members and their wives came to his home to congratulate him. He then put a question to them. He was determined to find out why he had been called, and so he said: "Brothers, I thought that when I preached for you that first Sunday, I made a miserable impression. And that impression was confirmed for me on the Sunday evening when none of you reacted to my sermon."

"As Zeelanders, we don't have an easy time expressing what we think about a sermon, Reverend," said Bart de Vaat.

The minister nodded. That much he had already figured out.

"But it was a sermon I will remember all my life," Bart de Vaat continued. The other farmers nodded in agreement. Then Bart de Vaat proceeded to tell the minister something about his own life and situation. He talked about his many doubts and about the conversation he had had with Melse on the outer dike in the deep of the night. He explained that Melse also had doubts, although he came to them from the opposite direction. Nevertheless, he and Melse had come to the same conclusion.

"Do you still have those doubts, Brother de Vaat?"

"If I must be honest about it, Reverend, I would say that I do sometimes doubt, even now."

He looked toward his fellow office-bearers hesitantly. The men were not inclined to open up their spiritual lives in the presence of others. Rev. Zomer understood what was meant by that look, and so he turned the conversation in a less personal direction.

*   *   *

Not long after that evening, he had a chance to talk with his elder in private, outdoors, on his farm. He said to him: "The doubting that you have been doing is sin, Brother de Vaat." The elder remained silent as he listened to the young minister. "When you make your home visits as an elder, how can you tell the members of the congregation to believe when you yourself are living in unbelief?"

Bart de Vaat looked at the young minister with his open-hearted, gray, little eyes, in which fear was reflected. "Are you saying that I can no longer serve in my office, Reverend?"

"Elders must be examples to the flock, Brother de Vaat, also when it comes to firmness and faithfulness in believing. If you are tossed about like a wave on the sea, you cannot be an example of firmness to others."

"But how do I get that firmness, that assurance, Reverend?"

"By believing."

"But what is it that I'm supposed to believe?"

"You must believe what you have confessed. Think back to when you made public profession of faith. It was very simple. You have to take God at His Word. He has said to you: 'I want to take Bart de Vaat as My child,' and now there is nothing that Bart needs to do other than to take hold of his Father's hand and believe the Father's assurance that he is indeed His child. That's all there is to it. That's what it says in the Word of God, and all you need to do is to say amen to it."

"But Reverend, there's also the doctrine of election to be considered — don't forget about that. Election is also part of the confession to which I have said amen."

"Election is not a doctrine given to frighten us but to comfort us, Brother de Vaat. Moreover, you must remember that the book of election is closed to us. You'll never get a chance to peek into it to see whether your name is written there or not. The certainty of election can be yours only if you believe through the Word. And so, if God preserves you from pain and distress and economic hardship in your life, all you need to do is to be thankful to Him. You need not ask for bad things to happen in your life — just ask Him for clarity. That's what our fathers all taught. You were baptized, and God accepted you as His child. You grieve the Holy Spirit when you start doubting whether you really are His child, Brother de Vaat. Learn to regard your doubt as sin, and ask God for forgiveness."

"Reverend, I believe you're right, but it's difficult for me to obtain such assurance. You people from the north sometimes think differently about these matters than we Zeelanders do."

"I've noticed that already, Brother de Vaat, but we all have the same Bible with the same content, whether we are Zeelanders or not."

"I want to bow before the Bible, Reverend."

"I know that, Brother de Vaat." The minister then shook hands firmly with his elder and departed on his bicycle, whistling.

A week later he had the same sort of conversation with David Melse, but this time in the living room, with mother Beth and Uncle Joris and grandfather Melse present as well. Except for mother Beth, they all doubted and struggled with the same sort of problem.

Mother Beth was sitting there nodding, with tears in her eyes. She was confirming what the young minister was saying; she was in complete agreement with him.

When Rev. Zomer stood up to leave, Grandfather said: "If Jacob Jobse were here, he would agree fully with what you have been saying, Reverend."

"And who is Jacob Jobse?"

"He's a friend of ours from Walcheren. He'll come here sometime on a visit, and then you can also make his acquaintance, Reverend."

"I'd love to meet him," said Rev. Zomer. Then he departed on his bicycle, whistling as he headed for the dike.

Rev. Zomer was struck by the similarity between the massive outer dike and the Word of God. If the Word of God no longer spoke to the people of Zeeland, the tormenting waters of mysticism would seep in and eventually wash the dike away. The dike, the Word of God, would have to hold if the low, fruitful polders of this rich land, which was also rich in terms of spiritual inheritance, were not to be flooded and become silted with the deadly salt of a subjective, self-willed religion.

Rev. Zomer was happy that he had wound up ministering among the people of Zeeland. It was fruitful territory for the seed of the Word. He found he could help these people along.

By this point he was starting to understand why they had called him after the sermon he had preached on that unusual Sunday. In an intuitive way, they had recognized their need of his message.

198

They had picked up the sound of the Word which they no longer understood in all its fine nuances and deep tones, but which they still knew to be the voice of the Good Shepherd.

*   *   *

As Rev. Zomer bicycled to the village, he remembered that he had also been sent out on an errand by his wife. He was supposed to go to Van Dyke, the grocer.

He propped up his bike against the front of the little store and stepped inside. Mrs. Van Dyke heard the bell ring and shuffled into the store from the living quarters, stroking the creases out of her colorful apron. Right behind her came her twenty-two-year-old son, "Mad Martin," who was mentally retarded because of his water-head. He was her only son and the greatest challenge she faced in life.

"Hello, Reverend," she said by way of greeting.

Rev. Zomer nodded and proceeded to explain that his wife had sent him to pick up a pound of sugar and a package of butter.

"Certainly, Reverend, the more, the better, if I may say so. We shopkeepers like to sell a lot of stuff — true or not?"

Mad Martin remained standing in the entrance to the shop. A silly grin came over his face and he said: "You're the minister."

"Yes, Martin, I'm the minister."

"Now, Martin, you go right back into the house," said his mother. "There's nothing for you to do here." But Martin remained standing right where he was, shaking his big head. He remained quiet for a few moments and then said anew: "You're the minister."

Mrs. Van Dyke took hold of her son by the shoulder and repeated: "Now you go inside — right now!"

Martin obeyed, but as he was going down the hallway his hoarse voice sounded: "When the world perishes, you will all perish, and you're the minister. Ha, ha!"

Mrs. Van Dyke shook her head. "I'm afraid he's acting up again," she sighed. "He always gets this way in the spring and in the fall — it happens when the leaves start to grow on the trees and when they fall. That's when he acts up. Sometimes he also gets strange when there's a full moon. It's quite something when you have such a boy around the house."

Rev. Zomer nodded and steered the conversation in a different direction. "I see that a lot of the shops have been renovating. Shouldn't you folks also renovate your shop, Mrs. Van Dyke?"

"What sort of idea do you have of us, Reverend? Did you think we would have so much money that we'd be able to do such a thing? Can't you understand, Reverend, that a boy like Martin costs a lot of money?"

Just then Mr. Van Dyke came shuffling down the little hall into the shop. "Good day, Reverend," he said.

"So, Mr. Van Dyke, I was just asking your wife why you people don't renovate your shop. It seems that the whole village is busy with renovations. It looks as though things are going quite well with the shop-keepers nowadays."

Mr. Van Dyke shook his head. "But we can't join in with that sort of thing. We have to be very careful with our money."

"Oh, come on, now. Surely things aren't that tight for you! You do quite a bit of business here, and you also do some work on the side, don't you? What work do you do on the side?"

"Some of this, and some of that, Reverend. Whatever I can find that will earn me a little bit of money. Sometimes, when I have the chance, I buy a few piglets and chickens and rabbits. If a man means to keep supporting his family, he has to be willing to try anything."

Mr. Van Dyke came over to the display table and stood next to the minister. He shook the dust off his Zeeland trousers, which looked as good as new. "New trousers, Van Dyke?" asked Rev. Zomer.

"I can well understand why you would think so," Mrs. Van Dyke quickly interjected. "It's still the very same pair of trousers that he got married in, and that was thirty years ago. You would never think those trousers were that old, would you, Reverend?"

"What's that, Mrs. Van Dyke? Are those trousers really thirty years old?"

"Yes, and from those trousers you can see just how thrifty we have had to be all these years. After we had been married for a year or so, the trousers began to wear out at the knees, and so I had to replace that section. A little later the back part of the trousers began to wear out, and so I sowed a new section in there. In time, the new patch on the front by the knees began to wear out again, and so it's gone on, back and forth, for thirty years now. Tell me — is it still the same pair of pants or not, Reverend?" She laughed heartily at her own little story.

Rev. Zomer could see that Mr. Van Dyke had a very thrifty housewife looking after him. Still, he did not quite know what to say by way of response.

Mr. Van Dyke kept brushing off the new section that formed the front of his thirty-year-old trousers. It was clear that he approved heartily of his wife's work. He nodded toward her benevolently.

Just then Martin appeared again in the back entrance to the shop. With his stick he pointed to Rev. Zomer. He grinned and said: "You're the minister."

Gravely he shook his big head back and forth as if he wanted to get rid of it, almost as though it were a heavy burden that was too much for his underdeveloped torso to bear. He wagged his stick at his father and mother and cried out hoarsely: "When the world perishes, you will perish too!"

Again his mother sent him to the living quarters. Rev. Zomer paid for his groceries and said goodbye to Mr. and Mrs. Van Dyke. The bell of the shop door gave forth a cracked, unpleasant sound, which pained his eardrums just as much as the hoarse outcry from the throat of Mad Martin.

While he was putting the groceries in the basket of his bicycle, he thought to himself: What am I supposed to believe here? Are these people really as poor as they make out, or do they have a stash of money somewhere? Could it be that they've been keeping some money back from the income tax authorities?

Sometimes you just couldn't figure things out in this village. There were people who acted as though they were very well off but actually had nothing, whereas there were others to whom you felt you should definitely give something, but it turned out that they had plenty of money.

Next to Van Dyke's grocery store was the smith's establishment. Just then the fat smith stepped into his automobile — brand new, a luxurious car. He seemed to have plenty to spare from his sale of all those modern farm machines. His place was full of the latest equipment from English and German factories — well-known brands. He had tractors, heavy machines with conveyer belts, combines, and Jacob's ladders, which were able to move the sheaves to be stored up to the highest part of a big barn.

The smith was doing excellent business. It was partly because the farmers were getting an unbelievable amount of money for their produce. Moreover, the harvests were almost as big as they had been before 1944, when the Germans put the island under water. The misery of that time now seemed far in the past, and life was better than ever.

The smith had a broad smile on his face as he nodded to the minister. He was not a man for going to church, but he was a bit too plump to be ill-tempered. He liked to be on friendly terms with everyone.

Just as Rev. Zomer was getting underway, following his route past the smith's shop, a farmer emerged from it, pulling a horse on a rope. One of the men in the shop gave the horse a tick on its hindquarters, but the horse stayed right where it was. The farmer, named Van Driel, then indicated to the minister that he wished to say something to him. The minister got down from his bicycle.

"Reverend, I'd like to detain you for a moment."

Rev. Zomer nodded. Van Driel was a faithful church-goer, a member of the congregation with a big heart. Rev. Zomer liked him.

"My son would love to make public profession of faith before he does his military service. Would you have any objection to that, Reverend?"

"Not at all, Van Driel. I welcome such willingness in a young man who wants to take care of this matter before he leaves home. When will he be leaving?"

"In about four weeks it will be his turn."

"Just tell him to come and call on me," said Rev. Zomer. "And how are things going at home with your wife?"

"Just fine, Reverend. Just as well as they could possibly go. I have such a wonderful wife!"

Rev. Zomer smiled when he heard this enthusiastic endorsement. "You should know, Van Driel. How long have you two been married?"

Van Driel took off his cap and scratched his bald head. "Let's see, I'll have to figure that out for a moment, Reverend. It must have been some twenty-three years ago that we got married. Yes, that works out. We hope to celebrate our silver anniversary in 1954. Will you come to the celebration, Reverend?"

"That's still a long way away, Van Driel. Let's hope that we'll all be here to see that day."

"Well said, Reverend. We're creatures of the day — isn't that what the Bible says? But if we do live to see that day, I hope to set out a lot of flowers, because I have such a terrific wife, Reverend."

Van Driel then proceeded to tell Rev. Zomer all about his wife. Up until 1940 he had been an ordinary hired hand on someone else's farm. But because his wife was so good at saving money and worked so hard herself, she managed to set aside something of their minimal income to the point that they were able to rent a piece of land and begin farming on their own. That had always been his ideal. The years after 1940 had been good ones for him. The prices gradually rose, and he was quite successful in his work as a farmer. At the moment he had some sixteen cows in his barn and was working a fairly good-sized piece of land. He also had a son who was a tremendous support to him. All of this was due to his wife, he told the minister.

"But I'm sure you yourself weren't sitting still all this time, Van Driel."

"I can tell you that I worked like a horse, Reverend. But that doesn't do any good if you have a wife who throws your money out the window — true or not?"

"I have to agree with you there," said Rev. Zomer.

The minister got on his bicycle again, and Van Driel headed home, leading his horse. Van Driel's little farm was just outside the village on the road that led to the outer dike. But before Rev. Zomer reached the parsonage, he got involved in another conversation. This time he was stopped by the wealthy farmer Koster, who touched the brim of his cap and said: "Reverend, may I have a word with you?"

Rev. Zomer jumped down from his bicycle and looked the proud and prosperous farmer in the eye.

"My name is Koster — you've probably heard of me. I'm a farmer on 'Rest Haven.' I'm not a member of your church, but I'd like to ask you something. If I am correctly informed, Melse's son Henry is engaged to your wife's sister."

Rev. Zomer nodded to indicate that this was true. He wondered where Koster wanted to go with this information.

"Well then, I'd like to ask you if the plan is that your sister-in-law will wind up on the Melse farm when the two of them are married. You're not from a farming family yourself, and I believe your wife isn't either. Doesn't her family come from Gelderland?"

"Yes, you are correctly informed."

Then the story came out. Koster indicated that it would not be a good idea to bring such a girl as the minister's sister-in-law to that rundown little farm. After all, it would be hard to make a good living there. And financial worries would in turn mean an unhappy marriage — at least, that was Koster's opinion. He indicated that he had seen the girl and that she was certainly a nice-looking young woman, but he also suggested that she would not make much of a farmer's wife, especially not on such a little farm where they would have to work hard each and every day. To make such a farm thrive, an experienced wife from a farming background would be needed — otherwise it wouldn't work. It would be much better for Henry if he would go with her and settle in Gelderland after they were married. Henry had been in Indonesia and surely had learned quite something there. He could go a long way in this world if he put his mind to it. He could do much better than to become a small farmer who had to work until he was crippled and bent over, like his great-uncle, Joris Melse.

Rev. Zomer listened attentively. Although he was young, he had enough knowledge of human nature to understand that there was something this farmer was keeping to himself. There was a reason for his interest in this farm, and it had nothing to do with Corinne's welfare.

"What sort of interest do you have in all of this?" asked Rev. Zomer, thereby putting the question directly to Koster.

The farmer responded in kind, without hiding anything: "Yes, I do have a personal interest in this matter. I have long had my eye on that piece of property. Long ago I thought that once Joris Melse was finished farming there, it would be best if that piece of land was added to my farm. The two are right next to each other, and I still have a son at home who could do something with that land."

"So you want *your* son to work on that tiny farm until he's bent over?"

"That's a whole different matter. My son could get some land added to the farm from my own place. I would see to that. So you can see, Reverend, that I'm being open with you. Now you have to tell me whether you think such a farm would be a good place for someone like your sister-in-law. She and her husband-to-be would not be able to make much of it there — true or not?"

"That's not something I can easily judge, Koster. I'm afraid the two of them will have to decide that for themselves. It's just as you said: Henry Melse has enough common sense to be able to weigh the risks, if indeed there really are risks to worry about."

Rev. Zomer stood ready to mount his bicycle and pedal away, but Koster was not about to let him go. The farmer took out a cigar box and offered Rev. Zomer one of his expensive cigars.

"No thank you, I only smoke cigarettes."

"I don't have any cigarettes with me."

Rev. Zomer took a cigarette from his own package. Then he offered the farmer a light.

"I heard that when you were a student you were active in the resistance against the Germans," said Koster. "I can certainly respect you for that. I also had to do some things against that bunch, and they sure did me a lot of harm."

"Oh, that was a long time ago," responded Rev. Zomer. "We have to be able to forget and go on."

"Were any of your brothers killed in the war?" asked the farmer.

"No, we all came through safely."

"Then I can understand why you talk that way. But it was different with me. I lost a brother to the Germans — they gunned him down as though he were no more than a beast. And they chased me off my farm by sticking a gun into my chest. They let the water flood my land, and they chased my animals out of the barn. Even so, there was this one time when I shook hands with one of the Krauts." Koster now seemed far away in his thoughts; it was as though he was staring at some point in the distance. And so the minister got to hear the whole story.

"Yes, it was when they started letting in some ocean water to flood the land. There was this Kraut standing on my land, and he was blubbering like a little kid. It was such a weird sight! I went up to him and said: 'What do you see that makes you blubber like that?' And Reverend, you'll never guess what came from his mouth as he continued to sob. He said: 'When I see the water flooding that beautiful land of yours, I think of my own farm back in Germany. I'm a farmer too, and I find it an awful sight to see the land being flooded.' So what do you think of that, Reverend? I can tell you that I was so moved by what he said that I shook the fellow's hand and said to him: 'Even though you're a Kraut, I still find you a faithful fellow.' Even he had to laugh through his tears. But I can tell you that's the only time I have ever shaken hands with a Kraut. As far as I'm concerned, they are and remain a bunch of Laban's thugs."

Koster still was not done talking. He suggested: "If your future brother-in-law were to emigrate to Canada, I would be able to do something for him there. My son has a large farm in Canada, and I'm sure he'd be able to help Henry Melse get a farm too — a farm four or five times as big as what he could get here. What you should do, Reverend, is try to get him interested in that idea. Your wife's sister would have a much better life in Canada than here on that little farm belonging to Joris Melse."

"It sounds as though it would be very worthwhile for you to see Henry Melse set sail for Canada, Koster."

"I'm being perfectly honest with you. This is now the third time I've said that to you. My farm has been in a direct line of descent from father to son for two hundred years. I'd like to keep it that way. But if I don't make my farm bigger than it is now, my second son will also go to Canada. And then I won't be able to keep up, now that they're starting to farm in the American way with those huge pieces of farm equipment and all. I have to try to keep my head above water when all these changes are taking place. Now, my older son, who's already living in Canada, is coming to Zeeland for a visit. My younger son is getting married this winter, and my older son wants to be at the wedding. I'd like to have everything arranged by that time. I'll have a talk with him, but you, Reverend, should also put in your good word. And if everything works out the way I propose, I'd like to see you at the wedding too. Do we have a deal, Reverend?"

Rev. Zomer smiled again. He looked into the eyes of the rich farmer, which were open just a crack at this point. His eyes now seemed more gentle than when the conversation began. Rev. Zomer began to understand something of the concern in the farmer's heart. He asked: "When is your son planning to get married, Koster?"

"I think about the end of January. The date has not yet been set, but it will be somewhere in that vicinity. And if you'd like to be part of the festivities, then I'll count on it: you and your wife must both come. But now I have to push on. Think about what I said today, Reverend."

Finally Rev. Zomer got onto his bicycle and managed to peddle home unhindered with his butter and sugar, for which his wife had been waiting for a long time. "We have an invitation to attend a wedding — when the son of a farmer named Koster gets married."

Through this unexpected message, Rev. Zomer managed to distract his wife's attention and thereby escape the scolding he would otherwise have gotten for staying away for so long. She looked at him in amazement and asked: "What are you telling me now, William?"

He proceeded to give her an account of his journey through the village. Ida responded with: "Hmm!" Then her kitchen needed attention again.

*   *   *

That afternoon, when the young minister stood in his study looking out the window and thinking, he saw many village inhabitants dressed in black. They were on their way to the church outside the village. Apparently there was a weekday service planned, at which an itinerant preacher would present a message.

The guest preacher, who had found lodging in the home of one of the small farmers, was wandering along the street with his host. He was a small man with a very unusual appearance. He was wearing a three-cornered hat and a fancy pair of pants with clasps — the type of clothing that had been in style in the seventeenth century at the court of Louis XIV, the French king. Soon such clothing became the accepted way for all the men to dress. But whereas such clothing had been ultra-modern back in the seventeenth century, it was now worn to suggest modesty and humility.

The two men walked along with their heads bowed and seemed to have very little to say to one another. The people in the street seemed to regard a church service as an occasion for a great show of piety.

As he looked out on the scene in the street, Rev. Zomer got to thinking about this curious village community of which he was now a part. In spiritual respects, the people in the village were divided into three streams. Yet the village formed a strong community. It was only when the people went to their respective churches on Sunday that they did not greet one another.

There seemed to be an impenetrable wall between their church life and their natural existence. As they went about their business and daily work, they were ordinary, sober, hard-working, thrifty people. They were not to be distinguished from their fellow villagers who attended one of the other churches. But just as soon as a conversation about spiritual matters sprang up, they would undergo a change: mysticism would then issue from their mouths. All their activity and energy, along with their sobriety and their everyday attitudes — all of this would then melt away, to be replaced by passivity and indolence, for then they could not get any further than to sigh that they, too, had hopes that eternal life would one day be theirs.

During the church service about to be held, this one theme would also set the tone for a full two hours as the visiting minister preached. Indeed, it would be held before the assembled crowd as the very content of the gospel.

Rev. Zomer knew just how it would go. His experiences in the two years that he had served in the village as minister had taught him a great deal in this respect.

He watched thoughtfully as the people shuffled past his house and observed that there were a number of members of the big church among the ones going to hear the preacher in the old-fashioned clothes. He was also aware that the spiritual undertone in the lives of most of the people in the village was about the same. In his own congregation he encountered it repeatedly. He thought of Joris Melse and his brother Dirk, also of David Melse and some others who always seemed to sink back into the despondency of being unwilling or unable to appropriate God's promises for themselves.

Indeed, there was a great deal of work to be done here as yet. But he could not say that the soil was unfruitful. Among most of the people he encountered a willingness to bow before the majesty of the Word of God.

What always struck him is that, despite the difference in direction that seemed to be reflected in the existence of the three churches, the village remained a tight-knit community. The people knew they were one; they were well aware that they were all of the same blood. They all went to the same smith to have their horses shoed; they went to the same miller to have their grain ground; and they encountered one another at the same grain-exchange. And when you looked carefully into family relationships, you were amazed to see how many of the people were related to others in the village in some way or other — sometimes very closely. Yes, despite all the surface differences, they were one, all those Zeelanders.

They had become one in their common battle against the enemy, which always disputed their right to the land they lived on — indeed, their right to existence as such. Could it be that the centuries-old struggle against the sea explained something of their somber, heavy character, their stubbornness, and the strength they always kept under such tight control? Might it also explain something of their mysticism, their complete sense of dependence on God their Creator, which sometimes degenerated into a fatalistic belief in a destiny that could not be avoided, a belief that then led them to become somewhat passive?

Now it was quiet in the street leading past the parsonage. By this time the people would all be listening to the minister in his antiquated costume as he told them about the things that inevitably and unavoidably lay ahead for them — in other words, what would strike all who were not among the elect. And he would undoubtedly go on to emphasize that the elect were *very few* in number.

"Sheep without a shepherd," thought the young minister.

Chapter 11

When grandfather Melse went to church on that memorable Sunday morning in January, he was not aware that this would be his last service. It had been a number of years since he had felt free enough to take his place at the table when the Lord's Supper was celebrated.

For some weeks, Uncle Joris had not been able to go to church because of his rheumatism. Therefore he was at home listening to a church service on the radio.

When Rev. Zomer gave a short introduction to his sermon, he announced that his text was taken from John 14, the first verse: "Let not your heart be troubled: ye believe in God, believe also in me."

"Now, it is well known that you believe in God," said Rev. Zomer. "There is not one among you who doubts the existence of God, but what good is God to us if we do not also believe in Jesus as the one who saves us from all our sins? Here Jesus makes an appeal to believe in Him as well — and then not as someone who once lived and played a role in history but as your personal Savior. Therefore He wants to see you come to the Lord's Supper this morning, so that you will be present at the breaking of the bread and the pouring of the wine, eating His sanctified body and drinking His purifying blood to the complete forgiveness of all of our sins."

The sermon was delivered in an alluring voice, and it spoke very deeply to grandfather Melse, who did not dare stay in his pew this time. He was one of the very last ones at the Lord's Supper table, and his hand trembled when he accepted the bread and brought the cup to his lips. Still, he *did* eat and drink, and he heard a word of deliverance spoken about his life, an assurance of the forgiveness of sins. He gave ear to the rich promise that there was also a place prepared for *him* in the Father's dwelling. Such was the effect of Rev. Zomer's sermon — or better, such was what the Holy Spirit was pleased to accomplish through the faithful service of the Word in the life of that old, broken, weary man.

That Sunday afternoon Dirk Melse stayed home from church. He was not feeling well, and so he kept his brother Joris company. Together the two old men sat on opposite sides of the table before the window and looked out over the yard toward the outer dike. It was a cold, wet, uninviting winter day. Uncle Joris felt the cold and the dampness keenly because of his rheumatism. There was a red, glowing pot on the stove. The wind whistled through the chimney.

"So you partook of the Lord's Supper today?"

Grandfather nodded. There was a bit of a smile on his thin, bloodless lips.

"If there is something prepared for you, then you are blessed indeed."

"I think it's also prepared for you."

Uncle Joris looked at his crippled hands, which were bent inwards from pain, and said nothing. He did not dare add his "Yes" to what his brother had just said. Neither did he find himself able to say "No." He simply sighed and let his hands sink to his knees once again.

"We're almost at the end of the road. And now it will all be a matter of whether you and I know what it's about, Joris."

Then Dirk Melse proceeded to give his brother the gist of the sermon that had moved him so deeply, explaining it in his own manner. Uncle Joris listened with interest. When his brother finally fell silent, he said: "That piece from John's gospel — you should read it for me, if you could."

Grandfather picked up his glasses and looked up the well-known chapter in the Bible. In a trembling voice he repeated the words of Christ about the many mansions. Finally he got to the fourteenth verse, the one that seemed to sum it all up: "If ye shall ask any thing in my name, I will do it."

"Let that apply to the two of us too, Joris. I want to lay down my head on that promise. I have no other ground upon which I could die. And you're in the same position."

By that point tears were rolling down Uncle Joris's cheeks. "But I haven't lived in accordance with the Bible," he sighed.

"It's the very same way with me," said Grandfather, "but I want to lay myself down on the basis of Christ's blood. That's what has to count for me — otherwise, I don't see a way out for me."

Uncle Joris nodded in agreement. That was what it all came down to — he knew it. His hands, long plagued by rheumatism, sank to his knees.

*   *   *

On Monday Grandfather remained in bed. He was coughing and having trouble getting his breath. The doctor came to look in on him, and so did Rev. Zomer. They could tell that he was dying.

It was getting toward the end of a dark, somber, misty, wet month of January when Grandfather fell gravely ill. From his sickbed he made it known that he wanted to see Jacob Jobse one more time.

Laura wrote a postcard to Beveland with the message that Grandfather was very ill and that he would love to see Jacob and Joan come and visit for a few days. Almost at once the Melses got a response: Jacob and his wife would arrive on Friday evening. They had arranged for their children to be looked after, and they sent their best wishes to Grandfather.

*   *   *

Corinne was visiting William and Ida in the parsonage, for it was to be Henry's birthday on Sunday. That week she came out to the farm to look in on Grandfather. She also went into the barn with Henry and walked along the stalls in which the cows were kept.

Henry was pleasantly surprised by how she took to the barn. It appeared that his fiancée had an interest in farming, for she already knew the cows by name. In the corner stall was Jans, the oldest of the cows. Corinne caressed Jans between the horns. In the next stall was Bertha; with her large, glassy eyes she looked toward Corinne, her head elevated, as though she was waiting for her turn to be petted. And she got her turn, as did Lies and the other three cows. There were six cows, all outstanding milk producers.

There was only one workhorse left in the horse stable. Henry tried to have the work done by machines as much as possible. Nowadays you could rent machines, and the wages you had to pay to laborers were simply too high. But he still kept Bles on the place.

When Henry entered his stall and filled his trough with some clover, the horse whinnied with gratitude. Corinne also entered the stall and went over to the trough, looking on with considerable interest as Bles devoured the clover which he reached through the wooden slats. Henry fetched a pail of water and held it before Bles. Eagerly the horse sucked up the water. Corinne was surprised at how quickly the water in the pail disappeared. "It's amazing what such an animal has for a stomach," she observed.

When the horse had had enough, he lifted his head, and a little trickle of water ran down his black lips. Then he went back to eating the clover in the trough.

"Grandfather is very sick," observed Corinne.

Henry nodded. "We fear he won't be with us much longer. He seems so totally run-down, as though he is suddenly used up. And he was always so strong — never sick."

"But we have to remember that he's eighty-one years old."

"Yes, that's a whole lifetime. And I'm somewhat worried that Uncle Joris will follow him soon. Those two have grown so unbelievably close that I can hardly imagine the one living on without the other."

As they left the barn, Corinne shivered. "What miserable weather it's been this month!" she said. "We've had nothing but mist and wind and rain, and never a bit of sunshine. In such a winter it must be lonesome behind this dike. Is that what you find, Henry?"

Henry looked at her and said: "As long as I don't have you with me, I'm lonesome — that's for sure. But we can get married whenever we want. This week there's a wedding at 'Rest Haven.' Bert Koster is getting married. It will be quite a feast, I'm telling you. We would never be able to put on something on that scale. I believe that as many as fifty guests are going to be present. You can imagine what that will entail! The whole village is talking about it."

214

Then Henry changed the subject slightly and said: "If we wanted to go to Canada, we could do so. Koster's elder son has come from Canada expressly to be present at this wedding feast. He's willing to help us get ahead in Canada under the condition that Uncle Joris's farm will be reserved for Bert — that's Koster's younger son — at some point in the future. What do you think — should we go?"

"If you go, I'll go with you."

"I'd rather stay here."

"Me too."

"Well then, that's just what we'll do." Henry took his fiancée in his arms. They were standing behind one of the farm buildings where the wind could not get at them.

"You silly boy!" she laughed. "Is this a place to stand hugging and kissing?" She fended him off when he tried to embrace her again and ran off toward the house.

That afternoon, when Henry walked with Corinne back to the parsonage in the village, it was already twilight, although it wasn't very late yet. There was a very strong wind at their backs, and so they moved at a good pace. But they came to an abrupt halt when they were startled by Mad Martin, the young fellow with the water-head, who suddenly jumped out in front of them, waving a large walking stick in his hand. He had been hiding behind a bush. "When the world perishes, our village will perish, and you will perish with it!" Mad Martin pointed his walking stick at Corinne and repeated his somber prophecy. Then he shook his head wildly back and forth, screaming into the wind.

Corinne shuddered and pressed up close to Henry, who was also startled by this unexpected and lugubrious sight and was thrown off stride for a moment. Henry then said: "Martin, come on now, stop trying to frighten people. Now, quickly, back home with you! You shouldn't be out here so late in the day. Quickly now — understood?"

Henry drew himself up to his full length, knowing that only a show of force would make an impression on this mentally disturbed young man. But Martin again waved his walking stick above his head. His head was swaying back and forth as though it would soon prove too heavy a burden for his body to bear.

"The world is perishing and we're all doomed, done for!" he screamed. Then he set off toward the village in a great hurry.

"What a horrible experience!" said Corinne.

"Did he frighten you that much? Well, he startled me too. All of a sudden he stood there before us when we weren't expecting him. But you have to bear in mind that every village has its idiot. So don't make anything of it. He doesn't really harm anyone. It's harder for him than for anyone else. But he's disappeared now. Come on, let's be on our way."

Corinne clung firmly to Henry's arm. He could feel that she was still trembling. When they were finally in the parsonage and she took her coat off, he was alarmed to see how pale her face was. "I believe Mad Martin really did upset you," he said. She nodded. There were tears in her eyes.

Henry was alone when he headed back to the farm. He had a very hard time of it. He had to walk bent over because he was facing a fierce wind that came at him from the northwest.

*   *   *

In the village, Koster's elder son was called "the Canadian." The stories he told here and there got discussed in many a home.

When he came to call on the fat smith, he was somewhat surprised to see the latest models in the way of farm implements on display in his shop. But for the Canadian this visit quickly became an occasion to hold forth about all the latest machinery and equipment that had just come from the factory in Ottawa. The farmers in the Netherlands did not yet have access to such modern mechanical aids. For example, there was a new kind of plow that was very good for smaller parcels of land: you could use it for almost anything.

The Canadian gave the smith some earnest advice: he should come over to Canada and see for himself whether this very unusual machine would not be just the thing for the farmers in Zeeland. Moreover, it wasn't even expensive. If he would import that machine and make it available in Zeeland, he would have it made. While offering this advice, the Canadian gave the smith a familiar clap on the back.

The smith was listening carefully. He asked the Canadian for the address of the company making the new plow. You never knew when such information might come in handy. Now that he had gotten a taste of prosperity and liked the idea of earning a great deal of money without doing much for it, it seemed that nothing was enough for him. He dreamed of having a very large shop with all the latest farm machinery on display, and then he would sell the equipment all over the island. As for his former trade as a smith — well, he could do without that sort of work now.

"You're living in a dinky little country here," said the Canadian. "I wouldn't want to live here again for all the money in the world. I just don't understand how that Henry Melse can be so foolish. He would have it made over there in Canada. He could step right into a farm of some eighty hectares of the very best land, and he'd also have some capital to get the place going properly. But he's decided not to do it — he'd rather stay tied to his mother's apron-strings. And so he'll work himself into the ground on that little farm of his uncle's — until he's also bent over with rheumatism."

The smith thought to himself that the Canadian talked just like his father. But he did not want the Canadian to know what he was thinking, and so he nodded without saying a word. Since the Melses might become customers of his, he felt it would be better to be cautious about what he said.

As for the Canadian, he seemed to have become quite free and bold. The young Koster went on to tell about the many advantages that Canada offers. No hassle with social legislation, no restrictions on building, no commissions governing the appearance of this or that — none of that nonsense. You lived in a free land over there, and everyone could do what he thought was in his own interest.

While he was busy talking with the smith, Bartelse, a goat farmer, came and joined them. Bartelse's wife Jenna was known to be the most slovenly housewife in the whole village. As Bartelse stood there scratching himself continually, he was providing proof that she came by her reputation honestly.

Bartelse figured he would take the wealthy Canadian down a peg or two. He shoved his disheveled, dirty cap back on his head and began to scratch his red hair. "You'd be crazy to let people see the dark side of that country of yours over there," he said. "But I've also heard it said that it's not all peaches and cream in Canada. I could give you a few interesting examples if I wanted to."

The Canadian looked down on his opponent with great disdain. He pulled up his nose and said: "Yes, man, you're completely right. It's a miserable country over there, if you ask me — but there's one respect in which it's much better there than this dinky little country here."

"And what might that be?" asked Bartelse.

"They have no fleas and lice over there."

The smith burst out laughing. He laughed so hard that he wound up slapping his fat knee. He dared to laugh because Bartelse was not a customer of his and never would be. "That's a good one!" he said. "That sure is a good one! Great joke, Bartelse."

Bartelse understood all too well what was meant by the joke. He pulled his cap down over his forehead and said: "If there are no fleas over there, I'm sure there are all kinds of other nasty critters. But never mind, I've got to get going. Good day, fellows."

The Canadian took a look at his gold wrist-watch. Then he adjusted his colorful Canadian tie and pulled it up right under his chin and got into his automobile. He explained that it was time for him to go and pick up his father, who was visiting the notary. They were planning to ride back to the farm together.

The smith looked through the car window for a moment and threw in a last word: "As for those new machines from Ottawa, I'm going to think it over. There might really be something in it for me!"

"Okay," said the Canadian, stepping on the gas, thereby ensuring that the car would make an impressive racket as it sped away. After he picked up his father, the two rode together toward "Rest Haven." When they were halfway home, Mad Martin suddenly jumped out of the bushes and took up a position in the middle of the road, waving his walking stick. It was only by braking sharply that the Canadian managed to avoid an accident. Koster began to swear, and his son screamed through the car window: "Hey, what do you think you're doing? Do you want to be run over and killed?"

"The world is going to perish, and you will perish with it!" screamed Martin hoarsely. Again he shook his water-head vigorously. His improbably large forehead manifested folds of fat of the kind one would expect to see on a baby. His small eyes stared fearfully at the big farmer, who was shaking his fist.

"That weirdo is enough to give me the creeps," said the younger Koster angrily, as he got the car going again.

"There must be a storm brewing," responded his father. "That's why the boy is acting up again."

"It's because of all the inbreeding that goes on here on the island — that's why there are so many idiots running around."

Koster laughed out loud. "Are you crazy, son? Have you forgotten that your mother and I are also cousins? Are you telling me that you're an idiot too?"

"There are exceptions," responded the Canadian. "But if you ask me, there are more than enough idiots running around with a screw loose. Why don't they come to Canada, where there's plenty of land and many women to choose between?"

The Canadian made a nifty turn and drove down the lane leading to "Rest Haven."

Koster knew his son well enough to understand that his bad mood was not entirely due to the incident with Mad Martin. His elder son could string people quite a line about Canada, for he had to convince himself that it was a wonderful place. Even with all the prosperity he enjoyed over there in Ontario, the boy was missing many good things that his fatherland made available to those who were well off — comfort, culture, and the cozy sociability of life in a proper Dutch home. And now it was almost time for him to return to that almost endlessly large land where everything was still basically at a colonization stage. That was the real reason for his bad mood.

On Tuesday the boat was to depart for Canada. Koster had made an arrangement with the mayor to have Bert's wedding take place on Monday. Then his oldest son would still be able to attend the wedding celebration. It would be a very memorable occasion — an old-fashioned farmer's wedding of the sort that Schouwen and Duiveland were well known for. His Canadian son would have something to exaggerate about when he got back to Canada.

*   *   *

When it was Friday, Henry Melse went to pick up Jacob Jobse and his wife Joan from the bus. He stopped at the Van Dykes' shop for a few groceries requested by his mother.

Just then Mad Martin's mother was busy adding up the accounts for the day; the money box was standing on the table. When she heard Henry enter the shop, she closed it quickly and noisily and shoved it under the bed. She had not expected that she would have to serve any more customers at that late hour.

Van Dyke was surprised at how quickly his wife had managed to hide the money box. He lit a fresh pipe.

Henry got the groceries he needed and then said: "That Martin of yours threw a real scare into my fiancée this week. You people must forbid him to do such things. He's the kind of fellow who gives people the creeps."

Mrs. Van Dyke shook her head sympathetically, as if to say: "Tell me about it." She did not know just what was wrong with Martin, but it had been a very bad week and they did not know what to do to control him anymore. He hardly slept at all. He went around screaming, and he kept wanting to go to the outer dike. Never before had they had so much trouble with him as just then.

Mrs. Van Dyke had already said to her husband on occasion: "If we had enough money, we would be best off putting him in an institution, because we can't hold out forever with this sort of behavior here at home."

"But where would people like us get that kind of money?" responded her husband. "We don't have a red cent, and it costs quite something to maintain such a sad case in an institution. Still, if there doesn't come a change in his behavior, that's where he'll wind up."

"Where is Martin now?" asked Henry Melse.

"How am I supposed to know? He wanders everywhere, all over the village. He has it in his head that the world is perishing, and he just keeps moving from one place to another. Once this week, in the middle of the night, he got out of bed and went up on the outer dike. My husband had to go and haul him away from the sluices. We really have a lot to put up with, if you ask me."

Henry said farewell and went his way. Soon the bus arrived, and Jacob Jobse helped Joan out the narrow door. At once he asked: "How's it going with you folks? How is grandfather Melse doing? Do you think he's really getting to the end?"

Henry nodded and gave him a brief rundown. According to the doctor, the end could come at any time. Grandfather's life was flowing away, like a lamp that was burning out.

"As long as the lamp of God's Word is shining for him, everything else will fall into place," said Jacob. "What weather we had on the way over! The boat was tossed about on the waves. I thought that at any moment Joan would come down with seasickness. The captain told us that there's some really bad weather on the way. The water is already high, and by Sunday we are to expect a spring tide."

The covered wagon with Bles hitched to it was standing ready in front of the smith's shop. Bles had a horse blanket over his broad back to protect him against the biting cold.

As they rode away, they found themselves facing a northwesterly wind as they headed for the outer dike. Bles had to strain against the harness with his chest just to keep the carriage moving forward.

"A fine horse!" observed Jacob.

"A wonderful horse, a gentle horse. We surely would not want to miss him."

"Yes, a farmer gets very attached to his animals," replied Jacob. "I've heard it said that a farmer sometimes loves his animals more than he loves his wife."

"Now, now, Jacob!" said Joan. "What sort of thing is that to say? Who would ever be so foolish as to say such a thing?"

"You don't hear me saying it, do you? But I'll tell you, some farmers are mighty peculiar characters. Oh boy!"

Henry could not help but laugh. He was the same old Jacob Jobse, even if his hair was starting to turn gray.

When they arrived at the farm, they found David Melse standing at the door waving to them by way of greeting. Jacob was a very welcome guest.

Soon he was sitting at Grandfather's sickbed. "Do you recognize me?" he asked.

"Do I ever!" said Grandfather with a weary smile. "I'm so happy you decided to come!"

"Of course I came! I'd have to be a really rotten, uncaring person *not* to come under these circumstances. But tell me, how are things with you? Are you coming to the end of the road, Grandfather?"

"Yes, Jacob, I think this is the end."

"And what will happen then?"

Grandfather immediately understood what Jacob meant. "I believe things are in good order with me, Jacob. The last Sunday I was in church, I was able to come to the Lord's table. And I hope I will soon be at His table forever in the house of our Father with its many rooms."

Grandfather was panting. Jacob could see that it was very difficult for him to speak. He took the old man's hand and addressed him with a tender, gentle voice that one would not have expected from him: "In that case everything is in order, Grandfather. Just be still for now. I've already heard what I was hoping to hear. You're exactly where you need to be. All the rest will take care of itself. Just lay your head down in peace. A little later I'll come and sit by your bed again for a while."

Then he stood up and left the sickroom. Grandfather Melse drifted off to sleep. His breathing was still labored, heavy, and irregular.

In the other room, Jacob said to David Melse and mother Beth: "He won't be with us much longer, if you ask me. But he will come to a good end — that much I could pick up for myself. And that's what really counts, after all."

Then he addressed himself to the old man who was in the room with them and said: "I suppose you'd be Uncle Joris — right?"

Uncle Joris nodded. He was staring straight ahead, with a vacant look on his face. In these last weeks, his bond with his brother had become particularly tight. The conversations between the two of them on Sundays when the others were at the afternoon service had made a very deep impression on his soul. When he looked at his claw-like hands, he considered them in an entirely different light than before. He viewed them as washed in the blood of Jesus, even though that thought was still so enormous in his mind that he could not understand it.

But that he would soon have to go on *without* his brother was a reality he could not yet accept. Again and again the others in the house saw him go quietly to the sickbed and stare at Grandfather's face. Then he would return with tears in the corners of his eyes and stand silently at the table or by the stove. Few words passed over his lips.

When it was time to go to bed, Jacob Jobse said: "If you folks have no objection, I'll take the first watch, sitting up with him in his room. Perhaps, if it proves necessary, Henry could sit with him for the rest of the night."

Mother Beth did not think this was a good idea. She pointed out that Jacob had just arrived from his journey. It was not necessary for him to stay up — she would do it instead. But Jacob prevailed and got his way. "You just make me a strong cup of coffee — as black as possible. Then I'll be sure to stay awake. And if something happens, you can count on me to awaken all of you at once."

Finally all was at rest in the little farm by the outer dike. Jacob was sitting in the sickroom where there was a small petroleum lamp. He observed Grandfather's breathing, which was becoming weaker and more irregular.

Most of the time Grandfather appeared to be unconscious. But once in a while he would come to. In a whisper he would then ask how things were going on Walcheren. He did not seem to remember that Jacob no longer lived there. In his own mind he was busy with

Walcheren. He was thinking about Rev. Verhulst and the Germans, and he asked whether the harvests on Walcheren were good again. Rev. Verhulst preached in a very different way than the minister over here. Rev. Verhulst was more a man for preaching judgment, whereas Rev. Zomer brought out the riches of the gospel for sinners who were bogged down in doubt. "We need comfort, a lot of comfort," he said to Jacob.

"That's exactly right, Grandfather," replied Jacob. "You're putting the emphasis just where it belongs. The gospel is a joyful message — all too often we forget that."

Then Grandfather stopped talking, and his breathing became more labored. Jacob could not help but think about a song he had learned many years ago: "The closer I get to my Father's house, the stronger my yearning for my eternal dwelling, and for the festival of my King, and for the end of the battle." That song applies here, he thought to himself.

At about three o'clock in the morning, Jacob woke up the others in the house. When they gathered around the bed, the end came. Grandfather extended his hand to each of them in turn, with Uncle Joris, his brother, coming last. He held Uncle Joris's crooked fingers in his hand and was still holding them when he uttered his final words: "The blood of Jesus Christ purifies us from all our sins . . ."

He gasped a few times and then he was silent — forever still. Grandfather was home.

Uncle Joris pulled his deformed hand from his brother's grasp and began to sob. He understood the message completely. He sensed that the word of deliverance about the blood of Christ was also spoken for him and about him. And now he had only one desire: to follow his brother — the sooner, the better.

No longer were his deformed fingers an unbearable hindrance for him. Now that they were wet with his own tears, he could see them properly, for although his hands had indeed been greedy and had reached out constantly for money, *Christ* had taken hold of them. By reaching for those crippled hands, He had also taken hold of Uncle Joris's soul, his life.

Chapter 12

Then it was Saturday morning, January 31, 1953 . . .

A powerful storm was brewing. A northwesterly wind came roaring down from the Arctic. It blew with tremendous force, following a course that would brook no resistance. It blew over the very top of Scotland and along the western coast of Norway and into the North Sea, that age-old funnel that narrows into the English Channel.

The northwesterly storm swept up the water before it. The water turned into foam as the rolling seas moved toward the south, smashing the coasts of England and Denmark and advancing steadily on the Dutch coast. Finally the water reached a point where, seemingly, it could go no further, a point where the great rivers joined the sea and encircled the islands of South Holland and Zeeland.

The water kept rising and rising. The hurricane was like a whip in the hands of a giant who drove the water ahead toward all the people collected in one place in the south, where they had no way out.

Helping this hurricane along was the complex relationship between the sun and the moon, which kept pulling the water toward the southeast. The water being swept ahead had come from hundreds of miles away. It roared and foamed in a veritable paroxysm of breaking wrath and threw itself at the lowlands along the sea, where there were little ridges called dikes rising up in the air to keep the sea at bay.

Those little dikes — behind them lay Holland, whose land was well below sea level. There the people worked and slept and ate and drank. There they were born and there they died — below sea level.

It seemed as though an angry fist had repeatedly come down on the water at points that were gigantic distances apart, smashing the mirror into all kinds of pieces. And now it was no longer a mirror; instead it was a boiling, swirling, foaming, black-green mass that was being pulled and pushed by forces and powers that far transcended any human understanding. The water rose in an ever more intense fury because it encountered resistance — the resistance offered by weak human forces, the resistance of a bit of earth with some stone blocks piled on top of it . . .

The water kept rising and rising. In this hour the danger was ever nearer.

*   *   *

That Saturday evening Henry had accompanied his fiancée to the parsonage, where she was staying. It was just after six o'clock when they both got on their bicycles and headed for the village, following the path at the foot of the high sea dike. The wind was now so strong that there could be no thought of bicycling on top of the dike.

They had the wind at their backs, and so they got to the village very quickly. The sky was dark — ominously so. Heavy, black clouds sped across the sky toward the southeast, as though they were fleeing animals.

When they were inside the parsonage, Rev. Zomer said: "I believe it's getting quite nasty out there, isn't it?"

"There's a tremendous storm brewing," Henry replied.

"At seven o'clock we'll hear what the radio has to say."

The reports on the radio were disturbing. The Weather Service in De Bilt told them that the coastal provinces were to expect a severe storm that evening. Angry, powerful winds would be blowing toward the south, coming from a west-to-northwest direction. There would be fierce winds and rapidly moving cloud cover, with some rain and hail — perhaps even snowstorms.

The radio also had a report for the ships at sea: they were cautioned to be on the alert for wind and storm. The earlier warnings issued were now being replaced by still more severe warnings. And then there was a report for those who guarded the dikes. They were told that from the northern and western part of the North Sea there was a very serious storm approaching from a north-by-northwest direction. The storm was growing in extent as it moved into the southern and eastern part of the North Sea. It was expected that the storm would continue throughout the entire night. Rotterdam, Willemstad and Bergen op Zoom were instructed to be ready for dangerously high water levels the next afternoon.

Rev. Zomer turned off the radio. He offered: "It doesn't look so good."

Ida asked: "Do you suppose we could have a problem with high water here?"

"I don't think so," said Henry. "Our dikes are high and strong. And they are inspected regularly. Something very, very unusual would have to happen before the water would penetrate here."

In the meantime, the wind outdoors was blowing so hard that the blinds began to move. The wind could be heard howling through the chimney of the parsonage.

"I'm going to head home at once," said Henry.

Corinne accompanied him to the door. "Till tomorrow, then. I'm afraid it will be a rather sad birthday for you. Your grandfather is gone, and now this horrible weather."

"Good night," he replied. He set out bravely on his bicycle, but once he was outside the village he stopped pedaling. There was no way he could bike into such a wind. And so he simply pushed his bicycle along, with the top part of his body bent over. Slowly he progressed down the dark road leading to the sea dike. And when he reached the dike, he took the path that followed the dike, where there was a measure of shelter against the wind. At least he could breathe properly.

At one point he was frightened by a scream above his head. He looked up and saw Mad Martin standing right on top of the dike. His silhouette formed a very strange contrast to the dark clouds scudding by overhead. Martin was waving his stick above his head again.

"If the world perishes, we are all doomed too!" he cried in his hoarse voice. "We are doomed — the world is perishing!" he shouted, by way of repetition. His words were snatched away by the howling storm and could hardly be understood. Henry heard only bits and pieces of what he was saying.

"You come down here right now, Martin — quickly!" screamed Henry. "You shouldn't be up there! Surely your parents are out looking for you. Quickly now, you have to go home."

Martin came down from the dike and stood before Henry. He was still waving his stick around and saying: "If the world perishes . . ."

"Now you be quiet, Martin, and go home, I'm telling you. Otherwise I'll bring you there myself. Shame on you for letting your parents get so worried! You must never do that, Martin, never! Now, home with you — and be quick about it!"

"I'm going, I'm going!" cried Martin. Again he shook his big, heavy head. As he departed, Henry could hear additional snatches of his cries penetrating even the howling storm.

But Martin did not go home. As he was making his way down the road back to the village, he suddenly turned a corner and headed down the long lane leading to "Rest Haven," where the Koster family was sitting around the hearth. With his stick he knocked against the heavy shutters and cried anew: "The world is perishing, and you are doomed. The world is perishing . . ."

His stick made the shutters shake. Soon the door was thrown open angrily, and Martin found Koster standing before him. With rude curses on his lips, the farmer grabbed Martin by the shoulders and pushed him down the lane leading off the farm. When Koster finally let the boy go, Martin lost his balance and wound up rolling in the mud. With difficulty he got to his feet and cried out: "You are doomed when the world perishes! You . . . you . . . !" Again he waved his stick above his head, but he shuffled down the lane when he saw the farmer coming after him.

As for Koster, he waited until the boy had actually disappeared from his property. Then he went inside and closed the door tightly. He turned off the light above the door, and again it was dark.

But Martin did not go back to the village. Once more he went to the outer dike and climbed up the steep slope. He had to crawl on his hands and knees to get there, taking hold of little bits of grass. When he got to the top, he faced a wind that seemed to have the strength of a hurricane as it raged over the concrete De Muralt Wall. The wind came right at Martin and took his breath away.

It was with considerable difficulty that he rose from his knees and stood on the concrete path along the wall, his fingers clawing at the sharp edge of the concrete wall. He looked over the Scheldt, where the turbulent water was seething. The stormy wind blew foam into his face. He licked his lips and tasted the salty mist.

Then he cried out as though he were an animal, took hold of his stick, and stood with his back to the storm, leaning against the concrete wall. He waved his stick over his head as his voice went out anew: "When the world perishes, you are all doomed!" His screams seemed to break apart into little disconnected bits of sound as they were overpowered by the thunderous hurricane. Nothing of what he was shouting reached the ears of a single inhabitant of the village . . .

*   *   *

When it was time to go to bed, David Melse reached for the Bible and read Psalm 77, a psalm of persecution: "Thy way, O God, is in the sanctuary: who is so great a God as our God? Thou art the God that doest wonders: Thou hast declared Thy strength among the people. Thou hast with Thine arm redeemed Thy people, the sons of Jacob and Joseph. The waters saw Thee, O God, the waters saw Thee; they were afraid: the depths also were troubled. The clouds poured out water: the skies sent out a sound: Thine arrows also went abroad. The voice of Thy thunder was in the heaven: the lightnings lightened the world: the earth trembled and shook. Thy way is in the sea, and Thy path in the great waters, and Thy footsteps are not known. Thou leddest Thy people like a flock by the hand of Moses and Aaron."

Then they all knelt before their chairs, and David Melse led them in an evening prayer. They prayed for protection from all danger during that stormy night. They also asked for new strength for the Sunday that was to come . . .

Grandfather was lying upstairs in the small room. With a night light David Melse went into the room to take one more look at the still and seemingly joyful countenance of his dead father, whose hands were folded in a posture of prayer. Grandfather was now at rest: no longer could pain and danger affect him.

*　　　*　　　*

"Father, what could be bothering Bles?" asked Henry. "That horse is *so* restless. He stands there stamping, and the cows are also feeling distressed. Shall I go and take a look at them?"

"We'll go out there together, Son, but I don't think there's anything to worry about. It must be the storm that's bothering the animals. It certainly is frightening weather. You have to feel sorry for the people who are at sea."

Carrying a storm lantern, they walked across the farmyard. Melse took a firm grip on his son's arm in order not to be blown over by the powerful wind. He tried to say something to Henry, but Henry could not understand a word. They were relieved when they were inside the barn and could close the door. "What awful weather, Son!"

There was nothing unusual to be seen when they looked at Bles. His nostrils were wide open, and he shook his head in a way that reminded Henry of Mad Martin. "The horse is restless — that's for sure," said Melse. "I think it's mainly because of the storm."

It was the same way with the cows. Jans and Lies began to moo when Henry and his father came into their part of the barn. But who could understand the language of the animals? Melse threw some feed into their trough. Then he caressed Jans' neck and said: "You just stay calm, Jans. You're nice and warm here in the barn. After a while, the bad weather will pass." Then the two of them closed the barn door and made their way with difficulty through the fierce wind.

When they were finally at the door of the house, Henry paused and said: "Shall I go to the outer dike, Father, and take a look to see just how high the water is now?"

"Why would you do that, Son? You'll just wind up with pneumonia. Tomorrow it will be somewhat calmer again. Just come inside — we should both get to bed."

Henry went directly to sleep, but sleep eluded mother Beth. "Why are those animals behaving so strangely?" she asked her husband. "Just listen to Bles. He stands there stamping constantly. Do you suppose he's suffering from some sort of stomach pain?"

"I don't think so," said David Melse, reassuring her. "It must be the storm."

Finally even mother Beth went to sleep. But Jacob Jobse was still lying awake. He, too, heard the noises the animals were making, and he was very uneasy about the water. He remembered what the boat captain had said about an extra high tide.

"What are you thinking about as you lie there?" asked Joan.

"Oh, nothing," he said, as he turned over to lie on his other side. "I'm just listening to the storm." Finally he fell asleep.

The one who had the most trouble getting to sleep that night was Uncle Joris. He also heard the unrest of the animals, and he understood that the storm must be making them nervous. There was something remarkable about this stormy night. He could not remember a previous winter storm during which the animals in the barn had been so restless.

His crippled body was tossing and turning, for the storm had made his rheumatism even worse than usual. In particular, his right leg was causing him almost unbearable pain. And so he lay there listening to all the noises coming from outside the house; some of the time it even seemed that he could feel the house shaking.

The tiles on the roof were clattering. The noise was making him uneasy. He was especially bothered by all the racket that Bles continued to make.

Finally he lit a match and held it up to his watch. Exactly two o'clock. He decided he could not stay in his warm bed any longer. With difficulty he pulled on some clothes. He put on a jacket for good measure. Moving quietly, so as not to disturb anyone, he slipped out of his room. He went to the side of the house that was sheltered from the storm and opened a shutter to look outside. It was a strange sight that met his eyes. There was a blanket of snow covering everything, but he could hear rain was coming down hard on the tiles on the roof. He wondered how in the world such a thing was possible.

The noise made by Bles and the continuing mooing of the cows finally lured him outdoors. He opened the door and at once felt some ice-cold water streaming along his feet. He hesitated for a moment. Then, instinctively, he began to walk through the water in the direction of the barn. He now understood that the animals were standing in water. He took a couple of steps. He hesitated. At the corner of the house, where the stormy wind was at its fiercest, he stood still in the middle of the ice-cold water. His teeth were chattering.

He decided to turn back and summon help, for he now saw that the situation was much, much worse than he had realized at first. But a stream of water knocked him over, and he did not have enough strength to get to his feet. He was drawn along by the force of the water and propelled in the direction of the barn. He tried to hold onto a fence post as he passed it by, but in vain. With great force he was swept along until his head hit a post right by the barn door. And there he remained. Uncle Joris had followed his brother — and quickly.

*   *   *

Joan thought she had heard something down on the first floor, and so she woke her husband up. "Jacob, listen! What could possibly be going on down there?"

Jacob sat straight up in bed. "That doesn't sound good to me," he said, as he listened, holding his breath. Then he jumped out of bed and opened a shutter. "Everybody out of here!" he screamed. "There's water everywhere!" He slipped into his pants and began to wake up the others in the house. At once they realized that Uncle Joris was gone, and they understood that he must be outside somewhere.

The water was already half a meter high in the rooms on the first floor. "We'll have to stay upstairs," said David Melse.

"No, we have to get outside!" Jacob shouted back. "If we go upstairs, we'll drown before long. The dike must have broken somewhere, and it's now the time of the extra high tide. The water will soon be even higher than the roof. We all have to get out of here and climb onto the dike."

"You just go ahead," said David Melse. "Henry, you take Mother with you. I'll first go and release the livestock. The cows have to be saved."

"It can't be done, Father," replied Henry. "It's already too late."

"I *have* to do it! I'm not going to let those animals drown."

"Then I'll go with you."

"You stay with your mother and get up on the dike as quickly as you can," said David Melse, giving his son an order. Henry obeyed.

They walked through water that was up to their waists. They didn't even have time to get dressed properly. Henry took hold of the top rail of the fence that led to the edge of the property, and with his other hand he held onto his mother. Laura also took her mother's hand, and with her other hand she held onto the fence. Jacob held onto the fence as well. And so they got to the edge of their property and began to ascend the stone steps up to the dike, where they would have solid ground under their feet.

As for David Melse, he had taken hold of the fence that led to the barn. He hoped he would find Uncle Joris, but he saw him nowhere.

In the barn the cows were mooing, and Bles was still stamping his feet. By now they were up to their bellies in water. Melse cut the cows loose and tried to get them to leave the barn. The horse was quite willing to follow, with his head up in the air and his nostrils wide open, but when the cows felt the icy wind blowing alongside their warm heads, they did not want to leave their warm stall. Melse then proceeded to use some force. Lies and Jans followed him, but the rest of the cows retreated and stayed in the barn.

Melse knew he had no time to coax them further, for the water level was rising relentlessly. With Bles in front of him and the two cows in halters behind him, he had enough support to be able to resist the flow of the water. By this point the water was up to his chest. The animals were willing and proceeded to the edge of the farm and up the dike until they finally found solid ground under their feet.

The water seethed as though it were possessed. It threw itself against the house and then coursed between the house and the barn as it swept across the land.

"It's not safe to stay here," said Jacob. "The dike has given way somewhere. We have to get to some other polder. Here the water can even get over the wall. Just look!"

Indeed, some of the waves were now flowing right over the top of the dike. Water was coursing down the slope to the land below. As they walked along the top of the dike, they had water under their feet.

Jacob and Henry looked over the concrete wall at the Scheldt. It was one boiling sea, full of foaming waves, right up to the level of the De Muralt Wall.

"If this wall gives way, we'll all drown," said Henry. "We have to see that we get to the village."

"That's out of the question," responded Jacob. "The village will be standing under water by this time. We have to stay on the dike and try to find a crossing point that will allow us to go to another polder — one that's still dry."

"In that case, we'll have to head toward the sluices."

They waded through the foamy water and waves along the wall in the direction of the sluices. On the outside of the dike was a heaving, seething sea, beyond which they saw only a pitch-black night.

There was nothing to be seen of the village. All the lights were out, and there was no longer any electricity. Henry began to think of the parsonage, and of Corinne. He pondered the possibility of trying to get to her. But when they were approximately at the point where a road led to the village, all he saw below was an abyss of turbulent water. He realized that anyone who ventured into that water would surely drown. Moreover, he knew that he could not be missed: David Melse still had his hands full looking after his animals, and so Henry had to take care of Mother and Laura. And then, he could see that the water was becoming still more violent as great waves washed over the concrete wall on top of the dike, which meant that the water on the inner side of the dike was treacherous too.

Finally the two women could no longer keep going. Jacob advised them to crawl on their hands and knees along the concrete wall. Then they would have some protection from the wind and the water. They found that this worked somewhat better, but it also slowed their progress.

"Maybe, Father, you should leave the animals to their own devices at this point," suggested Henry.

"No, Son, if I leave them behind, they'll drown," screamed Melse in response. "We have to keep on moving ahead as long as we can. You just make sure you take care of Mother."

They continued to struggle along, crawling and bending over, until their knees were open sores. They were not wearing much more than their night clothes, with only a coat or jacket quickly thrown on as cover for the cold.

Henry was beset by his concern for Corinne. As for Jacob, he was very worried about his children. If the water was very high here, it would also be high on Beveland — indeed, it would be high all along the coast. There would be such situations everywhere.

Jacob realized that the flooding was not just due to weak places in the dike: there were abnormally high water levels that had forced the water right up to the top of the dike and then enabled it to wash away the inside portion of the dike. Such a process must be underway all over Zeeland. The sea water was piled up so high that it had to find someplace to go.

Jacob did not say anything to Joan about his worries. For the present it was enough of a struggle for her just to keep moving ahead.

In the thick darkness, with nothing more than a seething mass of water around them, they continued to creep forward slowly. They kept going for an hour and a half, until they finally arrived at the sluices, where there were other people who had found refuge there before them.

On top of the dike was a fine new house; it had been built after 1944 because the Germans destroyed the former house that stood there. More than a hundred refugees had already assembled at the house, but Henry did not see any of the village inhabitants among them. They were people from the polder who, like them, had gotten out just in time and thus had managed to save their lives.

Soon they heard that the break in the dike had been directly opposite Koster's farm, "Rest Haven." The Scheldt had forced its way into the polder through the breach in the dike. As for what had happened after that, no one knew.

The house was full of people. They were in the kitchen, in all the rooms, and even in the small barn. Everything was occupied.

There were people with drawn, pale faces, people who were wearing nothing more than their nightclothes. They had been forced to leap out of bed and run through ice-cold water with the wild, cutting, hurricane-force wind pursuing them, a wind blowing from the northwest, all the way down from the Arctic Circle. Children were crying. A woman had fainted. Others were weeping about possessions they had lost. Some told stories of family members who had drowned.

One woman was suffering labor pains, but there was no doctor or nurse to help her. A few of the women, mother Beth among them, were huddled around her, until the cry of her new-born baby brought a moment of stillness among the refugees. Dying and giving birth — even during this strange night the cradle stood next to the grave.

And then the stillness was broken in a most frightening way. The door was thrown open, and Mad Martin lunged into the room, with his stick dripping with water. His hoarse voice overruled everything else. "The world is perishing, and we're all doomed! The world is perishing . . . The world is perishing . . ."

They were all frightened for a moment. It seemed like a supernatural apparition in this night of judgment, death, and destruction.

236

David Melse had found a place for his three animals where they found shelter from the wind. He tied them up by the barn. He had just stepped inside when he saw Mad Martin standing there. "Be quiet now, Martin," he ordered. "Hold your tongue, boy. Understood?"

Martin fell silent. He found a place on the floor in a corner, and there he sat, lost in his own thoughts. He had wandered around on the dike all night, and his wandering had saved his life. His big head, with baby-like furrows on his forehead, sank to one side, and his mouth fell open. He began to breathe heavily. Mad Martin had finally found rest . . .

* * *

When Henry and his father went outside with Jacob Jobse, they saw tiny lights in many houses in the distance. The lights could be seen through windows up in the attics, where some people had managed to save themselves by finding refuge from the storm.

"Maybe we could have stayed in our house too," said David Melse.

"No way, Father," replied Henry. "Our house is much too low for that. By now the water will be over the roof. You can see for yourself that the water here in the polder is just as high as the water on the other side of the dike. Remember that the top of our house was not above the level of the dike."

"Then the remaining cows are lost, along with Uncle Joris."

"You could say that everything is lost."

"But you managed to save your own lives," said Jacob Jobse. "Uncle Joris is lost altogether. Yet I did hear him say that he was longing to follow Grandfather. So maybe, in light of what he said he wanted, this is not such a bad outcome for him — true or not?"

David Melse went outside to check on Bles, whose head was hanging low as he stood behind the barn in the shelter provided by the two cows. The horse was trembling with the cold as he pressed against one of the cows. When he felt Melse's hand on his wet flanks, he moaned. Then he made a whinnying sound to express his gratitude for deliverance.

237

It was a very long night . . . Mother Beth continued to help the woman who had just brought her first child into the world. It was a baby boy, who now lay sleeping in his mother's arms. The baby's father was sitting by the bed, weeping. The mother was smiling through her tears. The horrors of this night had receded somewhat for her.

It was a very long night . . . It remained dark, and the storm kept howling, without pause, without dying down. The storm just kept piling up water and driving it into the small funnel of the North Sea, where it rose ever higher and attacked the sea gates and tore into the dikes as though they were made of soggy paper.

The water streamed across the polders and lifted houses off their foundations. Cows drowned. People suddenly had to flee for their lives. They sat up in attics, in the highest branches of the trees, on the roofs of houses. They crept along on pieces of dike that were still standing, even though gouges had been taken out on both sides. Those bits of dike now looked like molehills in the seething water that continued to rise. How long would those pieces of dike hold out?

It was a very long night . . . There were some people who had managed to get onto a raft of some sort. They now floated over the heaving sea that was once the Scheldt, where they were fully exposed to the wind and the waves. There were fathers with dead children in their arms — children who had died because of the icy cold.

The water kept eating further and further, as though it were a greedy, hungry monster. It ate the land away and vented its wrath on the dikes. It ate into the clay soil of the polders. It slashed through holes in the dikes and made them into channels many meters in depth. With great energy it forced its way to places where it had never been. It was a torrential flood fed by an inexhaustible ocean.

*   *   *

As for Mad Martin, he sat in his little corner with his mouth hanging open. He was asleep.

238

Chapter 13

When Sunday, February 1, finally dawned after a night of horror, with the twilight gradually replacing the night, each passing moment brought additional revelations of the extent of the catastrophe.

David Melse had found a place for his two cows and his horse in a barn on the dike. The animals were dried off, and there was hope that the cows would soon be able to give milk again, since milk was so sorely needed for the children and the sick and those who were weak.

Most of the food in the house was quickly consumed by the scores of people who were present. The water supply had already been contaminated by brackish sea water, and no one knew how long the isolation would last. The two cows represented some relief in a situation of extreme need.

Jacob Jobse walked up and down on a little piece of dike that was still intact. He had his two hands deep in his pockets. He was thinking about his children. What would the situation be in Beveland? Would it be flooded too? Because there was no electricity, there was no news to be had by radio. The people taking refuge in the house on the dike knew nothing except what they could see with their own eyes. And what they saw made their hearts sink.

Once the twilight gave way to daylight, they beheld an immensity of water all around them. Everything had become a single sea. Schouwen and Duiveland were now completely under water. It looked as though a huge ship of enormous dimensions had sunk after cannonballs made holes below the water line. The command bridge and the masts and stacks were still sticking up above the water, but everything else had disappeared. Such was the impression made by the church towers and the windmills and the roofs of the houses and the tree tops that could still be seen above the great expanse of water.

When it got still lighter, the people on the dike could make out human beings behind the little windows in the upper stories of the houses. They could see that there were people waving bed sheets. They were signaling for help, but no help was at hand.

Jacob understood that something had to be done, but what? In his heart was a burning desire to hurry as quickly as he could to tend to his children, even if he had to go over in a rowboat. But he knew that the Scheldt was still anything but peaceful. The storm from the northwest had continued, and although the water level had subsided somewhat, it was still very high. Who could say what would happen at the next high tide?

While he was walking back and forth on the dike, his eye fell on a small inlet right by the dike. There he saw a boat half full of water. Then it came to him what he should do. He went to the owner of the house next to the inlet and said: "Would it be all right to make use of your boat? I'd like to drag it to the other side of the dike and then go and get people out of their houses."

The man nodded. He seemed to be in a daze and did not know what to do in such a situation. What Jacob proposed was fine with him.

Jacob and Henry discussed matters. They decided they would row into the polder together and see if they could get over to the village. They hoped they would find people there in need of rescue.

The two men dragged the boat over the dike and put it into the water on the inner side. The boat did not appear to have a leak: the water inside it had gotten there because of the flood.

"Are you coming with me?" Jacob asked Henry. David Melse wanted to come along too, but Jacob shook his head. Two men was sufficient. They had to keep open space in the boat for as many people as possible.

On the dike men and women were standing and watching them. They pushed off in the direction of the village. As Jacob and Henry made their way, they came upon cadavers of cows, horses, pigs, sheep, and goats floating on the water. It looked as though all of the livestock in the immediate vicinity had drowned. They also saw bales of straw and planks and beams and items of household furniture, including a children's chair and a fancy easy chair and even a door — chaos that was gradually drifting in the direction of the dike.

Once they got to the area where Koster's farm had stood, they could find no trace of "Rest Haven." The hole in the dike had allowed the water to rush straight toward the farm with an enormous force that pulled the large house right off its foundations, just as though it was supposed to be wiped from the earth. Yet a wedding celebration had been scheduled to take place at "Rest Haven" the very next day. It now appeared that there would be no wedding and that the Canadian would not be returning to Ontario.

When they got close to the village, Jacob Jobse and Henry Melse saw six houses next to one another that had all collapsed. The stream of water entering the village had swept them aside, but the resistance they had offered to the water had broken some of its force. As a result, the houses on the other side of the village were in better shape. Included among them was the parsonage. Henry could see Rev. Zomer with his child on his arm standing in front of a window in one of the upper rooms. Ida and Corinne waved to him from the other window. The first floor of the parsonage was flooded.

Henry rowed with all his might. The tears in his eyes kept him from getting a better look at the people in the distance. But he now knew that Corinne had survived!

When the boat pulled up by the house, there was just a short conversation, for Rev. Zomer refused to go along with them. "We'll just wait here," he said. "The direct danger has passed. We can hold out for a few days. We still have food in the house. It would be a mistake if you didn't first go and rescue the people who are in real need. There are a number of houses around that are about ready to collapse. There are people sitting up on the roofs. Go and rescue them first."

Jacob and Henry had to admit that he was right. They rowed their boat along the older, threatened houses and helped some of the people out of small upstairs windows and into the boat. They passed along a small farm where they got some people out of the trees. A boy of twelve years old had held his cat in his arms all night. He took the cat along in the boat. And so, having picked up fourteen people, they returned to the house on the dike, after prom-

ising others who asked for their help that they would return as quickly as possible.

The victims sat in the boat, completely drained by all the misery they had suffered. No one spoke a word. Theirs was a pain that made people silent. Moreover, they were completely chilled. All they wanted was rest and warmth.

It took some doing to get them lifted out of the tipsy boat. Then they were assigned the best places in the big house. They were given hot milk, which did them a lot of good and loosened their tongues.

Out tumbled a series of disconnected stories that ultimately came down to the same thing: they heard the storm thundering and the alarm being sounded, and when they opened the shutters they saw snow everywhere — or what they thought was snow. Actually, it was the white foam of the rushing water that had already taken possession of their land, their gardens, and their barns while they were asleep.

There were some who reported that they had lost a child or brother or father or wife or husband. In most cases it had happened because someone tried to save livestock or possessions. The power of the storm had been underestimated. Who would have thought that a strong man would not be able to wade through a stream of water one meter in depth? The surprising speed of the rushing water would take a person down and drag him along or get him entangled in barbed wire or smash his head against a pole or a rock — and then it was all over.

After hearing such a story, the women would begin to sob. A mixture of tact and authority would be needed in order to keep people's spirits up.

Jacob and Henry were relieved by a couple of other men who took the boat to go and rescue survivors. A great deal of hard work was done as more and more victims found a place on the dike, where it still appeared safe for the moment.

For the moment . . . They all knew that the water was continuing to eat away at the inner side of the dike. During low tide, the water would move rapidly through the holes in the dike and pull mud and stone and other material back out to sea, and when the tide rose again, the water would come rushing through the holes once more, causing further damage. There was no cessation, no rest. At any moment, new holes could open up in the dike. Even the dike on which the large house stood might begin to break up.

*   *   *

That Sunday did not bring them deliverance. It was not until the afternoon that they saw an airplane flying very low overhead. They waved at the airplane with sheets, and the pilot signaled in return.

But then it was back to waiting. Everywhere there were people still sitting in little rooms on the top floors of their houses, crying out for help.

Jacob and Henry still had not had a chance to go back and pick up Rev. Zomer and his family. And then it began to become dark. Schouwen and Duiveland were again covered by a film of darkness — another chilly, stormy night.

On the surface of the water floated all kinds of wreckage, including furniture and an unbelievable number of cadavers. Toward evening, the men pulled four human bodies from the water, including those of the farmer Koster and his wife.

The cadavers of cows and horses and pigs kept floating over to the edge of the dike. The legs of these animals were stiff and pointed upwards. Their eyes were glassy, and you could see the terror that death had created as the animals' eyes stared straight ahead. Their mouths were hanging open. Many of them came from barns that had held first-class cattle — the pride of their owners.

"What are you looking for now, my child?" David Melse asked Laura, when he saw her walking all by herself in the twilight along the edge of the dike.

"I'm trying to see whether I can find our animals among all the dead bodies," she said. And then she burst into a storm of tears. "I find it so awful, Father!" she sobbed.

"Come, come, my child," he responded. "We still have one another, and Jans and Lies and Bles were saved. Remember that there are quite a few people who lost absolutely everything. Don't cry, my dear child. Let's keep our gaze fixed on what we still have. We can still be thankful — true or not?"

Laura nodded and dried her tears. Soon she was in control of herself again and followed her father inside, where the people were sitting packed together or stretched out.

All that Sunday, Mad Martin had been amazingly still. It was as though he was in a daze after weeks of enormous tension. He sat in his corner, sometimes shaking his big head and sighing. Then he would go to sleep again, with a foolish grin on the turned-down corners of his mouth.

*   *   *

A small light was lit, and a bit of food was dealt out to the people. It looked as though many of the people were about to give thanks for the food individually. Then Jacob spoke up: "Melse, you were an elder when you lived among us on Walcheren. I would say, considering that there is no minister here and it's Sunday today, that you should lead us in some Bible reading and prayer. Then we'll at least have some sense that it has been Sunday — true or not?"

David Melse nodded. As he took a Bible in hand, a petroleum lamp was passed over to him. The people were silent as he paged through the Bible. Finally he said: "At our place it's customary to continue reading where we left off the day before. Yesterday evening I read Psalm 77, and so now it's time for Psalm 78 — providing you people have no objection."

No one said anything. He looked around the circle for a moment and saw nothing but pale and drawn faces. There was no objection to be read in those faces. He then read Psalm 78, which stems from Asaph and begins with a warning: "Give ear, O my people, to my law: incline your ears to the words of my mouth." The psalm continues with the stirring story of God's deeds performed in the midst of the people of Israel, including the deliverance from Egypt and the wonderful leading through the wilderness. But the people did not serve the Lord; they went their own way instead. Even when He had led them into the land of promise, they did not listen to Him but again followed paths of their own choosing. Therefore He punished the people by giving them over to the sword.

It was a long chapter, but David Melse realized that it would be disrespectful to break off at some point before reaching the end. Moreover, how could the psalm be broken in half? David Melse sensed that it was important to keep reading right to the end.

The people were continuing to show great interest. His voice was calm and clear. It looked as though the waters of death surrounding them on this day would make the psalm take on a new significance for them.

Each listener understood the psalm in personal terms. Am *I* the one who was so privileged that I wound up forgetting about the Lord? Am *I* being punished for my sins?

When Melse had read the last words in the psalm and folded his hands in order to pray, the hoarse voice of Mad Martin was suddenly heard from the corner where he sat huddled: "Now the world is not about to perish anymore! You can be sure of it! Now the world is not going to perish anymore . . ."

"You be quiet, Martin!" said Melse. Then he proceeded to lead in prayer, thanking the Lord that they had been spared, thanking Him that He was still willing to concern Himself with sinners and had left them His Word so that they might listen and turn to Him. He asked that those who were still in danger might be saved from the waters. He also asked that all might come to understand that these were the deeds of the Lord — clouds and wind and water are all commanded by Him and go just where He tells them to. Without His will, not a hair can fall from our heads.

These were simple words, and they came straight from David Melse's heart. Many listeners, with tears in their eyes, responded with an "amen."

Jacob listened very intensely. He recognized the David Melse he had known on Walcheren. After the "amen," he nodded to his best friend by way of encouragement and said: "And now I hope that all of you will enjoy your meal."

There was very little food, but at least everyone had something . . .

*   *   *

While they were eating, everyone was silent. The reading from the Bible had made quite an impression on the people — all kinds of them — who were together in the two big rooms. Present were people who never set foot in a church, people who could get along without God in their everyday life, indifferent people who had concentrated their desires for life on their earthly existence. In addition there were people of various different theological persuasions. There were some who were quite willing to criticize the faith convictions of other people and condemn them. But in this hour it was as though a different spirit ruled, now that all had come under the same judgment and were lying in the dust, so to speak, feeling defeated. It seemed that all had been touched by one and the same mighty hand. In this hour, everyone was placed before questions of the first order. They all faced the question: Why? And they all had to ask themselves: What now?

They would have loved to receive an answer from the Bible. For all of these people, without exception, knew that they had been touched by the hand of God. In this hour He had come into the lives of all of them. But they did not all know what God meant by these things and what He had in mind for them in the future. And so there was a deep anxiety in their hearts, now that their ordinary, everyday existence had been cut off and they beheld the ruins of their former life all around them.

They all knew very well that in this hour God had intervened in their lives — the same God who had given them the Bible so that they could learn His will. They all knew that there were connections to be made, but they did not know what those connections were. The uncertainty which this hour had brought into their life made them quiet and shy in the presence of others.

There was no opportunity for a normal night's rest. The few beds that were available had been placed at the disposal of the people who were sickest; the weak ones and the old people and the very small children were also looked after. As for the others, they just stretched out on the floor in all the rooms. After all the misery they had suffered for half the night and a very long day, they reacted to the tension they now endured by falling into a short but deep sleep.

Even now, the storm winds continued to put a strain on the windows as they howled over the roof and kept whipping up the water on the Scheldt. Yet the storm had subsided somewhat since Sunday morning.

*   *   *

Again Jacob did not have a good night. He kept worrying about his children. Joan asked him a few times what he thought of it all. Would the flood emergency have struck Beveland too? He tried to reassure her on this score. Her pale face and the tears in her eyes told him enough, even though she said nothing more about the subject.

But it was during this very same night that he once again found his old faith and confidence. He thought back to the night he had spent on the top floor of his little dwelling on Walcheren when he was also in a time of great need. During that fearful night he had been able to sing psalms with his wife. Wasn't the same God still there for him? Jacob chastised himself for worrying so much, and then he found his rest again. Finally he slept soundly and deeply, to the point that Joan was amazed at him.

*   *   *

When Monday morning brought a new day, the people stood on the dike and looked out over the polder. The water had returned to roughly its normal level, but there was nowhere a dry place to be seen. All of Schouwen and Duiveland was under water.

There were small boats making their way across the dike-encircled lake. The work of rescue had begun. There were planes circling above the villages. Over the dike, just above their heads, small airplanes whizzed by. They dropped parachutes with packages of food which seemed to land in just the right place. Through these actions, the people in their isolation found that their spirits were lifted. They now knew they were no longer on their own — deliverance was at hand!

David Melse said to Henry: "Shouldn't we now make an effort to get over to our farm? Perhaps we can find Uncle Joris, and we'll also have to find a way to take Grandfather away from there. The water is low now."

Henry nodded. During the night he had already been thinking along such lines. The day before, there had been no thought of being able to get to the house. The water was almost up to the roof, and there were strong currents.

They were not sure whether they should walk along the dike or go over in a boat. They decided to wait until the water was at its lowest and then try walking along the dike. Perhaps they could get all the way on foot.

But Jacob had also given the matter some thought. He said: "I'll hammer together a small raft from all the driftwood that has washed up here. Then we can get Bles to pull it over to the dike right by the farm. If the water gets too high, the raft can float."

"It's a good thing to have a carpenter at your disposal," said David Melse with a smile on his face.

It was a bit of a trick to get the boards and planks and beams that had washed up by the dike to fit together in the form of a raft. But it was accomplished, and Bles was harnessed to the raft. It turned out not to be all that difficult for him to start dragging the raft in the direction of the farm. The water had indeed sunk a long way.

When they finally stood before the farm, they saw that they would need the raft in order to get further. The house stood in at least a meter of water.

"We should first see if we can find Uncle Joris," said Melse. Using poles, they directed the raft here and there over the farmyard and along the walls of the farm buildings. Then Henry pointed to a section of barbed wire that separated the farmyard from the pasture. There they saw Uncle Joris entangled in the barbed wire by his clothes. It did not prove difficult to get him free and lay him down on the raft.

David Melse wiped Uncle Joris's face clean with his handkerchief and then looked him over carefully. Uncle Joris seemed unchanged, at peace, and in a deep sleep. His hands, which had been made crooked through rheumatism, were now normal and straight. They lay open in a posture of complete surrender, just as a small boy stretches out his hands eagerly to his father when he sees him approaching.

David Melse was deeply moved and said: "It went well with Uncle Joris at the end, just as with Grandfather. It's a good thing he did not survive all this misery. He has now found bliss."

The men maneuvered the raft over to the door of the house. "You stay here by the raft, Melse," said Jacob. "Henry and I will take our pants off and go through the house in our underwear. If we can, we'll bring Grandfather out."

Melse nodded in agreement, and so they proceeded. The ice-cold water made their legs very stiff and sent a shiver up their bodies. They found themselves walking into slime that got right between their toes. It was hard for them to stay on their feet. Driven by the cold, they hurried to get up the stairs to the second floor so that they would no longer have to stand in water.

Everything was wet; everything was covered with mud. Cupboards and chairs and tables drifted around. They walked up the slippery stairs and arrived at the upper rooms, which had also stood under water. They realized that if they had gone to those upper rooms instead of taking refuge on the dike, they would eventually have been forced to go up on the roof. Many other people had figured that they would be safe on the second floor and that the water would not go any higher than it had gone in 1944, when the Germans allowed the island to be inundated.

They found Grandfather in bed. Everything was wet, but he was still lying just as peacefully as when they had looked in on him for the last time on Saturday evening. They picked him up and carried him down the steps to the raft. They did not find him a heavy burden, and their mission was soon accomplished. He was placed next to his brother.

For David Melse it was almost too much when he saw his own father lying there dead.

"I'm going to go and look in the barn for a moment," said Henry.

Melse nodded but said nothing. Then he asked: "Shall I go with you?"

Henry shook his head. "Don't do that, for the water is ice-cold, and you'll wind up getting rheumatism. It's so cold you can feel it in the marrow of your bones. I'll just go alone."

Jacob jumped off the raft and went with Henry to the barn. There they found four milk cows lying with swollen bodies, their tongues hanging out of their mouths and their eyes protruding. Some of the planks in the wall of the barn had been torn away, and the water, full of brown scum, washed through the barn.

"If this place isn't dried out soon, the old barn won't hold out," said Henry.

Jacob looked around the barn and shrugged his shoulders. "The beams and joists are intact," he said. "As long as there's no new flood in here, this place can still stand quite a bit."

Again they waded outside. They didn't bother going into the shed where the pigs were kept. They figured it would be just as awful in there. There was no living creature to be seen anymore. The chickens had also drowned and had presumably been swept away with the flood.

"In Java I saw some horrible things," said Henry, "but when it's your own place, it's an even worse sight." He was speaking from the depths of his heart. He wondered how in the world his life could ever return to normal.

A couple of gasoline containers, cut in half, had been attached to the raft to make it float. And so the raft sat fairly high in the water. When they climbed back up onto it, they were out of the water.

They no longer had any feeling in their legs. Jacob thought back to his days on Walcheren during the war, when he had experienced the same sensation. The biting cold of the water was familiar to him.

Using poles they moved the raft back over toward the dike. Then they laid the two dead brothers next to each other on top of the dike, right against the inner concrete wall.

"And what do we do now?" asked Jacob.

David Melse had already thought it through. "High tide will be here in a while," he said. "Then you should come over here with a boat and take Grandfather and Uncle Joris away. I'll stay here with them until then."

"All by yourself, Father?"

"Yes, all by myself."

"But it may take a while."

"I know that, but I'll stay here and wait anyway. You get going now and tell Mother what the situation is over here."

Henry and Jacob Jobse looked at each other. But finally they both concluded that there was no other way. And so Bles was hitched to the raft again, after the gasoline containers were first set on top of it.

Melse leaned against the concrete wall. Grandfather and Uncle Joris were right next to him. And he had a direct view of the farm. He could see that it was covered by muddy water. In the barn were the dead cows. He knew that the land was being poisoned by the salt water, and that the furniture of which mother Beth had been so proud was getting ruined because it kept smashing up against the ceiling.

He was completely alone and lonesome as he stood there. Never in his life had he felt so forsaken as in this hour.

There was still a harsh, bitter wind blowing from the ice-cold northwest. He let himself sink to the ground at the bottom of the wall and leaned with his back against the concrete, so that he still had some protection. And he kept staring at the farm in front of him at the foot of the dike. The water was already beginning to rise.

How quickly it rose! He had seen the same sort of thing on Walcheren, when his farm there came under water. But there the water did not rise as high — it did not go much above the threshold. You saw the little waves scurrying along as the tide came in. And that's how it was here.

At first the water was only up to the lowest rail of the fence. Now that rail was completely under water, and the water played the very same game as it did on a beach where children had fun with their pails and shovels as they built forts and then let the water gradually cover them. In just the same way, the water covered the farm. As the little waves kept rolling over one another, they had an easy time taking possession of everything standing in their way.

David Melse kept watching the scene. The water was now up to the window frames. Of course it was just as high inside the rooms as it was outside. And in the barn and the other buildings, it was also rising. The cows would rise with the water and be pulled through the barn.

More and more waves came along and climbed higher and higher. It was not long before the top rail of the fence was also under water.

The water came from the Scheldt behind him. The Scheldt got it from the North Sea, which was an inexhaustible source, and then pushed it through an opening in the dike, an opening that became ever broader and deeper.

The tide came in . . . In time the tide would go out, but then it would come back in again, and then it would go back out . . .

Once in every twelve hours the house would be almost completely dry. One would almost feel the impulse to begin cleaning up. But within a few hours there would be water everywhere again. In their endless advance, the waves would cover everything they could reach. Melse knew all too well how it went. The water would bring in a lot of slime along with a new supply of salt, which would remain behind and penetrate the earth and eat into it like a cancer.

Over there was a corner of the farm on which he had decided to grow wheat this year. He had figured it all out already. In another spot he was going to grow sugar beets, and he also had a corner in mind for barley. Right behind the house he was planning to grow potatoes. In his thoughts he could already see the fields and the play of colors within them.

And now he admitted to himself that nothing would come of it. Even if the whole business could be dried out that very week, the salt already in the ground would have had its devastating effect, and so all his plans would come to nothing. He remembered that the water in the Eastern Scheldt is different than the water in the Western Scheldt. Emptying into the Western Scheldt is a river from Belgium that brings fresh water to the sea. But in the Eastern Scheldt the sea water would have penetrated as far as Bergen op Zoom. There was nowhere else for it to go. And so the salt content is much higher in the Eastern Scheldt.

There he sat and looked at the two old men overtaken by the sleep of death. Uncle Joris's hands were open in complete surrender, while Grandfather's hands were folded in a posture of constant prayer. How the sight moved him in this hour: he was stirred to the very depths of his being.

These two men were blood of his blood. Had they not gone through the same kind of anxiety and struggle in life that he now had to wrestle with? Perhaps it had been even more difficult for them. Who was to say? Who knew what Uncle Joris, with his twisted body, had dealt with in his life? And then he remembered how much Grandfather used to wonder and doubt. But somehow they had triumphed in the end. No, they were even more than conquerors.

Words from Psalm 42 came into David Melse's mind: "Why art thou cast down, O my soul? and why art thou disquieted within me? hope thou in God: for I shall yet praise him, who is the health of my countenance, and my God."

Yes, it was indeed a beautiful psalm. But then, Job did not sing such a psalm when he sat on the dung heap, surrounded by the ruins of what had once been a happy life. And so David Melse thought about Job. He reflected that in this hour he looked somewhat like Job. Here he sat next to two dead bodies, facing a farm that was sinking away in the mud, facing a barn in which dead cows were floating in the water, facing land that was poisoned by salt. And there was no prospect of a harvest in the coming summer.

In this hour temptation came at him again — the same old temptation. It seemed that God had utterly forsaken him. All that he formerly believed turned out to be self-deception. He told himself that he was one of those whom God had rejected. He had been thrown on a pile with the godless and sinners — people who did not bother about God and His commandments. He asked himself: How can you, sitting on the ruins of your life, continue to believe that you are a child of God? Just the evening before you read a psalm aloud and you prayed before others. The people should know what's really going on inside of you now. How do you dare take God's name on your lips in public?

David Melse remained just where he was, seated with his back against the concrete wall. All through his body he trembled at the prospect of the continuing cold. If only he had some tobacco and a pipe! But even that small comfort had been taken away. His pipe was out there somewhere in the salt water. It was probably floating around in one of the rooms.

Again he was struck by how rapidly the water rises when the tide comes in. There was nothing more to be seen of the fence. The windows were more than half covered by water. It looked as though the farm was sinking away into the depths. After a while, when the tide went out again, everything would come back into view, if only for a while. And then the water would begin to rise once more. There was no way to stop the process, and there was nothing to be done. It looked more like a game the devil was playing than something brought about by the hand of God.

He reached into his pocket for his watch and discovered that it was gone too. He remembered that on Saturday evening he had taken it out of his work clothes. The watch was also ruined.

If mother Beth ever managed to enter her house again, she would have the same sort of experience. One day she would reach for this and the other day for that, only to find that the thing she was looking for was no longer there. There were hundreds of things that you would really miss, once you needed them.

"And in all of this Job did not sin . . ." It was almost as though a voice outside of himself was calling out to him, rather than the voice coming up from within his thoughts.

"But I *am* sinning," said Melse, almost aloud. He wanted to cry out to God and say: "This hour is *so difficult* . . . If only I could have the assurance that I am — and will remain — Thy child . . ."

Then he thought again of Bart de Vaat, who also doubted whether he was a child of God, but for a different reason — because it all went so well with him in the world. What had become of Bart de Vaat? Was he still alive? Had he also lost everything? Did he still have his wife and children? And if God had now chastised him, would he be satisfied and say: "Now, at least, I know that I am Thy child"?

Sometimes strange thoughts fly through a person's mind. What was it that Rev. Zomer had said? "Never go by the facts alone — they will leave the truth concealed. Live by the Word."

Live by the Word? Also in this hour? What did the Word have to say in this hour?

David Melse did not know where to turn. He did not know anymore what he should think. All he seemed to experience was the hot breath and anger of God. And then he began to ponder Rev. Verhulst's sermons about God's judgments and His hand of chastisement. What would Rev. Verhulst say about this hour? Wouldn't he say that God had a dispute with His people?

And what about Rev. Zomer? What would he say about this hour? He would probably profess that he didn't have the answer. He would say: "Facts in themselves do not provide us with the light of revelation. Only the Word gives us revelation, gives us what God says."

Also in this hour? Now that everything is destroyed and there is nothing that can be saved? Do the facts now tell us nothing apart from the Word that is supposed to shed light on the facts and explain them?

David Melse did not know where to turn with his thoughts. He looked at the two dead men, who were lying there peacefully beneath an open sky as a testimony of God's grace. They had transcended all hardship and struggle. Still, David Melse remembered how they had doubted and wrestled with things throughout their lives!

Again he shivered. He was still wearing wet clothes, the same clothes he had worn when he fled through the water at two o'clock on Sunday morning. The cold was making him feel stiff. He stood up.

How quickly the water rose! Wave after wave came rolling along. It was just as it had been with the Germans during the war. First came the storm troopers, who quickly conquered everything, and then came masses of soldiers who poured across all of Zeeland and proceeded to rule as if everything belonged to them. That was just how the waves went about it. They proceeded to take possession of the land like a hungry animal throwing itself on whatever it finds in its path.

Melse stood up with his hands in his pockets. His thick clothes had been soaked and were very slow to dry, and so his pockets were also wet. He peered across the brown-green water, with the frothy waves always moving over the land. And what did those waves bring into view? Furniture, doors, bits of a ceiling, beams, dead cattle, straw. He could see that his own hay-rack was also adrift.

Suddenly, on a bale of straw, he saw a cat. It was Morris, his own cat, clinging to the bale. Gradually the bale drifted closer. And then he saw a dark living thing nestled up against the cat. It was a big black rat which pressed up against the cat's body in order to save its own life. Morris did not seem to mind. Morris, that big, fierce hunter of rats, sat peacefully with the rat on a bale of straw as if the two had signed a peace treaty.

For a moment Melse's thoughts were diverted by this sight. So it is also among people, he thought. Yesterday he had read aloud from the Bible and prayed with people who otherwise would not pay any attention to him on a Sunday because they belonged to another church. Also on hand for the occasion were indifferent people who never showed up in any church, along with some people who thought they were special and looked down on others for their church-going. They had all listened hungrily because they wanted to hear from the Bible what God had to say in this hour.

In this hour oppositions were reconciled, not only among people but even among animals. It could go the same way with the entire population of the Netherlands. In this hour a unity could be born in which opponents — even people who could not stand each other — would extend a hand to one another and help each other in a spirit of fellowship.

The bale of straw came closer and closer. By this point Morris recognized his owner, for when David Melse called out to him, Morris proceeded to meow in a doleful way. Meanwhile, the rat pressed itself stiffly against the cat's body, apparently trying to keep warm. It was an amazing sight. Morris did not react to the rat. The white foam of the water passed over the bale of straw once more, and Morris shook his head.

Finally the bale came right up against the side of the dike. With one good jump Morris was on the dike and immediately began to rub his head against Melse's leg. The rat was on the dike too and quickly began to look for a place to go. But the cat turned his head and saw that the rat was running away. In three energetic jumps, Morris was right on top of the rat and sunk his teeth into its neck. There lay the rat on its back, dying. Morris returned to his owner.

At that moment an inner aversion to the cat sprang up in the farmer's heart. He could have kicked the cat. But then he thought to himself that this was simply instinct — the cat knew no better. He was simply doing what he was designed to do. Again the cat rubbed his head against Melse's leg and meowed in doleful way.

That's just how things go, thought Melse to himself, and that's also how it will be with us as human beings. This hour is sure to pass. There will come a time when we each go back to our own little church again. And then we will remember our little quarrels, and the wrath of God will have to come again . . .

Together on a single bale of straw — that sort of thing can only happen when the waters of death are all around us.

Again the water was very, very high . . . Nothing more could be seen of the fence rails — only the tops of some of the hedges were now visible. The fruit trees stuck up their naked branches as though crying out for deliverance from the water. Stuck in the branches were many bits of hay and straw that remained hanging there even when the water subsided. The hay and straw served as an indication of how high the water in its unchecked power could rise.

The water came splashing against the walls of the houses, as though they were simply made of clay. How long would Melse's own house withstand such pressure? Melse shook his head. He realized that this hour was much worse than anything he had experienced on Walcheren during the war. In this hour it was as though God was making a joke of his entire life.

Next to him lay the two dead men, and he was called to keep watch by them. If it were not for this duty, he would flee from this place, which looked to him ever more threatening and grim. He knew that this hour would remain burned into his soul. He would look upon it as God settling accounts with him. And in his doubt he mumbled: "Rev. Verhulst, could it be that you were right after all? Was my son on the wrong path when he died?" Could it be that his son had undertaken to resist the wrath of God?

He covered his eyes with his hand. The chill that ran through his legs and arms again prompted him to pace back and forth for a while. He walked along the dike to the point where there came a bend. And then, in the distance, he spotted a boat approaching. It was not the rowboat that Henry and Jacob had used but a motorboat, and it was moving at quite a speed. He could see that Henry was on board and was waving to him.

The boat raced across the foaming water and headed right for the spot where the two dead bodies were resting. Uncle Joris and Grandfather were taken on board. Melse picked up the cat and stepped into the boat. Then the boat set off again, but it did not head back to the sluices. Instead it went right across the polder to an inner dike, where some evacuees had assembled, waiting to be transported further. On this inner dike David Melse saw Rev. Zomer and his family.

He learned that there had been some contact with the world outside. Jacob Jobse had already heard that the Katse Dike protecting South Beveland had held and that his children had nothing to worry about as far as water was concerned. That was an enormous relief to him.

Jacob said to Joan: "Now it's my duty to stay here for a while yet, because there's work to be done." Joan nodded graciously. She knew that her husband was not a man to walk away when there was work to do.

*   *   *

With each low tide, the water level got closer to normal. Eventually the main part of the village began to dry up, making it possible for people to use ordinary transportation for part of the day to move the bodies that were still turning up. The victims of the flood now tried to save as much as they could in the way of their possessions.

Jacob and Henry worked their way down the main street of the village on a barge. On one side of the street, where the central thrust of the flood had broken through, stood the smith's house and also the house occupied by the Van Dykes, the parents of Mad Martin. The smith's wife and children had survived; they had managed to flee to the neighbors on the other side of the street.

But when the flood waters began to rise, the smith thought he still had time to get his car running; he thought he could use it to take his family out of the village. When the water broke through, it pulled the car right off the road and deposited it in the ditch. And that's where the smith was found, behind the steering wheel, with the door shut tightly. He would not be selling any more farm implements. His supply of expensive farm equipment now stood in his shed and around his workplace, drenched by salt water and rendered filthy by the briny mud.

When Henry and Jacob went by the grocery store owned by the Van Dykes, they saw that the police were busy taking out the two bodies. The police had found a supply of money in the house — some seventy thousand guilders. Even while she was fighting for her life, Mrs. Van Dyke clung to the money chest: she had her arms wrapped tightly around it.

The little store in which all that money had been earned no longer existed. The raging flood had swept right across the property, taking all the merchandise with it. There were still a couple of walls left, lending partial support to the small building. The roof slanted dangerously: let the high tide come in once or twice more, and it would surely collapse.

Among the dead found in the village were Koster's children, including the Canadian, the son who had emigrated to Canada so that he would be safe if the Russians ever overran western Europe.

*   *   *

In a small village in the northern polder of the island, where it was still dry, Jacob Jobse went to a carpenter shop to help make coffins. They were needed first of all for Uncle Joris and Grandfather, but also for people who had come to the island to join in the wedding festivities at the Koster farm. Large coffins were required for full-sized adults, but some small, narrow ones were needed as well, and even some tiny ones for children who did not yet know their right hand from their left.

Jacob shook his head as he went about this sad work. He paid no attention to the sweat on his brow as he thought about his own

children, who had been spared, and also about Joan, whom he had been permitted to keep.

The carpenter kept bringing more wood from his supply, and soon he was wondering whether he would have enough. There were more and more people coming to him with orders, and he knew there were many corpses waiting for burial, lying on the hard blue slabs of stone in the big church . . .

*   *   *

There was a great deal of work to be done on the inner dike. Because of the flood, the subsidiary dike had become the main dike protecting the island. Every time there was high tide, the sea water came at the soft slope, carrying all kinds of driftwood with it, such as crates, planks, parts of a roof, and even heavy beams that had come from some barn or other. Much of this wood wound up digging into the soft slope of the dike and making holes in it.

This floating refuse needed to be cleaned up if the dike was not to be eaten away. Bags of sand would have to be set in place to repair the weak spots and fill in the holes. Therefore a great many able-bodied men came to the inner dike to join in the work, for that dike was now the main barrier protecting the people from the sea.

Day and night they were hard at it, those young fellows. There was no time to eat or sleep, for there was important work to be done!

Chapter 14

It was only gradually that people came to realize that the disaster of February 1 was a national catastrophe. Not only had a large hole been made in the Schelphoek on West Schouwen, with the result that almost the entire island was flooded, but Duiveland, with its many smaller polders, had no less to endure. On Duiveland the number of victims was much greater than on Schouwen: in the large polder on Schouwen, the water was not able to rise very quickly, and so the people had a chance to flee. But in the small polders on Duiveland the people were overtaken before they could react. The water approached like a high wall: in no time at all it flooded the little polders. The people had no chance to save themselves. There were small villages with hundreds of victims. It was the same situation on Flakee, in the Hoeksewaard, on South Beveland by Kruiningen, by Wolfaartsdijk, and in many other places as well.

Every news report was laden with the most somber communications, including totals of human beings and animals that had perished. The animals were quite a problem too. A special commission was charged with the responsibility of gathering up the cadavers quickly in order to prevent infection. There were piles of dead cows and horses and pigs and sheep and goats lying alongside the dike.

$$* \qquad * \qquad *$$

Bart de Vaat was also involved in the cleanup. One day he was working by the dike when, unexpectedly, he found David Melse standing before him. It was their first encounter since the flood. They shook hands and looked into one another's eyes. "And how are you doing?" asked Melse.

Bart de Vaat shrugged his shoulders and turned the question around. Melse then told his sad story.

Bart de Vaat responded: "As for me, I can do nothing but give thanks. My farm is on fairly high ground, as you know. With the help of my sons, I managed to get most of my furniture up to the second floor, and so it's safe. I also succeeded in rescuing quite a few of my cows by moving them to higher ground. By this point my place is fairly dry. So I didn't come out of it too badly."

Then the two farmers looked one another in the eye. They were both thinking of their encounter on the outer dike in the deep of the night. Melse shrugged his shoulders and said: "I guess I'd have to say that you're fortunate to have come off so well. You have much to be thankful for, my friend."

"And I certainly am thankful. Only, I ask myself what I have done to deserve this."

Also in this hour, the facts had not provided him with any light of revelation. The great question mark in his life remained.

*   *   *

Rev. Zomer managed to get hold of a pair of coveralls so that he could join in the work. The people chuckled when they observed that he was not very handy with a shovel. He did his best to fill the bags with earth; by watching other people, he soon figured out how best to do it. Even though his hands were covered with blisters, he was not about to give up.

In the course of the week more help arrived, including some soldiers from Brabant. Among them were some big fellows who looked like trees and could each do the work of two men. They came from various different regiments, and they immediately understood that it was not a time to complain about a difficult assignment.

They respected the minister in the blue coveralls who worked very intently, even as the tip of his tongue kept circulating around his lips. They saw that he was a fellow who could talk but also know how to remain silent when it was time for deeds to speak.

And then there was a new phenomenon to be noted in the village — the preacher with the three-cornered hat and the pants that looked like they belonged in a museum. His face was more drawn and earnest than ever. The previous evening he had preached in the village for a small group of people. He talked about the

French soldiers helping to restore the dyke

judgments of God over the people of Zeeland and drew attention to the message that God was sending by way of this catastrophe. According to him, the overwhelming flood and its aftermath contained books full of revelation light. Somehow he managed to shake from his sleeve what God meant to say through all the things that had happened.

And now he stood there with his hands behind his back, watching the work going on. With his pale, earnest face he stared at the soldiers and waited for the right moment to address the hard-working men and shed some revelation light, light that had now been strengthened by this catastrophe. But he got no such opportunity.

A sturdy Brabant soldier looked up for a moment and examined the strangely dressed figure standing before him. He stuck his shovel in the ground and wiped the sweat from his face. Without taking his eyes off the strange phenomenon for even a moment, he proceeded to roll a cigarette. Just when the minister with the three-cornered hat wanted to put up his finger to indicate that he meant to speak some words of admonition, the soldier spoke up loudly, making sure his companions could hear. He asked: "Who in the world are you? Which regiment do you belong to?"

At once a wave of laughter rippled through the men working on the dike. The minister turned red and shook his head. He understood that this was no place for him to cast his pearls before swine. He turned his back on the scoffer and disappeared.

The soldiers did not follow him for long with their eyes. The dike needed to be strengthened!

American soldiers helping to restore the dyke

Rev. Zomer was standing among the soldiers. They knew that he was a minister too, but — minister or no minister — they saw that he knew what a shovel is for. And that was precise why he did get opportunity to carry out his work as a minister in the midst of these soldiers, even as they all sweated and panted to strengthen the dike.

Eventually one of the Brabant soldiers found it too much to have to look at all the drowned animals with their tongues hanging out of their mouths. He said: "Seeing that you're a minister, maybe you could tell me why the dear Lord, if He wants to give us human beings a good one on the head, also makes all those dumb animals suffer a martyr's death."

Rev. Zomer responded by giving him a short account of the story recorded in the Book of Jonah — how God spared Nineveh partly because there were so many cattle in that great city. God loves His creation, including the animals. And if He allows a great many animals to suffer and die in the Netherlands, it must be causing Him great pain. Since it is plain that He *did* allow all those animals that are not possessed of reason to drown in the flood, it must be because He wants to force people to listen to what He says in the Bible.

That evening in the barn, when Rev. Zomer could talk with the exhausted young men in a more relaxed way about the message of the Bible, he encountered Van Driel, the man who had spoken to him so enthusiastically not all that long before the flood about the silver wedding anniversary he was hoping to celebrate in 1954. Van Driel was the man who was so happy with his wonderful wife. He had told Rev. Zomer that between the two of them they had built up a little farm. But now it appeared that his wife had drowned. Still, her body had not been found.

Rev. Zomer found himself facing a man bowed down by the greatest sorrow. "Van Driel, how are you doing?" he asked.

Van Driel nodded but said nothing. He swallowed, and then he swallowed again. With his shirt sleeve he tried to wipe the tears from his eyes. But still he said nothing.

Rev. Zomer then asked: "Van Driel, did you listen to what I was telling the soldiers just now?"

The man nodded, and again he wiped his face with his shirt sleeve. His Adam's apple went up and down rapidly, and he was blinking, as if to hold back more tears.

Rev. Zomer understood that if Van Driel began to talk, there would be no holding back the tears. But why should that be such a bad thing? Why should a man be ashamed to cry? Is it necessary to always appear strong and in control?

"Van Driel, don't be ashamed of your tears, man. The Bible tells us that Jesus also wept when He stood by the tomb."

Then Van Driel finally broke free and began to sob. He kept trying to wipe the tears from his eyes with his sleeve. Rev. Zomer simply stood there, saying nothing. He thought back to the joy with which this man had told him about his wife, the wonderful wife who had joined him in building up a life together, so that he went from being a hired hand to being the owner of a small farm on which she joined him in working hard day and night and saving money — in everything being one with him. Rev. Zomer could still hear Van Driel's words: "I have such a wonderful wife in her, Reverend!"

Finally Rev. Zomer said to the sobbing man: "I have no words of comfort for you, Van Driel. But this Bible" — at that point he laid his hand on the small Bible he carried with him — "has the comfort you need. Through His Word God is also speaking to you, especially in these sad circumstances. If your life is right before God, Van Driel, you'll get the comfort you need. Read His Word. All I can do is promise to pray for you."

Van Driel then walked with Rev. Zomer into the dark night. It was blustery and cold. The wind was blowing off fields that were still flooded. In the light shed by some storm lanterns, which looked like glow-worms in the distance, the two men saw that a number of dike workers were still busy strengthening the inner dike.

"I thank you, Reverend, for what you said to me just now," said Van Driel. Then he shook Rev. Zomer's hand and went off by himself.

"But what did I really say to him?" Rev. Zomer asked himself in amazement. "There wasn't really anything I could say."

*   *   *

Before setting out for his evacuation address that evening, Rev. Zomer climbed up on the dike once more. He trembled when he felt the cold wind blowing in his face. The water kept washing up against the weak slope of the dike. He saw light patches set off against the grass. The white places were bags of sand that had been brought in to strengthen the dike. But it was hardly a permanent solution: the water kept lapping up against the sand, and the sand would stream out of the sacks and be carried away. It all seemed to come to nothing — the work that we as human beings do. When God allowed His breath to strike the earth, what can *we* do about it?

It was dark over the water. The sky was black with threatening clouds. In the water lay villages, farms, churches, mills, and barns containing dead cows.

"And also much cattle . . ." If God was willing to spare Nineveh, partly on account of its cattle, how pressing must His message now be, considering that He had allowed this catastrophe to strike Christian Zeeland. Would the Netherlands understand the message? Would she listen? "O Lord, grant that they will listen to Thy Word!" prayed Rev. Zomer. He shivered again and then went down the dike. He followed the road that led to the house where he and his family had found temporary lodgings.

*　　*　　*

A few days later the body of Mrs. Van Driel turned up. She had drowned during that very first night when she fled outside. She was right by the house located on the farm she had built up together with her husband.

At her grave, too, Rev. Zomer recited the Apostles' Creed, the confession of the church of all ages, in which we find these words: "I believe in the resurrection of the body and the life everlasting."

In a field of grass close to the inner dike were the graves of over a hundred people who had drowned. Each grave was marked by a black cross with the date of birth and the name of the person buried there. But there were also graves bearing the inscription "Unknown Man" or "Unknown Woman." And then there were some very small graves. The rows of graves kept growing . . .

*　　*　　*

Jacob Jobse helped make many coffins. He shook his head from time to time as he thought about his own wife and children. And then he would sigh: "Lord God, who and what am I, that this should *not* strike me? I'm no better than the rest of them . . ."

He said goodbye to David Melse and his family. With tears in her eyes, mother Beth thanked him for all that he had done. Jacob looked at her with eyes full of amazement, not knowing what it was that they should thank him for.

Joan was just as pale as ever. But her gentle smile was still on her face. "There's one thing that really amazes me," said Jacob. "If Joan should suddenly be pulled from her warm bed during the night and go outside in the winter cold in just her night clothes, you can be sure that she would have a lung infection the next day. And now? She was out during that cold winter's night wearing only her nightclothes, crawling along the dike on her hands and knees for an hour and a half, with waves of ice-cold water washing over her, and then for almost three days she walked around in those same wet clothes — and look at her now! She's still the same old Joan. She doesn't even have a cold! If that's not God's special protective care, then I don't know what is! Oh boy!"

With tears of gratitude in his eyes he departed, taking Joan with him, after assuring the Melses that if worst came to worst, there would always be a small place for them to stay on South Beveland.

A small rowboat took Jacob and Joan across the flooded polder to the outer dike, where a fishing boat that had come from Yerseke was waiting to take evacuees away. Joan kept waving with her white handkerchief until there was just a small dot to be seen. This sight reminded mother Beth of Jacob's story about Joan's white cap which he kept watching while he was on his sickbed and she walked all the way to Wolfaartsdijk to get that healing water. "And he's still the same Jacob," she said . . .

*   *   *

And now it was spring. Low and high tide continued to succeed one another. There were some sarcastic people who held an anniversary celebration when the flood poured over the polder for the 250th time.

It was May . . . The fruit trees in the water were now in full bloom. The sun shone down upon them, and the water was so beautifully still. The sight was like that of a young girl on her deathbed when her blossoming young life is suddenly cut off. The blossoming trees seemed to signal rich promises: the reflection of the snow-white blossoms could be seen in the calm water. But David Melse was aware that they were promises that would *never* be fulfilled.

He was standing with Bart de Vaat on the outer dike. The two men were looking at all this beauty that made them both shudder. They knew that once the time of blossoming was over, the branches would die off and no fruit would ever appear on those trees.

Meanwhile, on the other side of the inner dike, which was the area that had been spared during the flood, the farmers were out working on their land. The fields were being plowed and planted. Blossoms were appearing on the fruit trees, even though the land in the polder was completely surrounded by the sea. It was just one dike that had made the difference between life and death.

The two farmers stood on about the same spot where they had talked deep in that night of despair, when they had encountered one another walking on the dike. Bart de Vaat said: "I have come to understand the 'nevertheless' of faith. The Bible talks about possessing things as though you do not possess them. Sometimes the things in the Bible sound like riddles, but in His own time God enables us to understand these things."

Together they walked further. Then David Melse stopped again. "And this is the place where Uncle Joris and my father were laid out on the grass when we went back to claim their bodies."

"They came to a good end," said Bart de Vaat.

Melse thought about the Uncle Joris's crooked hands, which had straightened out in death. And then he thought about all the doubting his father had done. "What God does comes only to a good end," he said, as he looked over his farm covered with seawater.

"I agree with you completely. It all comes down to whether you have faith."

The two farmers had both found the faith that conquers all. Through struggle and doubt they had somehow gotten past the bitterest hour of their life. The jubilation of victory was theirs.

*   *   *

And now it was summer . . . Low tide and high tide continued to succeed one another. The sarcastic people could celebrate anniversary after anniversary, because the salt continued to eat away at the earth.

The fruit trees were now completely spoiled. It was the middle of the summer, but to look at them you would think it was winter. Their dead branches were completely bare. They seemed to be sticking up above the salt water in order to beg for help.

Chapter 15

A tug-boat passed through a hole in one of the dikes as it headed for the Scheldt. It was the *Holland,* a small, spirited, powerful boat belonging to the Van Buren brothers, who were entrepreneurs from Werkendam.

The captain of the boat had a boil on his neck and could only turn his head with great difficulty. When he wanted to say something to his guests standing next to him by the wheel, he had to turn his entire body toward them.

His guests were Henry and Corinne. They had been invited to travel by boat to the big hole in the dike that protected Schouwen. They were going to have an opportunity to see the work that was going on at "Life Struggle," which was near the Zierikzee harbor. They wanted to see something of the restoration project that was now underway in a grand effort to get Schouwen and Duiveland back on their feet. And so they were traveling to the notorious Schelphoek, the great hole in the dike, around which an emergency dike of some four kilometers in length would first have to be built.

The boat passed right through the deep channel which the streaming water had dug out in the polder. Two of the Van Buren brothers were on board. They were sturdy, energetic fellows, but their colleagues and the other engineers surveying the situation on Schouwen and Duiveland called them "the Patriarchs," because they were faithful church-goers, people who still believed in God and went to church each Sunday.

Apparently such faithfulness was unusual in the ranks of the men working to repair the dikes. But the "Patriarchs" were not ashamed of their exceptional position in this regard. They attended the services led by Rev. Zomer in his temporary quarters. They joined in the prayers when God's blessing was asked over the work being done to restore the dikes. They knew they were utterly dependent on that blessing, for without it their labors to restrain the water would never be crowned with success.

The *Holland* steamed ahead in an almost passionate race to the huge hole in the main dike, where the water had dug out a channel some thirty-five meters deep and where there was a waterfall to be seen with every change of high and low tide. The houses then disappeared from sight in the stream of water, and the land came to be covered with mud. As a result, no farmer would later be able to find the markers that defined the borders of his property.

Later . . . And just when would that be? By this time it was summer, but the water still covered the polder, just as it did on the first day of February. High and low tide continued to succeed one another. But at least hard work was being done on the foundations of reconstruction!

Specialized workers were busy preparing the mattresses made of osier twigs. Those mattresses were half a meter thick. When the tide was out, they would be dragged over to the dike where they were needed and carefully covered with blocks of basalt which had been brought in from outside the country. Then the combination would be carefully sunk into place. In this way a proper foundation was set in place in the seabed. Each such unit had to be situated in exactly the right spot — it was a matter to be figured out right down to the centimeter.

This was exactly how our fathers prepared the foundations for the dikes four hundred years ago, using rather primitive tools — no dredging machines or draglines or tug-boats. Nevertheless, they managed to pull Holland out of the water. Anyone today who proposes to wrest Holland and Zeeland anew from the stranglehold of the water-wolf will need to take lessons from our fathers who lived centuries ago.

Even today, there is no other or better method that has been found. If one were to throw sand into the depths, the alternation of high and low tide would quickly carry it away. If one were simply to throw in basalt blocks, the sea bed below them would gradually be washed away. But if one first lays a bed made of osier twigs covered by basalt, the sea bed is protected. The thin foundation of osier twigs is more solid than the most heavily reinforced concrete.

On such a foundation a new dike can be built, a dike that will keep out the sea. The hole in the dike can be repaired, and the polder can then be restored.

All kinds of equipment had been assembled — machines for sucking up sand and mud, drag-lines, tug-boats, huge Rhine barges. There were a great many men who were busy controlling all this equipment, looking like little black industrial dolls.

Each time a basalt block was put into place on a bed of osier twigs, the sea foam rose high into the air. Once the solid foundation was ready, the sand machines could go to work. Gradually, where there had once been a big hole, the new dike began to emerge above the waterline.

"We're standing with our backs to the wall," the head engineer said one day. "We're engaged in a life-and-death struggle with time. The dike simply *has* to be there by the time fall rolls around. If the hole should still be open at that point, a new evacuation would have to take place. And then it would be an open question whether Zierikzee could stand. The same could be said of Brouwershaven. And as for the inner dikes on Schouwen, which have now taken over the job of keeping out the water, they, too, would no longer be able to hold. Finally one would have to ask whether Schouwen and

Duiveland might not become undersea territories permanently, which is what happened some time ago to Reimerswaal."

And so there was a great deal of tension involved in the work of the men who were busy figuring things out with their pencils and rulers. The same thing was true of the work being done by the men operating the heavy shovels and mechanical equipment. The promise that the dikes would be closed before the fall storms would simply *have* to be kept. It was a matter of honor and duty.

In the few dry places on this large island, the people waited in groups, anxiously wondering what would happen. The Zeelanders had seen their homes and farms covered by the turbulent water. Yet there was no place in all the world that they loved quite so much as this land of their distress. In their hearts they just could not get away from it. They *yearned* for the sight of the noisy machines that would eventually pump the water away — that deadly enemy that was out to destroy and annihilate everything a person owned in this world. If only the island could be dry . . .

If only they could see the last high tide going out and know that there would not be another one to follow. Then the stinking mud on which you could never get a footing would gradually change into a hard crust in which there would eventually be fissures as it

dried up. And then the houses — at least, those that were still standing — could be reclaimed. The mud could be shoveled out, and everything inside could be washed . . .

There was hope, but there was also the fear that it would not work. It was still possible that the fall storms would destroy what had been built up and that every low tide would again be followed by a high tide. And so the people lived between hope and fear: these two took turns washing over the tortured souls of the Zeelanders just as regularly as high and low tide flowed across the land.

*　　*　　*

Henry and Corinne had been given a look at this titanic enterprise. The *Holland* was now bringing them back. The tugboat captain with the stiff neck, who was from Rotterdam, explained the technical side of the work on the dike. He seemed to know just about as much about these things as the people of Zeeland themselves. It was almost as though he had a small farm in the polder, lying under the water somewhere behind the broken dike.

The little boat was producing quite a wake in the water of the Scheldt. The sun scattered an abundance of gold shimmers over the waves. Snow-white clouds drifted slowly in a northwesterly direction. Seagulls made lazy circles all around the boat. Everything was beautiful and good and pure here on the river.

But when Corinne looked over the railing at the water that murmured so innocently alongside the boat, it was as though her eyes were repeatedly drawn to some sort of strip or dark object out there in the waves. She was well aware that there were still people who were missing. They might be floating dead right in this stretch of water. She could not get away from the thought, and so she trembled each time it came to mind.

They drew alongside the point in the dike right by Uncle Joris's farm. A small bit of the roof-line of the house could still be seen above the dike. Would she wind up living just behind this dike one day?

As Henry looked at her, he could tell what she was thinking, and so he assured her: "When everything is dried up, things will quickly be in order again, I promise you."

She nodded.

"On Walcheren we went through the very same thing. You are amazed at how quickly the ground becomes fruitful again. You just have to work the ground with gypsum and artificial fertilizers. And then, if there's a reasonable amount of rain, the earth quickly changes and becomes useful once more. It goes so fast! Just look at the Wieringermeer Polder — how quickly they're bringing in a rich harvest there, even though that land had always stood under sea water."

Again Corinne nodded. The captain with the sore neck turned to the side to look at his guests. He smiled benevolently. "Just wait," he said, speaking like a real Rotterdammer. "They'll soon close

those holes in the dikes, and then we'll get a very heavy sea dike along the coast. When that happens, you can get rid of all the little inner dikes. Zeeland is going to become a beautiful province, and I plan to come here and settle down with my wife once I'm retired. Then I'll drop in at your place for a cup of coffee and some of

those delicious Zeeland pastries. You have tasty things here that are not to be gotten anywhere else in the world."

Corinne laughed. As for Henry, he peered over the dike toward the tower in his village and thought about Rev. Zomer, his future brother-in-law, who was waiting for his church and parsonage to dry out. He thought about his father and about mother Beth, who were also waiting, waiting . . . They were waiting for the last low tide that was not to be followed by a high tide.

Then he looked deep into his fiancée's clear blue eyes. "Do you think you would dare to live with me here once the whole business has dried up? My mother is also yearning to make a new start."

Corinne understood perfectly well what he was getting at. She assured him: "With a mother like yours to help me and with a husband like you at my side and with a God above who directs all things, I would dare to live right next to a sea dike."

"Good — I'm glad to hear you say it," said Henry. The Zeeland blood coursed through his veins, pumped by a strong and healthy heart. Within him was a deep yearning to continue the struggle for life in this land that was once again being wrested from the grasp of the murderous sea.

Israel's Hope and Expectation by **Rudolf Van Reest**

G. Nederveen in *Clarion*: This is one of the best novels I have read of late. I found it captivating and hard to put down. Here is a book that is not time-bound and therefore it will never be outdated.

The story takes place around the time of Jesus' birth. It is written by someone who has done his research about the times between the Old and New Testament period. The author informs you in an easy style about the period of the Maccabees. . . Van Reest is a good storyteller. His love for the Bible and biblical times is evident from the start. He shows a good knowledge of the customs and mannerisms in Israel. Many fine details add to the quality of the book. You will be enriched in your understanding of the ways in the Old Testament.

Time: Inter-Testament Period   **Age: 15-99**
ISBN 0-921100-22-1   **Can.$19.95 U.S.$17.90**

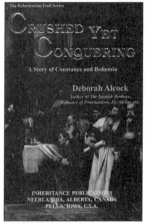

Crushed Yet Conquering by **Deborah Alcock**

A gripping story filled with accurate historical facts about John Huss and the Hussite wars. **Hardly any historical novel can be more captivating and edifying than this book.** Even if Deborah Alcock was not the greatest of nineteenth century authors, certainly she is our most favourite.
— Roelof & Theresa Janssen

Time: 1414-1436   **Age: 11-99**
ISBN 1-894666-01-1   **Can.$19.95 U.S.$16.90**

Quintus by **R. Weerstand**
A Story About the Persecution of Christians at the Time of Emperor Nero

The history of the Church in A.D. 64 is written with blood and tears. This book, based on historical facts, relates what happened in Rome in the summer of that year. It is a gripping chronicle. In the story we meet Quintus, the central character. He is a typical Roman boy, who through a number of ordeals experiences the grace of God.

Time: A.D. 64   **Age: 12-99**
ISBN 1-894666-70-4   **Can.$9.95 U.S.$8.90**

Against the World - The Odyssey of Athanasius by **Henry W. Coray**

Muriel R. Lippencott in *The Christian Observer*: [it] . . . is a partially fictionalized profile of the life of Athanasius . . . who died in A.D. 373. Much of the historical content is from the writing of reliable historians. Some parts of the book, while the product of the author's imagination, set forth accurately the spirit and the temper of the times, including the proceedings and vigorous debates that took place in Alexandria and Nicea. . . This is the story that Rev. Coray so brilliantly tells.

Time: A.D. 331-373   **Age: 16-99**
ISBN 0-921100-35-3   **Can.$8.95 U.S.$7.90**

Hubert Ellerdale by W. Oak Rhind
A Tale of the Days of Wycliffe

Christine Farenhorst in *Christian Renewal*: Christians often tend to look on the Reformation as the pivotal turning point in history during which the Protestants took off the chains of Rome. This small work of fiction draws back the curtains of history a bit further than Luther's theses. Wycliffe was the morning star of the Reformation and his band of Lollards a band of faithful men who were persecuted because they spoke out against salvation by works. Hubert Ellerdale was such a man and his life (youth, marriage, and death), albeit fiction, is set parallel to Wycliffe's and Purvey's.

Rhind writes with pathos and the reader can readily identify with his lead characters. This novel deserves a well-dusted place in a home, school, or church library.

Time: 1380-1420   **Age: 13-99**
ISBN 0-921100-09-4   **Can.$12.95 U.S.$10.90**

With Wolfe in Canada:
or, The Winning of a Continent by G.A. Henty

Through misadventure the hero of the story, James Walsham, becomes involved in the historic struggle between Britain and France for supremacy on the North American continent. The issue of this war determined not only the destinies of North America, but to a large extent those of the mother countries themselves. *With Wolfe in Canada* will take the reader through many battles of this conflict. Meet a young George Washington and General Braddock as they fight the French and Indians, join up with Rogers' Rangers, and learn of the legendary generals Wolfe and Montcalm. *With Wolfe in Canada* is a model of what a children's book should be with its moving tale of military exploit and thrilling adventure. This classic provides a lesson in history instructively and graphically, whilst infusing into the dead facts of history new life. Mr. Henty's classic *With Wolfe in Canada* is a useful aid to study as well as amusement.

Time: 1755-1760   **Age: 14-99**
Cloth ISBN 0-921100-86-8   **Can.$28.95 U.S.$19.99**
Paperback ISBN 0-921100-87-6   **Can.$20.95 U.S.$13.99**

The Romance of Protestantism by Deborah Alcock

A wonderfully warm and loving book about the beauty of Protestantism. This topic, too often neglected and forgotten, has been revived by the author in a delightful way. Glimpses of our Protestant history are strewn in our path like jewels, whetting our appetite to read on and discover the depth of our history. Too often our role models tend to be found outside of our Christian heritage "to the neglect of the great cloud of witnesses, the magnificent roll of saints, heroes, and martyrs that belong to us as Protestants." This book is not only for adults. Young people and even older children will find riches in its depth which will encourage and build up to carry on the work of God in our own day and age.

— Theresa E. Janssen, home educating mother

Time: 1300-1700   **Age: 12-99**
ISBN 0-921100-88-4   **Can.$11.95 U.S.$9.90**

Under Calvin's Spell by Deborah Alcock
A Tale of theHeroic Times in Old Geneva

They had now reached the Forte Neuve, by which they entered the town, with many others who were returning from the Plainpalais. As they walked along the Corratorie they met Berthelier and Gabrielle, taking the air, as the afternoon was very fine for the season of the year. Both the lads saluted; De Marsac with a flush and a beaming smile.

"I did not know you knew them," said Norbert.

"Oh yes; did I not tell you I was going to see them? Master Berthelier's sister, Damoiselle Claudine, and I are fast friends. Some years ago when I came here first, a mere child, I was one day in the market, looking about me and buying cherries or the like, when I saw this poor damoiselle being frightened half out of her senses by a group of angry, scolding fish-women. That was before such good order was put in the market, and in all the town, thanks to Master Calvin. She had told them, quite truly, that they were trying to cheat her. I fought her battle with all my might, which in truth was not great, and at last brought her home in triumph. She was much more grateful than the occasion required, and has been my very good friend ever since. I — they — they are all good to me, though lately, being much occupied with my studies, I have seen them but seldom."

"Do you not think the young damoiselle very pretty?" asked Norbert. "I do."

"She is beautiful," Louis answered quietly; and the subject dropped.

Time: 1542-1564	Age:14-99
ISBN 1-894666-04-6	Can.$14.95 U.S.$12.90

John Calvin: Genius of Geneva by Lawrence Penning
A Popular Account of the Life and Times of John Calvin

The publishing of this book is a direct fruit of the reading and publishing of *Under Calvin's Spell* by Deborah Alcock which is a great novel and gives a very good description of life in and around Geneva. However it tells little about Calvin himself. As a result I read Penning's book and was quickly convinced that both books should be published as companion editions, Alcock's book being the introduction and Penning's book the "full" story. Also today the world needs to know it's most important historical facts and since upon the mouth of two witnesses the truth of a matter is to be established we send out in these two books the true story of John Calvin.

Calvin is perhaps the most important person who lived after Biblical times (seconded by Martin Luther, William of Orange, Michael de Ruyter, and William III of Orange). To know and understand how the Lord has used these people in the history of His Church and world will stir in any reader the desire to follow them in their footsteps.   — Roelof A. Janssen

Time: 1509-1564	Age:15-99
ISBN 1-894666-77-1	Can.$19.95 U.S.$16.90

The Spanish Brothers by Deborah Alcock
A Tale of the Sixteenth Century

"He could not die thus for his faith. On the contrary, it cost him but little to conceal it. What, then, had they which he had not? Something that enabled even poor, wild, passionate Gonsalvo to forgive and pray for the murderers of the woman he loved. What was it?"

Time: 1550-1565	Age: 14-99
ISBN 1-894666-02-x	Can.$14.95 U.S.$12.90

Doctor Adrian by Deborah Alcock
A Story of Old Holland

Doctor Adrian was a scholar living in quiet seclusion in Antwerp, the Netherlands, until a fugitive Protestant preacher and his daughter Rose sought sanctuary in his rooms. Before he knew it, he became involved with the Protestant cause, and eventually embraced it in theory. When the persecution of the Reformed was stepped up, Doctor Adrian made the dangerous journey to Leyden with his family. They survived the siege of Leyden, along with Adrian's sister Marie. When the siege was lifted by the fleets of William of Orange, they moved to Utrecht. Doctor Adrian's faith in the Reformed religion died when he experienced the loss of some of his loved ones, but a new faith in the Author of that religion took its place.

This is a tale of a doctor and his contact with William, Prince of Orange, and of his spiritual journey.

Time: 1560-1584   Age: 12-99
ISBN 1-894666-05-4   Can.$15.95 U.S.$13.90

Love in Times of Reformation
by William P. Balkenende

N.N. in *The Trumpet*: This historical novel plays in The Netherlands during the rise of the protestant Churches, under the persecution of Spain, in the latter half of the sixteenth century. Breaking with the Roman Catholic Church in favor of the new faith is for many an intense struggle. Anthony Tharret, the baker's apprentice, faces his choice before the R.C. Church's influenced Baker's Guild. His love for Jeanne la Solitude, the French Huguenot refugee, gives a fresh dimension to the story. Recommended! Especially for young people.

Time: 1560-1585   Age: 14-99
ISBN 0-921100-32-9   Can.$8.95 U.S.$7.90

The TowerClock Stopped by J. DeHaan
A story during the time of the Reformation

An amazingly true story about a surprise attack by the Spanish army on Sluis, a small city in a southern coastal province of The Low Countries, now known as The Netherlands. The Dutch fought for their freedom from Spain in an eighty-year war, from 1568 to 1648. The surprise attack on Sluis is part of that war.

"As soon as I finished reading this book, I had to check Motley's *United Netherlands* to see if these amazing facts really happened! Yes, the Towerclock truly stopped!"   — Roelof A. Janssen

Time: 1606   Age: 8-99
IP0000008516   Can.$9.95 U.S.$8.90

Coronation of Glory by Deborah Meroff

The true story of seventeen-year-old Lady Jane Grey, Queen of England for nine days.

"Miss Meroff . . . has fictionalized the story of Lady Jane Grey in a thoroughly absorbing manner . . . she has succeeded in making me believe this is what really happened. I kept wanting to read on — the book is full of action and interest."
— Elisabeth Elliot

Time: 1537-1554   Age: 14-99
ISBN 0-921100-78-7   Can.$14.95 U.S.$12.90

The Governor of England by Marjorie Bowen
A Novel on Oliver Cromwell

An historical novel in which the whole story of Cromwell's dealings with Parliament and the King is played out. It is written with dignity and conviction, and with the author's characteristic power of grasping the essential details needed to supply colour and atmosphere for the reader of the standard histories.

Time: 1645-1660   Age: 14-99
ISBN 0-921100-58-2   Can.$17.95 U.S.$15.90

The William & Mary Trilogy
by Marjorie Bowen

The life of William III, Prince of Orange, Stadtholder of the United Netherlands, and King of England (with Queen Mary II) is one of the most fascinating in all of history. Both the author and the publisher of these books have been interested in this subject for many years. Although the stories as told in these books are partly fictional, all the main events are faithful to history.

F. Pronk wrote in *The Messenger* about Volume 1: The author is well-known for her well-researched fiction based on the lives of famous historical characters. The religious convictions of the main characters are portrayed with authenticity and integrity. This book is sure to enrich one's understanding of Protestant Holland and will hold the reader spell-bound.

D.J. Engelsma wrote in *The Standard Bearer* about Volume 1: This is great reading for all ages, high school and older. *I Will Maintain* is well written historical fiction with a solid, significant, moving historical base . . . No small part of the appeal and worth of the book is the lively account of the important history of one of the world's greatest nations, the Dutch. This history was bound up with the Reformed faith and had implications for the exercise of Protestantism throughout Europe. Christian high schools could profitably assign the book, indeed, the whole trilogy, for history or literature classes.

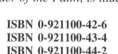

C. Farenhorst wrote in *Christian Renewal* about Volume 1: An excellent tool for assimilating historical knowledge without being pained in the process, *I Will Maintain* is a very good read. Take it along on your holidays. Its sequel *Defender of the Faith*, is much looked forward to.

Time: 1670-1702   Age: 14-99

Volume 1 - *I Will Maintain*	ISBN 0-921100-42-6	Can.$17.95 U.S.$15.90
Volume 2 - *Defender of the Faith*	ISBN 0-921100-43-4	Can.$15.95 U.S.$13.90
Volume 3 - *For God and the King*	ISBN 0-921100-44-2	Can.$17.95 U.S.$15.90

The Lion of Modderspruit by Lawrence Penning
The Louis Wessels Commando #1

A wonderful historical novel in which Penning has interwoven love, pathos, and loyalty. The conflict the Boers endure with England involves not only a fight to maintain their independence (to which the British agreed in 1881) but also a deep religious significance. Louis Wessels, eldest son of a well-established Transvaal Boer family, is betrothed to Truida, a Boer maiden living in the British colony of Natal, and educated in British-governed schools. When England sends over thousands of troops to invade the independent Boer colony of the Orange Free State, causing the Boers of the Transvaal Colony to prepare to invade Natal, the two lovers are confronted by more than a political conflict — two loyal hearts separated by loyalty to conflicting causes. The horrors of the war drag both Louis and Truida through heights of joy and depths of despair. How can these two hearts, beating strongly for each other but also strongly for their separate causes, ever be reconciled? On which side is justice to be found?

Time: 1899 **Age:11-99**
ISBN 1-894666-91-7 **Can.$10.95 U.S.$9.90**

The Hero of Spionkop by Lawrence Penning
The Louis Wessels Commando #2

A company of twenty-five horsemen with an officer in command galloped into the yard. They jumped down, fastened their horses to the young fig trees which bordered the broad driveway, and in silence awaited orders from their commanding officer.

He carefully scrutinized the terrain and set out five soldiers as watchmen. Five others were ordered to make a thorough search of the barn. Ten were posted at the various exits from the house and with the remaining five the officer entered the livingroom . . .

"Do you have a Boer from the Transvaal hiding here?" asked the officer.

"If I should deny it, you wouldn't believe me in any case, Lieutenant."

Time: 1900 **Age:11-99**
ISBN 1-894666-92-5 **Can.$10.95 U.S.$9.90**

ALL FOUR IN ONE

Journey Through the Night by Anne De Vries

After the Second World War, Anne De Vries, one of the most popular novelists in The Netherlands, was commissioned to capture in literary form the spirit and agony of those five harrowing years of Nazi occupation. The result was *Journey Through the Night*, a four volume bestseller that has gone through more than thirty printings in The Netherlands.

"An Old Testament Professor of mine who bought the books could not put them down — nor could I."
— Dr. Edwin H. Palmer

"This is more than just a war-time adventure. The characters have vitality, depth and great humanity."
— *The Ottawa Citizen*

Time: 1940-1945 **Age: 10-99**
ISBN 0-921100-25-6 **Can.$19.95 U.S.$16.90**

Captain My Captain by Deborah Meroff
author of *Coronation of Glory*

Willy-Jane VanDyken in *The Trumpet*: This romantic novel is so filled with excitement and drama, it is difficult to put it down once one has begun it. Its pages reflect the struggle between choosing Satan's ways or God's ways. Mary's struggles with materialism, being a submissive wife, coping with the criticism of others, learning how to deal with sickness and death of loved ones, trusting in God and overcoming the fear of death forces the reader to reflect on his own struggles in life.

This story of Mary Ann Patten (remembered for being the first woman to take full command of a merchant sailing ship) is one that any teen or adult reader will enjoy. It will perhaps cause you to shed a few tears but it is bound to touch your heart and encourage you in your faith.

Time: 1837-1861	**Age: 14-99**
ISBN 0-921100-79-5	**Can.$14.95 U.S.$12.90**

He Gathers the Lambs by Cornelius Lambregtse

A moving book, written not only with deep insight into the ecclesiastical, religious, social, and historical situation in which the story takes place, but also with a warm, rich understanding of a child's soul. Every page of the book carries proof that it was eked out of the author's own experience. It is written from the inside out, and the people who appear in it are flesh-and-blood people as they walked the streets of southeastern Zeeland. Zeelanders with a mystical character . . . who had great difficulty appropriating in faith the redemptive deeds of the covenant God.

Also beautiful in this story are the descriptions of the natural beauty of the island on which it takes place. The author views nature with a loving but also with a knowledgeable eye. The landscape through all the seasons. . . But what is most striking is his knowledge of the soul of a child, a knowledge born out of love.   — Rudolf Van Reest

Subject: Fiction	**Age: 14-99**
ISBN 0-921100-77-9	**Can.$14.95 U.S.$12.90**

By Far Euphrates by Deborah Alcock
A Tale on Armenia in the 19th century

Alcock has provided sufficient graphics describing the atrocities committed against the Armenian Christians to make the reader emotionally moved by the intense suffering these Christians endured at the hands of Muslim Turks and Kurds. At the same time, the author herself has confessed to not wanting to provide full detail, which would take away from the focus on how those facing death did so with peace, being confident they would go to see their LORD, and so enjoy eternal peace. **As such it is not only an enjoyable novel, but also encouraging reading.** These Christians were determined to remain faithful to their God, regardless of the consequences.

Time: 1887-1895	**Age: 11-99**
ISBN 1-894666-00-3	**Can.$14.95 U.S.$12.90**

The Dort Study Bible

An English translation of the Annotations to the Dutch Staten Bijbel of 1637 in accordance with a decree of the Synod of Dort 1618-1619

Rev. Jerome Julien in *The Outlook*: This is a wonderful addition to a home, church, school, or minister's library . . . Originally, these notes were commissioned by the Great Synod of Dort, 1618-1619, along with the Staten Bijbel, a completely new translation of Scripture. In a very real sense, this is probably the earliest study Bible ever produced. We might say of it that it is a short commentary on the Bible.

This volume, the first of what is planned, D.V., to be a republication of the whole set of annotations, contains an historical sketch — written most likely by Theodore Haak, and other documents from the 1637 Dutch edition. There is also an account of a gold coin produced by the States General of the United Netherlands commemorating the Synod. This coin is also stamped in gold on the front and back covers. (It *must* be added that the binding is beautiful!) Inside the front and back covers are reprinted the title pages of the Dutch Staten Bijbel and the English translation by Haak, dated 1657.

The notes are preceded by an introduction to each Bible book, and a summary at the head of each chapter. While the notes on Genesis are much more detailed due to the nature of the content, many insights are found on all the pages. These notes might not be what you would read in a commentary published today, but they give concise explanations of the verses. Regularly, they give cross references to other Biblical passages which shed further light on what God says in the text. Also, these notes give a historic-redemptive understanding of the Bible history. Ministers, as well as Bible students, will find helpful information here, as well as ideas to develop.

For those who might be interested, the position on creation days is "that night and day . . . made up one natural day together . . . comprehending twenty-four hours" (see Genesis 1:5). Further, the Book of Genesis lays open God's "everlasting covenant." The note on Genesis 17:7 states that it is "Everlasting for all believers in Christ . . ." This subject is discussed at great length in the appropriate places.

Of what value is this new, but very old set of notes? Some scholars might look with disdain on a republication of these notes. Yet, historically they have value because we can read in English what our fathers at Dort taught and believed concerning Biblical teachings other that those well explained in the Canons of Dort. It is foolhardy to cut ourselves off from our heritage, as so many wish to do today. Now, what has been readily available in the Dutch language for the last 350 years, is in a newly translated and typeset English edition for our reading and spiritual benefit.

Further, this volume has a practical value. For those who still attend church society meetings, or for those involved in Bible studies, here is a concise and helpful Reformed commentary. Its format allows it to be on the table with our Bibles, Psalters, and notes.

This is an ambitious project which Inheritance has undertaken. We must be grateful for their dedicated work. It is the hope of this reviewer that the day will come, beginning now, when this set will not only be displayed in many, many homes, but also well worn through use. In this day of seemingly shrinking interest in the Reformed Faith we and our children must be grounded in God's Truth!

Vol. 1 Genesis and Exodus	**ISBN 1-894666-51-8**	**Can.$24.95 U.S.$21.90**
Vol. 2 Leviticus - Deuteronomy	**ISBN 1-894666-52-6**	**Can.$24.95 U.S.$21.90**
Vol. 3 Joshua - 2 Samuel	**ISBN 1-894666-53-4**	**Can.$24.95 U.S.$21.90**